Praise for

The Case of the Not-So-Nice Nurse

"Maney has penned a mystery with tongue-in-cheek homoerotic hilarity that's simultaneously fun, nostalgic, and completely contemporary." —**Los Angeles Reader**

"Maney flawlessly lampoons the torpid style of both children's books and lesbian mysteries where similarly nothing happens without at least three changes of clothing and a good, hot meal..." —**SF Weekly**

"In a gem of a book-length parody, the author faithfully hews to the narrative and plotting style of juvenile series fiction, her remarkably straight face making the goings on all the funnier. I loved this book..." —**Ellery Queen Mystery Magazine**

"Maney, who evidently grew up bent in a straighter-than-thou environment, has had a field day with our conventions. Wittily, subversively, she has exposed the underbelly of America: it's softly rounded, and warm." —**Toronto Globe and Mail**

"[An] artful, hilarious send-up of girls' fiction of the past... Many a fan of the (Cherry) Ames and (Nancy) Drew series will be delighted by this wonderfully wry parody—and rewarded by a not-bad mystery, too." —**Booklist**

"Utter kitsch, done with class and distinction. Mabel tools the pages like an expert, in the process bringing up a lot of dialogue about the role of lesbianism in the 'gay' 90s, albeit subtly." —**Your Flesh Magazine**

"Girl-detective fiction fashioned with a gusto and much self-parody...Maney delivers a strange tale of missing nuns, lesbian romance and much hapless do-gooding detective work. Fun at its most Sapphic, this is one mystery that you should get to the bottom of!" —**The Pink Paper**

*The Case of the
Good-For-Nothing
Girlfriend*

Nancy swiftly and expertly roped Cherry in.

A Nancy Clue Mystery

The Case of the Good-For-Nothing Girlfriend

by Mabel Maney

CLEIS
PRESS

Published in the United States by Cleis Press Inc., P.O. Box 8933, Pittsburgh, Pennsylvania 15221, and P.O. Box 14684, San Francisco, California 94114.

Book design and production: Pete Ivey
Frontispiece: Susan Synarski
Cleis logo art: Juana Alicia

Printed in the United States
First Edition
10 9 8 7 6 5 4 3 2 1

Library of Congress Cataloging-in-Publication Data

Maney, Mabel, 1958–
    The Case of the good-for-nothing girlfriend / by Mabel Maney
        p. cm.
        ISBN 0-939416-90-5 (cloth) : $24.95.—ISBN 0-939416-91-3 (paper) : $10.95
        1. Women detectives—United States—Fiction. 2. Young women—United States—Fiction. 3. Lesbians—United States—Fiction.
    I. Title
    PS3563.A466C36
    813 .54—dc20   94-29820
                                                                    CIP

Contents

For Miss Lillian Bee of the Milwaukee Bees, and for M. P. K.

Special thanks to the nurses of Cleis Press—Deborah Barkun, Leasa Burton, Frédérique Delacoste, Maura Farrell, Lisa Frank, Pete Ivey, and Felice Newman—for their keen editing abilities, unflagging good humor, and eternal patience.

CHAPTER 1

A Maddening Mishap

Pretty, titian-haired detective Nancy Clue, known to all for her keen sleuthing abilities, up-to-the-minute fashion sense, and gracious finishing-school manners, kicked the right front tire of her modern convertible in frustration and burst into tears.

"I can't believe it! This is the second time today something has happened to this automobile! First that tire blew in Boise, and now this! Oh, it's maddening!" Nancy sobbed.

The attractive girl, clad in a simple powder blue summer skirt and crisp white blouse with a Peter Pan collar that gave her a charmingly innocent air, flung herself over the front of the snappy automobile and gave way to a fervent fit of wailing that made her traveling companions jump back in alarm.

The four girls accompanying her on the trip looked at each other in bewilderment. Just minutes before, Nancy had been leading the group in a merry sing-along, and now she was writhing on the hood of her 1959 canary yellow Chrysler convertible, tears streaming down her pretty face.

They had just finished a rousing round of "Row, Row, Row Your Boat" when the car had hit a rather large rock and made the most awful clanking noise before rolling to a dead stop at the side of the road. And just when they had almost reached Pocatello, Idaho, where they'd planned to stop for a nice supper before driving across the border to the majestic mountain state of Wyoming.

Nurse Cherry Aimless, Nancy's close chum and a native Idahoan, had warned them to use caution while traversing the roadways of eastern Idaho, but the five girls had been so engrossed in their own amusements, they had become careless. Cherry scolded herself for not paying closer attention. She knew from her many experiences during family car trips to keep an eye out for the rocky road ahead. Now, just hours into their trip, their automobile was damaged, perhaps beyond repair!

"And Nancy's on the verge of hysteria," Cherry noted with her keen nurse's eye. "Not only that, she's in danger of becoming downright mussed," she thought in alarm.

Under normal circumstances, Nancy Clue, who had solved enough baffling mysteries to earn a well-deserved reputation as a first-rate sleuth, was the model of feminine decorum. She was accustomed to keeping a cool head while solving cases that baffled even the professionals, and emerged from every escapade with nary a hair out of place. For Nancy was as well known for her attractive hairstyles as she was for her ability to remain unruffled during the most trying circumstances.

But now the young sleuth was facing one of the most hair-raising experiences of her life.

Nancy was headed home to River Depths, Illinois, to confess to the murder of her father, prominent attorney Carson Clue, who had been found shot to death eleven days earlier in the tidy kitchen of his comfortable, three-story suburban brick house!

"I *must* get home and expose the terrible truth about my father, and free Hannah!" Nancy cried through her tears. She pummeled the hood of the fancy car with her small fists. *"I...simply...must...get...home!"*

The Clues' longtime housekeeper, Hannah Gruel, had insisted on selflessly shouldering the blame for the death of Mr. Clue in order that Nancy might remain free, and so had confessed to shooting the popular attorney during a domestic dispute.

"I told that man time and time again to stay out of my kitchen while I was baking," Hannah had declared as she was led away in handcuffs to the River Depths jail. There she remained, awaiting trial for murder, due to begin in just over two days' time.

It was only because Nancy had been in such a state of shock after the shooting that she had agreed to Hannah's scheme. At the housekeeper's urging, she had headed for far-away San Francisco to start a new life. Once there, Nancy had been drawn into the exciting mystery of *The Case of the Not-So-Nice Nurse,* where she had become fast friends with the four girls who were now standing back helplessly as their new chum took out her frustrations on her nifty automobile. This fascinating case, which had started in San Francisco and led the girls to a dark dungeon outside the city, had ended on a happy note. Using just their wits and a pair of handy handcuffs, the five chums had managed to escape from their captors—a group of nefarious clergymen—free a convent of kidnapped nuns, and outwit the evil priest who had masterminded the devious plot to murder the nuns and steal their land.

Luckily, the five chums had been quickly exonerated in the priest's subsequent death, and it was then Nancy had decided to go back home and set the record straight about what had *really* happened in the three-story, Colonial style brick house at 36 Maple Street. The startling news that Hannah had suffered a heart attack in prison had made Nancy even *more* determined to get home as quickly as possible, for Nancy was terribly afraid that Hannah's weakened heart wouldn't survive the strain of a courtroom drama.

"If only I hadn't agreed to this scheme, perhaps Hannah wouldn't have become ill," she admonished herself over and over again, until she was sick with worry. She would do anything to get Hannah out of jail, even if it meant telling her terrible secret to all of River Depths!

Nancy was positive that once people heard the truth about her father, she would immediately be cleared of any wrongdoing in his death. "Once they hear how *truly* dreadful he was, there will be no question but that I did the right thing; the only thing I could have possibly done!" she had assured her companions. When her chums expressed their fear that *she* might be charged with murder, Nancy confidently brushed aside their doubts

"Any sensible person will certainly understand that I *had* to shoot Father," she assured them. "Besides, everyone in River Depths knows I never lie. Why, Police Chief Chumley, who has called on me many times to help solve particularly baffling cases, has declared that he trusts me as much as anyone under his command."

If truth be told, Nancy *was* one of River Depths' most important girl citizens. Tales of her exciting adventures were reported by newspapers everywhere, and the young sleuth was recognized wherever she went for her keen logic, upstanding behavior, and attractive outfits. Why, just the year before, Nancy had received the coveted River Depths Outstanding Girl Award. True to her modest nature, she had been surprised and flattered by the accolade, and had promptly donated the twenty-five dollars in cash that had accompanied the bronze plaque to the River Depths Home for Troubled Girls, a worthwhile institution Nancy had visited on many occasions on missions of charity.

She assured her friends that in River Depths her word was as good as gold. "Besides, I have irrefutable evidence that proves my father's crime," she had told her worried chums, adding, in a confident tone, *"Not that I'll need it!"* Safely hidden away in the secret bottom drawer of her hope chest at home were documents that would prove her father's guilt *beyond a shadow of a doubt*—letters written in Carson Clue's own hand. Once authorities saw this evidence, Nancy was sure she would *instantly* be absolved of any wrongdoing in his death!

"Little good that evidence does me here, though," Nancy groaned. "I may as well be a million miles away," she thought glumly as she slid off the hood of the car, not even caring that her travel outfit was now wrinkled beyond repair. "At the rate we're going, Hannah will have been tried and convicted already by the time we get there. Or worse! I'll never forgive myself if Hannah dies a murderess!" Nancy wailed. "Never!"

She fumbled through her summer straw handbag for one of the starched, white monogrammed handkerchiefs she always kept on hand. She discovered, with dismay, that she had run out of clean hankies!

"Could things get any worse?" Nancy wailed as she threw up her hands in despair. She jumped up and ran screaming from the car.

She didn't know where she was headed, and, frankly, she didn't care!

CHAPTER 2

To the Rescue!

 Cherry rushed after her distraught chum, a fresh hankie in one hand and her stainless steel travel thermos in the other. Cherry had thoughtfully purchased the sturdy, practical thermos earlier that day.

"A cool cup of water is just the ticket when dealing with emotional flare-ups," she thought cheerfully.

Cherry knew that water, along with the right amount of rest and plenty of tasty, nutritious food, was an essential component to good health. So, unfortunately, was peace of mind—something Nancy hadn't had in a very long time.

"It's not good to overexcite yourself in this warm weather," Cherry murmured in a soothing voice, trying to calm her near-frantic friend.

If truth be known, Nancy and Cherry were *more* than just friends. Despite the warmth of the humid, July day, Cherry shivered when she recalled the evening she had first set eyes on the lovely, titian-haired girl. Little had she realized *that night* she would find love beyond her wildest dreams!

Just one week before meeting Nancy in San Francisco, Cherry Aimless, R.N., an attractive, dark-haired girl with a bubbly nature and a burning desire to help others, had been a happily overworked ward nurse at a big-city hospital in Seattle. A vacation to the city by the bay had changed her life forever—for not only had she been caught up in an exciting mystery, she had also fallen deeply and truly in love, and with her longtime idol, Nancy Clue!

Until that trip, Cherry had been content with reading about the young detective in newspapers and magazines. It was well known throughout the nurses' dormitory at Seattle General Hospital that Cherry spent much of her free time filling scrapbooks with carefully clipped articles and photographs of her favorite detective. Cherry took the teasing about her enthusiasm for the girl sleuth with good grace. She knew hobbies were a relaxing way to spend one's leisure time, and no one needed to relax more than a hard-working nurse!

And no nurse worked harder than Cherry, whose cheerful presence and attention to duty made her a favorite among patients and colleagues alike. Cherry loved nursing, especially in her trim white uniform, dashing royal blue cape, and perky cap with its dark blue stripe that proclaimed she was a proud graduate of Stencer Nursing School, class of 1957!

So what if Cherry spent a tidy sum of her weekly salary on special leather-bound scrapbooks for her ever growing archive of Nancy Clue stories?

"At least it keeps me off the streets," she joked to her nurse neighbors before shutting the door to her room for an evening of clipping and pasting. No one was a more eager hobbyist than Nurse Cherry Aimless!

The kidding had stopped the day the attractive nurse solved *The Case of the Vanishing Valium* and exposed the dastardly deeds of young Dr. Kildare, who was pilfering dangerous drugs from the hospital supply room. After that, the nurses were frank to admit that Cherry, with her dancing green eyes, shiny black curls, and curvy figure, was proof that beauty and brains could walk hand in hand.

But never in her wildest fantasies could Cherry have imagined that one day she'd actually come face to face with Nancy Clue!

Although Cherry sorely missed the hustle and bustle of the overcrowded, understaffed hospital, where the patients seemed to *really* need her, she knew her place was by Nancy's side. For although she had taken a vow to be a big-city nurse—a soldier, really, in the fight against ignorance, filth, and disease—Cherry knew that there was one person who needed her most right now. And although she was dressed as a civilian, she was as much a nurse in her pretty pink taffeta party frock and dressy gold sandals as she was in her trim, starched white uniform, perky cap, and cunning cape.

It was Cherry Aimless, Registered Nurse, who put her own wants and needs aside in order to keep a cool head during Nancy's outburst. Cherry knew that Nancy's temper tantrum could send her blood pressure soaring! Why, Cherry might be called upon to perform a medical procedure right there by the side of the dusty road, where their automobile had rolled to a stop. She was somewhat reassured, knowing that her first-aid kit was securely stowed in the back seat of the car.

"If you just relax, we can put our heads together and find a way out of this spot," Cherry said in a soothing tone. "A cool head always prevails." She handed Nancy a clean handkerchief. Cherry always kept plenty on hand for times just like these.

"But I want to go *now!*" Nancy cried, crumpling Cherry's white cotton hankie and throwing it to the ground.

Cherry picked up the now germ-laden handkerchief and put it in her pocket. She took a fresh one from her white patent-leather purse and held it ready in her hand. In a calm voice that she hoped would stop her excitable friend from working herself into an even more heightened nervous state, Cherry explained that car trouble was not unusual during a long auto trip. "Especially if one is trying very hard to get someplace in a hurry. Accidents are bound to happen," she said in a firm yet soothing tone. "And you have to admit this wasn't the most carefully planned trip," she added.

" 'Many a trip is spoiled by poor planning,' " Cherry quoted her mother, Mrs. Doris Aimless of Pleasantville, Idaho, a sensible woman with lots of helpful advice. She felt a flash of guilt when she thought of her mother, who was no doubt worried sick about the whereabouts of her only daughter. Cherry had raced out the door earlier that day, and right in the middle of the mid-day meal!

Cherry vowed that she would call home as soon as she could, and assure her mother she was safe and planning on eating well-balanced meals. But until she could find a public telephone, she had another, more urgent, matter to contend with. Nancy was becoming dangerously overwrought, and it was Cherry's job to see she didn't make herself sick with worry.

"You told me yourself you've been involved in a lot of scrapes," she said, adding, "and, eventually, you've found a way out of each of them."

"But I've never been in such a precarious predicament before," Nancy wailed. "I should have flown home," she added anxiously. "What was I thinking when I suggested we drive cross-country in a little over a day's time? At the rate we're going, we'll never make it to Illinois in time to stop that trial!

"If I had flown, I'd be home by now, and Hannah would be free," she said, a gleam of steely determination in her blue eyes. She checked her slender, diamond-faced watch. "Let's see—it's almost six o'clock now. I could hop a bus back to Boise and catch a late flight to Chicago. I could be home first thing in the morning," Nancy schemed.

Cherry could scarcely believe her ears. Surely Nancy didn't mean that she wanted to go off on her own? "Airplane travel may be faster," Cherry thought, but she also knew, as a nurse, that cabin pressure could prove medically unsettling for someone in Nancy's unstable emotional condition. "Surely you don't mean that!" Cherry blurted out. "We've got *two and a half* whole days before the trial begins—why, that's plenty of time to get there!"

Cherry knew the foursome could provide valuable assistance to Nancy in her time of need and was just about to point that out when Nancy wailed, "Oh, I don't know what I mean," put her head in her hands, and gave way to a fit of weeping.

"I've got to make her calm down," Cherry thought, grabbing her chum by the hand so she could secretly check her heart-rate. Just as she suspected—it was awfully fast!

"I'll make her listen to reason; I've just got to," Cherry thought. A determined glint came into *her* sparkling, emerald-green eyes. She *must* get through to the hysterical girl. Cherry thought fast and hard.

"Why, once I decided to visit my Aunt Beatrice in Boise at the last minute, and on the bus I realized that I had neglected to pack any toiletry items!" Cherry exclaimed dramatically. "I had to borrow hair pins and cold cream from my aunt all weekend. But it all worked out and we had a delightful time. Now, see?"

CHAPTER 3

Oops!

Nancy looked puzzled, but Cherry's story had done the trick. She was no longer crying. This time she accepted Cherry's handkerchief gratefully, mopped her face, and ran a hand through her tangled hair.

At Cherry's urging, Nancy took her compact from her purse and applied a fresh dusting of powder to her pert but now shiny nose. Light pink lipstick completed her look. She then brushed her tangled titian hair until it shone.

"Feeling better?" Cherry asked.

Nancy admitted that she *did* feel much improved.

"A girl must always look her best and be prepared for the worst," Cherry said cheerfully.

Nancy smiled wanly but said nothing. Cherry could tell her mind was miles away. Sixteen-hundred eighty-six miles, to be exact.

They sat for a while on a big boulder in quiet contemplation before Nancy uttered a big sigh and stood up. "I guess if we're ever going to get out of here I should take a look at that darn automobile and see what can be done," she said resolutely, sounding once again like the sensible girl with whom Cherry had fallen truly and deeply in love.

"How brave she is," Cherry thought, her heart leaping with joy when she realized that Nancy must have abandoned her plans to fly home. "I'll bet we'll be out of here in a jiffy! We'll be speeding through the majestic mountain state of Wyoming before you know it!" she bubbled.

Cherry felt a thrill when she imagined how exciting the sightseeing would be as they traveled through the picturesque and colorful state, with its many recreational pleasures. Nancy looked unconvinced, so, as they walked back to the car, Cherry kept up a chirpy chatter, hoping to cheer up her cynical chum. "We can have supper in nearby Pocatello while the car's being fixed. After all, we do have to eat in order to keep our strength up," she added.

"A nice dry martini would sure hit the spot right now," Nancy admitted, sounding a bit calmer.

Was it Cherry's imagination, or was Nancy sounding almost cheerful? Cherry smiled. Who else would have thought of having a cocktail but Nancy? Golly, she was so sophisticated, she always knew the right thing to do!

"I'll bet Midge knows a lot about cars," Cherry guessed as they walked back to the convertible. "I'll bet she'll get us out of here in no time at all."

She had to smile when she thought of their tall, strong traveling companion, Midge Fontaine, the only girl among them with the upper body strength necessary to get the car moving if it wouldn't start on its own. Cherry had met the muscular Midge during her recent adventure in San Francisco. Although Midge, a handsome girl with a take-charge attitude and a tendency to tease, and Cherry, a small-town girl with a bubbly, eager-to-please nature and a habit of blushing at the slightest provocation, were as different as two girls could be, they had become fast friends during their recent adventure.

A case of mistaken identity had brought the two unlikely chums together. Dark-haired Cherry and Midge's longtime girlfriend, the lovely Velma Pierce, bore an uncanny resemblance to one another, resulting in a scary mix-up that had put the vivacious Velma in grave danger! Luckily, Cherry and Midge had been able to save her and had become good friends in the process.

"Only, Velma's more stylish than I am," thought Cherry, who frankly felt like Velma's drab little sister in comparison with the older, more glamorous girl.

Cherry, a sweet, simple girl from a small farming town, had to admit she was more at home in a plain, starched white nurse's uniform or the simple, cotton frocks she favored, than in the revealing get-ups Velma wore with such aplomb. "Plus Velma is always impeccably groomed, while I'm usually slightly mussed and my curls are all asunder!

"Who would have guessed that their picture-perfect romance began under the most trying of circumstances, while Midge was an inmate at a women's prison and Velma was her teacher?" Cherry thought to herself. She shivered when she thought of how Velma had risked her own safety to smuggle Midge out of jail, and how the devoted pair had spent years hiding from the police. It was the most romantic story ever!

Lucky for Midge, they had met Officer Jackie Jones in San Francisco, who had not only helped them solve their exciting mystery but had used her influence to wipe Midge's record clean.

"Midge is no longer an escaped convict, but a productive member of society," Cherry gave a happy sigh. "And she and Velma make an awfully attractive couple," Cherry thought dreamily. "Midge's masculine outfits, slicked-back hairstyle, and rugged good looks perfectly complement Velma's feminine frocks and movie star glamour. They're a perfect match," Cherry thought.

"Where is everybody?" Nancy worried aloud, pointing toward the car. Cherry got her mind off fashion fast when she realized with a start that Midge was no longer where they had seen her last, leaning against the side of the car smoking a cigarette.

For that matter, Velma, who was usually never far from Midge's side, and the fifth member of the little group, Lauren Rooney, a spunky girl of sixteen who dogged the devoted couple "like a bad reputation," as Midge was wont to joke, were nowhere to be seen!

"We mustn't waste another minute out here," Nancy fretted, looking around frantically for the missing girls. "If we're to get to town and find someone to repair our automobile tonight, we'd better move fast."

"They must have wandered off to enjoy this splendid scenery," Cherry realized, noting that dusk was settling over the valley where their car had broken down. Cherry sucked in a swift breath of astonishment as she gazed at the dazzling pinks and reds of the summer sunset reflecting off the lofty mountain ranges surrounding them. Little wonder her native Idaho, with its rugged mountain ranges, rolling farmlands, and swiftly flowing rivers was often referred to as the Gem State!

She stifled an urge to break out in a resounding refrain of the state song, a melodic tune sung each morning in all Idaho schools, right after the Pledge of Allegiance. Cherry contented herself with humming the first stanza of "Here We Have Idaho" under her breath.

"Brrrr. It's started to get chilly," she shivered, folding her arms across her bosom and skipping ahead to the car so she could retrieve her sensible white cardigan sweater, which she had left in the back seat.

"Oops!" Cherry cried in embarrassment when she flung open the back door and got a sudden surprise. She turned a brilliant shade of crimson.

She had found Midge! And Velma, too!

Pocatello Bound

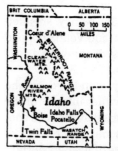

"I'm gonna have to push this thing to town," Midge declared as she slammed the hood of the car in disgust.

Cherry quickly consulted the map of Idaho she always carried in her purse. If her calculations were correct, downtown Pocatello was only a few miles away. "We'll get there before it's completely dark," she was pleased to note.

Before Midge could start pushing, Cherry jumped into the back seat and grabbed her travel first-aid kit. She wanted it to be in easy reach in case Midge hurt herself.

Midge had to grin when she saw the attractive girl emerge holding the white metal box with the red cross emblazoned on the side. Every time Midge saw the comely, dark-haired nurse, she was amazed at the resemblance the girl had to her own Velma. In fact, the two looked so much alike that one night just eight days earlier, Midge had found herself in the embarrassing position of pinching the wrong girl! Luckily, besides being a first-rate registered nurse and crackerjack detective, Cherry had turned out to be a good sport as well.

While Cherry was girlish in every sense of the word, Midge disguised her more feminine attributes with a cool attitude. She was frankly passionate about two things and two things only: her cocker spaniel Eleanor, left at home in Warm Springs, Oregon, and "the other love of my life," the beautiful, curvaceous Velma, who had hopped back into the car and was at this very moment using the rearview mirror to refresh her lipstick and run a comb through her shoulder-length, shiny black hair, styled in an attractive page boy.

Midge snapped back to reality just in time to hear Nancy and Cherry chorus in alarm, "Where's Lauren? We can't possibly go until Lauren gets here! Where could she be?"

Midge flushed a little. "A while ago she expressed an interest in the natural beauty of our surroundings, so I suggested she take a walk," she admitted. "But I warned her not to go too far from the car," Midge added with concern in her voice. She called for their young friend, but there was no answer. "Everyone stay here," Midge ordered. "I'll go get her." She ground out her cigarette under the heel of her black penny loafers, kissed Velma good-bye, and strode off.

Cherry busied herself tidying the car, Nancy sneaked behind a bush to change into a fresh outfit, and Velma hopped up on the hood of the automobile and began applying a coat of polish to her long, tapered fingernails.

"Aren't you at all worried?" Cherry wondered as she brushed cookie crumbs from the white leather interior of the snappy convertible. She was frankly amazed at Velma's cool demeanor. "Lauren's lost, we're stuck on some back road, and, only moments ago, Nancy was on the verge of near-hysteria!" Cherry cried.

Velma grinned and patted the spot next to her. Cherry hopped up.

"Relax," Velma said kindly, squeezing Cherry's arm. She rummaged through her purse and tossed a bottle of Pearly Pink nail polish in Cherry's lap. "Those girls of ours are *always* involved in some little adventure, aren't they?" she added conspiratorially.

Cherry smiled. Velma was right. She hadn't thought about the consequences of being in love with someone as busy as a famous girl detective. She hoped she was up to the task! "How did you get so wise?" Cherry blurted out. "About people, I mean?"

"I've lived with Midge for eleven years," Velma laughed. "Honey, I could write a book!" The two girls laughed merrily. "You know what I think is the cutest thing?" Velma added with a chuckle. "I realized today that Lauren is turning into a miniature version of Midge!"

"It's true," Cherry agreed. "Earlier, when we stopped for sodas, I watched Lauren walking toward the car and thought, she's beginning to walk like Midge."

"That strut's kind of cute on a kid, don't you think?" Velma grinned. Then she got a dreamy look in her eyes. "When I see Lauren, with her scruffy clothes, tough attitude, and bossy ways, I think, that's what Midge must have been like as a young girl. I wish I had known her then, before five years in that women's prison made her so—"

"What do you think of this color on me?" Cherry cried loudly, cutting Velma off. "Do you think this particular shade of pink polish really complements my dress?" She flung her hands about, trying to warn Velma that Nancy was headed their way. Velma got the hint. Cherry was trying to keep unpleasant topics out of earshot of the distraught detective.

"I think that color *is* you, Cherry," Velma said enthusiastically. "Oh, hi, Nancy, you're back."

"We were just discussing nail polish," Cherry explained. She gave her chum a quick peck on the cheek. "What do you think of this color?" Cherry asked, holding out one hand. Nancy agreed with Velma that the pale pink polish looked especially nice with Cherry's pink taffeta outfit. "You *do* look good in pink, Cherry," Nancy said.

Cherry blushed prettily at the praise. "And you look enchanting in that full-skirted, sleeveless, paisley-print, silk chiffon summer dinner dress you've selected! It's darling! And I love that beaded sweater you've casually tossed over your shoulders. It looks like you're ready for a gay evening."

"I'm afraid my summer straw bag isn't nearly fancy enough for this outfit," Nancy admitted ruefully. It was the only purse she had with her! "Imagine forgetting to pack a dressy purse! What must I have been thinking?"

Cherry tried to steer Nancy away from serious topics. "I love your pearls!" she enthused, taking a closer look at the luminescent beads around Nancy's neck. "You have so many nice things," Cherry gushed, remembering the sapphire and diamond starburst brooch and earring set Nancy had worn the night they met.

"Hannah insisted I pack my portable jewelry case," Nancy explained, pointing to her purse, where she kept the small white leather case with its assortment of fine jewelry and some fun costume accessories, besides. Her face suddenly grew grim, and the sparkle went out of her pretty blue eyes. Cherry knew she was thinking of Hannah, whose only jewelry now was a prison identification bracelet. She quickly tried to change the subject.

"Brrr, it's getting chilly, isn't it?" Cherry cried. She buttoned her sweater all the way up to her chin and rubbed her hands together. But her thin cotton sweater proved to be poor protection against the evening mountain air.

"Let's see if I've got something warmer," Nancy said. She went to the trunk of the car and removed the largest of her three-piece powder blue travel set. She snapped open the suitcase. "Velma, this black cashmere topper coat will look nice with that yellow sheath you're wearing," she said. The hip-length coat fit Velma to a tee. "And, Cherry, this is a little dressy for your summer frock, but it will keep you warm," Nancy said as she handed Cherry a pink wool coat with dolman sleeves and a big shawl collar. Nancy shrugged on an old red car coat, explaining ruefully, "It's this or a brocade evening stole."

Cherry stared in amazement at Nancy's suitcase, which was stuffed with all sorts of fashionable frocks and gay accessories. Cherry had left home in such a hurry, she hadn't had time to pack any spare outfits, and she was frankly nervous about having to wear her lovely taffeta frock with its dressy shirred skirt and tight-fitting bodice, all the way to Illinois. Taffeta wrinkled so!

"Help yourself to anything in there, Cherry," Nancy offered. "While your dress is pretty as pie, it might not be the best travel get-up. Besides, the weather can be capricious, and to be really comfortable while traveling, one should be equipped with two sets of day clothes and warm evening togs."

"You mean I can wear anything in this suitcase?" Cherry exclaimed. Why, outside of a department store, she had never seen so many lovely things! Cherry squealed in delight when Nancy shook the wrinkles out of a red and white polka dot sleeveless cotton frock and handed it to her.

"Pair this with my white broadcloth jacket, lined in red satin, and a red cinch belt, and you've got a summer classic," Nancy pointed out. "Or, if you'd like something more playful, how about a rickrack-trimmed, bright cotton broomstick skirt, perfect for patio parties? Or don this black linen scoop-neck sheath with a simple strand of pearls, and you're ready for a night at the symphony."

Cherry grew wide-eyed with wonder as she surveyed the contents of Nancy's suitcase. A sea green creamy crepe dress with a tulle stole; long and short soft gloves in the three most necessary colors; piles of cool, zip-up-the-back ladylike

shirtwaists with matching belts and coordinating handkerchiefs; stylishly simple linen shifts with matching shortie jack-
ets lined in satin; full-skirted sundresses just right for gay summer frolics; and shoe bags stuffed with velvety mules, satiny
sandals, foldable flats, canvas espadrilles, ankle-strap high
heels, and cork-soled sandals with uppers of soft calf.

Cherry fingered a deliciously soft, snow white angora
sweater set with matching pearlized buttons—the exact
same one she secretly longed for each time her birthday rolled
around, but had never been lucky enough to receive. And there
was one each in minty green, pale pink, creamy yellow, powder blue, luscious lavender, and sophisticated black, too.

"I'm afraid I was in somewhat of a tizzy when I packed,"
Nancy explained in a bemused manner. "Some of these things
are last year's fashions!"

But Cherry was too busy to pay any attention. She wondered what it was like to have an angora sweater set for each
day of the week. Suddenly her pink taffeta frock, which had
seemed so daring and sophisticated two years ago when her
mother had made it, now seemed downright dowdy!

"I may not have Nancy's nice things, but I do have one thing
that is never out of fashion," she realized. "I have something
I wouldn't trade a suitcase *full* of matching angora sweater
sets for—the proud uniform of a registered nurse!

"Besides, when I'm wearing my whites, I never have to
worry about looking out of place," she consoled herself as she
stroked the soft angora sweaters. "My crisp uniform, cunning
cape, and perky cap draw admiring glances wherever I go!"

Cherry swelled with pride as she thought of her car-trip
uniform tucked securely in the bottom of her travel first-aid
kit, next to a freshly polished pair of sturdy white shoes and
an extra cap. Nurse Cherry Aimless was ready to swing into
action the minute the call to duty came!

She almost reached for the uniform right then and there
when she saw Midge and Lauren walking toward the car and
realized with alarm that Midge was all bent over! To Cherry's
great relief, it soon became clear that Midge was doubled over
because she was carrying a big rock and not because she had
hurt herself. "Phew!" Cherry thought.

"Guess what we've got?" Midge groaned as she unceremo-
niously dropped the small boulder on the ground next to the girls.

"Midge, be careful!" Lauren hollered.

"It's just a big dumb rock," Midge shot back. "You can't hurt it."

"Can, too!" Lauren argued as she carefully placed her arm-load of smaller, yellow stones on the rear floor of the convertible before running to retrieve the large rock. "This is a fine specimen of a serpentine rock, and I don't want it chipped," she said, polishing the dark green, white-veined rock with the sleeve of her dirty red sweatshirt.

"She was mountain-climbing and wouldn't come down until I agreed to let her bring some of the Pocatello Peaks with her," Midge explained. She stared at Velma's new coat with keen interest. "This is nice," she murmured to Velma, stroking the front of her thick, luxurious wool coat. "Did you girls go shopping while we were gone?" Midge joked.

Just then, Cherry noticed the glare of oncoming headlights about a quarter mile down the road. "There's a car coming our way," she yelled, adding, "Maybe they'll give us a ride to town, and Midge won't have to push the car after all."

They turned on their headlights and honked excitedly so the driver would see them, but, to their utter amazement, the middle-aged man wearing dark glasses and a straw hat pulled low over his face zoomed past!

"Yoo hoo! Help!" Cherry yelled as she raced after the dusty brown Impala. The woman in the passenger seat turned around, and Cherry got a good look at her frightfully over-bleached hair, garish red head scarf, and white plastic sun-glasses before the car picked up speed, leaving the girls in a cloud of dust.

"How terribly rude!" Cherry cried as she took a clean han-kie from her purse and wiped her face. "I know they saw us! Why, that woman looked straight at me!"

"When we get to River Depths, I'll have Police Chief Chum-ley run a check on all known dusty brown Impalas," Nancy said hotly. "I'll bet they've many outstanding traffic citations. Someone needs to explain the rules of the road to them."

The episode had lit a fire in Nancy. She traded her cork-soled wedge sandals for a pair of ballerina flats and positioned herself behind the car.

"Heave ho, girls!" she cried.

CHAPTER 5

That Special Something

Midge gave a great big satisfied sigh. "Those *were* the best mashed potatoes I've ever had," she groaned as she licked the last of the gravy from her fork and pushed her plate aside.

Cherry beamed. "Idaho *is* the Land of Famous Potatoes, Midge!" she cried before taking another bite of her delicious, creamy Potatoes Au Gratin—perfectly baked spuds smothered in a rich cheddar cheese sauce and topped with a mound of sour cream.

"How are your French Fried Potatoes, Lauren?" she asked their teen-aged friend, who was hungrily gulping down thin strips of fried potatoes smothered in catsup. Lauren nodded and kept eating. She was especially hungry after her rock-climbing adventure.

Cherry glanced anxiously at Velma, who was busy checking her makeup in her compact mirror. "Her Hash Browns are getting cold," Cherry worried, knowing that the dish was most delicious when eaten piping hot. Cherry noted, too, with dismay, that Nancy had barely touched her plate of Scalloped Potatoes—generous slices of potato floating in a delectable mushroom sauce. "Although she has managed to consume two vodka martinis, that's not nearly enough nutrition for a girl on the go." Cherry knew Nancy was anxious to know the fate of their damaged automobile, now in the hands of a capable mechanic at a garage just around the corner from the Pocatello Potato Palace, where the little group was enjoying the fine local cuisine.

The nice mechanic had promised to report back to the group as soon as possible as to the condition of their vehicle. While Cherry sincerely hoped the damage would require no more than a simple repair job, she had to admit she wouldn't at all mind staying the night in Pocatello, a lovely little town nestled in a peaceful valley, ringed by the famous Pocatello Peaks. "Nancy could surely benefit from some of this refreshing mountain air," Cherry thought, taking a peek at her chum. Nancy was staring anxiously into her empty martini glass. "If I don't stop her, she's going to worry herself sick about Hannah," Cherry realized with alarm.

"Isn't it lucky we met a mechanic willing to work this late on a Friday night, and for no extra fee besides?" she remarked in a cheery tone, trying to get Nancy to look at the bright side of their predicament. "We were fortunate to meet such a helpful person."

"Mel thought you were pretty swell, too," Midge grinned. "Especially when you dropped your purse and bent over to pick up your things just as that gust of wind blew through the garage."

Cherry flushed hotly, and promised herself she'd never remove her undergarments again, no matter how hot the day!

"A true professional is on call twenty-four hours a day, Midge," she retorted, hoping Nancy wasn't taking Midge's teasing seriously. "Nancy must be terribly jealous," Cherry thought. "Why, Midge as much as said I deliberately used my feminine wiles to charm the auto mechanic!"

Cherry put her arm around Nancy, hoping to squelch any doubts as to her loyalty to her one and only true love! "Ignore Midge," she wanted to cry. "I would never do anything to jeopardize what we have."

Cherry noted with relief that Nancy wasn't paying one bit of attention to her. She was, in fact, busy scribbling notes on the paper coaster that had come with her drink.

"I was just writing down what I intend to do when we get to River Depths," Nancy explained. "When I'm working on a case, it helps to keep track of things." She showed them her list.

1. *Get Father's letters from secret hiding place*
2. *Confess to killing Father*
3. *Pick up Hannah from prison*

"Although I probably won't really need the evidence, since the Chief will believe me based on my fine reputation alone, immediately free Hannah, and declare the shooting a case of justifiable homicide," she pointed out, putting a question mark next to the first line.

Midge groaned, rolled her eyes, and shot Velma a disgusted look. Velma gave her a placating smile. Although Midge hadn't come right out and said it, Velma could tell her girlfriend was none too keen on Nancy's plan.

"Nancy, I'm not so sure—" Midge started, but Velma cut her off.

"Why don't you call the Chief now and tell him the whole truth? Then we won't have to rush so to get to River Depths," Velma suggested.

"Oh no, Velma," Nancy replied. "I must tell the Chief *in person*, and I must hand him Father's letters as I'm telling him, so that he understands fully the gravity and delicacy of the situation. But," she added as she rifled through her summer straw bag then tossed it on the table. "If anyone has any nickels I could borrow, I am going to try and contact Bess and George again."

Cherry handed over her red leatherette coin caddie, which she always kept filled with an assortment of change. Nancy jumped up and raced for the corner telephone booth situated in the rear of the restaurant.

Nancy had so far been frustrated in her attempts to contact her friends George and Bess, and inform them of her impending arrival. George Fey, a girl with a boy's name, and Bess Marvel, a giggly, plump girl with a sweet nature who was never far from George's side, had been Nancy's closest friends for years, and together the three chums had solved many an exciting mystery.

Midge sighed and shut her mouth. For now she'd hold her tongue about Nancy's plans. Besides, wasn't Velma always saying she was too quick to jump to conclusions? Midge leaned over the table and speared a potato from Nancy's plate. "It's a sin to let good food go to waste," she declared as she gulped down a big bite of Nancy's yummy Scalloped Potatoes. Cherry was just about to warn Midge about the health hazards of sharing food when she noticed that Midge had turned her attention from the plate and was now staring at the front of the restaurant with a bemused grin on her face.

"What does Midge find so amusing?" Cherry wondered. She looked across the crowded restaurant and was startled to see their mechanic standing in the doorway; only, in place of the oily overalls and cap favored by those whose work brought them in contact with many greasy items, Mel had changed into pressed, pleated trousers and a crisp white shirt.

And she was headed straight for their table!

"I'm going outside for a smoke," Midge declared suddenly, jumping up from the table and racing toward the door.

"I'm going to powder my nose," Velma said, following Midge.

"I'm gonna go to the garage and make sure my rocks are safe," Lauren said, hot on the couple's heels.

Cherry turned bright red. Her heart raced at the thought of being left alone with Mel. "Why, I wouldn't even know what to say to her," Cherry gulped. After all, she was only a nurse—what did she know about auto repair?

CHAPTER 6

A Chance Encounter

"What's the news?" Midge asked in a sincere tone as she slid into the seat facing Cherry. Cherry blushed when she looked up and saw the great big grin pasted on Midge's face.

"Mel said the car can't possibly be ready until morning, but she has her assistant working on it right now while she drives to the next town to pick up a much-needed part. We can have it back first thing tomorrow," Cherry reported. Cherry was frankly relieved that Nancy had not yet returned to the booth. How was she going to break the bad news?

"Is that all she said?" Midge wanted to know.

Cherry turned bright red. "Something big is broken," was all she could remember of the detailed discussion she had had with Mel about the state of their automobile. Cherry had tried hard to concentrate but had suddenly become all light-headed when the handsome, husky girl with short gray hair, large expressive blue eyes, and a ready grin had slid into the booth next to her. Although potatoes were one of Cherry's favorite foods—after all, they *were* loaded with essential vitamins and minerals—she had suddenly lost her appetite! Not only that, she had noticed the most unusual feeling in the pit of her stomach. She had hoped the potatoes weren't spoilt.

While Cherry had tried to pay attention as the girl drew diagram after diagram of the underbelly of their car, she had found herself staring instead at Mel's large, strong hands, so deftly sketching complicated mechanical parts Cherry couldn't possibly understand. "She has the strong, yet dexterous, hands of a surgeon," Cherry had thought, noting with her keen nurse's eye that Mel had taken extra care to scrub her short-clipped nails especially clean that evening.

"I think it's going to be very expensive, Midge," Cherry gulped, quickly adding, "But Mel said if we didn't have the money, I could leave my address and she would bill me."

"That's very generous of her," Midge grinned as she lit a cigarette.

"People in Idaho are famous for their desire to help others, Midge. Why, did you know that there are more nurses here per capita than anywhere else in the United States?"

Midge looked impressed.

"She even worried whether we had sleeping arrangements for the evening," Cherry continued.

"*Did* she?" Midge raised one eyebrow. "How very kind of her. What did you tell her?"

Velma suddenly appeared at Midge's side. "Her time in the ladies' lounge certainly wasn't wasted," Cherry thought, noting Velma had changed into casual Capri slacks topped with a snug peach sweater. "She looks like a movie star."

"I *always* get dressed up on Friday nights," Velma explained her festive outfit. Cherry admired her sophisticated French twist hairdo, exotic green eye shadow, and bright peach lipstick. Her bangle bracelets made a cheerful clatter as she playfully punched Midge on the shoulder. "Move over," she said in a bossy tone. Midge moved.

"Cherry was just telling me that nice mechanic offered her a bed for the night," Midge filled her in.

"She did no such thing," Cherry shrieked. Cherry could never tell when Midge was pulling her leg, and more than once in the eight days since she had first become acquainted with the handsome blonde, she had found herself dizzy with confusion. For good-natured Midge had a gentle teasing manner that made Cherry forget her sworn duty to stay calm at all times. "When I reminded her that there were five of us, she helpfully directed me to a nearby inexpensive yet clean motel," Cherry whispered urgently, her face all aflame.

"Ignore her, Cherry," Velma said in a soft tone. She turned to Midge. "You're such a tease," Velma lightly admonished her girlfriend, giving her a little pinch on the thigh.

Midge flushed with pleasure. "*I'm* a tease?" she murmured, putting an arm around Velma and pulling her close. "That sweater should be against the law," she sighed, as she nuzzled Velma's neck.

Cherry hurriedly pretended to be engrossed in the menu. She hadn't fully recovered from her embarrassment earlier that evening, when she had opened the car door to discover...

"Let's get dessert, shall we?" she cried. "I see the special tonight is sweet-potato pie. It looks good, doesn't it? Why don't I go get Lauren and we'll all have pie?" she babbled nervously. In her confusion, she grabbed Nancy's summer straw bag instead of her own patent-leather purse, and fled. But before she could get out the door, she slipped on a wet spot on the linoleum floor and fell smack into a man and a woman waiting to be seated.

"Watch it, girlie," the man growled as Cherry bumped into him and sent his straw hat and dark glasses flying. She flailed about, trying to stop herself from falling, and finally gave up, plunging face first into the bosom of a middle-aged woman outfitted in a shockingly casual shorts ensemble and silly Roman sandals. Nancy's summer straw bag flew open, and her white leather jewelry case slid under a nearby booth.

"Mother says a real lady would never wear shorts in public," was all Cherry could think as she went down.

CHAPTER 7

Mysterious Strangers

Cherry's cheeks were as red as a summer tomato. "I'm so sorry!" she exclaimed as she took her hands off the strange blond-haired woman.

"Well!" was all the woman had to say as she glared at the flustered nurse.

"Next time be more careful," the man barked. "You could have hurt my wife!"

"I'm so sorry, ma'am" Cherry stammered. "I'm a nurse. Perhaps I should give you an exam to make sure I haven't hurt you." She looked closely at the woman, giving her a quick visual check for bumps and bruises. Her eyes grew wide when she realized that the woman she had almost knocked to the ground was the very same passenger of the brown Impala that had passed them on the road earlier that evening.

"It's you!" she cried.

The woman's eyes grew big in alarm. "I don't believe we're acquainted," she said icily. She hastily donned a pair of cheap white plastic sunglasses.

"No, it's you. Now I'm sure of it," Cherry insisted. "A man in dark glasses and a straw hat, and a woman with blond hair, a red scarf, and glasses *just like yours* passed us on the road outside town," she explained excitedly. "You were in a dusty brown Impala."

"I'm sure I don't know what you're talking about," the woman glared at Cherry. "You must have us mixed up with some other people. Now, please stop before you further embarrass me."

"Can't you see my wife is very sensitive?" the man hissed. "Why don't you leave her alone!"

Cherry felt dizzy with confusion. What a horrible mistake she had made! "I'm sorry," she blurted out. "If there's anything I can do—"

She was just about to offer the woman a fresh handkerchief when the husband waved Cherry away and snapped in an angry tone, "I think you've done quite enough already." He hastily retrieved his hat and glasses and donned both, pulling the hat low over his face. "Now, just leave us alone before you *really* do some damage."

Cherry was stung by the man's harsh words. Tears filled her eyes. She who had given so selflessly to others now stood accused of deliberately harming another human being! She tried to explain that she had slipped accidentally, but the indignant couple would hear none of it. They turned their backs on Cherry. "Miss, we're in a big hurry. Could we please be seated?" the man snapped at a passing waitress carrying a plentiful platter of potato pancakes.

"Please," Cherry tapped the woman on her shoulder. "At least take an adhesive bandage with you. You might find a scratch later, and it's best to keep germs and dirt out of an open wound." She fished in the purse under her arm and realized with a start that she had left her handbag at the table and had taken Nancy's summer straw bag by mistake.

"If this is Nancy's purse, then where is Nancy's jewelry box?" she exclaimed after a quick but thorough check of the bag's contents. Now she really felt like crying! The jewelry box was gone!

In a flash, the strange couple was back at her side. "Did you say you've lost a jewelry box?" the woman asked in a helpful tone. She put a hand on Cherry's arm. Her angry demeanor had vanished. In its place was a friendly face full of concern.

"Yes, it's my friend's, and it's chock full of expensive things, like sapphires and diamonds, not to mention family heirlooms," Cherry explained. "It was in this purse a minute ago. It must have flown out when I bumped into you."

"You mean, when *I* bumped into *you*," the woman insisted. "Really, it was all my fault. I can be so clumsy at times! I was just telling Harold—he's my husband—well, I was just telling him that you seem like the nicest young girl, and so helpful, too! Isn't it funny how you confused us with another couple? They say everyone's got a twin somewhere."

"That's true," Cherry blurted out, relieved to find a reasonable explanation for her mix-up. "As a matter of fact, I recently met a girl who looks a lot like me and—" But before she could tell the fascinating story of her recent adventure, the woman patted Cherry on the arm and said, "Let's all look for your jewelry box, shall we?"

"We're sure to find it," her husband Harold said heartily. "Miss, you go look behind the counter while the wife and I search under the tables. I think I saw something fly from your handbag and land back there. Now isn't that the darndest thing?"

Cherry slipped behind the counter and searched with all her might, but could find nothing more than a handful of pennies and some after-dinner mints covered in dust.

"Did you lose something?" a nice waitress bent over the counter and asked her.

"Yes, a small, white leather case, with a little brass latch and the initials N C stamped in gold on top!" Cherry cried.

"Does it look like the one that man has in his hand?" the waitress wanted to know.

Cherry looked at Harold. He was standing there with a big smile on his face. And in his hand was Nancy's jewelry box!

"Oh, thank you!" Cherry exclaimed as she raced over to him. "I don't know how to repay you," she bubbled. "My friend has tons of nice jewelry at home, but still!" She breathed a sigh of relief. "If we hadn't already eaten, I'd ask you to join us. The Potatoes Au Gratin here are simply delicious. We're in a bit of a hurry ourselves," she confided. "We've got to get to...well never mind. We're just in a hurry. But our car's been damaged, and a nice mechanic recommended this restaurant, and a motor court for the night, too. The Pocatello Komfort Kourt. Mel said it's inexpensive but clean. Oh, I can't even begin to thank you!"

"I should be thanking you!" Harold enthused.

Cherry looked puzzled.

"I mean, for your perfectly charming company," the man added hastily. He handed Cherry the jewelry box with a flourish.

"Perhaps we'll meet again!" Cherry cried to the nice couple. She waved good-bye and headed back for her booth, clutching the precious case in both hands.

"I imagine we will," the man murmured softly. His companion raised one over-plucked eyebrow.

"I imagine we will," she echoed with a sly smile.

CHAPTER 8

An Important Assignment

"Guess what silly thing I almost did?" Cherry cried the minute she got back to the booth. But she forgot all about her adventure with the nice couple when she spied Nancy's tear-streaked face. "What's happened?" Cherry cried, as she slipped into the seat next to Nancy and threw her arms around her chum.

"The police are after me!" Nancy choked out.

"What?" Cherry shrieked in surprise. "How did they find out you killed your father?" she cried.

The noisy restaurant, packed with the supper trade, suddenly grew very quiet. Cherry cringed when she realized everyone had heard her. The family behind them was peeking over the top of the booth and staring at the girls in alarm.

"We're rehearsing a play," Midge said in a loud, calm tone. "*Hamlet.*" That seemed to do the trick. People went back to their many delicious potato dishes and left the girls alone.

Nancy quickly filled her chums in on the terrible news. She took care to keep her voice down. "When I couldn't get in touch with either Bess or George, I decided to call the prison and try to speak to Hannah directly, to let her know I'm on my way. I pretended to be Hannah's sister and took care to disguise my voice. The head matron said Hannah couldn't be summoned to the telephone because two members of the River Depths Ladies' Club had come to call and were giving her a permanent wave so she'll be ready for her trial Monday morning."

"That's not so bad," Cherry blurted out. "At least Hannah will look her best. Sometimes a new hairdo is the perfect medicine when you're blue."

Nancy shook her head. "There's more," she whispered dramatically. "There's an All Points Bulletin out on my car!"

The girls gasped in horror.

"I don't want to be picked up on the way," Nancy whispered fearfully. "What if we're spotted and have to tangle with some local police who don't know me the way the Chief does?" she shivered. "Without my evidence, I couldn't possibly tell my story to anyone. And Chief Chumley is the only one who can help me!" Tears trickled down her cheeks.

"I'll just disguise your license plate; that's easy," Midge said in a calm, commanding tone that let them know she wasn't at all shaken by the news that state police would be looking for the snappy convertible. Midge's time behind bars hadn't been all for naught, for she had learned many useful things. "And then we'll—" But she clammed up quickly when Lauren reappeared holding a big red rock.

"What's the matter with you guys?" Lauren asked. "Did someone die?"

Midge shot her a dirty look. "Lauren, be quiet," she ordered.

"How come no one's saying anything?" Lauren insisted. She stared at Nancy's tear-streaked face. "Is she blubbering again?"

"Lauren, go play with your rock," Midge said gruffly. But Lauren just stood there.

"Lauren, why don't you go to the candy shop across the street and get some sweets?" Cherry suggested.

But Lauren didn't budge. "What's going on?" she demanded to know.

"I sure could go for some bon-bons," Velma purred. She reached into Midge's shirt pocket and took out a dollar. "Lauren, would you be a dear and get me some chocolates?" she smiled prettily.

Lauren beamed from ear to ear. "Sure!" she said, snatching the dollar from Velma's hand. "Coconut cremes or fruit centers?" she wondered excitedly.

"I'm sure whatever you choose will be just right," Velma murmured.

Lauren flushed with pleasure. "Watch my rock," she called over her shoulder as she raced out the door.

"Smart-aleck kid," Midge muttered under her breath as she watched Lauren eagerly do Velma's bidding.

Cherry smiled. She had never seen Lauren so cooperative as she was with Velma. When Cherry had first met the brash teen, she had frankly been taken aback by her obvious lack of good breeding. Since then Cherry had tried to set a good example for the young girl. It looked like her example was finally beginning to pay off!

"Now if I could only get her to take some pride in her appearance, I know I could transform her into the graceful young lady I know she really is," Cherry thought dreamily. "An attractive, polite, nice-to-be-around girl. The kind of girl who thinks first before she blurts out unpleasant thoughts." As an older, more experienced girl, Cherry knew it was her duty to show Lauren the way to womanhood.

"With the cops out looking, we've really got to keep Nancy's identity a secret until we can get her home. What if the kid goofs and gives her away?" Midge groused.

"That's a very real concern, Midge," Cherry said solemnly.

"She's smart enough to understand the gravity of the situation," Velma declared. "Besides that, she's *hardly* a child! May I remind you, Midge, that she's only a year younger than you were when you went to prison?"

Midge threw up her hands in mock defeat. "Again, I am wrong and you are right," she joked. "Happy?"

"Almost," Velma said, giving Midge a sweet smile and batting her thick, dark lashes. She planted a big kiss on Midge's cheek.

Midge grinned. "I say we go and check out that motel the mechanic recommended. I'm ready for bed!"

"Good idea, Midge," Cherry said, checking her sturdy nurse's watch. It was nine p.m. "It's still early, but it would be wise for us to get a good night's sleep. And I've got a full evening ahead of me yet. I simply must wash my hair and rinse out my undergarments, plus get out my maps so I can figure the quickest route through the Rocky Mountains tomorrow. Besides," she added, lowering her voice to just above a whisper. "I feel creepy knowing the police are looking for Nancy. The sooner we get inside and away from prying eyes, the better."

"I agree," Midge said in a stage whisper. She made a big show of furtively looking around. "See that man over there in the gray suit? The one smoking a pipe?"

Cherry nodded. She stared at the man perched at a counter stool, reading the newspaper while eating a baked potato.

"I'll bet he's an undercover cop," Midge whispered. "Notice his rubber-soled shoes? They wear them so they can follow people around and not make a squeak."

"Pretending to be engrossed in the evening paper is a good ruse," Cherry whispered back earnestly.

"Keep an eye out for him," Midge warned.

"I will," Cherry answered solemnly.

"You're a good detective, Cherry," Midge winked.

Cherry beamed. She tarried so as to get a good look at the man on the stool. "He's clever to act so casual; as if he's really here for supper," she thought. Cherry was so intent on watching the strange man's every move, she bumped smack into Lauren on the way out of the restaurant.

"Careful!" Lauren cried, clutching a gold and white candy box tied with a pink bow. "These are for Velma. Where did she go?"

"The others have run ahead to the motel," Cherry explained helpfully. "I stayed behind to—" But Lauren took off, cradling the box of sweets to her chest.

Cherry took one last look at the man shadowing them; then, confident that she could identify him later, headed for the motel and a good night's sleep.

CHAPTER 9

A Horrible Mix-up!

"What a horrible mix-up!" Cherry cried as she kicked off her flats and flopped onto the double bed she would share with Nancy that night. "I can't believe the motel manager thinks Midge is a man and won't let her in the room with us!"

The girls had thought their luck was finally changing when they spied the Pocatello Komfort Kourt, a neat row of rustic cabins with a panoramic view of the surrounding Peaks. They were inexpensively priced and, by all appearances, clean and comfortable.

Under normal circumstances, right now Cherry would be exclaiming over the knotty-pine paneled interior of their cozy cabin, the thick moss green chenille bedspreads, and the modernized bathroom with its hot and cold running water. "You've got all the amenities of a big-city motel," the manager had said, pointing out that each cabin had many modern conveniences, "including a radio."

It was when he opened the door to cabin number thirteen and Midge marched inside that the manager had exclaimed, "Men are not allowed to stay with young ladies in my cabins!"

Cherry almost chuckled, but stopped short when she realized he was talking about Midge!

The manager had taken one look at Midge's short hairstyle, men's trousers, and bulging biceps and had jumped to the mistaken conclusion that he and Midge were of the same ilk. And, to Cherry's surprise, the usually quick-tongued Midge did nothing to correct the man's mistake!

"Unless you can prove these girls are your sisters, you're not staying in that room, young man. There'll be no hanky-panky going on in my Komfort Kourt," the manager had reiterated.

Cherry was just about to blurt out, "That's no man—that's Midge!" when Midge had shot her a sharp, warning glance

that said, "Keep quiet, Cherry." For some reason, Midge had apparently thought it best to go along with the man's mistaken impression.

Poor, tired Midge, who had practically pushed the car to town all by herself, was being forced to make her bed on a little cot behind the front desk, for there were no more rooms available at the Komfort Kourt, or, for that matter, anywhere in Pocatello!

"There's a philatelist convention in town, and everyone's full up," the manager had explained. "You're lucky there was just a last-minute cancellation; everything else has been booked for months."

The girls had already handed over six precious dollars for the cute, cozy cabin, and it seemed the only thing they could do was stay there for the night, even if it meant splitting up the little group.

"I'm surprised Midge didn't argue with the manager," Cherry remarked to Velma as she dropped a quarter into the metal box at the head of the bed, lay back, and let the vibrating motion soothe her tired muscles. "All she had to do was tell him she's a girl, and she'd be in here with us this very minute. I'm going out and tell Midge to do just that," she declared. "Just as soon as I'm done relaxing."

"That's not a good idea," Velma cautioned as she kicked off her leather-bottomed flats and lay down on the bed next to Cherry.

Cherry was frankly puzzled. Why, it seemed like a sound idea to her!

"In some towns, girls dressed as boys aren't exactly welcome with open arms," Velma explained.

Surely Velma was teasing, Cherry thought. But when she looked at Velma, she could see by the frown on her face that the older girl was serious!

"Midge could get into big trouble if she's found out," Velma said, "The manager would probably call the police in to run us out of town."

"You mean, there are places where it's against the law for a girl to wear slacks?" Cherry exclaimed.

Velma nodded.

"But you're wearing slacks," Cherry pointed out.

"They're girl's slacks," Velma explained. "Don't you see?"

Cherry didn't see, but she nodded anyway. She didn't want Velma to think she wasn't sophisticated. Besides, the long day was catching up with her, and she was beginning to feel dizzy with fatigue. "Maybe I'm too tired and wrinkled to understand anything right now," she thought. Cherry felt lucky, and a little guilty for it, knowing her sweetheart was close by. Nancy was just in the next room, taking a warm bath.

"Midge and Velma belong together always!" Cherry thought, her head aching from thinking of the silly thing that was keeping them apart. Cherry let the relaxing vibrating motion of the motorized bed calm her throbbing head.

"Poor Midge," Cherry sighed. "She's going to miss out on a swell evening. I thought later we could all wash and set each other's hair. Then we can play some games." She had noticed a deck of playing cards in the top drawer of the bedside table, along with some postcards and a complimentary pen with the name of the motel on it. "It will be just like a Friday night at the nurses' dorm," she told Velma, smiling as she recalled the many swell times she had had while lying in her narrow single bed, just inches away from an identical one occupied by her roommate, Nurse Cassie Case, a perky brunette with a warm smile and an infectious laugh. The two nurses had spent many pleasant hours laughing and chatting well into the night, giving each other relaxing back rubs and engaging in fun pillow fights.

Cherry suddenly had a grand thought. What if they put vibrating motors on the nurses' beds? "It would be soothing after a long day at work." She made a mental note to suggest just that, once she got back to the hospital.

"I guess Midge is lucky the manager offered her that little cot behind the desk," Cherry remarked. "Although, I'm sure she would prefer a hot bath and a nice comfy bed. Plus, she's going to miss out on all the fun."

"We won't tell her the beds vibrate," Velma whispered conspiratorially.

"Okay," Cherry agreed. There was no use rubbing salt into Midge's wounds!

Velma got up off the bed and hopped into her shoes. "I'm going to go and see my sweetie," she said.

"See if you can find Lauren while you're out there," Cherry suggested. "It's taking her an awfully long time to get one bucket of ice."

"She's probably hanging out with Midge, learning how to spit or something," Velma said in a teasing tone. She powdered her nose, refreshed her lipstick, and threw her coat over her shoulders. A chiffon scarf tied around her pretty dark hair completed her evening ensemble.

"You look beautiful!" Cherry enthused. "Have a swell time. Say good night to Midge for me."

"Thanks, I will," Velma smiled. "Now, you know, I won't be back for a while," she warned. "Are you two going to be okay all alone?"

Cherry blushed.

Velma grinned. "Say good night to Nancy for me," she said. "On second thought, give her a great, big kiss good night!"

Cherry turned beet red. She was having that very same thought!

"I'll knock three times before coming back in, okay?" Velma promised. "Remember. Three knocks," she repeated as she went out the door.

Now Cherry was really red! Her heart began racing wildly. Alone with Nancy! All day she had been dreaming of being near Nancy, of putting her arms around the attractive, titian-haired sleuth, of...

Her time ran out, and the bed came to an abrupt halt. Cherry was so lost in her dreaming she practically slid off!

She was just debating whether to spend another quarter when the washroom door flew open and Nancy emerged, wrapped in a bath towel that left her lovely legs and shapely shoulders bare for all to see.

Cherry thought she had never seen anything so fetching as Nancy standing there in the doorway with the mist from the steamy room swirling about her, her cheeks all rosy, and her damp, trademark titian hair curling softly around her flushed face.

"Golly, she's the most beautiful girl *ever*," Cherry thought breathlessly. She felt a sudden pulsating sensation somewhere deep inside. It was her heart beating a mile a minute! Cherry slipped a quarter into the metal box, and, ever so slowly, the bed started to move.

Nancy said nothing, but just walked toward her with a friendly look in her eyes. She gave Cherry a sweet smile. "Wouldn't you be more comfortable if you got out of that tight outfit?" Nancy murmured.

Cherry felt faint. She quickly unzipped the back of her dress and lay back on the bed, closing her eyes. She awaited Nancy's soft kiss.

After a moment had passed with no kiss, Cherry opened her eyes and found, to her dismay, that Nancy had slipped into a white flannel nightgown, matching terrycloth robe, and plush slippers, and was busy tidying the room.

"Thanks for letting me bathe first," Nancy said cheerfully as she neatly hung her dress and slip on a hanger, wiped the dust from her shoes, and put her pearls in her white leather travel jewelry case.

"Help yourself to any of my pajamas," Nancy said, when she realized Cherry had unzipped her dress. She threw Cherry a quick kiss and slipped under the covers next to her. "How odd. The bed's moving," Nancy mused aloud before proclaiming, "I'm so sleepy I can't possibly stay awake one more minute! Good night."

Cherry blushed all the way to her taffeta neckline. "But you'll catch cold if you sleep with wet hair!" she wanted to protest. But she was too late, for Nancy was already fast asleep.

47

CHAPTER 10

What a Coincidence!

"A red nine goes on a black ten," Cherry said under her breath as she scrutinized the cards lying in a neat progression in front of her on the bed. "One, two, three," she counted out the cards from the stack in her hand. She flipped the third card over. It was the jack of clubs.

Cherry shivered a little. She got up to get her sweater, taking care not to wake her sleeping chum. It had been almost an hour since Velma had gone to see Midge, and in that time, Cherry had rinsed out her lingerie, scrubbed Nancy's handkerchiefs until they were squeaky clean, and selected an attractive yet comfortable travel outfit for the next day: a generous full skirt of the prettiest violet with practical front patch pockets and a cream-colored cotton dotted swiss short-sleeved blouse that was simplicity and coolness personified.

"Velma and Midge are probably out enjoying the refreshing evening mountain air," she thought as she opened a window and took a deep, cleansing breath. But what could have possibly happened to Lauren? Cherry was tempted to go and see for herself, but quickly changed her mind. What if Nancy awoke and found herself alone in this strange cabin? No, it was best to stay put, Cherry decided. She ducked her head out the door and looked around, but her chums were nowhere to be seen.

"I'd best go ahead and wash my hair," she thought, realizing with alarm that if she didn't do it soon, her hair would be damp when she retired for the evening. She looked longingly at the soft, warm bed and the sleeping girl curled up on one side. It *had* been an especially long day, she thought, barely stifling a yawn. But before she could give in to temptation, she came to her senses.

"One is never too tired nor too busy for good grooming," she scolded herself as she gathered up her travel kit containing her cold cream, shampoo, brush, comb, toothbrush, and bobby pins and marched into the bathroom. Ten minutes later, she had washed and towel-dried her thick, curly hair, pinned it off her forehead, applied a thick layer of cold cream to her face and neck, and was happily splashing about in warm, sudsy bath water.

"Jeepers," she thought. "Mel said she'd be back here at the crack of dawn with our car, and I'll bet it's ten o'clock already. If I'm going to be fresh for the morning, I'd better hurry!" She felt good knowing their car was in Mel's strong, capable hands. "She's awfully nice," Cherry smiled to herself. "So eager to help a girl in need!"

Cherry hummed a gay tune as she gave every inch of her body a rigorous rubbing with her soapy washcloth. When she was finished, she was truly exhausted and ready for bed! "I won't even wait for Velma and Lauren to return," Cherry decided. "We can do our hair another night." She jumped out of the tub and into the pale yellow nightie, neatly trimmed with lace, that she had selected from among Nancy's many lovely things. After wiping the cold cream from her face, she gave her teeth a good scrubbing, gargled with a mild antiseptic, and put a dab of rose water behind each ear. A pretty yellow satin ribbon tied atop her head completed her look.

Cherry stifled a yawn. She could think of nothing nicer right now than slipping between fresh sheets and falling fast asleep.

Suddenly, she heard the door to the room creak open. For a moment Cherry thought Lauren might have returned, but changed her mind when she realized the boisterous young girl was incapable of being so quiet. "Why, Lauren even makes noise when she's standing still," she smiled.

Cherry knew Lauren, as a typical teen, was prone to the hormonal urges and emotional conflict that afflict all girls. Luckily, Cherry had taken a human development course in nursing school, and so felt equipped to really understand Lauren!

"Velma must be back," Cherry realized. "That's funny, though. She was going to knock three times to warn me she was coming in. Well, it's just as well that Velma forgot to use the secret code; she might have waked Nancy." Good thing she had left the door unlocked so her friends could come in quietly!

Cherry opened the bathroom door and tiptoed out to greet

her friend. "Did you two have fun?" she whispered, before realizing that the person standing in the middle of the room wasn't Velma at all! It was the casually dressed, middle-aged, blond-haired woman from the restaurant, the one Cherry had nearly knocked over earlier that evening. And right next to her was her helpful husband, Harold!

"Eek!" Cherry cried as she dropped her travel kit and hurriedly folded her arms over the front of her nightie. "Why didn't I don the matching robe?" she chastised herself.

The couple looked as surprised to see Cherry as she was to see them. Their mouths dropped open at the sight of the startled nurse.

"We must have the wrong cabin," they chorused in alarm.

Cherry pointed to her sleeping chum and signaled for them to be quiet. To her great relief, they understood and immediately lowered their voices.

"We took your suggestion and decided to stay here for the night," the man whispered as he backed out of the cabin.

"I'm terribly embarrassed," the woman said, taking care to keep her voice low. She sounded truly alarmed! "Our cabin must be the one right next door. I must have mixed up the numbers on the door," she smiled, explaining, "It's awfully dark out."

"The manager should really put more lights outside," Cherry agreed. "Why, a person could fall and get hurt!" After tossing on a robe, Cherry borrowed Nancy's flashlight from her purse and pointed the couple toward the correct cabin. "You were really lucky to get a cabin," Cherry whispered to them. "And how odd that it's the one right next to ours."

They all agreed it was a happy coincidence.

"And lucky for us, we opened your door by mistake," the woman gasped. "What if we had wandered into some else's room? Someone we didn't already know. Why, they might have thought we were thieves!"

They all had a good laugh at the thought. Cherry bade them a good night. "I must get back indoors. Wet hair and cool mountain air are a sure prescription for a cold," she explained.

"You know best. After all, you're the nurse," Harold agreed. "Goodnight, miss, and thank you, once again, for all your help," Harold said.

Once back in the room, Cherry took care to lock the door

before slipping into bed next to Nancy. Velma had the key and could let herself and Lauren in. Goodness knows how many people could walk into their cabin by accident!

"I could be directing people towards their rooms all night," Cherry thought sleepily. She had to giggle at the thought. In the course of her career, she had been many things. A Cruise Nurse on a ship bound for the high seas, a Department-Store Nurse called in to handle the fainting spells at a big girdle sale, even a Dude-Ranch Nurse for a summer. But she had never been a tour guide, or a Cabin Nurse, for that matter, although she would most certainly throw on her uniform and come running whenever and wherever a call for help reached her ears!

Her thoughts drifted toward the friendly couple staying next door. At first she hadn't thought they were very nice and had been put off by their cheap, garish clothing. But they had turned out to be lovely people. "To think I accused them of being those awful people in that dusty brown Impala who passed us by," Cherry admonished herself. "It just goes to show, you can't judge a book by its cover." It struck Cherry as funny that they had run into each other two times in one day. "By now we're practically old friends!" she chuckled to herself.

"Mother was right. You do meet the nicest people when you travel," she thought as she snuggled up to Nancy and planted a little kiss on her soft neck. Nancy didn't respond, so Cherry closed her eyes, and a few minutes later, she, too, was sound asleep. So sound asleep, in fact, that she didn't hear the urgent whispering going on outside her door, or the rattling of the knob, or the angry cries followed by retreating footfalls.

All Cherry knew as she drifted through layers of sleep was that she was in her beloved home state with her true love by her side. What more could a girl ask for?

CHAPTER 11

"Adieu, Idaho"

"Good-bye, majestic mountains! Good-bye, raging rivers! Good-bye, lush, green forests!" Cherry cried as she drove their newly repaired convertible across the Idaho state line and into the rugged state of Wyoming. She felt a little teary as she left behind her beloved Idaho. Who knew when she would be back to partake of its natural splendors?

Cherry turned her mind to the trip ahead. According to her calculations, and barring any complications, it would take them ten hours to cross Wyoming, upon which time they would be halfway through their trip. "Then there's only Nebraska and Iowa, and, before you know it, we'll be in River Depths!" She shivered with excitement when she thought of the picturesque ten hours ahead!

"Girls, did you know that today we'll be traveling through some of the finest scenery in the country?" Cherry chirped cheerfully. She checked her sturdy nurse's watch. It was just after eight a.m. They had been on the road for about an hour.

"In another four hours, we'll be crossing the Rocky Mountains, one of the world's main mountain systems. That will be the perfect time for us to stop and have a nourishing lunch and stretch our legs while viewing some of the most spectacular scenery in all of America! Aren't you excited, Midge?"

Midge, who was curled up on the passenger side of the front seat with her eyes closed, just smiled.

"We'll miss the Grand Tetons," Cherry continued, "We're too far south, and we shouldn't really take the time to go out of our way. It's really a shame, though, don't you think? I've always wanted to see them, haven't you?"

Midge groaned, which Cherry took as a yes. Who in her right mind, if given the opportunity, wouldn't want to see such a sight?

Cherry made a mental note to send her mother a picture postcard showing the spectacular scenery from this strange and enchanting land. Funny, when she had called her mother just a half hour before, she had received no answer. Oh, well! It was a lovely Idaho day, and her mother was probably out tending her rose bushes before the summer sun got too high in the sky.

"Look! There's a meadowlark!" Cherry called out in excitement, pointing at a yellow-breasted bird flying overhead, while taking care to keep one eye on the road. It would never do for them to have another car mishap like the one they had had yesterday, for that repair had taken all but thirty dollars of their car-trip kitty. Thirty dollars would be plenty for meals and gasoline, for the girls planned to drive all day and all night until they reached Illinois. "We'll be fine, barring any unforeseen disasters," Cherry thought.

Cherry was positive they'd have no more trouble like the day before. Seeing the meadowlark was a good sign, she thought with a smile. "It's the official state bird of Wyoming, and, despite its name, it's not really a lark at all," she informed her traveling companions. "It's a blackbird, although it does live in the meadows, just like a lark. I guess you could say they're not related, but they are neighbors," she chuckled.

"I sure could use some coffee from that thermos," Cherry hinted to Midge. "There's nothing better than a cup of good, hot coffee drunk outdoors," she added. "Don't you think? Midge? Are you listening?"

"Don't I think what?" Midge grumbled sleepily. Midge had gotten up at six a.m. with the rest of them, and stayed awake just long enough to gulp down a cup of black coffee, smoke a cigarette, and, using tape from Cherry's first-aid kit, alter the letters of Nancy's license plate so as to throw the police off their trail. Then she had sacked out in the front seat.

Cherry peeked in the rearview mirror. Why, everyone's asleep, she realized with a start. "They're going to miss this glorious morning," she thought. Using the car horn, she merrily tapped out the first verse of the Wyoming State Song. That did the trick! "They'll thank me for this later," Cherry told herself as her sleepy chums jumped awake.

"Cherry wants a cup of coffee," Midge muttered to Velma as she suddenly sat up. Velma was sitting in the back seat behind Midge, and the box containing the thermos, paper cups, and a sack of oranges—a gift from that nice mechanic, Mel— was at her feet.

"And an orange, too, if you don't mind. Peeled and split into sections. You'll find a clean handkerchief in my purse right next to you on the seat, Midge. You can put the orange on that," Cherry added.

"And an orange, too," Midge crabbed. "Peeled and split into sections. You'll find a clean handkerchief in her purse. You can—"

Velma pinched her girlfriend. "Perhaps I'd better sit up front and let old sleepyhead stay back here," Velma proposed.

Midge readily agreed. "You come up here first," she said, as she rubbed the sore spot on her arm.

Before Cherry could stop the car so the two girls could trade places safely, Velma tossed the thermos of coffee over the seat, then hiked up her skirt and slip, too, straddled the seat, and swung right into Midge's lap.

Midge put her arms around her girl and buried her face in the bosom of Velma's soft sweater. "Can I just stay like this until we get to Illinois?" she murmured happily.

Velma smiled and ran a hand through Midge's hair. "That would suit me just fine," she answered dreamily. She gave Midge a long, lingering kiss. Midge moaned.

Cherry turned bright red. "Golly, Midge, in some states, it's against the law for three adults to ride in the front seat of a car," she explained. "And I haven't my *Road Guide to State Motoring Laws* with me. We don't want to call any attention to ourselves, remember?" Cherry reminded them. "Besides," she lowered her voice to a whisper, "Do you think it's good for children to see people kissing?" She peeked in her rearview mirror. Lauren was sitting straight up and staring at the cooing couple with big bug eyes and the queerest expression on her face.

Midge groaned and gave her girlfriend one last kiss before taking her place in the back seat. "Wake me when we get to Illinois," she said miserably as she tried to make herself comfortable between Nancy, who was leaning on the car door and staring off into space with a sad look in her eyes, and Lauren, who was taking up more than her share of the seat. "I'll just sleep until then," Midge announced.

"That's silly, Midge," Cherry scolded in a light tone. "Why, there's plenty to do until then. We could see how many meadowlarks we could spot; I've already seen one so far. Or we could play the license plate game. That's where you try to spot cars from different states. Whoever spots the most variety wins," she explained eagerly.

"But there aren't many cars on the road," Lauren pointed out.

Cherry realized Lauren was right. Except for that brown car that had been keeping a steady distance behind them since they had left Pocatello, she had seen no other automobiles that morning.

"We could sing songs," Cherry proposed brightly. "When I was a Girl Scout, we always sang songs to pass the time. I could teach you one," she offered eagerly. "Does that sound like fun, Nancy?" Cherry asked her chum.

But Nancy said nothing. She just gave a great big sigh and turned her head toward the car door.

"I think that sounds like a grand idea, Cherry!" Velma cried when she saw how crestfallen Cherry was by Nancy's lack of enthusiasm.

"Teach us a song, Cherry," Midge chimed in. "But first, pass me that thermos, babe," she said to Velma. She filled a paper cup with the steamy, hot liquid, took a big sip, and said, "Okay, Cherry. Let's hear it."

In a clear, high voice, Cherry began singing a traveling tune. Soon her chums were singing merrily as they sped through western Wyoming. Everyone, that is, except Nancy who sat silently as if she were in another world—a world far removed from the gay little group.

CHAPTER 12

Shocking News

 "That's funny," Cherry frowned as she hung up the telephone receiver and stepped out of the booth. "That's the second time I've called home this morning, and there's still no answer."

Cherry had felt sure she'd catch her mother at home. After all, Saturday was her mother's wash day, and Mrs. Aimless always did everything on the right day. Mondays she baked. Tuesdays she canned fresh fruits and vegetables. Wednesdays she puttered in the garden and attended her ladies' club luncheon. Thursdays she dusted, swept, and turned the mattresses, and Fridays she washed windows, scrubbed the front steps, and changed the shelf paper in her kitchen cabinets.

"And *today* she should be home doing the wash," Cherry thought as she wrinkled her pretty brow, wondering where her mother could have possibly gone. "Perhaps she's in the basement starching Father's shirts and didn't hear the telephone," Cherry reasoned. "That must be it. Where else could Mother be?"

She forgot her mother's puzzling absence once she took her seat at the table and had a chance to peruse the menu, which was chock full of tempting treats. They hadn't had a real breakfast, only coffee and oranges in the car, and Cherry had been forced to abandon her plan of reaching the Rocky Mountains before stopping to dine when even Nancy admitted she was willing to lose a little travel time in order to stop for a snack.

"Besides, if we eat quickly; but not too quickly as to cause stomach-aches, we'll only be a half hour off schedule," Cherry realized. She took out her little red spiral notebook and neatly changed the estimated time of their arrival in the Rockies to 12:30 p.m.

Cherry had to admit she could use a bite to eat as well. When it was her turn to order, she was hard-pressed to choose between the special of the day, liver loaf sandwich, or a clear broth soup and raw-vegetable salad served with an assortment of crackers. She knew she should opt for the lighter lunch. Since she had already driven four hours that morning, she would no doubt spend the afternoon napping. A clear broth would be easier to digest, and she'd awake refreshed for her next driving shift.

"But who could sleep with all these beautiful peaks and valleys and ridges and canyons around her?" she thought, as she looked out the large picture window and spied the Rocky Mountains in the distance. It was a clear summer day, the blue sky stretched for miles, and even Nancy looked like she was beginning to perk up. Cherry threw caution to the wind and ordered the yummy liver loaf sandwich, creamed spinach, and an extra side of gravy.

The girls hungrily devoured their lunch. Cherry noted with approval that Lauren was taking bites of Velma's plate of mixed-vegetable salad. "All my lecturing about the essential food groups is finally beginning to sink in," she smiled to herself. "Now, if I can just do something about her table manners," Cherry thought in alarm as she watched Lauren wipe her mouth on her shirt sleeve.

"Lauren, that's what your napkin is intended for," Cherry told her nicely, pointing to the red-checkered cloth folded by the side of the girl's plate. "And, please take off your baseball cap when eating indoors. I could see wearing a hat if this were a picnic," she added, so the girl wouldn't think her hopelessly rigid. "You wish to be both pleasing and pleasant to others, don't you?" Cherry asked.

Lauren just scowled and pretended she hadn't heard.

"Why don't you take off your cap?" Velma wondered. "You have such pretty hair." Lauren blushed and did as Velma suggested.

Midge scowled. Cherry beamed.

"Let's go!" Midge cried suddenly in a testy tone. She gripped the back of Velma's chair. "Let's go, Velma," she said.

Velma gave Midge an imperious look. "I'm going to fix my lipstick," she said calmly. "Then we'll go." She headed for the ladies' lounge with Lauren hot on her heels. Midge followed them both.

From the little shriek that came a moment later, Cherry

knew that Midge had once again been mistaken for a boy. She saw the grim restaurant manager roughly escort red-faced Midge out to the parking lot.

Cherry gulped down one last bite of her scrumptious liver loaf. She realized that Nancy had barely touched a bite of her cottage cheese and gelatin salad, although she had managed to finish her cocktail! "Is there something else you'd like?" Cherry quizzed her, determined to get some nourishment in her friend.

"I'll be right back," Nancy murmured as she grabbed her purse and jumped up from the table. "I'm going to freshen up and then try to reach Bess and George again," she called over her shoulder.

Cherry stuck some crackers in her purse, hoping she would be able to talk her chum into eating something later. By the time she had paid the bill, tipped the waitress, and purchased a package of chewing gum, she had used up every penny of the pin money she'd squirreled away for small amusements.

She went out to the parking lot and found Midge, leaning against the trunk of the car smoking a cigarette with a sour expression on her face.

"How am I going to buy postcards to send to my friends?" Cherry wailed. But Midge didn't seem to hear her.

"Did you happen to see my girlfriend?" Midge wanted to know.

Cherry shook her head. "Come to think of it, I haven't seen Velma *or* Lauren since they had disappeared into the ladies' lounge ten minutes ago," she said.

"What do you think they're doing in there?" Midge wondered softly.

Cherry shrugged. "Trying out new hairstyles?" she guessed brightly.

Midge laughed bitterly. "I'll bet that's it," she said. But Cherry didn't think Midge sounded convinced. Cherry wished she knew what was bothering Midge all of a sudden. Oh, they had been through many an adventure together, and a girl couldn't ask for anyone braver or bolder than Midge Fontaine, but Cherry knew that under all that teasing and joking beat a real girl's heart. One that broke easily, Cherry suspected.

Midge was looking at Cherry queerly, as if she could read her mind. She dug through her pockets and came up with a dollar. "For your postcards," Midge smiled as she handed it to Cherry.

Cherry gave Midge a quick peck on the cheek. She put the worn dollar in her purse. "I'm going to wait until we get to the Rockies to spend it," she planned out loud. "They'll have the best scenic postcards."

"That's a good idea, Cherry," Midge said. Suddenly, she perked up. "Look, here's Velma."

Velma smiled as she crossed the parking lot to join them.

"What have you and Lauren been doing all this time?" Midge asked in a casual tone.

"Oh, just talking," Velma said. She got behind the wheel, took a chiffon scarf from her purse, and tied it around her hairdo. "I'll drive next, okay? I'm getting awfully antsy just sitting all day."

Cherry checked her little book. "It's really Nancy's turn," she said. "But I think it will be okay. I wish Nancy would hurry up and get out here," she worried aloud. "We're going to fall way behind schedule. And where's Lauren? It seems like she's always running off."

"Lauren will be out soon," Velma said. "Don't worry about her."

"I'm going to get a newspaper so I can check the weather report," Cherry decided.

"What do you and Lauren have to talk about?" Midge wanted to know once Cherry had left. She slid into the seat next to Velma.

"Girl stuff," Velma said in a casual manner. She took out her compact and powdered her nose.

"What kind of girl stuff?" Midge asked anxiously.

"It's a secret, Midge."

"Even from me?" Midge sounded hurt.

"Especially from you," Velma declared, refusing to budge an inch. She snapped her compact shut.

"Fine," Midge said, in a sullen tone.

Velma rolled her eyes. "You are such a big baby," she teased Midge.

"I'm in no mood to be teased," Midge grumbled. "I'm all sore because I had to sleep on a stupid cot all night—alone—and now—" Velma stopped her angry words with a big kiss.

"I *am* in a mood to be teased," Velma whispered. "If we

don't get somewhere soon where we can be alone, I don't know what I'll do," she sighed in Midge's ear.

Midge gulped hard. Golly, she loved her girlfriend!

"Let's get out at the next big town and take a train with a sleeper car to Illinois," Midge grinned.

Velma snuggled close. "What's on your mind, babe?" she asked. "I mean, besides—"

"Besides a long, slow train ride?" Midge laughed. Then she shrugged. "I'm worried about Nancy's scheme. You know how you're always telling me that I have to stop jumping to conclusions all the time? I'm trying, but, well, I just have a bad feeling about this plan of Nancy's to waltz into River Depths and spill the beans about everyone's favorite dad."

"I hope this time you're wrong, Midge," Velma said.

"Me, too. All in all, I guess I'd better stay," Midge admitted. "Someone on this trip's got to have a level head," she said, in all seriousness.

"And who would *that* be?" Velma giggled. "I don't know, Midge. I'd use a lot of words to describe you, but level-headed wouldn't be one of them." She whispered some of those words in Midge's ear until Midge turned bright red and pulled Velma close for a big kiss just as Cherry appeared back at the car with a horrified expression on her pretty face.

"Midge, Velma, look!" she shrieked. In her hand was a copy of the *Wyoming Buffalo Bulletin*. And on the front page was a photograph of Nancy, with the caption, *"Have you seen this girl?"*

Midge closely examined the photograph. "Why is Nancy wearing a tiara?" she wondered.

"Nancy was Miss River Depths 1955," Cherry replied. "I guess it was the most recent picture the newspaper had on file."

"We're safe then," Midge cracked. "As long as we don't let Nancy wear her crown outside of the car, no one could possibly spot her from this picture."

Cherry could see that Midge had a point. "Yes, this photograph is obviously a poor-quality reproduction and four years old, besides. And Nancy's hair is *much* more modern now than it was when this photograph was taken," she said. "Plus, today she's wearing a casual shirtwaist dress, suitable for car travel, and simple white moccasins. Surely no one will think she's anyone other than a girl on vacation."

"So there's no problem," Midge said. "Let's get the others and get out of here."

"But look, Midge, there's more!" Cherry cried as she scanned the news article below the picture. In a tremulous tone, she read the horrible story aloud.

DESIRE TO "RULE THE ROOST" MAY HAVE TRIGGERED CRIME, SAYS CRIMINAL EXPERT

River Depths, Illinois—Horrible housekeeper Miss Hannah Gruel, once celebrated for her prize-winning huckleberry pies, now sits in the cell which will likely be her home for years to come. Just twelve days ago, Miss Gruel shot her employer, prominent attorney Carson Clue, during a domestic dispute, leaving him to die on the floor of his newly refurbished Formica kitchen.

"I told that man time and time again to stay out of my kitchen while I was baking," Miss Gruel declared as she was taken away in handcuffs from the murder scene. Steely-eyed Hannah has maintained a grim silence ever since. River Depthians are left wondering, what made this simple housekeeper suddenly go berserk?

"Hannah Gruel obviously has a deep desire to dominate and one day she could no longer contain herself, and she snapped," said Prof. Melvin P. Merville, well-known expert and widely read author on matters of the criminal mind. "It's the classic Rule-the-Roost Syndrome, so common in frustrated spinsters who have trouble accepting male authority."

"Why, Nancy would be so upset if she knew the horrible things people are saying about Hannah! She'd probably have a hysterical nervous breakdown!" Cherry cried, waving her arms about in excitement. "I must hide this newspaper immediately," she said as she stuffed the paper in her purse. She snapped her purse shut just in the nick of time, for Nancy had come outside. By the look on her face, Cherry could tell she had had no luck reaching her chums, Bess and George. But she *had* combed her titian hair into an attractive ponytail.

"It's time to go," Midge breathed a sigh of relief upon

spying Lauren straggling out to join them. Lauren, Cherry, and Nancy climbed into the back seat and made themselves comfortable. Velma started the car and backed out of the parking lot, only to narrowly miss being rear-ended by a dusty brown Impala.

"Watch out, Velma!" Cherry cried, just in the nick of time.

Velma hit the brakes, and the Impala swerved and sped past them.

"Say, isn't that the same car that passed us back in Idaho yesterday?" Midge cried out.

"Oh, it couldn't be," Cherry countered. "Midge, you're so paranoid!" she teased.

Velma gave a little laugh and Midge tried to hush her by biting her neck, which only made her giggle harder. Soon everyone except Lauren was laughing joyously as they headed east into the system of canyons and peaks that made up one of the most noteworthy landscapes in the world. Cherry felt in her purse for the offending newspaper. She would throw it away at the first opportunity. Nancy must never see it!

Cherry put her hand in Nancy's and gave it a little squeeze. "Rocky Mountains, here we come!" she cried happily.

CHAPTER 13

A Cheery Hello

Dear Mother and Father,

Am having a splendid time. The Rocky Mountains are even *more* magnificent than I imagined! I'll call you when we get to River Depths (That's in Illinois, the "Land of Lincoln.") Today we drove by the famous Abraham Lincoln statue near Laramie, Wy. Imagine! It's twelve and a half feet tall and made completely of bronze! Mr. Lincoln certainly was tall! Ha! Ha!

On to Nebraska!

Much love, your daughter,
Cherry Aimless, R.N.

P.S. Is your telephone out of order?

CHAPTER 14

A Sudden Crash

"Oh, no!" Midge groaned as she and Velma climbed out of the car to survey the damage to their snappy automobile. Velma had taken her mind off the road ahead for only a split second, but it had been long enough for the car to veer off course and crash into a boulder.

Midge flipped up the hood, and then jumped back in alarm as clouds of steam came pouring out. She vowed that next time she would keep her hands to herself when Velma was driving. "But everyone was asleep in the back seat and I was all alone with Velma and I didn't know I'd cause an accident!" Midge moaned to herself.

The others, awakened by the crash, quickly scrambled out of the car. "Oh, no!" Cherry cried. "What's that leaking out from under the car?"

"What happened?" the girls cried in unison.

Midge turned bright red. "We had a little accident," she explained. "Is anyone hurt?" she asked anxiously.

Cherry grabbed her first-aid kit, pinned on her spare nurse's cap, and gave each of her chums a quick physical exam. She was relieved to find no one had been injured in the sudden shake-up. But their car was in a sorry state!

"Now we're never going to make it to River Depths!" Cherry blurted out without thinking. When she saw the expression on Velma's face, she immediately regretted her hasty words.

"I'm so sorry!" Velma exclaimed, on the edge of tears. "I must have lost control for a moment."

"No, babe, it's my fault!" Midge cried. "If I hadn't been poking around, er, never mind. I'm the reason we're in this jam, and I'll get us out of it, too.

"And we were almost out of this *darn* state," they heard her swear in displeasure. "Who'd ever have thought I'd be eager to get to Nebraska?"

"I'll help you, Midge," Nancy declared as she climbed atop the car and peered inside. Cherry thrilled to the sight of the attractive girl standing on the front bumper over the open hood with her legs splayed apart. "It's good to see Nancy back to her old self again," Cherry thought happily.

"How's it look?" Cherry fretted as she watched her chums fiddle with the complicated system of hoses under the hood. "Will it run?"

"That course I took in auto mechanics sure has come in handy on this trip," Nancy joked bravely as she hopped down off the bumper. Then her face grew cloudy. "I fear this car isn't going anywhere without a tow truck," she sighed.

Midge frowned. "The radiator's busted and all the vital fluids have leaked out," she added. "I'm sorry about this, Nancy," she added in a solemn tone. "I'll push it to the nearest service station."

Velma put her hands on her full, rounded hips and raised one shapely eyebrow. "I'll help, but first let me take off my high heels," she said, balancing herself against the car to remove her three-inch, T-strap summer sandals.

Midge assured her that she didn't need any help. She bent down and put her strong muscles to work, but the car wouldn't budge!

"Wait, we forgot to remove the suitcases," Cherry said. She snapped open the trunk and took out Nancy's three-piece powder blue monogrammed travel set and matching cosmetics case, Midge's battered leather valise, Velma's pink travel bag and Lauren's knapsack.

"Try again," Velma urged. This time, over Midge's objections, she added her weight to the force. But still the car didn't move.

Cherry peered into the deep trunk. "Maybe it's Lauren's rock collection. It's certainly grown since this morning," she mused. It took the girls almost ten minutes to clear the trunk of the many different boulders, rocks, and pebbles Lauren had picked up in the Rocky Mountains. "I hope she left some for the other travelers," Cherry said in concern.

"That darn kid!" Midge cried in an exasperated tone. "She's becoming a big pain in the neck! We've got enough to do without having to haul a mountain around with us. Who on earth would want this many dumb rocks?" Midge muttered. "Why can't she collect something small, like stamps or matchbooks? Whose bright idea was this to begin with?"

"I thought it would be fun and educational and keep her occupied," Cherry said meekly.

"Where *is* Lauren?" Velma jumped in. The girls looked around, but their sixteen-year-old traveling companion was nowhere to be found.

"Great. Now we have a disappearing kid on our hands," Midge said in disgust.

"I'll bet she's wandered off to find another rock," Cherry guessed. "According to my travel guide for the state of Wyoming, there are lots of interesting rocks in this area, like terra cotta and jasper." Cherry pronounced the exotic names carefully. She secretly thought it fun to travel cross-country, seeing new and unusual landscapes, people, and rocks. And although Lauren's collection *did* take up an awful lot of space, they really hadn't lost any time because of it. Besides, Cherry was really beginning to learn something about the fascinating world of rocks and minerals!

"She sure is a funny little kid," Velma remarked. "But sweet. Remember at the beginning of the trip when she told us her father was a rocket-ship engineer? Later she told me he was a geologist, and that's why she knows so much about rocks."

Cherry was astonished by this revelation. "At the Komfort Kourt this morning, when we were brushing our teeth, she told me her father was a *spy*," Cherry revealed. "And that her mother had been a circus performer and they met on a secret mission under the Big Top."

Midge burst into laughter.

Cherry looked hurt. "I'll bet there *are* spies in the circus," she said in a wounded tone. "My father says there's spies everywhere these days. You can't be too careful."

"You have to admit, that Lauren is quite a character," Midge chuckled.

Cherry frowned. "Lying is nothing to laugh at, Midge," she said. "That could be a sign of a serious disturbance that could lead to real trouble later. Why, Lauren could even become a juvenile delinquent!"

"Well, whatever her destiny, we can't go anywhere without her," Midge said. She leaned back on the hood of the car, took a cigarette from the pack in her shirt pocket, and lit one. "I'll go after her as soon as I have a cigarette."

"Fine," Nancy said in a brisk tone. "While you do that, I'll walk to town and engage a tow truck to get us out of this jam."

"Good idea, Nancy," Velma agreed. "I don't think Midge should push any more cars."

"A walk to town will be invigorating after a day in the car," Cherry pointed out. Then she blurted, before she could stop herself, "But how ever will we pay for the tow and repair? We only have twenty-four dollars left!"

"We should have taken that nice mechanic Mel up on her offer to bill us, and kept more money back in case of emergencies," Velma said.

"Or left Cherry as collateral," Midge joked.

"We'll put our heads together and come up with something," Cherry said weakly, hoping Nancy didn't notice her red cheeks.

"I know a way to make a few dollars fast," Nancy declared, patting her purse. "I think it's time to take a trip to the jewelry store."

Cherry was puzzled. This didn't seem like a good time at all for Nancy to go shopping! Then it dawned on her what Nancy meant. "You don't mean you're going to sell your precious jewelry, do you?" Cherry gasped. "Oh, no!"

"I've tons more at home," Nancy assured her. She sat down and dumped the contents of her travel jewelry case in her lap.

Cherry went over to get a closer look. She never tired of looking through Nancy's lovely gems. "I like this one best of all," Cherry said, picking up a small silver, diamond-studded brooch in the shape of a horseshoe. It fit quite nicely in the palm of her hand.

"This was Mother's," Nancy said sadly.

Cherry fingered the bauble, a hand-forged piece of silver cleverly bent into the shape of the luckiest of charms. Diamonds ringed the U-shaped piece. She turned it over and read the inscription aloud. "Rebecca Clue, May 1937."

Nancy explained the origin of the unusual brooch. "Mother was a talented equestrian, and she won this for jumping through hoops. Just a few weeks later, her roadster crashed and she perished in its fiery flames. I was too little to remember much, except that she was very beautiful, and very kind, and—" Cherry, whose keen nurse's eye missed nothing, spotted tears in Nancy's bright sapphire blue eyes.

"Let's see what else you've got," Cherry said briskly as she examined the baubles in Nancy's lap with keen interest. "How pretty!" she cried as she slipped her hand through two thin gold bangle bracelets dotted with diamonds and held them up so they sparkled in the bright sunlight.

"Those were my sweet-sixteen presents from Father," Nancy said, almost in a whisper.

Cherry gulped hard and quickly took off the bracelets. Golly, she was a lucky girl! She had a mother and a father, and even if Father was so busy with his real-estate business he sometimes didn't come home for days at a time, well, at least she had parents. And a twin brother, too, and a courageous Collie named Lady. Why, Nancy had nobody! Cherry quickly corrected herself. "Nancy's got me," she thought happily. Cherry just knew that, in time, she could make up for all the things Nancy had lost.

She looked sadly at her chum, who was holding up a simple pair of emerald drop earrings that exactly matched the color of Cherry's eyes.

"These should bring a pretty penny," Nancy said. "Enough for this repair, the rest of our expenses to River Depths, a whole bunch of fashionable frocks for you and Velma, overalls for Lauren, and a fresh pair of trousers for Midge."

While the other girls had plenty of outfits, thanks to Nancy, and Lauren had packed two pairs of dungarees, Midge had come unprepared and been stuck in the same pair of trousers for days.

"How like you to think of others first!" Cherry cried. "And while it's true that at this point Midge's pants should be burned, I don't need a new frock. I'd go naked first before letting you sell those earrings! Didn't you tell me those earrings were a family heirloom? Why, I'd walk the last one thousand one hundred fifty-seven miles to Illinois before I'd let you sell them," she declared stubbornly.

"You won't get nearly what those gems are worth," Midge remarked. "Besides, you'd better save them for later. There's no telling when you'll need to cash them in."

"I have plenty of money at home," Nancy assured them. "Besides, as the last living Clue, I'm sure to inherit everything."

"Not if you're convicted of murder," Midge thought darkly. She kept her mouth shut, though. Nancy had made up her mind, and Midge could see nothing she said would change that. "Maybe things will turn out for the best," Midge thought. But she didn't really believe it. Not for one minute.

"I'm going to walk to town," Nancy declared as she tossed her things back in her jewelry box. "I'm dying of thirst."

"I think a nice, cool drink would be refreshing," Cherry agreed.

"Let's go, then," Nancy urged. "My treat."

Cherry felt badly when she realized that from now on, everything was going to have to be Nancy's treat. Cherry had spent all her spare change on postcards to send to her parents, clever trinkets fashioned from native rock for her brother Charley, and packages of rock candy for her nurse friends. "Even if Nancy *is* the reason we're taking this trip, it still isn't right that she has to pay for everything," Cherry thought, vowing that once she got back to her job on the Women's Psychiatric Ward at Seattle General Hospital, she would save every extra penny until Nancy was paid back in full.

"Or maybe I'll find a nursing job in Illinois," she thought dreamily, "and I can pay Nancy back in person!" The last eight days had been the happiest time of Cherry's life, and Nancy's, too, she was sure! Cherry decided to wait a little longer before springing her dream on Nancy—the dream of becoming an Illinois nurse! Luckily, she knew there were always plenty of jobs helping unfortunate people wherever she went.

"As soon as this whole horrible murder mess has blown over, and Nancy is back to normal, I can let her in on my secret." Cherry thought with a smile. Golly, she could hardly wait to see the look on Nancy's face when she told her the news!

"We'll stay behind and find Lauren," Midge and Velma volunteered.

"Thanks, Midge and Velma," Cherry said. She was touched that her friends had offered to stay behind in the hot, dusty place. "Even though I'm sure they'd rather take a brisk walk to town, they know that Nancy and I want to be alone."

Before the girls began their walk into town, they changed into comfortable walking shoes. Cherry donned a pair of stylish penny loafers. Nancy chose a pair of leather-soled ballerina slippers. But there was one problem!

"These shoes don't go with my outfit!" Cherry wailed, looking ruefully at her flared skirt and soft blouse, which was just right for a long car ride, but entirely too fussy for a casual stroll. Nancy saved the day by pulling a matching red and white gingham skirt and blouse ensemble with a wide white belt from her suitcase.

Cherry ran behind a bush to change her costume, and minutes later she and Nancy were ready for their walk to town.

"According to our map, there's a town called Dust Bin two miles east," Nancy reported.

"Sounds romantic," Cherry thought dreamily. "We'll be back in approximately one hour," she waved good-bye. As soon as the couple was out of sight, Midge pulled Velma close.

"We're finally alone," Midge murmured happily, nuzzling Velma's neck while stroking her soft dark hair. "I finally get you all to myself."

Velma blushed. "I thought we were supposed to be looking for Lauren," she murmured as Midge pulled her toward the car.

"Oh, yeah," Midge said, all flustered. "I forgot. Stay here," she said. "I'll be right back." Within minutes, Midge had located their young chum. She was not at all surprised to find Lauren standing in the middle of a quarry. And in her hands was a large rock.

"I found a cool rock with a fossil of a crustacean in it!" Lauren called up in delight. "It's really keen down here—you guys should join me!"

Midge smiled. "Nancy and Cherry went to town to get help. Don't wander too far off. They'll be back in an hour," she called out.

Lauren flashed Midge the okay sign. Midge, convinced that

her motherly duty was done, raced back to the car...and to Velma!

She was delighted to see that Velma had assured them some privacy by putting up the top of the convertible and was now stretched out languidly on the wide, soft white leather back seat, using Nancy's plaid stadium blanket as a pillow.

"This is a great car, don't you think?" Midge grinned as she kicked off her penny loafers and climbed into the wide back seat. "It's costly to repair, but, boy oh boy, the back seat sure is big!" She slid one hand under Velma's snug shell top. "Gosh, Velma, the last few days have been torture!"

"You don't have to tell me," Velma replied huskily, hiking up her skirt and slip so she could wrap her legs around Midge's hips. She ran her hands down the front of Midge's white, short-sleeved Orlon shirt.

"Oops, there goes a button," Velma giggled as she wrenched it open. She moaned softly. "You know I can't stand to go more than a few days without you," Velma sighed.

Midge pushed up Velma's top to reveal voluptuous round breasts spilling over the top of her bra.

"Being kidnapped by that evil priest during our last adventure was bad enough, but a whole three days went by without, well..." Velma blushed prettily. "It's just that every time I'm around you, or even just *think* of you—" She took Midge's hand, and slipped it in her panties.

"Cherry was right. I *am* going to have to burn these pants!" Midge groaned happily.

"Oh, Midge," Velma breathed.

"Oh, Velma," Midge groaned.

"Oh—Lauren!" Velma suddenly hollered.

"What?" Midge cried, recoiling as if she had been slapped. She jumped up, hitting her head on the car roof.

Velma turned bright red. "I saw Lauren at the window," she hurriedly explained. By the time the girls had straightened themselves and tumbled out of the car, Lauren was gone. "Are you sure you saw Lauren at the window?" Midge cried.

"Here's proof she was here!" Velma cried, pointing to a large gray rock right outside the car door.

"Velma, we're in Wyoming. There are rocks everywhere," Midge insisted angrily. But when she took a closer look at the rock, she saw it looked just like the one Lauren had had in the quarry. "That darn Lauren *was* peeking through the window at us!" she fumed aloud.

"No, I wasn't," Lauren declared from her perch on a nearby boulder. She looked like she had been crying! "I was just going to show you my rock, that's all," Lauren gulped. "I didn't see anything, honest."

Midge blushed. Although she was upset by the turn of events, she wasn't nearly as upset as she had been a moment ago when she had heard Velma call out another girl's name!

"Oh, sweetie, don't cry," Velma begged as she ran over to the young girl.

"Are you mad at me?" Lauren asked in a quivering voice.

"I could never be mad at you, Lauren," Velma assured her. She hugged the girl to her soft bosom and kissed her on the forehead. Lauren beamed. "Let's put all these rocks back in the trunk before the tow truck gets here," Velma suggested.

Although she would rather have left the cumbersome rocks behind, Midge kept her mouth shut. The truth was, Midge would do just about anything to keep in Velma's good graces. The gang at the Miraloma Club back home, where Midge and Velma socialized every Friday night, often teased her about her devotion to her girl, but Midge just laughed it off. "The way some of our gang change partners, you'd think we were at a square dance," Midge often quipped.

She and Velma had known they were destined to be together *always* since the first day they laid eyes on each other at the women's penitentiary. Not that they hadn't had their fights! Midge could remember many a time in the early days when she'd been thrown out of bed and forced to sleep on the stiff, white vinyl sectional sofa.

"But all the bad times are behind us now," Midge thought with relief.

"Let me do that!" she cried when she saw Velma bending to pick up a rock. If she remembered correctly, some of Lauren's rocks were pretty heavy, and she didn't want Velma hurting herself!

CHAPTER 15

A Cunning Career Gal

"There. That's the last one." Midge wedged a large, black rock with a glassy surface and jagged, sharp edges, into the trunk. Although the trunk of the 1959 Chrysler was deep and wide, it had taken some doing to squeeze in all their luggage *and* Lauren's entire rock collection.

"Good thing we don't have a spare tire; we'd have no place to put it," Midge joked. "Golly, Lauren, how the heck did you fit these in here the first time?"

But the girl wasn't listening. She was busy fretting over her rocks. "I know there's one missing," she said. "I don't see my sample of cobaltite anywhere! One, two, three—"

Midge snapped the trunk shut and locked it. She pocketed the keys. "Lauren, you have dozens of rocks in there. What on earth is your mother going to say when you come home with all of these?"

"My mother has a rock garden," Lauren explained.

"I thought you said you live in a high-rise apartment in downtown San Francisco," Midge quizzed her.

A funny look came over Lauren's face. She thrust her hands into the deep pockets of her worn, dirty overalls and stalked away.

"What did I say?" Midge turned to Velma. "What's up with her, anyway?"

"She was really embarrassed earlier, Midge," Velma said. "I'll go after her. You stay with the car."

"No, stay here with me," Midge urged. But Velma didn't hear her, as she was already running after Lauren.

"I'll stay here and guard the car in case someone wants to steal these rocks," Midge joked sourly. It seemed to her Velma was always running after that girl. "She's gonna spoil her," Midge thought. She was fishing through her pockets for a cigarette when the tow truck pulled up. A good-looking gal with short gray hair and a friendly manner waved to Midge.

"This must be the place!" the driver cried as she hopped out of the truck cab and ran around to the passenger side, opened the door, and helped Cherry down.

"Thank you ever so much!" Cherry cried as the strong girl scooped her up in her arms and helped her safely to the ground. Cherry blushed as she buttoned her blouse, which had somehow popped a few buttons on the way down. Midge had to grin when she saw how red Cherry's face was. But her smile turned to a frown when she realized Cherry was alone.

Where was Nancy?

While the capable tow-truck operator got to work, expertly attaching hooks and chains to their automobile, Midge quizzed Cherry as to Nancy's whereabouts.

"She kept saying how much she needed a drink, so I got her a refreshing soda and left her in a cool spot under a big juniper tree next to the service station," Cherry explained.

"Not a martini?" Midge joked dryly.

"Why, it's awfully early to have a cocktail, Midge," Cherry pointed out. "We haven't even had supper! Oh, look, there's Velma and Lauren!" she cried. She had spied the pair walking toward the car arm in arm. And Lauren had a big smile on her face.

The girls piled into the cab of the tow truck. It was so crowded that poor Cherry had to sit practically in the driver's lap!

"Good thing I'm a good sport," Cherry thought as she balanced herself on the girl's strong right thigh. While the confident girl steered the truck over two miles of unpaved, bumpy road, Cherry busied herself asking pertinent questions about their destination, the town of Dust Bin, Wyoming.

"Did you hear that, Midge?" Cherry squealed in delight when she found out there was a square dance that very night. "Maybe we can go while the car's being repaired! It will be good for us to get some exercise after sitting all day in the car!" She wriggled about in excitement when she thought about how much fun it would be to do-si-do that very night!

"My, that was an invigorating ride!" Cherry exclaimed when they pulled up to the service station. She scampered out of the truck and fanned herself with her handkerchief.

The driver donned a pair of overalls, picked up a heavy box

loaded with all sorts of interesting tools, and got right to work on their automobile. Another girl clad in a similar fashion came over to assist her.

"Honey, we're here," Cherry called. When there was no reply, she ran to the back of the building and gave a cry of alarm when she realized Nancy was no longer in the cool, shady spot where Cherry had left her.

The mechanic's assistant informed them as to Nancy's whereabouts. "Your friend said she was dying of thirst, so I directed her to town," she said helpfully. "I offered her another cold soda pop, but she said she needed something stronger."

"She probably went to get a refreshing ice cream soda," Cherry realized aloud. "Golly, I'm tired. I sure could go for one, too. But first I simply must freshen up!"

Cherry disappeared into the washroom and came back five minutes later looking invigorated and relaxed, and with a new hairstyle and fresh lipstick, besides.

"What's that smell?" Lauren cried. She wrinkling her nose in disgust. "Pew!"

Cherry blushed to the tips of her toes. "It's Tabu, Lauren," Cherry said. The washroom had a perfume dispenser, so Cherry had dropped in a dime and chosen the exotic fragrance.

Lauren held her nose and pretended she was choking.

"Perfume is as important to a girl as scent is to a flower," Cherry told Lauren in a hurt tone.

Lauren started to laugh but stopped when she saw the disapproving look on Velma's face. "Uh, I was only kidding. You smell nice, Cherry," she said in a chagrined tone. "Really. And your hair looks...ah...different, too." She peeked at Velma, who was smiling in approval. Phew!

"Thank you, Lauren," Cherry replied. "As my mother always says, a girl can change her hair almost as often as she changes her mind. You know, Lauren," she continued, "with your long, thick hair, you could wear many different attractive styles. I've got some styling lotion and bobby pins in my purse if you'd like to step into the ladies' lounge with me and try something new."

Lauren scowled and tucked her long auburn braid under her baseball cap.

Cherry vowed to do whatever she could to guide the young girl along the perilous path to womanhood. "We'll fix her hair and get her some nice clothes," Cherry planned to herself. "I'll bet we'd find a really cute girl under all that dirt." Then she said to Velma, "Don't you think Lauren should do something with her hair? Something besides hide it?"

Velma cocked her head and took a good, long look at Lauren.

Cherry smiled when she saw Lauren turn bright red under Velma's penetrating gaze. "Why, Lauren really *does* care about her appearance!" Cherry thought. "She just doesn't let on."

"I don't know, Cherry," Velma replied. "I'm really not the best judge. While I like to do *my* hair in many different styles, what I really like on a girl is short hair." She lightly brushed the nape of Midge's neck with her hand. Midge smiled happily.

"Let's all go to town for an ice cream soda while the car is being repaired," Cherry suggested. "And then we'll be on our way."

The mechanic shook her head. "I'm afraid you gals are stuck here for the night," she said ruefully. "It'll take us all that time to fix what's broken under the hood, and, besides, the front right wheel-rim is pretty dented and I'll have to pound it out.

"It will cost approximately forty dollars," she added.

Cherry groaned. "Nancy will be *frantic* when she learns we're delayed yet another day," she said. "How are we going to get forty dollars for the car repair *and* money for a motel, not to mention other important things like snacks?" she cried aloud. She flung up her arms in despair and wailed, "Oh, we are never going to get to River Depths!"

"You're going to River Depths?" A smartly-coifed, middle-aged woman outfitted in a trim, cherry red, worsted boxy jacket and matching straight skirt, poked her head around the side of the garage and smiled at Cherry.

"I'm sorry, I didn't mean to interrupt, but did you say you were going to River Depths? River Depths, Illinois?" the woman asked. She put down the orange soda she was holding in one neatly gloved hand and slipped off her jacket to reveal a white nylon shell top that, despite the heat, looked band-box fresh.

She noticed Cherry staring wide-eyed at her. "You're wondering how it is I've been sitting in the car all day and I'm still perky as a daisy, aren't you? It's the miracle of synthetic fabrics," the woman announced grandly. Actually, Cherry *had*

noticed how wrinkle-free the woman's blouse was.

"Now, didn't you say you were going to River Depths?" the woman queried.

Without thinking, Cherry nodded her head.

Midge groaned. No one was supposed to know that they were speeding to River Depths with Nancy Clue!

"Marty, they're going to River Depths, too," the woman called to her friend sitting in the front seat of a white, four-door Buick. Her friend, a handsome brunette with a smart, short hairdo tinged with silver at the temples, smiled and waved at the girls before going back to studying her map.

"We're from the *Wyoming Buffalo Bulletin,* sent to cover the story of housekeeper Hannah Gruel, charged in the murder of attorney Carson Clue," the smartly dressed woman announced importantly. "Marty—that's my friend over there; her real name is Miss Martha Mannish, but everyone calls her Marty for short. Well, Marty and I decided to do some sight-seeing on the way; that's why we're driving. By the way, my name is Gladys Gertz. Miss Gladys Gertz. I'm the newspaper's society editor and Marty's our wedding photographer. I usually never get to cover exciting crime stories such as this, but because it's a housekeeper that did the deed, they gave it to me," she confided with a sunny smile. "It's my big chance to really dig up some dirt!" She took a starched white handkerchief from her black alligator handbag—which Cherry noticed perfectly matched her low-heeled pumps—and wiped her brow.

"Goodness!" Miss Gladys Gertz exclaimed. She took a reporter's thin spiral notepad and a pencil from her pocket.

"Tell me, why are young girls such as yourselves so interested in this trial?" she asked. "What fascinated you about this particular murder? Do you think it was a crime of passion or one of premeditation? In your wildest dreams, would you have guessed that after twenty-two years of devoted service Hannah Gruel would shoot her employer through the heart?"

"Er...ah...we don't know anything about a murder," Cherry blurted out. "We're going to River Depths because... because—"

"Because of a rock collector's convention," Lauren stepped in to announce. She raced to the trunk and brought back a chalky white rock the size of a bowling ball. "See, this is one of our finest specimens. It's a piece of bentonite, or, in other words, weathered volcanic ash. Want to hold it?"

"No, dear, I'll get all dusty," Miss Gertz shook her head. "I was so hoping to get the youth angle on this," she said, a disappointed look marring her pleasant features.

"We don't know *anything* about *any* trial," Midge repeated Cherry's words.

"But don't you girls keep up with current events?" the woman cried in bewilderment. "Ill health or not, housekeeper Hannah Gruel's trial will begin at nine a.m. Monday morning for the murder of prominent attorney Carson Clue. They say if she's too sick to go to court, they'll try her from her cot in the prison infirmary!"

"Oh, no!" Cherry cried. "Poor Hannah!"

Miss Gertz's eyes lit up. She scribbled some notes in her book.

Midge shot Cherry a warning glance. "Now that I think of it, we did hear about this Gruel person on the radio," Midge hurriedly interjected. "My friend here is the excitable type," she explained. "She's a nurse. Just mention a sick person to her and she's ready to run to her side. Aren't you, Nurse Aimless?"

Cherry nodded her head.

Miss Gertz patted Cherry's hand. "I'm sure you're a wonderful nurse, dear," she said. She shook her head. "It does seem a little queer that they're putting this Miss Gruel on trial even though she's so ill. Seems to me they're in an awfully big hurry to get this over with. And isn't it odd that Nancy Clue isn't there to see the woman who killed her dear father stand trial?" Miss Gertz remarked casually. "Last they saw of her, she was somewhere in California, wasn't she? Driving around in a big convertible. Now what color was that car again?" Miss Gertz wondered aloud. She rifled thought her notes. "Ah, yes, here it is. It was a great big 1959 Chrysler..." She sneaked a look at the girls. Midge struggled to maintain a neutral expression. Was it her imagination, or was Miss Gertz watching them with a sly gaze? "...painted robin's egg blue with white-wall tires! My, that sounds like a pretty car, doesn't it?"

The girls breathed a big sigh of relief.

The beep-beep of a car horn interrupted Miss Gertz's next comment. "Oops! There's Marty. I must be off!" Miss Gladys Gertz ran to join her traveling companion. "It's been nice talking to you girls. Perhaps we'll meet again! Toodle-oo!" she cried as she waved good-bye, hopped into the car and sped off.

"Nancy's not going to like this one bit!" Cherry cried, when the reporters were safely out of earshot. "We must take a vow not to mention one word of what Miss Gertz said. The last thing Nancy needs right now is more upsetting news. She's shown symptoms of acute anxiety on this trip. Anxiety is often most unpleasant," she declared.

Midge knew from experience the true nature of reporters. "They're just like vultures," she shuddered, remembering how the press was quick to vilify her in the shooting of her own father many years ago. "He didn't even die, and they still wanted to hang me," she recalled bitterly.

"Not one word of this to Nancy," Cherry warned Lauren as they retrieved their things from the car.

After securing directions to the Double-D Motor Lodge and Diner, they waved so long to the nice mechanics and headed downtown, three blocks due east.

"Don't you think Miss Gertz's look is understated yet elegant?" Cherry remarked to Velma. "Just perfect for a successful career gal."

Lauren rolled her eyes and looked at Midge. "Girls!" she said.

Midge grinned. "Yeah," she said, a dreamy look in her eyes. "Girls!"

"By the way, that was a good save," Midge praised Lauren as they set off behind Velma and Cherry. Midge was struggling to carry her valise as well as Nancy's three-piece, powder blue monogrammed travel set and matching cosmetics case, too. "About the rock convention and all. You're a sneaky little thing," Midge grinned. She stopped grinning when she noticed a dusty brown Impala pull into the service station. A middle-aged man wearing dark glasses and a straw hat pulled low over his face, was driving. The woman next to him was wearing a red head scarf and white plastic sunglasses.

"Why, that car looks just like the one that almost hit us earlier today at the sandwich shop," Midge thought angrily. "I'm going to go over there and give those people a piece of my mind," she fumed.

"Honey, are you coming?' Velma called.

Midge contented herself with merely glaring at the driver of the brown Impala, who hastily buried his face in a map. "Something about him seems odd," she thought. Then she shrugged. She had enough on her mind at the moment without worrying about some rude man. It had been a long day, and they still had to find a way to break the bad news to Nancy—the news that they would once again be stuck for the night. "And tonight I'm sleeping with Velma," Midge vowed to herself. "There must be some way, short of actually wearing a dress, that I can get into a motel room with her."

She became so engrossed in dreaming about her girlfriend, she didn't see the driver of the dusty brown Impala turn to his passenger, whisper excitedly, and point at the girls. And she was so busy hanging onto the luggage while trying to catch up to Velma, that she didn't see the driver get out of his car, amble over to the mechanics, and strike up a friendly conversation.

Had she noticed what was going on back at the garage, her dreaming of Velma would have dissolved into suspicious fuming about the motives of the strange couple!

CHAPTER 16

"Look Out!"

"This town looks just like a movie set for a Western!" Cherry cried in delight as they walked along the wooden sidewalk of Dust Bin. She exclaimed over the charming early Western reproductions everywhere—the dirt road, wooden sidewalks, big balls of tumbleweed blowing about in the soft evening breeze, the old wooden lampposts lining the street.

"There's even rope hanging on each lamppost," Lauren pointed out. "In case you want to tie up your horse. Keen!"

Soon they were at the Double-D Diner, designed to look like an old saloon. "This town is aptly named," Cherry complained cheerfully as she dusted her penny loafers with a clean handkerchief before stepping through the swinging wooden doors. The girls looked around the room, but Nancy wasn't among the handful of diners enjoying the $1.29 fried steak special.

"Where could she be?" Cherry worried aloud. "Perhaps she's putting on her face in the ladies' lounge," she remarked, dumping her first-aid kit on the floor and heading toward the back of the room to find her friend.

Lauren hopped onto a stool at the bar. She dug into her pockets. Mixed in with old candy wrappers and a green cat's-eye marble was enough change for a chocolate soda. She ordered, and when her soda arrived, she took a deep, satisfying slurp. "Want some?" she offered to Velma, who sat down and took a sip of the delicious concoction.

Cherry returned, looking dismayed and worried. She was too confused by the turn of events to warn them that they were in danger of ruining their supper. Where was Nancy?

"She's selling her beautiful jewelry!" Cherry gasped suddenly. "That's got to be it. That's why she insisted on being left behind while I accompanied that nice mechanic back to the car. Why, she lied to me!"

Midge had never seen such a fierce look in Cherry's eyes

before. "Velma used to get that same look whenever she had to pull me out of a fight," Midge remembered. "That look meant I was going to be sleeping on the couch."

"Hide all sharp objects," Midge joked as they watched Cherry race out of the diner.

Velma grinned. "Young love," she sighed. "I'm glad we're old married folks now," she said to Midge with a wink. She dug into her purse and came up with a handful of quarters. "Later on I was going to wrestle those pants off you and wash them, but I think we're going to be here for a while," Velma said. She put her quarters on the scarred wooden counter. "Bartender, another round for my friends."

But before the waitress could bring the three chocolate sodas, a loud scream brought the girls to their feet.

"Stop, thief!" they heard a girl cry.

"That sounds like Cherry!" Midge exclaimed as she raced out of the diner with Velma and Lauren at her heels.

"Look, Midge! Across the street!" Lauren cried. "That's Nancy and Cherry, in front of the Treasure Chest jewelry shop!"

The girls watched in horror as a tall, unattractive man with flaming red hair pushed Cherry out of his path so hard he knocked the hapless girl into the street. And right into the path of an oncoming car!

Nancy's quick thinking saved the day. She grabbed a rope from the post in front of the jewelry shop, swiftly looped it into a lariat, swung it over her head, and expertly roped Cherry in. The driver of the car slammed on the brakes just as Cherry was pulled back from certain death!

"Those rodeo lessons I took sure come in handy," Nancy grinned in relief as she hugged Cherry. In a flash, the other girls were at Cherry's side, expressing their relief that their chum was okay.

Two nicely dressed career gals with horrified expressions on their faces jumped out of the car and raced over to Cherry. They were the reporters the girls had meet earlier at the garage—the ones who were determined to find Nancy Clue!

"Oh, look. It's the reporters we met earlier at the garage— the ones who are traveling to River Depths to interview Nancy Clue," Midge said loudly.

Nancy sensed danger was near. She turned her head, dug into her purse, and found a gay chiffon scarf, which she quickly wrapped around her trademark titian mane. A pair of dark glasses completed her disguise.

"My dear, are you all right?" Miss Gladys Gertz fussed over Cherry. "I wasn't paying any attention to the road ahead," she confessed. "I was just looking at this darling Western motif and thinking about doing our rumpus room over in a similar style, and then suddenly there you were smack in front of me in the middle of the road!

"Why, I could have killed you!" she cried in horror, throwing up her glove-clad hands in alarm. "Oh!"

"I'm okay now, Miss Gertz," Cherry calmed the frantic woman. "Except for the rope burns on my arms, there was no harm done." Lucky for her, she had had the foresight to pack rope-burn salve.

"What on earth happened?" Miss Gertz quizzed Cherry. "Why did that rude man push you? Shall I call a police officer?"

"It was all a mistake," Cherry stammered. "I thought he had taken Nan...er...my friend's jewelry box, but now I see it's just fallen on the ground." She picked up the jewelry box, gave it a quick once-over, and was relieved to find nothing missing. "It was all a silly mistake," she stammered.

"That red-haired man *did* take Nancy's case," Midge thought. "Cherry's cry must have scared him into dropping it. Too bad these nosy reporters are here, otherwise I'd go after him," she schemed. "But by now he's long gone," she reasoned. She slyly surveyed the ground around them, but saw no clues.

"We must call the police and report this immediately," Miss Gertz declared, fishing through her purse for some change for the telephone. She handed a nickel to her companion. "Marty, be a dear and call the police and inform them that we've been accosted by a rather rude man!"

"It was all a misunderstanding," Cherry insisted, not wishing to alert the police to Nancy Clue's whereabouts. "Please don't go to any trouble on my account," Cherry begged. "Besides, we must get to the Double-D Motor Lodge and secure a room for the night."

"At least let us buy you dinner for all the trouble we've caused," Miss Gertz proposed. "Goodness, all this excitement's made me hungry." She grabbed Cherry by the hand. "We won't take no for an answer," Miss Gertz insisted. "Besides, Marty and I could use some fresh company. We've all but talked ourselves to death, haven't we, Marty?" Marty nodded but said nothing.

Minutes later the girls were back at the diner, seated around a large wooden table gaily outfitted with a red-checked tablecloth. While they waited for seven steak dinners with all the trimmings to be brought to their table, they fielded questions from the inquisitive reporter. One by one the girls introduced themselves, revealing nothing else. Everyone but Nancy, that is, who pretended to be too engrossed in the decor of the diner to pay attention to the conversation.

"I just love these horseshoe-shaped drink coasters, don't you?" Nancy exclaimed. "What a charming idea."

But Miss Gertz couldn't be ignored. "What's *your* name, dear?" she persisted.

"I'm...I'm...Miss Darcy New," Nancy said hesitantly. "Yes, Darcy New. From River...er...dale. Yes. Riverdale...er... California."

"What a pretty name!" Miss Gertz exclaimed. "Darcy. So unusual. Why, with your peaches-and-cream good looks and exotic name, you could be a movie star! I'll bet you are. I'll just bet. And you're in disguise. That's why you're wearing dark glasses. Am I right?"

Nancy nodded, then excused herself and raced for the ladies' lounge.

Midge dropped her voice to a dramatic whisper. "That *is* Darcy New, the movie star," Midge revealed. "But it's a secret. You see, Darcy New is the star of Twin Mountain's newest picture. It's called...um...er...*Chit Chat*. It's just about to be released."

Miss Gertz's eyes grew wide with excitement. "I figured as much!" she cried. "Not much gets past old Gladys here. But why are you going to River Depths? And why on earth does Miss New have a nurse traveling with her?"

Midge thought quickly. Hadn't Nancy once mentioned an adventure at a sanitarium in River Depths? "Darcy New's on the verge of a nervous collapse," Midge said solemnly. "Surely you've heard of the world-renowned River Depths Sanitarium? Specializing in nervous disorders? All the really *big* actresses go there."

Miss Gertz nodded. "Of course," she whispered excitedly, her eyes all aglow. "That's why you have a nurse along!"

Midge nodded. "That's right. But you can't let Darcy know you know,"

Miss Gertz put one hand over her heart. "Cross my fingers," she whispered solemnly. Marty nodded.

"Good," Midge said. "If word leaked out about Darcy going to the sanitarium, why, there's no telling what might happen. She could go over the edge, and that would put an end to a brilliant movie career. Do you want that to happen?" Midge added dramatically.

"Oh, no," Cherry whispered, forgetting for a moment that Midge was making the whole thing up. "Poor Darcy!"

Midge shot her a dirty look and kicked her under the table. Fortunately, Miss Gertz didn't notice. She was so overcome by Midge's sad story, she had covered her mouth with her handkerchief.

"Your secret is safe with me," Miss Gertz gasped out.

When Nancy returned to the table, the reporter winked at Midge and put on a cheerful smile. "Dear, you're here just in time for the main course!" Miss Gertz cried as she spied a waitress carrying plates of steaming food their way. "Before the food gets here, would you be a dear and give me your autograph?

"Oh dear, where's my pen?" Miss Gertz cried as she turned her pocketbook upside down, searching for her writing tool. "Got it! Now, what can you write on? I know. Sign your name on this newspaper."

Cherry gasped when she saw what was in Miss Gertz's hand—a copy of the *Wyoming Buffalo Bulletin!* Miss Gertz noticed her keen interest in the newspaper.

"Isn't that a charming photograph of Nancy Clue on the front page?" Miss Gertz asked Cherry. "And inside is the most delicious recipe for rhubarb pie. I must remember to save it. I'm always meaning to save things and then I simply forget. Oh, well, that's what happens when you're a busy reporter and have to keep all sorts of information stored in one little brain."

"My mother has an excellent recipe for rhubarb pie," Cherry said helpfully.

"May I see the newspaper?" Nancy asked softly. She autographed the front page with her alias while quickly scanning the story about Hannah. Her face grew grim.

"I think that criminologist's theory about Hannah's wanting to be the dominant female in the household is an interesting one, don't you?" Miss Gertz asked Nancy. "It may help in her defense, but ultimately I think it's an open and shut case, what with the signed confession and possession of a fingerprint-laden murder weapon. Shall I order you another martini, dear?" she inquired when she saw how alarmed Nancy had become.

"I have to make a very important phone call!" Nancy cried. She jumped up from the table and headed for the telephone booth at the back of the restaurant.

"My, she's a flighty little thing, isn't she?" Miss Gertz commented. "Actresses are always so squeamish when it comes to murder."

CHAPTER 17

A Startling Confession

"I have wonderful news!" Nancy announced gaily the minute they were safely in their room at the Double-D Motor Lodge and away from the nosy reporters. "I called Chief Chumley and told him to let Hannah go!"

"What?" Midge cried. "You didn't tell him that you shot your father, did you?"

"I thought you had planned to wait until we got to River Depths so you could tell him in person and show him your father's letters," Velma chimed in.

"I was," Nancy replied. "But when Miss Gertz showed me that newspaper and I realized how strong the case is against Hannah, I decided I couldn't wait. And the Chief wasn't *at all* angry with me. Once I told him why I had done it, and where I had hidden the evidence proving Father's crimes, he promised to free Hannah immediately!"

Midge said nothing. She had the most awful sinking feeling in the pit of her stomach.

"I'm so relieved!" Nancy cried as she grabbed Cherry and danced her around the room. "I don't know why I didn't think of this sooner. Police Chief Chumley is my best friend in River Depths, besides Bess and George, that is. He'll take care of everything. Why, he's the most respected man in town. No one will question his decision to turn Hannah loose.

"He even scolded me for not calling him sooner," she chuckled. "He told me to take my time coming home, and not to tell anyone what I had told him. And he promised to call me here as soon as Hannah is free!

"Then he hung up rather abruptly. He was probably in a hurry to rush off and fix things," she reasoned. "So, you see, everything is fine. Hannah will be released right away, so it doesn't matter so much that we're stuck here for the night."

"How wonderful!" Cherry cried. "This calls for a celebration."

"I've already thought of that," Nancy declared. She pulled a bottle of champagne from her purse, got glasses from the washroom, and poured drinks all around.

"Bottoms up!" Nancy laughed as she raised her glass.

Midge left her drink untouched. She was frankly concerned that Nancy had acted in haste. "Still, that reporter practically pushed Nancy into it," she realized. Was Miss Gertz really as dumb as she seemed? Suddenly, Midge was too tired to care. She kicked off her penny loafers and plopped down on one of the two double beds in their room at the Double-D Motor Lodge. This time they had been careful not to let the motel manager see her enter the room. Now all she wanted was to curl up next to her girl and fall asleep.

"I think I'll join you!" Cherry exclaimed, bouncing on the bed. She surveyed the rustic room, with its rough wood paneling and Western decor. "These lamps shaped like covered wagons are cute!" she cried.

Nancy drew the curtains, which were patterned with a handsome horse motif, took off her kerchief and dark glasses, and fluffed her trademark titian hair. "Phew! I didn't think we'd ever get rid of those nosy reporters," she exclaimed. "I was so excited after calling the Chief, I almost blurted out the whole story at the supper table," Nancy laughed. She refilled her glass.

"Miss Gertz would be aghast to know she just had supper with Nancy Clue," Cherry giggled.

"I can't believe they really thought I was a movie star," Nancy added. "Luckily, every year at Lake Winnebago Summer Camp I played Juliet to my chum George's Romeo, so I was able to come up with a convincing soliloquy," she grinned. " 'Romeo, Romeo, wherefore art thou, Romeo?' " she intoned in a dramatic manner. She put her hand to her head, pretended to swoon, and collapsed on top of Cherry.

They were startled by a sudden knock at the door. "It's those two dames," Lauren whispered as she peeked through a part in the curtains.

Nancy raced to the bathroom to hide.

Cherry opened the door to find Miss Gertz and her friend Miss Mannish standing outside, attractively attired in matching bathing costumes. Miss Mannish had on a darling pair of beach clogs, while Miss Gertz was clad in casual straw sandals. With towels wrapped around their hair turban-style, they made a gay sight. "We're going to the pool for a late swim," Miss Gertz bubbled. "Care to join us?"

Cherry checked her sturdy nurse's watch. Only thirty minutes had passed since their meal of fried steak, mashed potatoes, salad, vegetable medley, biscuits and gravy, strawberry pie, milk, and coffee. "Why, you'll drown if you swim so soon after a large meal," she cautioned.

Miss Gertz thanked Cherry for her thoughtful advice.

Cherry beamed. More than anything, she liked helping others best. She graciously declined their invitation, feigning sleepiness. "I must get my beauty rest," she joked, faking a yawn.

Miss Gertz and her companion bade the girls a pleasant evening. "Remember to wait at least thirty more minutes before getting in the pool," Cherry leaned out the door to call after them. "And don't hesitate to come and get me if one of you should get cramped while swimming."

Midge pulled Cherry inside and closed the door. "Cherry, don't give those busybodies an excuse to come around," she cautioned. "I think they already know too much," she said.

"Midge, a nurse's vow is sacred," Cherry said. She put her hand over her heart and intoned:

> " 'I solemnly pledge myself to pass my life in purity and to practice my profession faithfully. I will abstain from whatever is mischievous or disagreeable and will not take or administer any harmful drug. With loyalty I will endeavor to aid the physician in his work and devote myself to the welfare of those committed to my care. I will at all times put the needs of others first, as that is my solemn vow.'

"I took the Stencer Nursing School oath two years ago, and except for the night I killed that evil Father Helms in self-defense, I've kept it," Cherry said proudly.

Nancy emerged from her hiding place in the bathroom, her hair neatly combed and her lipstick refreshed. "I'm going back to that jewelry store and sell some things," she declared.

"No, Nancy," Cherry protested. "Besides, it's closed by now."

"There must be someone I can call." Midge thought a minute and shook her head. "Everyone we know is broke," she remembered. "And those are our friends with jobs!"

"Well, if I'm not going to sell my jewels, then the only thing to do is sell my story to those reporters," Nancy said, a determined look in her blue eyes. "I know the Chief said to keep quiet, but I'm desperate!"

"What?" Cherry cried. "And have your most personal business splashed all over the front page of every newspaper in America? I should say not," Cherry declared. She had an idea. "Let's go through all our belongings carefully; perhaps we can scrape up enough to pay our motel bill and part of the auto bill. We could leave something as a deposit and promise to wire the money as soon as we get to River Depths," she suggested. She took off her sturdy nurse's watch. "This must have cost at least $5.99," she said. "That's something."

"We could cozy up to those reporters in the morning and get another free meal," Midge suggested. "Maybe the idea of interviewing a movie star over breakfast will appeal to them."

Nancy brightened. "Those are both fine ideas," she said, cheering up a little. She dumped the contents of her summer straw purse onto the bed and surveyed its contents with her keen detective's eye.

"Besides my clothes, I've got one tube of Passion Peach lipstick, a gold compact engraved with my initials—that might be worth something. One flashlight. My favorite magnifying glass. A fingerprinting kit. My jeweler's eyepiece. The bill from yesterday's auto repair. Eight crumpled dollar bills and...twenty-five...thirty...thirty-five...forty-two cents."

She next emptied her jewelry box onto the bed. She held up her sparkling emerald pendant and earring set. "These were my coming-out present from Great Uncle Cedwick Clue, the industrialist and railroad magnate. I'll bet we'd get a pretty penny for them. Just as a last resort," she added quickly when she saw the frown on Cherry's face.

Her late great-uncle, a lifelong bachelor with exquisite taste in clothing, had been particularly fond of his great-niece and showered her with many lovely things, including frocks and shoes it had been his pleasure to select.

The thought of parting with Uncle Cedwick's gems brought tears to her eyes. Still, she would do whatever she had to do to get home to Hannah. "I may very well have to sell these come morning," Nancy realized. She separated her truly good pieces from her costume accessories, wrapped the genuine gems in a clean handkerchief, and put the bundle on the bedside table. "Later I'll polish each piece; that way, I'm sure to get more for them," she schemed, taking care not to let Cherry see what she was doing.

Midge next emptied her small, beat-up leather valise onto the bed. "One tee-shirt, my leather jacket, a pair of government-issue handcuffs, an ace bandage, and a can of Butch Wax." A quick search of her pockets revealed one worn five-dollar bill, two dimes, and a rumpled man's white cotton handkerchief smeared with lipstick.

Cherry giggled when she saw the soiled handkerchief. "Midge, I didn't know you wore lipstick," she teased.

"Only inadvertently," Midge explained, a grin lighting up her handsome face.

"Let's see what I've got in the bank," Velma said, reaching into her bra for her folding money. "Unfortunately, it's not much," she sighed, producing four one-dollar bills. She shook out her purse. Two lipsticks, a cake of black eyeliner, a small tin of eye shadow, a small vial of luscious smelling perfume, and a compact tumbled out.

Cherry dumped the contents of her purse on the bed. "I don't think I have any money left," she said. "But it's worth a look. Goodness, my purse is a mess!" she cried, as she sifted through the jumble of objects that had come pouring out of the smart patent-leather bag.

Lauren immediately pounced on a small, red vinyl zippered case. "This looks keen—what is it?"

"That's my sewing kit," Cherry explained. "Phew! I thought I had lost it yesterday after I finished sewing a rip in Velma's blouse. Midge, I don't know if you realize it, but you've lost a button," she told her chum. "Luckily, this kit has white and black thread, a little scissors, a seam-ripper, and a jar of shirt buttons. I'll fix it later. And here's my trusty Girl Scout compass!" Cherry cried in delight, picking up a little leather case and snapping it open. "I always keep it in my purse, just in case I get lost or someone asks me directions.

"I've got a spool of dental floss and a whole bag of travel toothbrushes. I purchased five of them yesterday in case any of you lose yours. So don't be shy!" she cautioned them. "Dental hygiene is an important key to good health!" she cried, staring directly at Lauren.

"Let's see what else I have," she said. "I've got a glasses repair kit; I don't wear them but so many people do. Here's the stylish manicure kit my mother gave me for Christmas. It's got everything you need for a professional manicure, all contained in this nifty brown leather-look case. If anyone wants to borrow it, you may. Just warn me, so I can sterilize it later," Cherry added. "Oh, look!" she cried, holding up a can of White-ola Shoe Polish. "Nurses must look their best at all times; it inspires confidence and trust in our patients," she declared. "That's why I always carry a bottle of all-purpose stain remover, too, which has come in handy many a time in the last two weeks.

"Here are my stamps in case I ever get any time to write to my nurse chums," she sighed. "I promised practically every nurse I know a postcard from San Francisco, and I've been so busy I haven't had time to send even one to my roommate, Nurse Cassie Case, an attractive girl with a winning smile and a ready grin."

"What's this?" Lauren asked, picking up a small pink plastic envelope the size of a comb.

"That's my collapsible plastic rain bonnet. See?" Cherry took the bonnet out of its cover and showed Lauren how it unfolded to make a nifty full-size hairdo shield.

"What's in your first-aid kit?" Lauren wondered, quickly bored with the rain bonnet.

Cherry opened the white metal travel kit with its striking red cross emblazoned on the front. "Here's my lightweight car-trip uniform and a spare nurse's cap in case I'm called to duty. This is my snake-bite kit," she said, opening a cardboard box to reveal razor blades and a pamphlet describing the deadly vipers. "According to my *Nurse's Guide to Snakes*, there are many different kinds of deadly reptiles in Wyoming," Cherry shivered.

"Lauren, don't open that package of wooden tongue blades!" Cherry cried, snatching the paper package away from the young girl just in the nick of time. "They're sterile! And put down my blood-transfusion kit!" she cried, taking two small plastic bags that resembled deflated hot-water bottles away from Lauren. Attached to each was a slender rubber hose.

"These are not toys," Cherry admonished her. "This is specialized equipment that could save numerous lives! Nurses aren't required to carry blood-transfusion kits, but I always do," Cherry explained. "In case we come across a highway accident, I want to be fully prepared.

"This is a rectal thermometer, Lauren," she said, showing her a glass tube encased in protective plastic. "It's been a godsend in the medical world. Its accuracy can't be beat." Lauren's brown eyes grew big with wonder. Cherry could see she had really made an impression on the girl.

"What else do you have in there, Cherry?" Midge wanted to know.

Cherry was pleased that all her chums were paying close attention to her little lecture. She felt downright important as she explained all the items in her well-stocked first-aid kit. "Here's an ice bag, good for bringing down high temperatures or providing cooling relief for a headache."

"Or a hangover," Midge half joked, looking Nancy's way.

Cherry frowned and ignored her. "Here's a pad of paper and pencil for making patient notes, sterile gauze and tape, an assortment of bandages, bottles of tannic acid, a small supply of rubbing alcohol in case anyone wants a refreshing rubdown later," she looked longingly at Nancy, who was too absorbed in her own thoughts to notice. Cherry continued her inventory. "I've got milk of magnesia for stomach upsets, mercurochrome for cleaning scrapes, spirits of ammonia for fainting spells, table salt and baking soda used in treating shock and as a protectant against radiation, too, and water purification pills.

"This is a bar of strong soap for scrubbing one's hands squeaky-clean," Cherry pointed out, holding up a small, paper-wrapped rectangular bar. "A good scrubbing, and then on with the rubber gloves, and you're ready for any physical examination!"

She showed them a little plastic kit containing a vial filled with clear fluid, and six small, sharp syringes. "This is precious bee-sting serum," Cherry said. "We owe a debt of gratitude to the hearty bee, who works so hard to pollinate our beautiful flowers, but one prick to an allergic person could spell certain death!"

"Oh!" the girls chorused.

"What's this?" Midge wondered, picking up a small vial of pink pills.

"That's Valium, Midge. It works wonders!" Cherry replied. She smiled when she saw Midge's eyes light up. "Sorry, Midge, I can only dispense this under the instructions of a doctor," she warned.

"Shouldn't these be in your sewing kit?" Lauren asked, pointing to a small packet of needles. "Those are for closing a deep gash," Cherry explained. "Oh!" she cried when she came across a stray razor blade. "This should really be in my snake bite kit," Cherry mused. "In case someone is bitten, I'd use this blade to make a series of shallow cuts in their skin and suck on the wound for at least 30 minutes," she explained.

"Nursing is really keen!" Lauren cried.

Cherry beamed with pride. She took pleasure in her profession, with its many selfless acts. She hoped that she could lead many young girls into her rewarding way of life. Maybe Lauren would be one of them!

Nancy sifted through the objects on the bed. "If we need to operate, we're in luck," she joked. "But we still need money. Lauren, what's in your purse?"

Lauren scowled. "I wouldn't be caught dead carrying a purse," she said scornfully, "especially with this cool pocket in the front of my overalls." She leaned over the bed and a handful of objects spilled out.

"This is our last chance to find something," Nancy said as she eagerly looked through Lauren's collection of assorted junk. "A slingshot. Marbles. Notebook and pencils. Two miniature plastic dogs—a collie and a boxer, I believe. One...two...three..." Nancy counted under her breath. "Seventy-seven cents. A crumpled pack of cigarettes—same brand Midge smokes. Matchbooks from every diner and soda shop we've been to. Plus three stainless-steel butter knives."

"You're not smoking, are you?" Cherry gasped. "Smoking is a disgusting habit that causes your teeth to yellow, not to mention the damage it does to fine fabrics." Although she was directing her comments to Lauren, she was glaring at Midge. "And why on earth do you have these knives?" Cherry picked up a utensil and examined it closely. "Why, these are from the diner where we had supper tonight. Lauren! You're smoking *and* stealing? What next? Mayhem and murder? Young lady, you are going to march right back to that diner and return these," Cherry commanded.

"Yeah, and exchange them for real silver ones we can sell," Midge joked. Midge quit kidding around when she saw the expression on Cherry's face. She could tell she was in for a scolding, too.

But before Cherry could light into Midge, Nancy noticed a bulge in Lauren's front pocket. "What's that?" she asked. Lauren took out a dull brownish yellow rock three inches in diameter. "That looks like gold!" Cherry cried in delight, momentarily diverted.

"That's just a junky piece of iron pyrite. I already have tons of it," Lauren explained. She tossed it into the metal waste-basket between the beds.

"That's it, then," Midge announced. "In addition to the twenty-four dollars in our travel kitty, we've got eighteen dollars and thirty-nine cents, Cherry's watch, and your gold compact, Nancy." But Nancy wasn't listening. She was staring at the wastebasket with the queerest expression on her face.

"Did you hear the thud that rock made when it hit the metal?" she asked, almost to herself. She got off the bed and fished it out of the wastebasket. "If I remember correctly, gold is heavier than iron pyrite," she murmured. Suddenly her eyes lit up with excitement. "This rock may be gold!" Nancy exclaimed. "Gold and iron pyrite look an awful lot alike; that's why pyrite is often called 'fool's gold.' I learned how to identify precious gems during *The Case of the Genuine Gimcrack*," she added.

"Cherry, do you have any aqua regia in that first-aid kit of yours?" Nancy half-joked. "Plus a high heat source, like a blow torch or a Bunsen burner?"

"No, but those are certainly excellent suggestions; I must remember to pick them up," Cherry replied.

Nancy furrowed her pretty brow. "If only we had a scale, or a way to fashion one out of nearby materials." Her keen eyes swept the room, searching for the raw materials necessary for her experiment. She grabbed a wire coat hanger from the closet and set to work fashioning a crude weighing device.

The girls gathered around as the determined sleuth worked feverishly on her contraption. What was Nancy up to?

Soon she had fashioned a makeshift scale. She then removed the powder from two compacts and attached them to the wire using clip-on earrings to connect the two.

"These compacts, when open, make handy measuring plates," she smiled. "And these will do for weights," she remarked as she twisted off the clasp of her opera-length strand of pearls and started piling beads on one side of the scale. While she worked, she explained her experiment.

"It's so obvious, I don't know why I didn't think of it sooner," Nancy said with a smile. "It's simple. Since we all know the specific gravity of gold is nineteen point three, all we have to do is calculate the specific gravity of this rock, and if it happens to be nineteen point three, or close therein, we've found gold!

"We can determine the specific gravity by weighing the rock in the air and then by weighing it once again, this time submerged in water. All we really need is a uniform measure of weight. Luckily, I have this long strand of small pearls which will do nicely as a counterweight. See?"

"Oh yeah," Midge joked. "Why didn't I think of that?"

"Sometimes the simplest solution is right under our noses, Midge," Cherry comforted her.

The girls watched breathlessly as Nancy piled pearls on the scale, then raced to the washroom to reenact the very same experiment in the sink. Would the rock reveal itself to be gold?

CHAPTER 18

Eureka!

"Now, the difference between ninety-six pearls and ninety-one pearls is five. If I divide ninety-six by five, I get nineteen point two!" Nancy cried triumphantly. "There must be just a hair of silver mixed in," she mused.

"It's gold all right," she added when she saw how puzzled her friends looked.

Eureka!" Lauren shouted. She jumped up and down on the bed. "We're rich! We're rich!" she shrieked.

"How rich?" Midge asked eagerly.

Nancy dug through her suitcase and took out her *1959 Guide to Precious Minerals*. "Gold is thirty-five dollars an ounce right now," she told Lauren. "We're not rich, but we've certainly got some nice pocket money here." Her eyes twinkled in delight.

Cherry's eyes lit up. "I remember seeing a gold-exchange shop next to the restaurant!" she cried. "And if I'm correct, the sign on the door said it opens at seven a.m."

"We'll go there first thing in the morning," Nancy planned aloud. "But until then, we mustn't let this rock out of our hands. It's our only way out of here."

A sharp knock at the door startled the girls. "Yoo hoo! It's Gladys Gertz and her friend, Martha Mannish. Are you girls okay in there? We thought we heard a shout."

Nancy stashed the rock in front pocket of her casual shirtwaist dress and hurriedly donned her earlier disguise of head scarf and dark glasses.

Miss Gertz knocked again. "I know you're in there because I can see your lights are on," she called through the door in an insistent tone.

"Not one word of this to those nosy dames," Midge warned. She opened the door. "Why, it's those nice reporters!" she exclaimed heartily. "How grand to see you again!"

"What took you girls so long to answer the door?" Miss Gertz quizzed them. Without waiting for an answer, she pushed past Midge and walked right into the room.

The two women had changed out of their swim costumes and were now attired in denim outfits—a skirt for Miss Gertz and dungarees for Miss Mannish, crisp checkered shirts, and pointy cowboy boots. Miss Mannish sported a festive kerchief tied at a jaunty angle around her neck and had a fringed suede jacket casually thrown over one broad shoulder.

"Your place is just like ours," Miss Gertz said, looking around the cozy room, "except, of course, we have only one bed." She frowned. "My dear, with your being a movie star and all, I'd think you'd have rented the Bonanza Suite. The manager let us take a peek at it—it's got darling wagon-wheel tables, a private telephone, and everything! But I guess if you're traveling incognito it's best if you keep a low profile."

Suddenly Miss Gertz whirled around and took a good, long look at Nancy.

Had Miss Gertz finally figured out who she really was?

"Now that you've revealed your true identity to us, why not remove your disguise? Wouldn't you be more comfortable, dear?" Miss Gertz queried.

"We're just on our way out!" Velma exclaimed, snatching up her lipstick from the bed. She linked arms with Nancy. "Let's go Darcy!" she cried gaily.

"Where are you going?" Miss Gertz asked excitedly.

"We're...er..." Velma stumbled for an answer.

Cherry remembered what the nice mechanic had said about the square dance that evening. "We're going to a square dance at the Round-Up Club," she said. "And we must hurry or we'll be late!"

"What a lucky coincidence—that's where we're headed!" Miss Gertz cried. A calculating expression crossed her face. "Wait! I've got a great idea. Let's go together. I've even got extra scarves." She dug deep in her handsome leather-tooled handbag and came up with a handful of brightly colored Western kerchiefs. "This way no one will have to feel silly by not being properly attired," Miss Gertz said brightly.

"Although, Darcy dear, I don't know what you're going to do. I believe that wearing one scarf around your head and another around your neck is formula for a fashion disaster," she added in a worrisome tone. Nancy declared that she would be satisfied wearing just the one scarf on her head.

Cherry rummaged through Nancy's suitcase, grabbed a few items, and disappeared into the bathroom, appearing a few minutes later in an attractive black felt circle skirt just right for dancing and an off-the-shoulder peasant blouse. Short white socks paired with black penny loafers gave her a sporty air. If she was going dancing, she was going in the right outfit!

Miss Gertz nodded her approval, and handed Cherry a red kerchief. Velma chose a pale yellow scarf that nicely complemented her peach shell top. Midge balked when it came her turn to select a kerchief. Like Lauren, she preferred to remain in her own, unadorned outfit.

"We're not leaving this room until you two girls play along," Miss Gertz declared, so Midge and Lauren grudgingly chose neckwear—Midge a deep blue kerchief and Lauren a light lavender. As soon as they left the hotel room, Midge ripped off the scarf and stuffed it into her back pocket. Lauren followed suit.

"Those dames are giving me a pain," Lauren whispered to Midge. "As soon as we can, let's ditch them and go to a movie." Midge nodded in agreement. But a half hour later, when Midge reminded Lauren of her plan, the girl was too full of warm peach cobbler and spicy apple cider to move from her comfortable resting spot atop a bale of hay.

Midge climbed up next to the contented girl and spent the next hour happily watching Velma, Nancy, and Cherry whirl around on the sawdust-covered plank floor. To everyone's surprise, Cherry proved to be quite an accomplished dancer. Over cider and cookies, she explained that she had had a dance lesson at a country-western bar in San Francisco the night she'd met Nancy.

"Look over there, Lauren!" Cherry cried suddenly. "They're giving rope-trick lessons."

"Keen!" Lauren cried. And off she went. For the next half hour, Lauren watched eagerly as various rope techniques were demonstrated. She returned to the group with a rope in one hand and a big grin on her freckled face. "Look!" she cried. "This one's called 'Walk the Dog.' " She tied a small loop in the rope and set it to twirling, keeping the loop just inches above the floor.

"My, you're good with your hands!" Velma exclaimed. Midge looked a little jealous.

Even Nancy, who had proven her rope-handling abilities beyond a shadow of a doubt, was impressed by Lauren's skilled handling of the rope. "Golly, it took me weeks to learn that trick!" she exclaimed, remembering how hard she had to work to earn her Rope-Trick Badge. The strict Troop Leader, Miss Jane Hathaway, had made Nancy tie knots over and over again until she was fully satisfied. "She was so nice to let me practice on her," Nancy remembered with a smile. "Anyone else would have lost patience after the first hour, but not swell Miss Hathaway!"

Nancy's thoughts were interrupted by Miss Gertz and Miss Mannish, breathless from a rousing Virginia Reel. "Goodness!" Miss Gertz cried, taking the kerchief from around her neck and wiping her face. "I'm bushed. What do you say we call it a night? Besides, I want to switch on the radio at eleven o'clock and hear the latest report about the murder trial. Do you think they've caught up with the elusive Miss Clue yet?"

The girls studiously ignored Miss Gertz, pretending instead to admire the crafts at a nearby booth. They tried to keep the mood light as they walked back to their motel—Cherry and Nancy humming a dance tune, Lauren practicing her rope tricks, and Midge and Velma happily holding hands. Soon Miss Gertz stopped talking about the case and instead busied herself exclaiming over the stars above.

Had the girls known what was going on back at their room, their cheery mood would have been shattered. For at this very moment, a shadowy figure was lurking outside their door!

CHAPTER 19

Unexpected Guests

"Good, we finally got rid of them," Midge said after they dropped Miss Gertz and Miss Mannish at their room. "I was going to pop her if she mentioned Nancy one more time," Midge scowled. "She sure has Nancy on the brain."

Cherry smiled. She knew what that was like!

When Lauren declared that she could go no further without a cold drink, the girls agreed to go to the diner adjacent to the motel and purchase refreshing beverages for consumption in their room.

"Then it's off to bed, as we have a long day ahead of us," Cherry reminded her chums. "I must freshen up," she decided, giving her friends her order for an orange soda. She skipped ahead to their room, humming a festive fiddle tune. Goodness, she was dusty.

When Cherry got to their room, she was surprised to find the door was unlocked. "That's strange," she thought, as she turned the knob and peered inside. "I thought I locked this. I must have been so nervous when Miss Gertz burst in and I had to tell that fib, that I neglected to lock the door." She looked around, but nothing seemed out of place. The contents of their purses were still in a big jumble on the bed.

"Mother would shriek if she could see how untidy we are," Cherry smiled as she walked over to the bed and began gathering her things. She realized she had been remiss to leave the contents of her first-aid kit lying about. "A child could toddle in here and accidentally ingest one of these medicines," she thought with a shudder as she put her supplies back.

Just as she was finishing her task, she heard the door slowly creak open. "I sure could use that soda!" she exclaimed, whirling around to greet her friends. She was startled to see a dark-haired man with his suit lapel pulled high over his face racing out the doorway, with Nancy's jewelry case in one hand!

"Stop, thief!" she screamed for the second time that day. But her throat was parched from an evening of laughing and chatting, and all that came out was a pathetic croak.

"I mustn't let him steal Nancy's precious possessions," she thought, racing out the door after the man. "Thank goodness I'm wearing flats," was her second thought.

She did her best to keep up, but she fell further and further behind.

"I'm going to lose him," she thought frantically. She spotted her chums lingering outside of the diner. Unaware of the drama unfolding before their eyes, they were casually leaning on the porch rails, sipping sodas and laughing. Nancy spotted Cherry and waved to her.

Cherry thought fast. How could she alert them to the danger at hand—and quickly? Suddenly, she had the answer. She took two clean white handkerchiefs from her pocket, and, using them as flags, signaled her distress. Thank goodness that during her stint as a Cruise Nurse aboard an ocean liner, she had learned the Coast Guard Distress Signals.

Nancy, who was well-versed in all forms of communication, immediately translated Cherry's message for the others. "Stop that man with the untidy black hair. He's got your jewelry case," Nancy repeated slowly. "Oh," she exclaimed. "He's got my jewelry case!"

Midge leapt into action with the others hot at her heels. They chased the thug down the sidewalk and had almost caught up to him when he disappeared around a corner and raced down an unlit side street, his dark coat and black hair blending into the inky night. They heard a car screech to a halt, a door slam, and a engine roar.

"He's gone!" Cherry cried in alarm. "How very odd that there are two jewel thieves in this very same area," she said, remembering the ugly incident earlier that evening in front of the jewelry shop. "One with flaming red hair and the other with untidy black hair. Oh, dear!"

"What's this?" Nancy asked excitedly, snatching a strand of black fiber from the ground. Using the flashlight she always kept in her pocket in case of emergencies, she examined her find. "This is from a cheap wig," she determined. "That man was wearing a shoddy disguise. He *must* be the same man who pushed Cherry earlier today. What a clever ruse," she added. "Now we have no idea what he really looks like!"

Luckily, Nancy had spent many a summer behind the scenes at the local Junior Theater, learning first-hand the materials of stage craft. She was particularly adept at recognizing disguises—a skill that had helped her in solving many mysteries!

"He's got your jewels!" Cherry wailed. "Oh, Nancy, can you ever forgive me? I forgot to lock our door, and a nefarious hoodlum sneaked inside and stole your jewels! I wouldn't blame you if you never spoke to me again," Cherry added. "Why, I may never speak to myself again! How could I have left the door unlocked? How could I have—"

Nancy grinned and kissed Cherry quickly to end her tortured lamenting. "He's got my jewel *case* containing only my costume pieces," Nancy laughed. "I left my good gems wrapped in a hankie on the bedside table." She reached into the pocket of her dress for the chunk of gold they had discovered earlier. "Luckily, I took this to the square dance. We're still going to get out of here tomorrow, and home to Hannah. That's what's really important."

"Do you think they'll come back when they realize they've got a case full of fake baubles?" Cherry cried worriedly.

Nancy nodded. "It's just possible they will. We know two things. He's in disguise and is likely to change his appearance again in order to fool us. Plus, he's got an accomplice, and they're traveling in an automobile. We've got to keep our wits sharp and our eyes open," Nancy cautioned. "Jewel thieves are a particularly cunning breed of criminal. They'll go to any length to attain what they want."

"Why, the next time I see a suspicious character, I'll run and get someone immediately!" Cherry vowed.

"And I can tie 'em up with my rope," Lauren planned as she practiced her double-hitch square knot.

The once gay little group, now sobered by the run-in with the thief, made its way back to the room. Cherry peered around every corner and even jumped once when she heard a sudden moaning noise from behind her. She was relieved when she realized it was only Midge and Velma.

"I've got to keep my wits sharp and my eyes open," Cherry thought, a chill of terror racing up her spine. She was determined, having been neglectful once, not to make the same mistake again!

CHAPTER 20

A Frantic Phone Call

"Coffee. Hot and black," Midge ordered as she slid her lanky frame into a booth at the Double-D Diner. She yawned and rubbed her eyes. It was practically against her religion to get out of bed before nine o'clock in the morning, but she figured it was the only way she could get some much-needed privacy.

"I haven't been up at the crack of dawn on purpose since that time my grandfather took me fishing when I was ten," she remembered. "Once every twenty-five years or so I'll get up and watch the sun rise," she vowed. "Builds character!" She yawned again. Between Nancy's tossing and turning and Lauren's snoring, Midge had gotten precious little sleep.

The waitress, a shapely number in a tight-fitting pink costume and frilly apron, smiled at Midge as she placed a cup of steaming coffee on the chipped Formica table. Midge took a big gulp of her favorite beverage.

"Not too strong, I hope?" the waitress purred, lingering at Midge's side even though the diner was quickly filling up with early-morning fishermen.

"Perfect," Midge replied. The waitress bent close to Midge and refilled her cup. Midge surveyed the curve of the girl's breasts under the thin cotton material of her uniform. "Er...ah...I'll need a few minutes to look over the menu," Midge stammered. She noticed that a large man wearing a loud plaid jacket was gesturing frantically at the waitress.

"Take your time," the girl replied in a smooth manner. "I'm here until two. That's when I get off. Two o'clock. In the afternoon—"

Midge hurriedly pointed at the menu. "I'll have this," she said, not even caring what she was ordering.

The girl took the pencil from behind her ear and flipped open her order book. "One Dish of the Day," she murmured.

"Would you like anything else? Anything at all?"

Midge blushed and shook her head. She watched the waitress walk away, swaying to the country music coming from the jukebox. "I'm not used to getting so much attention from other girls," Midge thought. "I've practically got the word 'married' stamped on my forehead!" She gulped down the rest of her coffee and lit her first cigarette of the day. "Can everyone tell that I'm starved for romance?" she wondered. She counted the days on her fingers. She realized with a start that she hadn't been alone with Velma for two days.

"*Two* whole days!" Midge moaned.

Her thoughts of Velma were interrupted by the waitress, back with a platter of food. "Sausage, flapjacks, fried eggs, grits, bacon, ham, homemade biscuits, jam, and grapefruit juice. Can I get you anything else?"

Midge shook her head dumbly, overwhelmed at the feast set before her. "At least I can eat all I want," she sighed, cracking the yolk of an egg with a fluffy biscuit before stuffing it into her mouth. She turned her attention to the newspaper she had picked up outside the diner. She was relieved to see no mention of Hannah's trial.

"What are you doing, Midge? Reading the newspaper?" Lauren slid into the booth and tried to get Midge's attention.

Midge groaned. What was Lauren doing up?

"Trying to," Midge replied. She was determined to have one quiet breakfast. Why, since they had begun their journey, she hadn't had one minute to herself.

"Can I have the comics?" Lauren wanted to know. She reached across the table, and clumsily knocked over Midge's coffee.

"Darn it, Lauren," Midge yelled, hastily trying to mop up the hot liquid with her thin paper napkin. "Cherry's right— you are headed for reform school." Midge had to grin a little when she said this. More and more, Lauren was beginning to remind her of herself.

The waitress appeared. She quickly mopped the table top and provided Midge with a fresh cup of coffee. "Would your little friend like some milk?" she asked.

"Milk?" Lauren scowled. "I'll take a cup of coffee. Make it black," she snapped.

"Milk," Midge mouthed. She noticed Lauren eyeing her plate of food, and pushed it across the table. "You can have some," she said, "but only if you promise not to do anything but sit there and eat."

"I promise. But, Midge—"

"Not another word," Midge scowled. "I want total silence." She took a sip of her coffee.

"But—" Lauren started.

"Not one word," Midge grumbled.

"Fine, but just don't blame me 'cause I didn't give you Velma's message."

Midge hastily put down her cup. "Velma gave you a message to give to me? Why didn't you say so?"

Lauren shrugged and took a big bite of ham. Midge looked annoyed.

"She wants to see you back in the room," Lauren finally spit out.

Midge jumped up from the table. "Stay here," she said. "Finish your breakfast and sit until I get back." Midge raced out of the diner and headed for their room.

"Hi, Midge," a cheery voice called out. Cherry, crisply outfitted in a pink poplin jumper and white blouse, was standing next to their newly repaired car, a paper sack in one hand and a newspaper in the other.

"That nice mechanic just dropped off the car," she reported. "Nancy has gone to sell our piece of gold and settle the repair bill. I'm going to tidy the car before we begin the last leg of the trip," she planned aloud. "And that nice motel manager gave me some boxes so I can organize Lauren's rock collection."

"Good!" Midge cried as she raced past her. She took care not to be seen by the manager and was relieved when she made it through the door. Midge's heart melted at the sight of Velma, curled up in bed, a pile of warm blankets near her feet. She kicked off her loafers, peeled off her shirt, and slipped under the covers.

For a moment Midge lay quietly, enjoying the way her body fit so perfectly with Velma's. She gently put her hand on Velma's hip and kissed the back of her neck. Velma moaned and wriggled closer to Midge.

"I've been waiting for you," she sighed, rolling over to face her girlfriend. She wrapped her arms around Midge's neck and pulled her close.

"Lauren took forever to give me your message—otherwise I would have been here minutes ago!" Midge cried out excitedly.

Velma grinned, roughly rolled Midge on her back, and climbed on top of her. "Did you lock the door?" she murmured.

Midge nodded as she worked feverishly to rid Velma of her pink satin pajama trousers.

Velma grabbed her purse from the bedstand. With one hand she swiftly emptied its contents on the floor. "I swiped this from Miss Gertz," she explained, holding up her yellow bandanna from last night's square dance. Within seconds she had expertly bound Midge's wrists to the decorative cattle horns on the headboard. "Nancy's not the only one who earned her Rope-Trick Badge," Velma grinned.

"I could use a free hand," Midge protested mildly.

Velma ignored her. She ran her tongue over Midge's breasts.

"Just for a minute?" Midge pleaded.

Velma bit her softly but said nothing.

Midge groaned and closed her eyes. She knew when she was licked.

A sudden knock at the door startled them both.

"Ignore it," Midge groaned, locking her strong legs around Velma's waist. Velma did her best, but it was difficult to ignore what came next.

"River Depths calling Miss Nancy Clue," a man's voice rang

out. It was the motel manager. Both girls had the same thought. It must be an emergency!

"We're coming," Midge yelled, trying to stop the man from shouting again. The last thing they needed was for those nosy reporters staying just three doors down to discover that Darcy New was really Nancy Clue!

Velma leapt out of bed, jumped into her clothes, and headed for the door. She whirled around and raced back to the bed. "Sorry, honey," she said, as she quickly untied Midge. Then she raced out the door.

Midge groaned and buried her head in the pillow. She was as close to tears as she'd ever been!

When Velma returned a few minutes later, she had a horrified expression on her pretty face. "Oh, Midge!" she cried. "The most horrible man was on the phone!"

Midge leapt from the bed where she had been anxiously awaiting Velma's swift return and raced over to her girlfriend. She held the trembling girl close.

Velma's story tumbled out in gasps and sobs. "When I went to the phone...I intended...to say...that I wasn't Nancy...but before...I could say...any more than 'hello,' a dreadful voice...came on the line. He said the most awful things," Velma gasped. She repeated his exact words. " 'Nancy Clue...if you know...what's good for you...you'll stay...away from River Depths lest a tragic fate...befall you.' Then he said...he'd make...sure...she spent the rest of her life...behind bars...if she didn't...keep...her...mouth...shut!" Velma cried. "Oh, Midge, what are we going to do? We can't let Nancy go back there now!"

"I will, too, go back," Nancy declared. They were surprised to see Nancy standing in the doorway, holding a sack of groceries, her cheeks aflame with anger. "I don't know why someone would try to scare me off, but it's not going to work," she declared. "I will not go to jail for the murder of my father when it was clearly a case of justifiable homicide!" she exclaimed. "What did the man sound like? Could you identify an accent or any unusual characteristics?" she quizzed Velma.

Velma shook her head. "It was hard to make out his voice," she admitted, adding, "It was all muffled. But I did hear a slight buzzing noise in the background. It must have been a bad connection."

"So he was disguising his true identity," Nancy deduced. "He was probably using the old handkerchief-over-the-receiver trick. It's popular with crooks who use telephones in their wicked misdeeds."

Nancy put her bag on the bed and took off her scarf and dark glasses. "When I called Chief Chumley yesterday, I gave him the phone number of the motel. Some criminal must have stolen it from a pad of paper on his desk. I'll bet he overheard the Chief talking to me and hatched his evil plan. My best guess is that he's setting a trap for blackmail," she concluded. "When we get to River Depths, this petty thief will probably be the first to contact us. I will simply turn his extortion attempt over to the Chief, and we will be done with him," she declared.

"Not a word of this to Cherry," Nancy pleaded. "You know how much she worries."

Just then, Cherry skipped into the room. She spied the bag of groceries. "Oh, good, you got the money and purchased food. Well, I've been a busy bee, too, while you've been gone. I've tidied the car and updated our driving schedule. Barring any more breakdowns, we should be in River Depths in exactly twenty hours and seven minutes, not counting rest stops and meals. Oh, Nancy!" she cried, throwing her arms around her favorite date. "I have such a good feeling about today. I just know that once we get to River Depths, everything will be okay!"

CHAPTER 21

"O, Nebraska!"

"I'm bored," Lauren complained as she surveyed the long stretch of unending fields before her eyes. "Aren't we ever going to get out of this flat place?" she scowled. "There's nothing to look at here besides miles and miles of stupid corn and boring wheat!"

Cherry gasped indignantly. "Nebraska is the heart of our nation, Lauren," she admonished. "Look all around you—see that wheat growing tall and proud?" Her voice cracked with emotion. "See it glistening gold in the sun? I'll tell you who lives here, Lauren. People who feed hungry folks with the toil of their hands." Cherry swelled with pride when she thought of the vast and rich resources of her country. "Despite heat and hail and dust storms and insects, hearty Nebraskans keep going!" she cried. "And why? To nourish people just like you and me, Lauren. To grow wheat so you can have your morning sticky bun, and the roll around your frankfurter, not to mention corn on the cob and other favorites.

"Look above you, Lauren," Cherry said as she threw her head back and squinted into the brilliant sunlight. "Have you ever seen a sky so radiant and rich in color? Have you ever seen such cottony clouds, racing across the prairie swells?"

Lauren had to admit that the sky *was* awfully blue.

"It will be dark as we drive through Iowa," Cherry warned as she checked her travel itinerary. "So soak up these broad fields, deep skies, waist-high wheat, fields of golden corn, and brilliant sunshine while you can, Lauren."

She was excited to realize they would reach River Depths right on schedule! They would cross the state line into Iowa at approximately six o'clock, stop for a yummy supper, then drive swiftly but carefully across Iowa, arriving at the Illinois border at approximately one o'clock in the morning. From then on, it would be a mere matter of hours before they arrived in River Depths. "And Nancy will see Hannah and finally put all her worries aside."

Cherry was a little disappointed that they would drive through most of corn country under cover of darkness.

"Iowa—now that's a most important state in the exciting story of our nation's food production," she declared. "Did you know, if you put Iowa's corn crop for one year in freight cars, the train would stretch from New York to California?" Cherry cried excitedly. "Nobody, however, would really do this," she was quick to assure them. "It's a good thing, too, because then we would have to do without things like corn syrup and penicillin and cornsilk for our face powder."

"Or corn chowder," Velma piped up. "Yum."

"And popcorn," Lauren added.

"Corn fritters," Nancy licked her lips.

Cherry settled into the cushy leather back, closed her eyes and soon was dreaming of rows and rows of silky golden wheat swaying in the gentle breeze. A few hours later, the crack of thunder, then the soft splashing sound of summer rain on the canvas convertible top roused Cherry from her restful sleep.

"Are you feeling refreshed?" Velma asked softly, handing her chum a cup of cool water. Cherry was pleased to see that Velma had remembered to fill their travel thermos. She took a generous gulp of the cool liquid and smiled her thanks.

"Have I been asleep for long?" Cherry asked Velma, who was sitting in the front seat next to Midge, who was still at the wheel.

"We're almost to Iowa," Velma replied.

"But Nancy's supposed to take the second leg of the Nebraska excursion!" Cherry cried. "Didn't you check the schedule?

"Nancy's sleeping," Velma whispered.

Cherry realized with a start that Nancy was stretched out in front of her on the floor of the back seat and was sound asleep.

"We stopped for lunch about an hour ago. You were sleeping peacefully, so we left you in the car. I'm afraid that Nancy overdid it a little and passed out," Velma explained.

"Good Midwestern cooking can have that effect on many people," Cherry remarked.

Velma made a funny face and passed Cherry a brown paper sack. "Er, yeah," she said. "Here's a meat loaf sandwich, some stewed tomatoes, and a nice piece of raisin pie for you."

Cherry hungrily downed the tasty lunch, then wiped her hands on a hankie. She settled back to enjoy the ride.

"Don't you think it's exciting to be in the middle of a storm, watching the sky turn all sorts of colors? Look over there! Is that lightning?" Cherry squealed as a flash lit up the sky.

Midge cracked a smile. Around Cherry, it was hard not to. "When I was a kid and it stormed, my grandmother and I would take the kitchen chairs outside and sit under the old oak tree and watch the sky light up," Midge remembered fondly. "You're not really supposed to," she chuckled. "But as my grandmother would say, there're worse ways you could go."

Cherry's eyes grew big with alarm. She could see now was as good a time as any for some weather-safety tips!

"Never stand under a tree or fix your television antenna during a thunderstorm," Cherry cautioned. "Stay away from sailboats and water as well. And if you come across a tornado, run to the nearest basement! A tornado is a whirlpool of air so violent that houses in its path may fly apart like matchsticks, and trains can be pulled right up off their tracks," she explained helpfully. "Did you know that next year, the United States Government has plans to launch weather satellites which will circle the globe every one hundred fifteen minutes at an average height of nine hundred miles, and report back threatening weather conditions, thus saving countless lives?" Cherry said in awe. "Imagine! Three times a day, the satellites will make snapshots of the entire earth!"

"Do you think weather is all they're interested in?" Midge wondered.

Cherry was puzzled. "What could you mean, Midge? Why else would the government put cameras up there?"

"Maybe they like to look at what people are doing," Midge guessed.

"Golly, Midge, you've got to stop being so suspicious!" Cherry cried. "What a thing to suggest. Why, that would be snooping, and that's downright un-American!" She shivered at the thought of a big camera in the sky taking her picture. "Of course it couldn't see through roofs, so no one could see me when I'm undressing," she reasoned. Still, the idea made her nervous.

Silly Midge! Always seeing trouble where there wasn't any. True, during their recent San Francisco adventure, Midge had been right about many things, including the true nature of the evil priest who had tried to kill them, but that was an isolated case, wasn't it? Cherry thought Midge could certainly do with a more positive outlook on life.

She lay back on the comfy white leather seat. "We're almost to Omaha," she thought dreamily. She wriggled on her side so she could gaze into her sweetie's face. If only Nancy would awaken and realize I'm here, Cherry thought wistfully. She lightly touched the sleeping girl's cheek and wished her awake. But Nancy slept on.

CHAPTER 22

At Long Last, Iowa

Cherry hummed happily as they crossed the Missouri River into Iowa. Although the river wasn't nearly so glorious as the raging Mississippi—a secret and eccentric river full of thick trees, tall grasses, birds, mosquitoes, deer and turtles, and an industrial artery with a ceaseless flow of traffic, as well—it was a nice tributary just the same.

"And I do remember a nifty song that travelers often sing as they pass over the Missouri," Cherry suddenly realized. She sang out, clear and true.

Oh, Shenandoah, I love your daughter,
'Way you rolling river!
I'll take her 'cross your rolling water.
Away we're bound, away, 'cross the wide Missouri!

She knew there were many more words, but for the life of her, those were the only ones she could remember. "Sorry, that's all I know," she said.

"That's quite enough," Midge grinned. She steered the car over the impressive concrete expanse that linked Nebraska and Iowa, stopping only to pitch a quarter into the box at the toll plaza.

"Midge, aren't you tired of driving yet?" Cherry worried. It occurred to her that Midge had spent an awful lot of time behind the wheel. "Next time we stop for gasoline, and have our tires and fluid levels checked, I'll revise the driving schedule so you get some time off," she declared.

"I don't mind driving," Midge said. "It gives me something to do besides just sit and think." She wanted to add, "and worry," but didn't.

"Thinking can be very wearisome," Cherry declared.

"Besides that, it causes those awful worry lines on one's forehead. I'll let you in on a little trick my mother taught me, Midge," Cherry shared helpfully. "Several times a day, for as long as you can, try to think of nothing at all. It works wonders! Oh, look!" she squealed, pointing to a roadside sign in the shape of a giant ear of corn.

WELCOME TO IOWA!

"We're finally here! Did you know, Midge, that the tallest corn ever grown was right here in Iowa? A farmer named Lawrence Flanders grew a stalk measuring twenty-three feet, two and a half inches tall!"

Midge grew wide-eyed in alarm. She said nothing.

Cherry checked her *Travel Guide to Corn Country*, which she had purchased at an earlier rest stop, listing all events and fairs throughout the corn belt. "If we were traveling only a few days later, we would get to see Plowing Day in Des Moines, where men compete on their tractors to see who is the best contour plower. The man who wins this is known for a year as the Contour King," she informed Midge. "For ladies, there is a slipper-kicking contest to see which lady can kick her slippers the highest. Oh, wouldn't that be fun to see, Midge?"

Midge was too busy chewing on a rope of red licorice to reply.

"It says here, this feature alone is worth traveling miles to see. Forty thousand people come each year to Plowing Day! I'll bet they need a lot of Fairground Nurses for that many people. Besides danger of sunstroke and hay allergies, people often overindulge on many delicious foods and get indigestion, I'll bet," Cherry dreamed happily.

"I can't wait to get to River Depths," she sighed. "Then all our troubles will be over. I'll bet Hannah's clad in a simple house dress and a crisp starched apron, baking up a storm while she awaits Nancy's return."

Midge didn't answer.

"She's probably too hypnotized by the miles and miles of corn fields, glistening crimson and orange in the light of dusk to respond," Cherry thought. "Don't you think so, Midge?" Cherry quizzed her. "Don't you think that soon all our troubles will be over?"

"I hope you're right, Cherry," Midge sighed.

Cherry unrolled her window and took a deep whiff of the rain-drenched fields. "There's nothing sweeter smelling than wet corn!" she cried out. She took another deep breath, intending to fill her lungs with the fresh country air, but found herself gasping and choking instead.

"Pew! What's that smell?" her traveling companions cried in unison as they jerked awake. They had unfortunately passed a pig farm!

"Where are we?" Nancy asked sleepily. She stretched her arms over her head and arched her back, stiff from sleeping so long on the floor of the car. "I could sleep forever," she yawned. "Maybe I will," she murmured. She lay back down and closed her eyes.

Cherry checked the Iowa map which she kept stored, neatly folded, in her skirt pocket. "We're only a few miles from Kornville," she reported. She checked her *Travel Guide to Corn Country* so she could inform her chums of the many fascinating facts about the nearby town. "It's a farming community with a population of thirty thousand. It's also home to many worthy state institutions, like The Industrial Home for Problem Girls, for example.

"Iowa provides institutional homes for those who have failed to become good citizens," Cherry was delighted to report as she read her booklet aloud. " 'Every effort is made to help them by emphasizing religious training and educating them in sewing, beauty culture and other domestic arts, and teaching them to be industrious.' "

She was further impressed when she saw hygiene and sanitation were taught as well. " 'Here girls are being taught clean living and right-thinking,' " she read aloud.

"Could we drive by there?" Midge wanted to know. "Do you think they give tours?"

"That would be fascinating and educational, Midge, but it says here it's only open to the public on the fourth of July, when townspeople are encouraged to visit the troubled girls and bring them picnic suppers," Cherry informed her. "Besides, if we had had time to stop anywhere, I would have insisted on a trip to Red Cloud, Nebraska, to visit the childhood home of Willa Cather. She was an important American writer who never married but instead devoted her life to her work, much as I do.

"Oh, look, Midge, there's even a school for the feeble-minded!" Cherry cried as she continued browsing through her book. "It's called The Iowa State School for the Feeble-Minded."

"That's a very original name," Midge cracked.

"It sounds like a wonderful place, too, Midge!" Cherry enthused. "Listen to this:

" 'Every effort is made to provide amusements and entertainment in order to make the lives of the more than twelve hundred unfortunate people here as happy as possible.' "

Cherry wondered if someday she, too, could be a Feeble-Minded Nurse.

"It's hard to believe there's anyplace more interesting than Nebraska, but Iowa is living proof," Midge remarked dryly. "Ouch!" she yelped.

"What happened, Midge?" Cherry cried. "Did a bee bite you?" She grabbed her first-aid kit, ready to spring into action.

"I was bitten, all right, but not by a bee," Midge laughed. At this, Velma, who had been napping with her head in Midge's lap, sat straight up. She took out her compact and applied a thick layer of lipstick to her full, pouty lips.

"Biting is a good way to spread germs and disease," Cherry cautioned them.

"Yeah, you heard the nurse. No biting," Midge agreed. Cherry smiled when she realized Midge was finally taking her professional advice.

"Then you'd better be good," Velma shot back at Midge.

Midge popped a cigarette in her mouth, lit it, and took a long drag. She looked sideways at Velma, a sly look in her eyes. "I *am* good," she said softly.

Velma grinned and slipped off her shoes. She propped herself against the car door, and stretched out with her feet in Midge's lap. "Yes, you are," Velma murmured as she stared at her girlfriend through half-closed lids. "You're *very* good," she purred as she wriggled about.

Cherry had to grab her first-aid kit fast to keep it from falling off her lap as Midge abruptly jerked the car to the side of the road and cut the engine. "I can't drive anymore," Midge gasped as she jumped out of the car and flung her body against the side of the snappy convertible. She was almost in tears!

Cherry was shocked to see how red Midge's face had

become. "And she's breathing so heavily, she must be about ready to hyperventilate," Cherry thought in alarm. She grabbed the paper sack that had been serving as their litter bag, jumped out of the car, and popped it over Midge's head.

"Oops, I forgot to empty it first," Cherry blushed as cookie crumbs, banana peels, and candy wrappers cascaded over Midge. "I'll clean up later," Cherry decided. She knew this was no time for second thoughts! Here was her chance to practice medicine in a faraway land with only her know-how, taut nerves, and the most rudimentary of medical equipment to get her by!

"Breathe deeply," Cherry warned her. "Or else you're going to hyperventilate, or faint, or worse! You're not too young for a heart attack or a stroke—one that could leave you incapacitated and in terrible pain for the rest of your life!" Cherry cried, trying to get her chum to relax.

Midge pulled the bag from her head, licked the cookie crumbs from her lips, and lit a cigarette. After a short rest by the side of the road, Midge was still a little pink, but she had calmed down considerably.

Once again, a cool head had proven to be the best medicine, Cherry realized with a smile.

"I'd better drive," Velma murmured as she hopped in the car, adjusted the front seat to accommodate her petite frame, positioned the rearview mirror for best visibility and tied a chiffon scarf around her hairdo.

"Are we ready to go?" Velma asked her passengers.

"Ready," everyone chorused. Everyone, that is, except Midge.

Velma switched on the engine. "You ready, Midge?" she asked in a light, teasing tone.

"Yes, Velma, I'm ready," Midge sighed from the back seat. Off they went.

"We'll be driving through Kornville in another hour!" Cherry cried excitedly. "Won't it be downright educational to see a real farm town up close? Wouldn't that be fun, Midge? Wouldn't you be excited?" she asked her chum, who seemed to be in unusually poor spirits.

"Yes, Cherry, if anything could excite me, that would be it," Midge sighed.

CHAPTER 23

A Surprising Encounter

"Isn't it picturesque here?" Cherry cried as they drove through residential Kornville. "All these darling little houses with their white picket fences. This sure looks like a swell place to live.

"Darn!" she cried upon spying a billboard advertisement announcing Kornville's Korn Karnival. "If we were only making this trip a little later, we could attend the annual festival. I read all about it in my book," she added. "A king and queen are crowned, and they reign over three whole days of fun, festivities, and crop-growing demonstrations."

Velma eased the car into a spot in front of a sparkling chrome and green-tiled diner. "I've simply got to powder my nose," she murmured.

"This is a good opportunity to call Bess and George again," Nancy declared. "Oh, darn, what did I do with my purse?" she worried aloud. Cherry handed Nancy her coin caddie, and Nancy and Velma headed inside.

"Is there any food left?" Lauren wanted to know.

Cherry shook her head. "We've already eaten the bag of apples, one dozen bananas, a box of chocolate bars, two loaves of bread, and the jar of peanut butter Nancy purchased this morning," she informed her.

Lauren scampered out of the car and headed for the diner.

"Lauren, come back. We're not scheduled to have supper for another hour," Cherry said, to no avail. Cherry opened her little red notebook where she kept accounts of gasoline expenses, mileage, and the driving schedule. "I didn't figure in time for unscheduled stops, so we've fallen slightly behind," she admitted. "Maybe we can get a sack of hamburger sandwiches and eat them in the car," she suggested, but changed her mind when she saw Lauren was already perched on a stool, sipping a soda.

"Oh, let the kid have her fun," Midge declared. "There's barely been a peep out of her all day."

Cherry realized Midge was right. "That long talk Velma had with her last night worked miracles," she remarked.

Midge looked puzzled. "What talk?" she wondered. "I didn't hear anything. We all went to bed at the same time; plus, I was up half the night, anyway. I would have heard something."

Cherry grinned. "Midge, you were out like a light the minute your head hit the pillow," she teased. "I was the one up all night—listening to you snore. Besides, you wouldn't have heard anything because Lauren and Velma went for a walk right after you fell asleep. Come to think of it, they were gone an awfully long time. I don't even remember hearing them come in," she mused. "Oh, I guess we are eating here. Look—Velma's joined Lauren."

Cherry suddenly spotted two old friends walking up the street toward the diner. "Yoo hoo," she called. "Why, it's that nice couple I bumped into back in Pocatello, the ones who helped me find Nancy's jewelry box when I accidentally lost it the other day!" Cherry cried to Midge as she waved to the blond-haired woman and her male companion, who pulled his hat low over his face and looked away. "What a happy coincidence that they would be in Kornville at the very same time! Oh," she added in disappointment. "They turned down a side street. Too bad you didn't get to meet them, Midge. They're quite nice. They probably didn't recognize me, as last time we met, I was in my nightie," Cherry chuckled.

"Huh?" Midge asked. She hadn't been paying attention.

"Are you telling me that Velma and Lauren sneaked out in the middle of the night to have a private conversation, and stayed away for hours?" Midge stared at Lauren and Velma through the plate glass window of the diner. They were sharing a soda and chatting amiably. Then Midge stalked off.

"Is it my imagination, or is she acting a little strange?" Cherry wondered. "Where are you going, Midge?" Cherry cried. "You'll miss supper. Shall we order some food for you?"

But Midge waved her away. "Suit yourself," she said. "I'm going for a walk."

"Oh, dear. Slushes, sundaes, burgers and shakes. Chicken-in-a-basket. Fish sticks and Bar-B-Que. Whatever will I order for her?" Cherry thought worriedly as she stared at the sign over the diner.

"What's eating Midge?" Cherry quizzed Velma once she made her way inside the sparkling clean chrome and tile diner. She perched on a stool, puzzling over her chum's odd behavior. "I've never seen her like this. She acted all queer, then she stomped off without saying where she was going. Something seems to be truly bothering her."

"What's the date?" Velma asked.

Although Cherry was puzzled, she opened her purse and checked the little calendar in her wallet. "It's July the eighteenth, why?"

Velma laughed. "It's just that Midge gets really edgy when, well, you know. When it's her time."

Cherry looked blankly at Velma.

"You know. When her visitor arrives."

Cherry blushed. Somehow, she never thought of Midge as having any visitors!

Lauren, who was perched on the stool next to Velma, giggled nervously.

"Lauren, menstruation is nothing to be ashamed of," Cherry scolded her. "Have you seen that little filmstrip—the one where the girl chipmunks go off into the woods to be alone for a few days?" she asked anxiously. "Well, if you have any questions, as a nurse, I'm the perfect person to talk to about intimate, personal matters in a simple, straightforward way.

"I'd better check my first-aid kit to make sure I've got an assortment of sanitary products on hand," Cherry whispered to Velma. She hopped off the stool. "When Nancy returns, make sure she orders a nutritious supper, as we've got a long journey ahead of us tonight," she said to Velma. "And get two chicken-in-a-baskets to go," she added on her way out the door.

When Cherry got to their car, she was startled to find a middle-aged dark-haired woman clad in a simple navy blue shift and navy pumps, crouched on the floor of the convertible.

"Oh!" Cherry cried in alarm. "I must have the wrong car." But she quickly realized it had to be their car, as her first-aid kit was lying in plain view on the back seat.

"Oops!" the woman cried as she jumped up and scrambled out of the car.

"What happened?" Cherry cried. "Did you trip and fall into our car? These convertibles are a real hazard sometimes," she added in a soothing tone. The woman had to be awfully embarrassed; why, her slip had been showing!

"Yes, that's it," the woman laughed as she brushed herself off, straightened her dress, and patted her short beehive hairdo. She took a red headscarf from her purse, tied it around her hair, and donned a pair of white plastic sunglasses. "Well, I simply must be going. My brother Howard is probably sick with worry wondering what has happened to me!" she cried as she raced off.

Cherry smiled and hopped in the car to make a quick check of the feminine products in her first-aid kit. "What's this?" she wondered as she spotted a colorful piece of cardboard lying on the floor of the convertible. Why, it was the jack of clubs from the playing deck from the Pocatello Komfort Kourt!

Cherry grew wide-eyed in concern. "Lauren must have stolen the deck, and this card fell out of her pocket," she reasoned. "This is the second time I've caught her stealing. Is Lauren a kleptomaniac?"

But she forgot all about her worrisome young chum when she spied Nancy's summer straw bag crammed under the driver's seat. "So this is where Nancy's purse went to," she smiled, pleased to have found it. While she was startled to see Nancy's purse was wide open, she was equally relieved to find everything in its place, including the handkerchief-wrapped bundle of jewelry.

"I'll have to tease Nancy later about being so careless with her things," Cherry grinned. "It's unwise to leave your purse in the car. Why, someone could step on it!"

CHAPTER 24

Eager Anticipation

"A package of corn-on-the-cob holders for my mother, corn syrup for Head Nurse Margaret Marstad, a box of rubber erasers cleverly shaped like the state of Iowa for the nurses at the hospital, and for my good friend, Nurse Penny Perkins, a lovely wooden pencil box with the Iowa motto, 'A Place to Grow,' carved on top."

Cherry showed Lauren the charming, inexpensive gifts she had purchased at the Kornville Five-and-Dime while she was wandering through downtown looking for Midge. She found herself taken with the cute little town and its quaint shops.

"And, look, I got a whole box of assorted, discarded books and magazines at a second-hand book shop. I found a wonderful book that will make a fine addition to my medical library!" Cherry enthused. "It's the *Women's Medical Guide* by forty specialists. It has a section devoted to the treatment of kleptomania. Do you know what that is, Lauren? It's a nice word for someone who steals. Plus there are many sections explaining the psychology of women and all sorts of personality quizzes and guidelines so you can diagnose and treat mental disorders right in your own home!" Cherry cried excitedly. "With pictures, too."

"That should come in mighty handy," Midge joked.

Cherry whirled around to greet her friend. She was happy to see that Midge had returned, and in better spirits. Cherry's eyes sparkled. She was tempted to let Midge in on her little secret. She *was* planning to specialize in nervous women, all right, but not at Seattle General Hospital!

"What's this?" Midge wondered, picking up a slim volume entitled *Secrets of Life*. "I could use this right now," she joked.

"It's by Walt Disney, Midge," Cherry explained. "It's all about the mysterious worlds that exist right here on earth, about plant life and the insect world, fresh-water ponds and the jungles. Did you know that there is great wonder and beauty all around us, Midge?"

"Yeah," Midge cracked. "Her name's Velma."

Cherry had to smile. When it came to Velma, the usually unruffled Midge didn't even try to mask her ardor. Cherry knew she and Velma were lucky to have such devoted girlfriends.

"Speaking of Velma, I purchased these women's magazines for her," Cherry said. "They're chock full of decorating hints and tasty recipes."

"Velma's mother is always sending her articles from magazines like these so she can try out new things on me," Midge laughed.

"I *did* see a yummy-looking recipe for a new weiners 'n' beans casserole in one of them," Cherry remembered.

Midge laughed. "No, I mean she's always reading those advice columns about love and marriage and stuff. She's always scheming new ways to trick me into changing—trying to get me to talk more, you know, stuff like that."

Cherry wondered what she meant. Midge was always cracking jokes and tossing off funny remarks. Why, Cherry thought Midge talked plenty!

"Where is my girlfriend?" Midge wondered.

"Velma's powdering her nose while Nancy's on the telephone, calling Bess and George again," Cherry reported. Cherry frowned as she thought of her own unsuccessful attempts to reach her parents by telephone. She had called them three times in the last two days, and each time her efforts had been for naught. Where could her parents be?

Cherry absentmindedly handed Midge a white paper sack. "I got you some chicken-in-a-basket," she said.

Midge perched on the hood of the car and hungrily downed her supper. "Let's get some coffee to go, shall we?" Midge suggested when she was through.

Although normally she didn't partake of any artificial stimulant, Cherry agreed to the plan. "I want to be wide awake when we cross the mighty Mississippi and see Illinois, the Land of Lincoln, for the first time ever!" she enthused. Illinois was the heart of the Midwest, and Cherry didn't want to miss one scenic sight. All day long she had been sneaking a peek at the description of Illinois in her *Travel Guide to Corn Country*: "It is a flat state. It has a natural topographic monotony."

Cherry shivered as she anticipated the view that would unfold before her eyes. Even if Illinois weren't so naturally exciting, it would be to Cherry. After all, it was Nancy's home state!

CHAPTER 25

A Queer Quiz

"What would you rather be able to do—fly or be invisible, and why?" Lauren asked, ready to take down their answers. "Midge, you first."

"Why on earth do you want to know?" Midge sighed. They had been traveling for four hours now, and Midge was beginning to feel a little weary. She longed for some peace and quiet. Moreover, the closer they got to River Depths, the more anxious she became. Midge was convinced that Nancy's telephone confession to Chief Chumley had been a bad idea. What if they were met at the city limits by a police escort who took them right to jail?

"I've compiled a questionnaire from various quizzes in the *Women's Medical Guide*," Lauren explained. "I'm going to figure out what you are, exactly. I've made a chart with everyone's name on it. If you answer these questions, I can give you an accurate description of your personality type.

"Now, what would you rather be able to do—fly or be invisible, and why?"

"Fly," Midge said curtly.

"Because?" Lauren prompted her.

"Because then I could leave this stupid car and fly to River Depths!"

"You sure are a crab," Lauren scowled. "In fact, you're all a little crabby tonight."

"I'm cheerful," Cherry pointed out. Cherry was in the front seat beside Nancy, her map of Illinois spread over her lap. Cherry was as excited as Midge had ever seen her.

"Yeah, Cherry, but you're cheerful all the time," Midge retorted. "Even first thing in the morning."

Midge made it sound like it wasn't a good thing at all, Cherry thought.

"I've been meaning to talk to you about that," Nancy teased, giving Cherry's thigh a little squeeze.

"Yeah. Happy people are annoying in the morning. Well, they're annoying at any time, but *especially* first thing in the morning," Midge declared.

"Oh, Midge, you'll feel much better when your visitor finally gets here!" Cherry cried as she reached over the seat to put a sympathetic hand on her chum's arm. "Velma told us you always get like this."

Midge shot her girlfriend a pained look. "Thanks, Velma," she grumbled.

"Midge, if you need any sanitary products, I've got plenty," Cherry added helpfully. "I've got belts and pads and pain reliever in my purse. You don't have to ask. Just help yourself. Regular and," she turned around to wink at Lauren, "Junior Miss."

"It's okay, Cherry," Midge said hastily. Lauren just turned scarlet.

"Midge, are you cramping?" Cherry continued. "We can stop at a service station and I can fill my hot water bottle," she offered.

"I'm fine, Cherry," Midge said as she slumped against the car door, using her jacket as a pillow.

"Can we get back to the quiz?" Lauren wanted to know. "Velma, you're next. Would you rather fly or be invisible?"

"Could I do both?" Velma asked.

Lauren thought about it for a minute. "It would throw off the study, but if you really want to pick both, I can redo the whole thing."

Velma smiled sweetly. "I'll pick flying, then."

"Why?"

"So I could fly away from my grumpy girlfriend, of course," Velma replied with a smile.

"Excellent," Lauren grinned.

Midge put her arm around Velma and pulled her close. "You know why I'm so grumpy, don't you?" she said softly. She dropped her voice so no one could hear what came next. But whatever she said, it sure made Velma turn red!

"Let's continue," Lauren said in a gruff voice. "Cherry?"

Cherry knew her mind on this matter. "I'd fly. If I were invisible, I wouldn't need to wear my uniform, and that would

be like going naked and I wouldn't like that at all. I'd only fly in slacks, of course," she added.

"Nancy, you're last," Lauren prodded.

Nancy thought a while before answering. "If I could fly, I could leave right now and get home to Hannah. But being invisible would certainly have its advantages, wouldn't it?" she mused. "What if I could have been invisible? Then none of this would be happening, would it, if I could have really made myself disappear?"

Midge leaned over and put a hand on Nancy's shoulder. "You know, the mood I'm in today, if you hadn't already killed your father, I'd do it for you," she said. Cherry smiled. Midge could be really sweet when she wanted to be!

"Was that fly or be invisible?" was all Lauren wanted to know.

"Let's move on," Midge suggested.

Lauren sighed and wrote "undecided" next to Nancy's name. "Okay, but it's going to throw off Nancy's score," she grumbled before she read the next question.

"Question number two. Which would you rather be? A lumberjack or a librarian?"

"Librarian," Nancy, Cherry, and Velma said in unison. They didn't have to think twice about that one!

Lauren looked at Midge and without saying a word checked the lumberjack box next to her name. "Number three."

Midge groaned. "How many questions does this quiz have?" she asked.

"Sixty. And you are all going to answer every one of them."
Lauren fumed. "Question number three. Now, pay attention.
This is a true or false question. 'True or False. I am attracted
to mannish women.' "

Velma burst into laughter. Midge began pinching her,
which only made her laugh harder. Soon all the girls were giggling—everyone except Lauren, that is, who was scowling.

"Fine. If you're not going to take this seriously, I'm not
going to analyze any of you," she fumed.

"Why don't you read aloud, Lauren?" Cherry asked.
"Read something from the Walt Disney book. That will be
soothing."

"Yes, you have a lovely voice," Velma chimed in. "I could
listen to you all night."

"Okay!" Lauren cried eagerly. "I'll read about ants."

Cherry thought that sounded nice. Ants were so industrious.

"It says here that an ant is made of three sections, and if
it's ripped apart, each section can go on living for a short time.
After the head is cut off, the jaws can go on biting; the middle part, with its six legs, can go on running and kicking, and
the rear can stab enemies with its stinger. Here's a color photograph of a ferocious battle between a red ant and a black
ant," Lauren leaned over the seat to show Cherry. "The red
ant doesn't even have a head, and it's still fighting! Look, its
head is lying next to it on the ground! Do you see?"

Cherry felt a little woozy. Although she was a nurse and
saw medical emergencies everyday, she had to admit she was
a bit squeamish when it came to bugs; although, if need be,
she would use her medical skills to nurse one back to health.
She just hoped that never happened!

"That's very nice, Lauren," Cherry said weakly. "Why don't
I read aloud?" she suggested. She opened *Woman's Home
Companion* and scanned the index for an interesting article.
"Oh, look, there's a nice story about Mamie Eisenhower's fall
wardrobe."

"I don't care if Mamie Eisenhower walks around naked,"
Midge declared. "Isn't there anything more interesting in
there?"

Cherry was a little hurt by Midge's remark until she remembered Velma's warning. She scanned the magazine for some-

thing that would please Midge. "Here's an article with over thirty-five new hairstyle tips!" Cherry cried. She looked at Midge. Midge frowned. Cherry folded the page back so she could come back to it later. After all, she was always interested in finding new ways to style her stubborn, curly locks.

"Here's an interesting article," she said. "It's a scientific look into the future by a panel of experts. Does that please you?" Cherry joked.

Midge lit a cigarette and grinned. "Read on," she said.

"Twenty years from now we'll preserve food by atomic-ray sterilization," Cherry read aloud.

"Twenty years from now, we'll be able to buy psychoanalysis insurance to protect us against mental illness," she continued. "Like kleptomania and lying," she added, sneaking a peek at Lauren to see if she got the hint. Lauren only looked bored.

"Twenty years from now, we'll have a mood counter, like a Geiger counter, that tells you what your husband's disposition is when you want to discuss a new hat," Cherry continued.

"I could use one of those," Velma teased. Midge groaned good-naturedly. "What else?" she asked. Cherry was pleased to see she had helped Midge get her mind off her troubles.

"Twenty years from now, men will help with the housework even more than they do already!" she read the last of the list.

The girls had a good, long laugh.

"Goodness, the future certainly looks very exciting, doesn't it?" Cherry cried.

Lauren yawned. "I can hardly wait," she said sleepily. She put her head on Velma's shoulder and fell fast asleep.

Midge put her head on Velma's other shoulder and stretched out as best she could in the crowded back seat. She, too, promptly fell asleep.

Cherry finished reading quietly. She didn't care what anyone else thought, she was interested in Mamie Eisenhower's fall wardrobe. "I might pick up some fashion hints," she decided. "Besides, Mamie seems like a genuinely nice person, although I'm not sure I care for her hairdo."

CHAPTER 26

Crossing the Mississippi

Midge awoke with a start. "Where are we?" she yawned, looking over at Nancy, who was staring grimly ahead, her eyes fixed on the road. They were the only travelers on the lonely highway. Midge gave a little shiver and slipped on her leather jacket.

Cherry and Midge had switched places hours earlier when Cherry realized she was too sleepy to be an effective helpmate to Nancy. "Whoever sits in the passenger seat has a big responsibility, Midge," Cherry had cautioned her chum. "There are maps to read, hankies to dispense, and one has to keep the driver alert and entertained!"

After agreeing to assume Cherry's duties, Midge had promptly fallen fast asleep. The last thing Midge remembered was Cherry's squeal of delight as they crossed the Mississippi River. "Now I've seen everything," Cherry had declared after they had crossed the wide, wild river with its stout dikes and thick masses of foliage. "Look at those powerful, modern barges lashed together, piled high with coal. Or is that yellow sulphur?" she had cried excitedly as their headlights illuminated a typical river scene for all to see.

"What a pleasant, cool place to be after a long trip on a dusty road," Cherry had then murmured before falling asleep.

Nancy had been content to drive for a while without benefit of Cherry's cheery chatter, but now she was a little lonely. She was glad Midge was awake.

"We're almost to River Depths," Nancy answered back, taking care to keep her voice low so as not to wake the others, who were sound asleep.

Midge checked her watch. She was surprised to find it was

almost three a.m. "What happened to Cherry's driving plan?" Midge joked, pretending to be alarmed. "We're off schedule! Seriously, Nancy, aren't you sick of being behind the wheel?"

Nancy shook her head. "I'm wide awake," she assured Midge. "Besides, I know this route better than anyone. Illinois has some pretty treacherous roads, especially in the dark."

"I'm telling Cherry you drove while fatigued," Midge said in a teasing whisper. "And I'll just bet you haven't even stopped once to stretch."

Nancy stifled a giggle and offered Midge a cigarette from the pack in her lap. Midge accepted gratefully.

"Does Cherry know you smoke?" Midge gasped when she realized Nancy was holding a lit cigarette.

"I was smoking the night we met, but Cherry was probably too drunk—oops!" Nancy clapped one hand over her mouth. "I mean, it was probably too dark for her to notice."

Midge grinned and lit a cigarette. "I had a feeling you two weren't telling the whole truth about how you met," she said. "That little story about Cherry's spending the night tracking you down is a lie, isn't it? How did you two spend that night?"

Nancy had the good grace to blush. She tried to change the subject, and quickly.

"Oh, look!" she cried excitedly, pointing to a large, well-lit roadway sign, set back at the side of the road, surrounded by stately Sycamores.

WELCOME TO RIVER DEPTHS
"HOME OF GIRL DETECTIVE NANCY CLUE"

Midge was impressed and, for the first time, a little relieved. Maybe Nancy was right. Maybe everything would be okay. "I guess people here really do like her," Midge thought.

"My house is in one of the older suburbs at the far end of town," Nancy explained. "We won't pass through downtown now, but later, if you like, I'll take you on an official tour. It's really an attractive place, with lots of fine old homes. And you'll never be wanting for entertainment here, either. We've got a grand theater that dates back to the turn of the century and a very good library with all the latest novels. And two cinemas.

"In a couple of days, we can all drive up to Lake Merrimen and cool off. My chums Joe and Frank Hardly summer there with their Uncle Nelly. There's a beautiful lake where you can participate in all sorts of water sports."

Midge laughed. "I'll worm the truth out of you sooner or later about how you and Cherry met," she promised. "You might as well come clean now. Besides, you know Cherry will spill the beans as soon as I lean on her. Why, you know she can't keep a secret."

Nancy chatted on about River Depths, hoping to divert Midge's attention from the topic at hand. She had promised Cherry not to breathe a word of their steamy first encounter during their recent adventure in San Francisco!

She busied herself pointing out interesting landmarks. "There's the famous River Depths Sanitarium," she said, as they passed a stately white stone mansion set back among elm trees. She turned a teasing eye to Midge. "That's where the famous movie star Darcy New is staying," she chuckled, adding, "Luckily, I once mentioned we had a sanitarium in River Depths so you could use it in your tale to throw those reporters off my trail!"

Nancy filled Midge in on more details about the institution. "It used to be the Frenshaw mansion, and until twenty-two years ago, people from town went there regularly to perform skits and otherwise lift the spirits of the patients. Then suddenly the ghostly figure of a woman in white began appearing on the grounds, accompanied by the most ghastly screams," she reported. "And since then, no one's dared venture there."

Nancy continued. "A few years ago I called and asked Head Psychiatrist Doctor Fraud if I could investigate the sightings, and somehow Father found out, and he refused to let me go there. He said he feared for my safety." She shivered. "I tried to sneak onto the grounds, but was driven back by two fierce dogs.

"Oh, look!" she exclaimed, pointing out a large brick building set back among majestic maple trees. "There's River Depths High. It's a very attractive campus, don't you think? My chums George and Bess work there now. George is the girl's physical education instructor and Bess heads the home economics department."

Midge thought the campus, with its spacious, manicured grounds and grand marble buildings, looked more like a university than a high school. "When did you graduate?" Midge asked.

"Oh, we didn't go *there!*" Nancy cried. "Bess, George, and I attended Miss Edger's and Miss Cramp's School for Girls in nearby Lakeview, a private girls' school specializing in Manners, Deportment, and Civilized Culture.

"We're now passing the Park of Roses, where Hannah wins first prize for her beautiful blooms every year at the Festival of Flowers. Oh, dear. I hope the gardener's remembered to prune her rose bushes and trim her morning glories," Nancy fretted. "How dreadful if she had to come home to withering vines!

"Mr. and Mrs. Tickerson live down this way!" Nancy exclaimed as they passed Old River Road. "Poor Ted Tickerson. It was so tragic the way he died!"

"Do tell," Midge begged.

Nancy filled Midge in on the unfortunate accident at the River Depths Men's Club that had claimed the life of Ted Tickerson, her frequent escort at many country club dances, and River Depth High's most outstanding quarterback.

"A stuffed moosehead unexpectedly fell off the wall and right onto poor Ted's head, killing him instantly!" Nancy cried. "It happened during Ted's induction into the club. It was a sudden shock!

"He was certainly a fun escort for high school dances, even if I did have to karate-chop him a few times when he got fresh," Nancy remembered with a little grin. "He had an awfully pretty sister," she added wistfully. "Her name was Theresa, but everyone called her Terry. Boy, she was sweet."

Midge grinned and lit another cigarette. "How sweet?" she wondered aloud.

Nancy blushed when she remembered how many times she had agreed to double-date with the Tickersons, knowing all the while that the first chance the girls got, they would ditch their dates and spend the entire evening giggling together in the powder room.

"She left town suddenly a few years ago," Nancy added sadly. "I heard she joined the Navy." It was obvious to Midge that Terry Tickerson still occupied a very special place in Nancy's heart!

"Tell me more about this Terry girl," Midge urged.

"Nothing to tell," Nancy said briskly as she made a sudden sharp right turn into a circular, tree-lined driveway and brought the car to a halt in front of a stately, three-story brick home, circled with tidy hedges.

"We're home," she said, putting the car in park and turning off the motor. Nancy grew suddenly quiet. The animated, chatty girl of a few minutes ago had disappeared. In her stead was a girl shuddering in dread.

"I don't want to awaken Hannah," Nancy worried aloud. Suddenly, she wanted to be anyplace but here!

"We don't have to go in," Midge said softly. "We can go to a motel. I can come back later and get what you need."

"No, I must go in," Nancy said firmly. "I must see Hannah." She bounded out of the car, a flashlight in one hand and her keys in the other. She raced up the stairs and crossed the wide front porch with a determined stride. To her surprise, her key wouldn't fit in the lock!

"That's odd," she murmured, trying the key over and over until she determined that there was no hope of opening the door. Just then her flashlight flickered and went out. "Drat!" Nancy exclaimed, remembering that she had neglected to add batteries to her shopping list. She hated being caught without fresh batteries in her purse!

She turned around and bumped smack into Midge.

"Oops!" she exclaimed. "Midge, my key won't work." Nancy suddenly remembered Hannah kept a key to the back door under a flower pot, and ran to check. But there was no key under any of Hannah's begonias.

Next they tried the cellar door, but it, too, was locked tight. And the windows were secured as well! Nancy was just about to pound on the door and awaken Hannah when she realized she had lost sight of Midge. "Midge, where are you?" Nancy called softly.

"Over here," Midge called back. "I'm stuck."

Midge was dangling halfway through a small cellar window that hadn't been locked. "You're headed for Hannah's canning room," Nancy whispered, giving her a shove. "There's about a ten-foot drop onto a large oak table. Careful, there might be—" But she was too late. From the sound of jars crashing to the ground, Nancy knew that Midge had indeed landed on Hannah's canning table.

Nancy carefully hoisted herself through the window. "Are you all right?" she asked Midge.

Midge groaned. "Yeah," she grumbled, helping Nancy off the table. "I hit my head, but it's okay. Velma always says it's the hardest part of my body," she grinned.

A creaking noise from the room directly above them startled the two girls. "It's Hannah!" Nancy cried excitedly.

"Who's there?" a deep, harsh voice demanded. "I've got a gun and I'll shoot!" The footsteps grew louder.

"That's not Hannah!" Nancy cried. "Whoever it is, he's coming this way!"

Before the girls could find a hiding place, the basement door swung open. Light streaming in from the upstairs threatened to give them away. They took cover behind stacks of old newspapers tied in tidy bundles and piled almost to the ceiling.

"I'll bet it's the same man who threatened me over the telephone," Nancy whispered, her ire raised. She picked up a jar of Hannah's homemade marmalade and took aim.

"Reveal yourself," the sinister voice demanded. But the girls stayed hidden. "All right, I'm coming after you," the voice snarled.

The light snapped off. It seemed like hours before their captor began his descent. Although the girls couldn't see a thing in the dark basement, a slow shuffling sound from the direction of the staircase alerted them to his movement.

"The bottom step squeaks something awful," Nancy whispered. "Wait for that sound; then pelt him with these jars." Midge nodded and quietly gathered up jars of marmalade. She wanted them to be close by if one round wasn't enough!

A sudden sharp click made Nancy jump. "He really is armed!" she thought fearfully as she recognized the sound of a gun being cocked.

The soft shuffling noise grew closer. "Any second now," Nancy thought, holding her breath, waiting for the creak of the bottom step that would alert them to the stranger's presence.

Suddenly, a small furry animal raced over Nancy's foot, causing her to jump in alarm. Her flashlight fell out of her pocket and hit the cement floor. A thin beam of light flashed on just long enough to reveal the feet of the approaching stranger.

Nancy gasped in horror, for the light revealed muscular, hairy legs shod in brown leather slippers—her father's slippers!

"He's alive!" she shrieked, before fainting right into Midge's strong arms.

CHAPTER 27

A Delightful Surprise

The overhead light burst on, and Midge was delighted to find their stalker was a handsome, dark-haired girl with short wavy hair and a shocked expression on her face. And right behind her was a curvy blonde clad in pink flannel pajamas and bunny slippers. The ears on her slippers quivered as she raced down the stairs.

"Oh, Nancy!" the girls cried in unison. The dark-haired girl slipped off her plaid bathrobe and covered Nancy, who was out cold.

"What have you done to her?" the blonde cried in alarm. "And who are you?"

Midge knew immediately who they were. Why, Nancy had spoken many times about her closest chums. "You must be Bess and George," Midge grinned. A sudden pounding at the front door interrupted their introductions. "That's the rest of our gang," Midge explained.

Bess trembled with fear. "You're part of a gang? You kidnapped Nancy, that's why she's been gone so long. You have, haven't you?" She jumped behind her chum. "Honey, do something," she fretted.

The brunette looked Midge square in the eyes. "Who are you, and how do you know our names?" she demanded in a gruff voice.

Midge quickly explained her presence in the Clue basement. A relieved grin broke over the brunette's handsome face. She put out her hand and gave Midge a hearty handshake.

"There's tons more to tell," Midge added. "But let's get Nancy someplace more comfortable and let the others in before they wake up the whole neighborhood." She scooped up Nancy and carried her up the stairs to the comfortable couch in the Clues' attractively furnished living room.

By the time they opened the door and let in the rest of the

girls, Nancy was beginning to revive. Nancy laughed in relief as she spied George. "I'm all dizzy with happiness!" she exclaimed. "George, for a minute there, when I saw you on the stairs, I thought you were...well, never mind. I'm home and I'm safe, and that's all that matters! Oh, Bess and George, how I've missed you!" she cried, throwing her arms first around Bess, an attractive plump girl with a soft halo of white-blond hair, then around George, a handsome girl with a tomboy's disdain for feminine apparel.

The three chums had been thick as thieves since their first meeting seventeen years earlier at Miss Margie's Ballet School. Although George was eventually asked to leave the school when she refused to don a tutu for her part as a sugarplum in a school production, the trio had been inseparable ever since and had solved many exciting mysteries together!

"And here's Gogo!" Nancy exclaimed happily as a little white terrier raced into the room and jumped onto her mistress. The perky little dog covered Nancy's face with kisses.

"We've been taking care of her since Hannah called us at Lake Merrimen after the murder. And we've been worried sick about you," Bess scolded her wayward chum. "Where have you been? Why didn't you call us?"

"I'll tell you everything later," Nancy promised. "But now I must see Hannah. I know I really shouldn't wake her, but I'm so eager to see her! I'll bet she was thrilled when Chief Chumley let her out of jail! Hannah, I'm home!" Nancy cried, joyously jumping off the couch.

George and Bess exchanged puzzled glances. "Hannah's in jail, Nancy," George said softly. "Charged in the murder of your father. Jury selection for her murder trial begins later today."

Nancy looked stunned. "I know that!" she cried. "But I thought...I mean, Chief Chumley promised me he would..." was all she could gasp out before falling back on the couch in deep swoon. Bess watched in alarm as Cherry pinned on her cap and efficiently took Nancy's pulse. "Why does Nancy have a nurse with her?" Bess asked. "Oh, she's not sick, is she?"

Cherry assured them that Nancy would be just fine. "She's had an awful fright and needs some rest," she explained. Midge and George carried Nancy to her attractive, blue and white second-floor bedroom, leaving her in Cherry's capable hands.

"I'll take over from here," Cherry declared as she unzipped her chum's frock and loosened her undergarments.

While Cherry tended to her patient, Bess and George explained their presence in the Clue house.

"A couple of nights ago the house was burglarized. When we heard about it, we decided to stay here to prevent further break-ins," said George.

"When we moved in, I found Nancy's lovely old hope chest on its side, and the sweaters she stored in there strewn in untidy heaps all over the floor. I set everything in order," Bess added. "I didn't want Nancy coming home and knowing someone had been in her bedroom."

"Yes. Then we had all the locks changed. We tried to scare you away because we thought you were the thief," George interjected.

"What did the police say?" Midge asked.

"Well, since it appears nothing was taken, there was no major investigation," George replied.

"For the life of me, I can't figure out what the thief was after. The Clues have many lovely and expensive things, and nothing is missing," Bess mused. She then sighed in relief. "Golly, I was so scared when we heard that noise in the cellar, I shot right out of bed, didn't I honey?" she turned to George, who grinned and put an arm around Bess's plump waist.

"Yeah, you shot right out of bed and ran and hid in the closet," George teased. Bess blushed. It was a well-known fact that George was the bolder of the two.

"I was simply deciding which pajamas to wear," Bess explained unconvincingly. "If we were going to catch a crook, I wanted to do it dressed!"

George shot her a delighted grin, but then her grin faded and she grew solemn again. "Why did Nancy think Hannah would be here?" she wondered. "Hasn't she read a newspaper in the last two weeks? They're full of stories about Hannah."

Midge quickly filled them in on the events of the last week and a half. "So Nancy did go to San Francisco as reported," Bess said. "That's where she met that nice nurse!"

"We didn't know whether to believe news reports that said she had been working a case there," George explained. "We don't know what to believe anymore. The newspapers are reporting the existence of iron-clad evidence against Hannah, but we know that she couldn't possibly have committed murder!"

Velma nodded. "When Nancy heard that, she called the Chief and..."

"...and gave him information that would allow him to release Hannah and drop all charges," Midge finished, purposely keeping her information vague.

"So that's why Nancy thought Hannah would be here!" George cried. "What could Nancy have told him to make him release Hannah?" she wondered.

"How much do you know about this case?" Midge asked Bess and George.

"You tell it, honey," Bess shivered.

George started from the beginning. "The day Nancy's father was shot, we were at our cabin at Lake Merrimen. We got a frantic telephone call from Hannah. She was so upset that at first we could barely make out what she was saying."

Bess picked up the story. "She made us promise to tell the police that Nancy had been with us that day. She begged us to lie, saying it was a matter of life and death. But before we could question her, she hung up."

"We'd do anything for Hannah, so we agreed," George blurted out. "The minute the police were through questioning us, we started looking for Nancy. That's all we know," George said sadly. "Mr. Clue is dead, and poor Hannah is languishing in the River Depths jail. We've scoured this house looking for clues to the real murderer, but haven't found a thing," she added miserably. "We just know that evidence

leading to the true killer must be in this house somewhere.
There must be someone Carson Clue crossed, someone angry
enough to exact revenge at the point of a gun!" She jumped
off the couch and paced about. "It looks like Hannah is going
to stand trial for murder, and there's not a thing any of us can
do about it!"

"Why, Hannah is incapable of harming anyone!" Bess cried
out.

"Even creepy old Mr. Clue," George added, half under her
breath.

Midge and Velma exchanged a knowing glance. "What do
you mean by that?" Velma asked.

"Ignore George," Bess said lightly. "She's got some strange
idea that Mr. Clue was, well, a little odd."

Midge glanced at Velma. Should they tell Bess and George
the real circumstances surrounding Carson Clue's death?

But before they could speak, Lauren, who had been busy
playing with Gogo all this time, took care of that. "Nancy
killed her father!" Lauren blurted out. "Now, what do you
have to eat in this house? Golly, I'm hungry."

"There's some yummy deviled eggs in the refrigerator and
half a chocolate cake on the kitchen table," Bess said, pointing Lauren toward the kitchen. When Lauren was gone, Bess
exclaimed, "Golly, where'd you get her? The very idea; saying Nancy killed her father! Why, she must be so lightheaded
from hunger, she's imagining things. Why, Nancy would never,
ever..."

But Bess stopped talking when she saw the expression on
Velma's face. She gasped, and put her hand over her mouth.
"You mean, it's true? Nancy really did kill her father?"

"It was justifiable homicide," Velma said hurriedly.

"He deserved it," Midge stated firmly. "He did unspeak-
able things to Nancy!"

"I knew he was too perfect to be true," George said, springing up from the couch and pacing around the charmingly decorated living room. "There was always something suspicious
about that man," George shuddered. "He was a little too
attached to Nancy, if you ask me."

Bess shivered. "He had a penetrating glance that always
made me feel like he could see right through my clothes," she
admitted. "I never said anything to Nancy about it because

I didn't want to upset her. Besides, I thought I might be imagining it."

"He was *always* commenting on your outfit or hairstyle," George remembered with anger.

"Once when I was eleven, I could have sworn I saw him peeking at me through a crack in the cabana at the country club while I was changing into my swimsuit," Bess recalled. "When I opened the door, I bumped right into him."

George hit the roof. "How come you didn't tell me?" she demanded.

Bess tried to comfort her sweetie, but George would have none of it. "She's impossible to calm down when she gets angry," Bess explained to Velma.

"Tell me about it," Velma sighed. "Why, the only thing that distracts Midge when she's like that is..."

"Excuse me!" Midge cried, her face red as a beet. "I mean, er, I'm hungry. Let's take this conversation to the kitchen, shall we?"

"I'm too upset to eat," Bess wailed, but once she spied Lauren attacking the luscious chocolate cake she had baked the night before, she changed her mind. She got a pitcher of cold milk from the refrigerator and cut generous slices of the delicious dessert.

"What is it about upsetting news that always makes food taste better?" Bess wondered. "And this is just about the most upsetting news I've ever heard. Whatever will we do?"

No one had an answer.

CHAPTER 28

A Creepy Tale

Midge groaned as she covered her head with a pillow and burrowed under the covers in an attempt to shut out the bright sunlight streaming in through the windows at one end of the small, simply furnished first-floor back bedroom that had been Hannah's residence for over twenty years. Midge tried with all her might to fall back to sleep, but couldn't. She checked the little alarm clock on the metal bedstand. It was seven a.m.

"I'm cursed," she thought, propping herself up. "You wake up early once in your life, and it ruins your sleep forever," she groaned.

Normally she would have delighted in finding herself awakened early in a deliciously cool room with Velma asleep by her side. "If we were alone, she wouldn't be asleep for long," Midge thought ruefully. She got out of bed, almost stumbling over Lauren, who was passed out in a sleeping bag on the floor. Midge had been too tired to argue when Lauren had followed them to bed.

She pulled the curtains shut so the others wouldn't be disturbed by the morning light. They had all stayed up to explain the unusual circumstances under which they had met. "Could it be only eleven days since we met Cherry and became embroiled in the search for those kidnapped nuns?" Midge asked herself in amazement. Why, she felt as if she had known Cherry and Nancy her entire life!

Bess had been shocked when she'd found out that an evil priest had been behind the dastardly kidnapping of the kindly nuns, but George said it didn't surprise her one little bit. Midge smiled. That George was a good egg, she decided as she carefully stepped over Lauren and pulled open the bedroom door. "What's this?" she wondered, picking up a small red rubber ball on the ground outside her door.

A white bundle of fur flew by, stopping just long enough to grab the ball from Midge's hand. It was Nancy's terrier, Gogo. "A terror's more like it," Midge grinned as she threw a plaid bathrobe over her pajamas, and made her way to the spacious, sunny white and yellow kitchen.

She was delighted to find a pot of fresh coffee already percolating. Bess had gotten up early and was taking fragrant buttermilk biscuits out of the oven.

"There'll be apple pancakes in a few minutes," she smiled at Midge. She motioned for her to be seated at the white and gold speckled Formica table and brought her a cup of coffee and a pitcher of cream.

"You don't have to wait on me," Midge protested, but Bess just laughed. "I always do the cooking, and George does the dishes," she explained. "Sit and eat," she added, bring a basket of biscuits and a plate of butter to the table. "Did you sleep well?" she asked.

Midge broke open a biscuit and slathered it with the creamy butter. "As well as can be expected with that little snoring kid in the room," she said.

Bess laughed. "Maybe tonight Lauren will feel comfortable enough in this strange house to sleep in the living room." Bess grew somber. She sat down across from Midge and poured herself a cup of coffee. "You might think I'm crazy, but..." Her voice trailed off.

"Go on," Midge urged. "I won't think you're crazy."

"I can't explain, exactly, but after hearing what you said about Nancy and her father, I just couldn't sleep. Why, I even got up to make myself a cheese and tomato sandwich, hoping that would put me to sleep, but still I lay awake."

Bess continued breathlessly, her brown eyes growing as big as saucers as she relayed her bizarre experiences in the Clue household.

"This house has always felt a little scary to me. Whenever I'm here, I feel like, well, I feel like I'm being watched. Like someone's standing behind me, watching everything I do." Bess shivered. "Until last night, when I learned of the horrible things that went on here, I thought I was just being silly." She blushed. "I'm not the bravest person," she admitted. "Last night when we heard you in the cellar, I made George pretend she was a man, and I stayed a safe distance behind her."

Bess leaned in close to Midge and dropped her voice to a whisper. "One night years and years ago I was sharing Nancy's room and I awoke in the middle of the night and thought I saw someone standing at the foot of my bed.

"I must have been dreaming, though, because when I turned on the bed-side lamp, the figure disappeared. I remember smelling the most luscious scent; I thought it was a perfume of some sort until I remembered that a large lilac bush grows right outside Nancy's bedroom window," Bess added.

Midge wanted to quiz Bess further about the strange incidents in the Clue household, both before and after Carson Clue's death, but Bess clammed up when she spied Lauren headed down the hall toward the kitchen. "No more talk like this, or we'll never get her out of your bedroom," Bess giggled. "Anyway, I'm always being a silly goose about things. Why, I'm even afraid of my own shadow. Don't listen to a thing I say about this house. I'm sure there's nothing to any of it."

Midge wasn't so sure, but she let the conversation drop, at least for the time being.

Lauren wandered into the sunny kitchen holding the waistband of her pajamas in an attempt to keep them from sliding down her slender frame. In the oversized pajamas, with her hair sticking up in unflattering angles, Lauren looked more like a kid and less like the smart-aleck teen Midge knew her to be.

"Why, she looks harmless," Midge realized. "How could I have ever suspected that she and Velma..." Her thoughts stopped when she saw the newspaper in Lauren's hand. It would certainly include coverage of Hannah's trial. Midge snatched the paper away from Lauren, and tried to think of a way to get her out of the room so she could freely discuss the trial with Bess. "You stink," Midge said bluntly. "Go take a bath."

"You're not my mother," Lauren replied tartly as she slumped into a chair and reached for a biscuit.

"That is one of the many things I am grateful for," Midge replied sarcastically. "Go take a bath," she ordered again, in a no-nonsense tone that surprised them both. "Now."

"Yes, sir!" Lauren saluted before snatching another biscuit. She put a third in the breast pocket of her pajama top, glared at Midge, and stomped off.

"There're fresh towels in the hall closet and bubble bath

beside the tub," Bess called after her. The slam of the wash-room door was Lauren's only reply.

"Honestly," Bess sighed as she mixed pancake batter. "She's an odd little duck. What on earth are you doing with her? And where are her parents?"

Midge lit her first cigarette of the day. "She's just a little juvenile delinquent we picked up along the way. I'm sure her family's glad to get rid of her," she chuckled.

Bess quivered in alarm. "Should I hide the crystal?" she wondered.

"Nothing like that," Midge assured her. "I have caught her in a few lies," she admitted. "Well, not really lies. More like creative story-telling. I get the feeling she's not happy at home and isn't too keen on returning. I am, though," Midge admitted. "We've been gone much longer than planned, and my long-suffering friends, Tom and Monty, have been caring for my pets all this time." She shuddered when she imagined what Monty's white wall-to-wall carpet would look like after boarding one dog, five puppies, a cat, and various, assorted rodents.

"One problem at a time," she sighed, scanning the news-paper. She almost knocked over her coffee cup, so shocked was she when she saw the *River Depths Defender*. For the entire front page was devoted to what the paper was calling "The Case of the Homicidal Housekeeper."

"Horrible Hannah," read the twenty-four point caption below a harsh jail-cell photograph of Hannah Gruel. Midge had never met Hannah, but she could tell from the wan look of her once-pleasant features that the elderly woman was suffering a great deal. "I can't believe this. Look!" Midge cried to Bess, who was absorbed in dropping evenly spaced dollops of pancake batter onto the hot griddle.

" 'Hannah's Recipe For Mayhem,' " Midge read a headline aloud in a shocked tone. "It says there's evidence Hannah tried to poison both Nancy and Mr. Clue during last year's Founder's Day Picnic by baking arsenic in a huckleberry pie. They even printed her recipe!"

Bess hurriedly wiped her hands on her apron and looked over Midge's shoulder. She shuddered when she saw how the newspaper had twisted and distorted kindly Hannah Gruel's life so as to make it appear that she was really a manipulative, scheming woman.

"It says here police believe Hannah's been squirreling away money for years!" Midge exclaimed. "Look at this photograph of a jar filled with coins. They're saying it's evidence of her successful scheme to steal money from Mr. Clue."

Bess gasped in horror when she looked at the photograph. "Why, I know for a fact that Hannah keeps her pin money in that jar. She makes extra money baking pies for the neighbors and uses her savings to purchase Christmas gifts for Nancy and Mr. Clue," she gasped indignantly. "What other lies are in here?" she cried, doing her best to flip pancakes while reading over Midge's shoulder.

Midge groaned as she rifled through the newspaper. "Most of the articles are about Hannah!" she cried. "Even on the society page, there's one titled, 'I Never Trusted Her.' " Midge read it aloud.

" ' "I never trusted that woman," Mrs. Milton Meeks, a prominent leader of the community, was overheard exclaiming at yesterday's Ladies' Club Luncheon honoring local poetess Miss Betty Pearl, whose recent publication in *Reader's Digest* has earned her accolades from around the state.

' "I knew the day Carson Clue brought that woman into his house no good would come of it," Mrs. Meeks declared after sampling a delicious luncheon of tuna salad and vegetable medley. She expressed concern that Hannah's actions would disrupt the happy harmony housewives and housekeepers of River Depths have always enjoyed. Others at her table expressed similar fears.

'A good time was had by all.'

"They're all the same," Midge sighed after a quick scan of the other articles. "There's even an editorial calling for a law to disarm housekeepers," she sneered as she threw the paper on the floor in disgust.

Bess plunked a platter of pancakes on the table in front of Midge and announced, "Why, Mrs. Meeks tried several times to hire Hannah away from the Clues. My mother overheard her cornering Hannah one night after a Ladies' Club meeting, where Hannah served her delicious blueberry tarts. She begged her to quit and come work for her!

"Although she was too much a lady to ever say so, Hannah never did like that Mrs. Meeks." Bess's pretty face flushed with anger. She twisted a dish towel in her hands. "If I ever see that woman on the street, why, I'll—" But before she could finish, the doorbell rang.

"Who could it be this early in the morning?" Bess wondered aloud as she hurried to answer it. "It's probably the milkman, unable to decipher George's note about extra butter." She pulled off her apron, dusty with flour, and ran a hand through her mussed hair. She flung open the door and to her great surprise saw the very same Mrs. Milton Meeks in the news article, standing on the Clues' front porch. And in her white-gloved hands was a casserole dish covered with a red-checkered cloth.

"Oh, Beth, dear, you're here!" Mrs. Meeks exclaimed in glee.

"It's Bess," Bess corrected, but Mrs. Meeks paid no mind. She sailed right past her and headed for the kitchen.

"Was I ever shocked and pleased to drive by earlier and see Nancy's car out front!" Mrs. Meeks cried.

"Nancy's asleep and can't be disturbed," Bess warned.

"So she *is* home," Mrs. Meeks' eyes twinkled in delight. "I wouldn't dream of waking her," she declared. "I just wanted to drop off this special tuna salad I prepared especially for her."

"Oh, hello young man," she said cheerily to Midge as she put the casserole dish in the refrigerator. "You must be one of Nancy's detective chums from Lake Merrimen. Now, which Hardly boy are you? Joe or Frank?" She reached in her handbag hanging from the crook of one arm and took out a pair of jeweled cat glasses. She balanced them precariously on the tip of her pug nose and stared at Midge. She gave her a good going-over.

"Young man, I'd advise you to not sit around the house in your sleeping attire," she warned. "Honestly, what will people say when they find out you and Nancy are staying in the very same house without a chaperone? Beth, does your mother know about this?"

Without waiting for an answer, she added, in a teasing tone, "Unless, of course, you two have a surprise announcement for us? The young man who marries Nancy Clue will be twice-blessed, indeed," she declared with glee. "Not only will he be getting a charming girl, he'll also be marrying River Depths' newest, and some say, richest heiress!"

Mrs. Meeks put a gloved hand against her powdered, rouged cheek and added, "Oh, I guess it's not nice to talk about money at a time like this, with the murder so fresh in everyone's mind and the jury selection for the trial beginning today." A devilish look came into her small, blue, beady eyes. "But a wedding might be just the thing to make everyone forget about that nasty crime."

Mrs. Meeks boldly helped herself to a warm biscuit. She daintily ate it, wiping crumbs from her thin lips with a monogrammed hankie from her purse. "These are quite good, Beth, dear. Not as good as Hannah's, mind you. Oops," she tittered. "I probably shouldn't be mentioning the poor dear's name in this house, should I?" She sighed. "Some people snap, just like that," she declared, illustrating her point by snapping her plump, little glove-encased fingers together.

She rustled through her purse and took out a compact and a tube of red lipstick. After reapplying fresh color, she added, "If I were you, Beth dear, I'd starting reducing now. You're sure to be a maid of honor, and those bridesmaid dresses, lovely as they are, are never very flattering to the, shall we say, fuller figure?"

Bess almost choked on her biscuit.

"And as for your friend George, well," Mrs. Meeks shuddered, rolled her eyes and sighed. "There's nothing anyone can do about her, is there?" Bess was too flabbergasted to say anything and for once Midge kept her mouth shut. She had a feeling it would be a good idea to keep her true identity a secret.

Mrs. Meeks snatched up another biscuit and raced out the door, leaving a trail of crumbs in her wake. "I must hurry off and tell everyone Nancy's back!" she cried.

For the first time since they had arrived in River Depths, Midge felt alarmed. There was something about Mrs. Meeks that made her shiver. "She's not nearly as flighty as she pretends," Midge thought, realizing that she reminded her of a cruel prison matron she had bumped heads with more than once during her stretch in the pen. "That Mrs. Meeks is one dangerous character," she said.

Bess wiped the tears from her eyes and blew her nose on the dish towel in her hands. "I'm a silly goose to let Mrs. Meeks get under my skin, but, golly, I'm awfully sensitive about my figure problem."

Midge looked at the attractively plump, feminine girl and said in a disgusted tone, "It's people like Mrs. Meeks who should be on trial, not Hannah." Midge was relieved to see Bess giggle a bit at this, but she knew by the look in her eyes that her feelings were still hurt.

"Everyone's always commenting about my weight," Bess sighed. "Why, you'd think it was a national disgrace that a girl carries a few extra pounds."

From what Midge could see, Bess was carrying those pounds in all the right places. She struggled to find a polite way to say so, but gave up and just blurted out, "Bess, as far as I'm concerned, you are one good-looking girl, and your girlfriend seems to thinks so, too."

At the mention of George, Bess's cloudy expression grew bright. She smiled, revealing darling dimples in each cheek. "Did Nancy ever tell you how George and I got together?" she asked. Midge shook her head.

"When I was nineteen, I uncovered a family secret," Bess began dramatically. "I was adopted! Mother was afraid I would be destroyed by the news, but I was elated," Bess revealed as she spooned sugar into her coffee and buttered a biscuit.

She blushed. "For a long time, I had known my feelings for George were more than cousinly, and I had the funniest feeling George felt the same way," Bess said, all starry-eyed. She stirred her coffee and continued her story. "One night we accompanied Nancy to a Happy Homemakers of America dance. When Ted Tickerson and his vivacious sister, Terry, joined us, I grabbed George and sneaked out the back way.

"Nancy used to be head over heels about Terry," Bess confided. "They had a terrible quarrel and Terry left town. Nancy's heart has been broken ever since. Anyway, I asked George to walk to the gazebo with me. I told her I wanted to see the stars," Bess giggled. "While she was pointing out the Big Dipper, I blurted out the news that we weren't related at all, and then I kissed her smack on the lips. George was so shocked, she tumbled backward over the railing. When I tried to help her up, she pulled me on top of her. That's where we were a half hour later when Nancy and Terry stumbled upon us.

"How did you meet your girlfriend?" Bess asked.

"In prison," Midge said nonchalantly.

Bess gasped. "Really?" Her eyes lit up bright as new pennies. "I bet you were the head of a gang, and Velma was your girl," Bess guessed dreamily.

Midge laughed. "Nothing as exciting as that," she admitted. "It's a long story, but…what's that smell?" she wondered suddenly.

"My pancakes!" Bess shrieked. She had been so engrossed

in swapping stories with Midge, she had forgotten all about breakfast! She ran to the stove.

"They *were* pancakes," Bess moaned as she scraped the now-blackened batter from the hot griddle. She mixed a fresh batch and soon perfect circles of luscious smelling hotcakes were bubbling away.

"You are some cook," Midge sniffed in appreciation.

"My job as the home economics instructor at River Depths High is to prepare girls for their future roles as homemakers," Bess said proudly. She laughed. "They say the way to a man's heart is through his stomach. I've found it works on girls, too. What's Velma's specialty?" Bess wondered as she expertly flipped the flapjacks onto a large platter. "Maybe we can trade recipes. I just found a new one for the most scrumptious Swedish meatballs."

Midge laughed. "I'll let you in on a little secret," she said. "But you've got to promise not to tell." She lowered her voice. "I'm the cook in the family," she revealed.

Bess laughed merrily at the thought of Midge in an apron. "Your secret's safe with me," she giggled.

"What secret?" Lauren wanted to know. She tripped into the kitchen, clad in a terrycloth bathrobe three times her size. Her dripping hair hung in a lank braid down her back. "While I was in the bathtub, someone stole my clothes," she announced, explaining her get-up. Her mouth dropped when she spied the platter of pancakes. "Pass the syrup," she said, hopping onto a chair and pulling the platter toward her. One pancake fell to the floor and was snapped up by Gogo. The terrier raced off with her treat.

"I'll make some more," Bess sighed as she watched Lauren pour half a container of maple syrup over her pancakes. "And I'd better go to the basement for another bottle of syrup."

Midge watched in amazement as Lauren threatened to polish off the platter of pancakes without once stopping for breath. "Come up for air, will you?" Midge gently scolded the girl.

Midge leaned back in her chair and lit a cigarette. "How'd you sleep?" she asked.

Lauren made a face. "Terrible. I heard a bunch of kissing noises right before I went to sleep. Jeez. Maybe I should stay in the living room tonight," she scowled.

"Be my guest," Midge replied dryly.

Velma dragged her sleepy self into the kitchen, her tousled black curls framing her face in the most haphazard, adorable way. She plopped down on the chair next to Midge and put her head on her shoulder. "When I woke up, there was a dog in bed with me, eating a pancake," she yawned. "Honey, it was just like home."

Midge gave her a long, lingering kiss on her full, pretty mouth.

Lauren threw down her fork and glared at the couple. She had lost her appetite.

"Goodness, Lauren, why the sourpuss? Morning, Midge. Morning, Velma." Cherry swept through the kitchen, sparkling with energy and attractively attired in a flowered, short-sleeved house dress that made her look even younger than her twenty five years. In her hands was a laundry hamper. "Velma, wait until you see Nancy's closets. Why, they're stuffed with all the latest fashions! I've never seen so many beautiful things. Nancy's locked in the bathroom, fussing over her hair," Cherry added. "I helped her pick out a nice sky blue linen suit and a simple white blouse with a Peter Pan collar. She wants to look her best when she goes to see Chief Chumley and straighten out this whole mix-up."

As a nurse, Cherry knew that often the confidence a girl got from knowing she looked her very best was better than any medicine.

"I wish she weren't so stubborn about doing this all by herself. I don't know why she won't let me go with her. I'm beginning to see a headstrong side to Nancy," Cherry admitted. "Although, she does know the Chief better than I do and is positive he's got a good explanation as to why Hannah's not out of jail yet."

Midge groaned. Why hadn't he already let Hannah go? "I still think we should consult an attorney," Midge worried.

"We'll just have to hope for the best," Cherry said cheerfully. "Now where's the door to the basement? I've got laundry to do."

Midge pointed the way. "Bess went down to get syrup," she said. "Come to think of it, she's been down there an awfully long time." A worried expression crossed Midge's handsome face. She ran to the basement door. "Bess, are you okay?" she called. But there was no answer.

"Bess!" she called louder. A low moaning sound reached their ears. Bess was in trouble!

CHAPTER 29

"Bess? Bees?"

"She might need medical assistance!" Cherry cried. Midge raced downstairs while Cherry ran to get her first-aid kit. Within minutes she had pinned on her nurse's cap and was heading for the basement stairs. Cherry threw caution to the wind and, putting aside her own safety, took the stairs two at a time. Awaiting her was a gruesome sight. Bess was sprawled motionless on the damp basement floor, surrounded by jars of canned fruit.

"I didn't know whether or not to move her," Midge said in a shaky voice as she watched Cherry take Bess's pulse. Cherry nodded her head. Midge had done the right thing, but there would be time later to let her know that! Cherry barked out orders. "Get all the warm blankets you can find. Wake up George. And bring me an ice bag!"

While the others raced about on their important missions, Cherry checked Bess for broken bones, all the time keeping an eye on her pulse. She was relieved to find that, outside of a badly twisted ankle, Bess had no major injuries. "If she's fainted, she should be coming to any minute," Cherry thought. But Bess's breathing grew more labored. Cherry checked her pulse again. She was shocked to find a large, sharp stinger buried deep in Bess's palm.

"Why, she's been bitten by a bee!" Cherry suddenly realized. She quickly injected Bess with the life-saving bee-sting serum she always carried in her first-aid kit. Within seconds, the color came back into Bess's face and her breathing steadied. After sterilizing her tweezers with a match, Cherry removed the barb from Bess's hand and cleansed the wound.

George arrived, her shaking arms loaded down with blankets. Right behind her was Midge, holding an ice bag. Velma and Lauren waited at the foot of the stairs, keeping out of Cherry's way.

"Is Bess going to be okay? What happened?" George frantically quizzed Cherry.

"She's fine," Cherry said. "She had an allergic reaction to a bee sting. Luckily, I had the right medication in my first-aid kit." She held up the stinger for George's inspection.

"Bess? Bees?" George gasped in surprise. "Why, she isn't allergic to bees. In fact, she was bitten several times while we were at Lake Merrimen, and she had no reaction at all!"

"That's odd," Cherry puzzled. She knew it was most unusual for someone to develop a bee allergy late in life. Cherry took a blanket from George, and, using some planks of wood she found nearby, fashioned an emergency stretcher. "Let's get her upstairs and comfortable, and then discuss her medical history," Cherry said. She tucked her patient into the stretcher, and George and Midge headed upstairs with their precious cargo.

"Ugh, what's that?" Cherry cried aloud as she stepped on something big and squishy. She examined the sole of her shoe. "It *was* a bee," she shuddered. "Here it is!"

Lauren whistled. "That's the biggest bee I've ever seen," she declared. Cherry had to agree. In all the bee-sting lectures she had attended, she'd never seen a specimen that size!

"Cherry, I've decided to wear my hair up, as you suggested," Nancy called out from upstairs. "Would you help me pin it into place?" But when she poked her head into the cellar and saw Bess being carried up the stairs, she gasped in horror, forgetting all about her hairdo dilemma. "What's going on down there?" she cried excitedly.

Cherry quickly filled her in on the shocking events, and Nancy hurried to make a comfy bed for Bess on the davenport. Bess quickly regained consciousness and within minutes, was her old, bubbly self. Cherry packed her twisted ankle in ice, and the swelling subsided. She showed Bess the bee, still stuck to the bottom of her shoe.

"I was standing in front of the cabinet, searching for syrup, and suddenly I felt a sharp pinch on my hand," Bess exclaimed. "Golly, that's the biggest bee I've ever seen!"

"Let me see your shoe, Cherry," Nancy said, explaining modestly that entomology was a hobby of hers. She grabbed a nearby magnifying glass and closely examined the specimen.

"This is no ordinary Illinois bee," she declared. "This is the deadly Killer Bee, from the most remote region of the Amazon. It's virtually unheard of in the United States," she said. "No wonder Bess had a reaction; the sting from this bee is fatal without the proper antidote!"

Cherry expressed relief that she had selected the all-purpose serum for her kit.

"But what is it doing in Illinois?" Nancy wondered aloud. "And in my basement?"

The girls gasped. Could it be that someone had planted the deadly insect, hoping to harm them?

"I'll know more after a quick phone call," Nancy said in a most mysterious manner as she headed for the den. When she returned, she had a puzzled expression on her pretty face. "I called my friend, Professor Delbert Dunwiddie at the Department of Agriculture." She explained that she had called upon his expertise while solving *The Mystery of the Insistent Insect*. "When I asked him if any deadly bees had been spotted recently in Illinois, he thought I was joking. I didn't tell him we had captured one in our home; I thought it best if we keep this to ourselves. At least for now.

"Before he hung up, he asked me if I thought Hannah would get the electric chair," Nancy choked out. She flung herself onto an overstuffed love seat and cried out, "There's only one explanation for this. That bee was put here on purpose. Someone is trying to harm us!"

When she heard this, Cherry almost dropped her emergency forceps. "Oh!" she cried. "How dreadful."

"What if there are more bees down there?" Bess asked in a shaky voice, wondering if the door to the cellar was securely closed.

"It's highly unlikely," Nancy answered. "Don't you think they would have stung us, too, with all the commotion we made?"

Still, Bess would not be mollified. "Shouldn't we check?" she wondered.

"That's a good idea, Bess," Cherry said. "I only have five more vials of bee-sting serum left, and there are seven of us here. That leaves one of us wholly unprotected." She shivered. "That's a chance I wouldn't want to take," she said. "Why, one of us could be stung and killed!"

"I believe there's some insecticide in the garage; Hannah

uses it to spray the aphids on her roses," Nancy remembered.
"Don't you worry, Bess. I'll go give the cellar a good dose of
poison." She checked the dainty gold watch on her right wrist.
"It's 8:20 a.m. now. Chief Chumley is always at his office by
nine o'clock. That leaves exactly forty minutes for me to fix
my hair, select the right shoes, and spray poison in the cellar, after which I will drive to the police station and find out
when he's planning to release Hannah and cancel the trial.
Golly, I'd better hurry!"

"But, Nancy, what if you get bitten?" Bess worried aloud.

Cherry was worried about that, too. Although she had
plenty of serum, there was no use courting disaster.

"Besides, the sting really hurts," Bess added. "Ouch. I'd go,
but I'm scared!" She clutched George by the hand. "Don't
leave me," she begged.

Quick as a flash, Cherry had the answer. In her first-aid kit
was a mosquito netting, left over from her two-week stint as
an Island Nurse. Nancy got her bird-watching helmet from
the hallway closet and draped Cherry's net over it, securing
it with the thin leather band that ringed the helmet. She put
on her thigh-high wading boots and tucked the ends of the
netting securely inside. Meanwhile, George ran to the garage
for a canister of insecticide.

What a sight Nancy made, covered in net and carrying the
metal pump filled with deadly fumes! Thick oven mitts from
the kitchen and a gas mask from her father's old army trunk
in the attic completed her costume.

"A girl can't be too cautious!" Nancy joked, before
adding, in a more solemn tone, "I'm going down now."

Cherry stood by, first-aid kit in hand. The girls clustered
around the cellar door until they could smell the first scent
of insecticide.

Velma opened the windows in the living room. "This stuff
stinks," she said. "I can't believe it's the same thing they put
on food crops."

"Velma, a good insecticide, properly used, makes our tomatoes plump and pretty and our apples so red and shiny. Why,
if food didn't look good, people wouldn't eat it," Cherry
informed her.

"There, I'm finished," Nancy said, coming back upstairs and
locking the cellar door behind her. "I didn't see any more

bees," she said, "But I did see something peculiar. It looks as though a hole had been bored through the thick concrete wall; a hole just big enough for a large bee to fly through!

"But who? And why?" Cherry gasped, floored by the discovery. It was seeming more and more impossible that the deadly bug had made its way to the Clue basement unaided!

"Someone deliberately drilled that hole," Nancy said. "Someone is trying to harm us and make it look like a freak accident!"

Bess shivered and reached for George.

"We needn't stay here one day longer," Nancy said as she discarded her protective gear. "As soon as Hannah is released from jail, I propose we go directly to Lake Merrimen for a few days. I have plenty of play clothes to go around," she added when she saw the doubtful look on Midge's face.

"That sounds grand," Midge said weakly. She wasn't so sure she should say anything to shake Nancy's confidence. After all, Nancy was old friends with the Police Chief. "It is entirely possible that all this will be settled with a minimum of fuss," Midge thought hopefully.

"Jeepers! Look at the time!" Nancy cried suddenly. She ran a comb through her titian hair and threw on some lipstick. She brushed aside the cup of coffee Cherry was trying to hand her, grabbed her purse, and raced out the door, but she was back in a flash. "I forgot my evidence," she grinned, taking the stairs to her room two at a time. "I'll bet the Chief was just waiting to see the evidence before releasing Hannah," she mused as she raced upstairs. "I'll bet that's it. He needs to see official proof, plus perhaps take a statement from me."

Nancy's loud shriek a moment later brought them all running. They found her prostrate on the floor, sobbing hysterically. "They're gone!" they heard her wail.

What she said next sent chills through her chums.

"Someone's stolen the letters from my secret hiding place!" Nancy cried.

CHAPTER 30

Purloined Letters

"Let's all look for them," Cherry suggested. "Maybe they're just misplaced. Often I *think* I put something in a special place, and then, to my surprise, find it someplace else! Why, the day I graduated with honors from Stencer Nursing School, I fretted for over an hour because I couldn't find my cap, and what do you know, I had already pinned it to my hairdo!"

Nancy shook her head. "I *know* I put them in the secret hiding place in my hope chest," she wailed. "They're gone!"

She got off the floor, wrenched open the maple chest, and glided her fingers over the smooth wood until she found the secret spot. The girls watched in amazement as a hidden drawer slid out from under the wooden chest. "I hid them in here!" Nancy cried.

"We must call the police and report a break-in!" Cherry gasped.

"They already know," Bess blurted out. "Two nights ago someone broke into this house and the only thing out of place was this hope chest!" Bess cried.

Nancy looked awfully upset when she heard this. "So, someone managed to find my secret hiding place and steal the evidence," she said. "No wonder Chief Chumley didn't let Hannah go! When he came to get the letters, they weren't there. Why, he must have thought I made the whole thing up, or that I was playing a terrible prank!"

Cherry gasped in alarm.

"There is someone afoot in River Depths who wishes me ill," Nancy added in an ominous tone. "My guess is that he'll be willing to give me back that evidence in exchange for a nice big reward."

Nancy took out the bundle of jewelry she'd been keeping in her purse since Dust Bin. "When he calls, give him *these* for the return of my personal papers!" she cried dramatically.

She threw the parcel on the bed, and the knot in the hand-kerchief came undone.

Cherry gasped. "Why would a blackmailer want a pile of small, dull, gray stones?" she asked.

A sick expression came over Nancy's face when she looked at the stones. "My jewels!" was all she could gasp out. "Someone has stolen my jewels!"

"And put these stones in their place," Cherry pointed out. "But who could have done this?"

"The jewel thieves, of course," Midge and Velma chorused. "They must have followed us."

"But how could they have gotten to your purse without your knowing it?" Cherry cried. She had a sinking feeling in her stomach. Could Lauren be responsible for this? After all, she had stolen three butter knives and a deck of playing cards.

"You couldn't have had your purse with you in Kornville, Nancy, because I distinctly remember you borrowed my hair-spray," Velma remembered.

Cherry gasped as she suddenly remembered something. "As we were getting ready to leave Kornville, I found Nancy's purse wide open and shoved under the seat!"

"Someone in Kornville stole Nancy's gems and left these rocks in their stead," Midge deduced. "No one knew Nancy was carrying these jewels except the jewel thief who snatched the case of costume pieces and got away." She shook her head. "They must have followed us all the way across Nebraska." Midge looked peeved. "I can't believe they followed us that many miles and we never caught on," she said in disgust.

"They must be very clever people," Cherry pacified her. "And, after all, they were in disguise, so it's not as if we knew who to watch out for. At least they got what they wanted, and are now probably many states away."

"Wait," Midge replied. "I remember seeing the exact same car in two different states. Remember outside of Pocatello when that dusty brown Impala passed us by? Then in Wyoming, a dusty brown Impala almost hit us. Remember, Velma? You were driving and had to stop short."

Velma nodded.

"Later, I saw that very same car at the service station out-side of Dust Bin. I got a good look at the driver. He was an unattractive man wearing a straw hat and dark glasses. With him was a blond-haired woman wearing a red head scarf and big white glasses. The pointy kind your friend Ethel wears."

"Cat glasses?" Velma guessed.

Midge nodded.

Cherry gasped. Why, Midge was describing the nice couple Cherry had bumped into the very first night of their trip! "Oh, Midge, those couldn't possibly be the jewel thieves! Why, they're just a nice couple on a vacation!" she cried.

Everyone looked at Cherry as if she were suddenly speaking in a foreign tongue.

"Come again?" Midge demanded. When she saw how shaken Cherry was, she softened her tone. "What is it, Cherry? What do you know?"

"I met them at the Pocatello Potato Palace," Cherry admitted. "They helped me find Nancy's jewelry box after it flew out of Nancy's purse."

"What?" her chums cried in surprise.

"I had picked up Nancy's purse by mistake," Cherry quickly explained. "You and Velma were necking and when I went to get Lauren, I bumped into them and somehow Nancy's jewelry box flew out of her purse. I was so upset, and they were so nice when I told them she had sapphires and diamonds and family heirlooms in the case. They seemed truly interested in helping me find it," her voice trailed off. She reddened.

"Do you remember anything else, Cherry?" Nancy asked. "Did you see them again?"

Cherry blushed furiously. "Just later that night when I helped them find their cabin at the Komfort Kourt," she admitted. "And in Kornville," she added meekly, "when I saw them outside the diner."

Midge groaned.

"But they can't be the thieves," Cherry added hurriedly. "When I went to the car to check in my first-aid kit for something, someone *was* in our car, but it was a brunette in a navy blue shift and a red scarf. She had tripped and fallen into our convertible.

"Oh," Cherry suddenly blushed. "She wasn't telling the truth, was she, Midge?"

Midge shook her head.

"It was one of the thieves in disguise, wasn't it?"

Midge nodded.

Cherry cringed. "I guess I'll have to turn in my detective's badge, huh?" she joked meekly.

"But we'll still let you practice medicine," Midge quipped. When she saw the tears in Cherry's eyes, she wished that for once she had kept her mouth shut. Golly, Cherry was as good a sport as they came!

"I'm the reason they knew about the jewels in the first place. Oh, Nancy, you must hate me!" Cherry cried. She burst into tears and flung herself on the bed. Nancy hurried to her side.

"Anyone could have made that same mistake," Nancy said as she hugged her pal to her bosom. "Don't worry. I have tons more jewelry."

"But the thieves got your diamond-studded, silver horse-shoe-shaped brooch," Cherry wailed. "The one from your mother."

Nancy put on a stoic show. "Never mind," she said bravely. "There are more important things to worry about, like getting Hannah out of jail!" She charged out of the room and down the stairs, calling behind her, "If the blackmailer calls while I'm out, take a message." They heard the front door slam shut and the roar of the snappy convertible as Nancy sped off.

"How could I have befriended jewel thieves and then watched while they stole Nancy's jewels in front of my very eyes?" Cherry sobbed. "You must think I'm an awfully silly goose, and Nancy must think she's got an awfully dumb bunny for a girlfriend! Some help I'll be in solving mysteries."

"You're just trusting and sweet," Velma tried to soothe her sobbing chum.

Midge came over to the bed and put an arm around Cherry. Then she did something she had never done before. Midge kissed Cherry right on the cheek!

"We all love you," Midge said, a husky tone creeping into her voice. "You're really a swell kid."

Cherry hiccuped happily. "Even though I made such a dumb mistake?"

"Why, Midge here has made many dumb mistakes," Velma volunteered. "Haven't you, Midge?" Her tone was light, but the look in her eyes was serious.

A sorrowful look shot across Midge's handsome face. "Yeah," was all she said.

CHAPTER 31

The Search for Nancy

 "Now I'm not hungry," Midge said, pushing aside her plate of cold pancakes. Bess offered to whip up some fluffy scrambled eggs, but Midge shook her head. "Not for me," she said. "I couldn't possibly eat. I'm too worried about Nancy." The others agreed. They were too upset to think about food.

"I must *really* be worried," Bess declared as she, too, gave up on her pancakes. "Why, this has never happened to me before. There has been many an adventure when I made Nancy stop the car so I could get a snack," she admitted. "But now..." She didn't have to finish her sentence. Everyone was thinking the same thing. Now they had the joyless task of waiting.

"I will have some more coffee, though," Midge said as she got the pot and poured fresh brew all around. The others agreed that a strong cup of coffee would help them think more clearly.

"Golly, Nancy's stubborn," George grumbled as she poured cream into her cup. "She's one of my best chums, and I love her to death, but that girl can be headstrong."

Bess agreed. "She's always the first one to offer help, but the last one to accept it."

Cherry bristled under the criticism. "Nancy's not stubborn, she's just independent," she insisted, her cheeks beginning to redden.

"You said so yourself you noticed a stubborn streak in her," Midge reminded Cherry. "Remember?"

"I know," Cherry sighed. "It makes me think that Nancy doesn't really need a nurse girlfriend after all. I can't just sit here and worry," she wailed as she got up from the table. She gathered the breakfast dishes and filled the sink with hot, sudsy water. After donning a pair of thick yellow rubber gloves she found in the cabinet under the sink, she plunged into the hot water and began furiously scrubbing the breakfast dishes.

"Careful, you'll wash the pattern right off that plate," Midge joked as she grabbed a dish towel and joined Cherry.

"You know, girls everywhere are always writing to Nancy, telling her how much they admire her, trying to get to meet her. Golly, Cherry, you must feel awfully lucky to have bumped into Nancy in San Francisco the way you did," George said.

Midge was about to tease Cherry about the night she bumped into Nancy, but stopped when she saw a fat tear roll down Cherry's cheek and fall, splat, into the dish water. Why, Cherry was crying! And Midge could just bet she knew what was causing her tears. "Nancy will be okay," Midge assured Cherry, giving her a little hug.

"After all, she's famous for getting out of tight squeezes," Bess chimed in.

Cherry wiped her face on the back of her rubber glove. "I just wish I could be more help," she wailed. "Nancy wouldn't let me make her breakfast or drive her to the police station. Why, she even left the sack lunch I packed for her." Cherry pointed to a small paper bag on the counter with Nancy's name printed on it in tidy cursive writing. "I even cut off the crusts on her lettuce and tomato sandwiches," Cherry hiccuped through her tears.

Bess handed her a dish towel, which she accepted gratefully.

"What if the Chief thinks she shot her father on purpose and that's why he hasn't let Hannah go, and he's planning to arrest Nancy for murder?" Cherry cried.

"I'm worried about that, too," Midge admitted. She took one last swallow of coffee and jumped up. "I'm going to the police station."

"Me, too," the others chorused.

Cherry put down a dish and threw up her arms in alarm. "I've got to bathe and find fresh stockings and set my hair!"

"There's no time for that," Midge declared. "Everyone get dressed. We'll meet back here in five minutes."

A sheepish look came over Cherry's face. "Eek!" she cried. "Midge, Lauren, I threw all your clothes in the washer last night after you went to sleep and forgot to hang them on the line. Why, they'll be sopping wet, and you haven't anything else to wear. I was trying to be helpful," she added, looking chagrined.

"Nancy has plenty of clothes in her closet," Bess said helpfully. "The hem lines will be awfully long on you, Lauren, but I can pin those up in a flash." Lauren blanched, but Bess wasn't paying any attention. She was busy examining Midge, who was a whole head taller than the rest of the them. "I believe you're about the same height as Hannah, Midge. Maybe we can find a simple shift in her closet that you could wear," Bess said hopefully.

Midge raised one eyebrow in alarm. "You want me to go out in a dress?" she cried. Except for the day Velma had been kidnapped by thugs, Cherry had never seen Midge look so upset! "I'd rather go out in my pajamas," Midge declared.

"Me, too," Lauren added in a defiant tone.

"By the way, where did you get that robe?" Bess wondered, touching Midge's plaid bathrobe.

"It is handsome," Cherry conceded, "but I hardly think now is the time to discuss Midge's wardrobe."

"I found it in the hall closet upstairs," Midge said.

"Then there must be more things here that Midge and Lauren could wear. Come to think of it, I don't think anyone's cleared out Mr. Clue's closet yet. The police were leaving that for Nancy, I believe," Bess directed.

"My mother went through his closet to find a suit for his funeral," George added. "She mentioned that he had scads of new clothes from all the best shops." She shuddered. "The only problem is, we have to go in his room to get them."

Although Midge was frankly repulsed by the idea of wearing a dead man's clothes, having to wear a dress would be much worse! "I say we go check out his closet," she said reluctantly.

George agreed to lead the expedition, while Velma, Cherry, and Bess disappeared into Nancy's room to select fresh outfits. Midge and Lauren followed George up the stairs to the room that was once the sleeping chamber of the late Carson Clue.

"The police have already searched this room for clues," George said, as she opened the heavy maple door leading to the large, dark-paneled room. "They claim they found threatening notes in here that Hannah had written to Mr. Clue," George added. The doubtful tone in her voice alerted Midge to what George thought of *that*.

"This is a creepy place," Midge decided as she looked at the heavy maple furniture and matching maple-paneled walls that gave the room all the charm of a cave. "It's so still and dark in here—like a tomb," Midge noted.

Lauren snapped open a shade. In the daylight, Midge could see that the walls were covered with framed documents and photographs attesting to Carson Clue's many civic deeds and social activities.

"It's *still* creepy in here," Midge shivered.

"Look on his bureau," George said, pointing to a large ornate silver-framed photograph of a handsome, smiling, middle-aged man with jet-black hair and stern expression. "That's *him*," she shivered.

"Is it my imagination, or do his eyes follow us around the room?" Midge wondered.

"There's not one picture of Nancy's mother in here. Don't you think that's odd?" George commented.

"I don't know," Midge replied. "Sometimes the picture of a lost love is the hardest thing to look at."

"I guess so," George said doubtfully. "Although, I wouldn't know. After all, Bess is my one and only love."

"Really?" Midge said, fascinated by this information. "You mean, you've never been with any other girl?"

George shook her head. "Never, and neither has Bess," she reported. "How about you?"

Midge looked embarrassed. "Well, it's a long story, but I was in prison for five years. There wasn't much else to do, besides set hair and learn to knit," Midge blushed. "And I was never very good with my hands. Well, not for things like that. But the minute I met Velma, I was finally in love. Although, my cellmate didn't take it too well." Midge clammed up when she noticed Lauren paying close attention to their conversation.

"I wasn't listening to your stupid conversation anyway," Lauren muttered.

George remembered the urgency of their errand and changed the subject. "Let's get you some clothes," she said, opening a door to a large walk-in closet. They were amazed to see stacks and stacks of blue-striped boxes of all sizes. George peeked in a few.

"Sweaters, shirts, cardigans; all sorts of things. And from the most exclusive men's stores in town," George noticed. "It looks like he just selected a whole new fall wardrobe. Too bad he won't be here to wear it," she sneered, sounding not at all sorry.

"I wonder if Nancy will mind?" Midge thought guiltily as she stripped down to her shorts and slipped on a pair of lightweight black suit pants and a crisp summer shirt. She noticed that George had selected a nice pair of sporty worsted blue slacks and a white shirt for herself. Thin, black leather belts completed their ensembles. Midge then slipped her feet into a handsome pair of brand-new black wing tips. She was delighted to find they were a perfect fit!

Midge admired her sharp new outfit in the mirror. "Every time I try to buy men's clothes I get chased out of the store, or I have to buy them real fast before the salesman figures out they're for me, and then I get them home and they don't fit or they're not really what I wanted," she explained. "And I've never had the money for good stuff like this," she said, appreciating the way the fine fabric felt against her skin.

"Those fit you perfectly, Midge," George said, handing Lauren a pair of men's casual slacks that would surely be many sizes too big. Poor Lauren struggled to keep the pants up on her slender frame. "You sure have small hips," Midge remarked as she put a belt through the loops on Lauren's trousers, and cinched it tight. She stood back and gave Lauren a good looking over. "You do look a little like me," she admitted grudgingly. Lauren grinned happily.

"When we get back, Bess can fix those pants for you in a jiffy," George promised Lauren.

Cherry, Bess, and Velma appeared at the door, dressed in gay cotton summer dresses. Cherry had tightly bound Bess's sprained ankle, and Bess had managed to slip her swollen foot into a comfy pair of summer moccasins. "Didn't you guys hear us?" Bess giggled. "Look, they're up here practically shopping!" she teased.

Velma let loose a loud wolf whistle when she got a good look at Midge in her handsome new outfit.

Cherry was pensive as the girls crossed the driveway and piled into George's jalopy.

"I'm going to assist Nancy whether she wants me to or not," Cherry decided as she took her place in the back seat. She was frankly anxious to get downtown and find her girlfriend. She was terribly worried about the state of her chum's mental health.

"And she didn't even have a chance to have her breakfast!" Cherry fretted as they sped downtown.

CHAPTER 32

Conflicting Reports

But Nancy *was* having her breakfast. Although Cherry wouldn't have agreed that a martini with three olives was a very nutritious way to begin the day, it suited Nancy just fine.

"Hit me again," Nancy said to the attractive, dark-haired, older woman behind the bar. Nancy took her drink to the far end of the bar so she could be alone. She had to get her wits about her and figure out what to do next. Earlier that morning she had been so full of hope, and now those hopes had been cruelly dashed, for when she had arrived at Chief Chumley's office, his deputy had informed her that the Chief was gone on a week-long fishing trip!

"I've got to think, only everything's such a muddle right now!" For the first time in her life, she was mystified as to what to do next.

"Another drink," she called out. She turned up her nose at the bowl of pickled eggs the bartender slid in front of her instead.

"You're going to need something to soak up those martinis," the woman pointed out, using the low, soothing tone she kept for the very young or very drunk. "This girl is a bit of both," she decided. "But she's not a regular. Not in this bar, at any rate. She does look awfully familiar, though," the bartender thought, puzzling over the identity of the girl in the chiffon scarf and dark glasses. But she couldn't place her.

"And I would have remembered her," she concluded, trying not to stare at the attractive girl perched precariously on the edge of her bar stool.

When Nancy got up to leave she was surprised to find her legs were all wobbly and were threatening to give way. "Why, I've had this much to drink many times and not had any trouble," she thought as she plopped into a chair to catch her breath. The bartender brought her a cup of coffee, which Nancy accepted gratefully. She sipped it slowly, and soon her cheeks were rosy again and her head had stopped spinning.

The bar began filling up with the noon crowd, buzzing excitedly about that morning's courtroom proceedings.

"Golly, this trial's going to be the most exciting thing to happen all summer!" a girl cried. "Weren't we lucky to get seats for the jury selection?"

"Why, I've never seen the courtroom so packed. There were reporters from all over. What a sight," her chum remarked.

Tears stung Nancy's eyes. "I must get to Hannah and let her know that I'm going to get her out of jail," Nancy thought urgently. But how?

She pulled her chiffon scarf close to her face and prepared to make her escape. But on the way out the door, she overheard something that made her gasp.

"It's too bad Miss Gruel's been assigned Gerald Gloon to defend her. Why, everyone knows he's just about the worst lawyer this side of the Mississippi," Nancy heard a woman exclaim.

Her companion nodded. "I overheard Chief Chumley telling Bailiff Brown that the housekeeper's goose is cooked for sure!"

"But the Chief couldn't have been in the courtroom," Nancy wanted to cry. "He's gone fishing." She realized someone was trying to keep her from talking to the Chief. But who? She raced out of the bar, jumped in her car, and headed once again for the police station. Her ears were buzzing with the dreadful things she had heard. Would she be able to save Hannah after all?

She would find a way to get to the Chief. She just had to!

CHAPTER 33

A Frightful Encounter

"Well, if it isn't my dear Miss Clue," Chief Chumley exclaimed as he hastily shut and locked the middle drawer of his desk upon spying Nancy—a rather disheveled Nancy, for she had had to climb in the back window of the washroom and then pick the lock on the Chief's door in order to gain access to his inner sanctum. The deputy had sworn the Chief was miles away by now, but Nancy had seen his car parked behind the station, between a dusty brown Impala and an old elm tree, and decided to take matters into her own hands.

Luckily, the girl sleuth had never met a lock that was a match for a good, strong bobby pin!

For a moment, the Chief looked surprised to see Nancy, but he quickly regained his composure. "Nancy, how are you?" the Chief cried warmly as he quickly closed the dusty old leather-bound tome in front of him, jumped up, and gave his favorite young sleuth a hearty handshake.

"It's so good to see you!" Nancy cried in relief as she sank into an overstuffed leather wingback chair and wiped her brow. She had sat in this chair many a time, puzzling over particularly perplexing mysteries with the Chief. It was good to be home.

"Your deputy insisted you're away on a fishing expedition," Nancy informed him. "I had to sneak in the back way," she explained, gesturing at her smudged suit and torn stockings.

"Now why would anyone say I was away fishing?" The Chief looked puzzled.

Nancy breathed a sigh of relief. Everything was going to be okay!

"Now Nancy, what's on your mind?" the Chief asked in a friendly manner as he took a seat behind his massive oak desk. Nancy thrilled to the sound of his words. That was what the

Chief always said when she came to him for help or to give him a clue she had dug up.

"I've got a case to crack and I need your help, Chief," Nancy joked back. "It's the case of the mistakenly imprisoned housekeeper."

Chief Chumley smiled. "Always chasing some mystery, eh, Nancy?"

Nancy grinned. "You should know, Chief," she joshed back. "You've been my partner in crime all these years." Her voice grew grim. She leaned forward and said, "Seriously, Chief, what gives? I expected to see Hannah home by now."

The Chief looked genuinely confused.

"When I called you from Wyoming two days ago and you promised to release Hannah, I assumed you would do so immediately," Nancy continued. "Before the trial began."

Chief Chumley lit his pipe, leaned back in his chair, and stared at Nancy. "I received no telephone call from you," he said in a flat, stern tone. "Why, I haven't heard hide nor hair of you since we wrapped up the case we were working on several weeks before your poor father's death."

Nancy could scarcely believe her ears. "Oh, why did I have two drinks?" she scolded herself. "Now nothing is making any sense! I must not be saying it right," she thought.

"I did call you, Chief!" Nancy insisted. "Remember? I told you that I killed Father. You weren't at all angry with me. In fact, you agreed yourself it was the only thing I could have done, given the circumstances."

"What on earth are you talking about?" the Chief thundered, his watery blue eyes flashing with anger. He jumped up and pounded his fist on the book in front of him.

"That book has the queerest title," Nancy thought. *Exotic Entomology Made Easy*. When the Chief caught Nancy staring at the book, he quickly turned over the tome and mumbled something about a roach problem in the jail cells.

"If this is some crazy attempt to take the heat off Hannah, it's not going to work," the Chief admonished. "Why, we've got enough evidence to put her away for a long, long time. While I'm impressed you would go so such lengths to free Hannah, this is one scheme of yours that isn't going to work, Nancy."

"This isn't a scheme, Chief Chumley. It's the truth," Nancy gasped in indignation. She jumped out of her chair but quickly fell back when the room began to spin before her eyes. "I told you on the phone...my father...he...it was justifiable homicide!"

"Just as I suspected," the Chief said. "You're drunk, aren't you Nancy? Drunk and imagining all sorts of ridiculous things. Your father was the most upstanding citizen River Depths has ever known. Everybody knows that."

He perched his stocky frame on the edge of his massive oak desk and clasped Nancy's soft, small hands between his large, thick ones.

"Now, you mustn't run around telling wild stories," the Chief chided her. "I think some little girl had too much sherry at luncheon," he said with a wink.

He buzzed for his assistant on his intercom.

"Miss Clue isn't feeling well," Chief Chumley informed his second-in-command, Deputy Dwight Drone. "Deputy Drone, take Miss Clue to Dr. Fraud for a thorough examination," the Chief ordered.

"Oh, no!" Nancy cried. "Chief, you've got to listen to me. You don't understand."

"I understand, Nancy," Chief Chumley replied calmly. "The strain of your father's death and Hannah's trial has caused you to think things that couldn't possibly be true. Why, I hear crazy stories like this all the time. But do they ever check out?"

In answer to his own question, he sadly shook his head.

"And you know why these stories never check out, Nancy?" the Chief said softly.

Nancy shook her head. She was too stunned to do anything more.

"Because there's never any evidence!" Chief Chumley hissed as he leaned forward and peered knowingly into the young sleuth's eyes.

Nancy stared back at the Chief in horror. Tears puddled up in her bright blue eyes. "But my evidence was stolen!" she wanted to blurt out, but she didn't get the chance. Chief Chumley escorted Nancy and the deputy through the station house and out the door.

"If I were you, I wouldn't attempt to tell such horrible lies." He squeezed her arm hard enough to cause Nancy to cry out in pain. "No one would believe you."

With that, Chief Chumley firmly guided Nancy into the back seat of the patrol car and slammed the door shut.

CHAPTER 34

A Meddling Matron

"Where could she be?" Cherry wailed as she gingerly slipped her swollen feet into a pan of hot water. They'd been all over River Depths—but no Nancy! "Why, we've been to the police station, the courthouse, and all of Nancy's favorite dress shops," she exclaimed. "Lauren, are you sure that when you managed to slip into the courtroom you didn't see Nancy?" Cherry quizzed the young girl for the tenth time that hour. Lauren assured her that Nancy had not been there. Cherry slumped dejectedly in her chair. "There's nothing we can do but wait," she sighed.

Velma put a kettle of water on the stove to make coffee.

"I'm starved!" Bess exclaimed, as she rummaged through the icebox for something to eat. "Here's some cheddar cheese, and I know there's a whole loaf of bread in the bread box," she planned out loud. "Yummy. Grilled cheese!"

"Sounds great," Midge said. "Let's eat and then plan our next move."

Although Cherry was certain she was much too worried to eat, she quickly changed her mind when she smelled the scent of fresh coffee and the delicious aroma of bubbling cheese wafting from the grill. "Nourishment will help me think more clearly," she decided, tucking a linen napkin over the collar of her dress as Bess put a platter of sizzling sandwiches on the table.

"These are great," Lauren said, gulping her sandwich in three bites. Bess passed her another. "There are two apiece, and I can make more," she said.

Cherry did feel a little better after devouring two of the savory sandwiches, but not much. She was still awfully worried about the whereabouts of her chum. "Where could Nancy be?" Cherry worried aloud. She checked her watch. "It's almost supper time. What if there's been an accident and Nancy's wandering around hurt and dazed? What if she doesn't even remember her name? I hope she's carrying proper identification."

"If that's the case, someone's bound to recognize her," Midge said, trying to calm down the frightened nurse. "She won't get far, not with the way her picture's been splashed all over the evening newspaper."

News had traveled fast that River Depths' favorite daughter was back in town. *The River Depths Defender* carried a front-page interview with Mrs. Milton Meeks.

"Fearless Socialite Pays Call to Horror House," the headline read. And on the society page was an announcement of the engagement between Nancy Clue and Frank Hardly!

Cherry heard footsteps on the back porch. "Maybe that's Nancy now!" she cried. She dried her feet, slipped into her shoes, and raced to the door, prepared to jump into Nancy's arms. "First a hug, and then a good scolding," she smiled to herself. "Darling, you're home!" Cherry cried as she flung open the door, threw open her arms, and flung herself at her intended. She was shocked to find the recipient of her embrace was a stout older woman, primly attired in a worsted gray suit and a ridiculous little gray felt hat decorated with blue-jay feathers that now sat all askew on her tidy brown curls. In her hands was a casserole dish covered with a blue-checked dish towel. On her face was the most astonished expression.

"It's meat loaf à la king," was all the woman could say.

Cherry turned beet red. "I thought you were someone else," she said shyly.

Bess recognized their visitor. It was Mrs. Thaddeus Tweeds, the president of the Women's Club, a Patroness of the Arts, and a close friend of Bess's mother.

"Hello, Mrs. Tweeds," Bess said, reaching out to help her with her dish. "Won't you come in?"

"Hello, Bettina, dear," Mrs. Tweeds replied as she stepped into the kitchen. "I tried the front door, but no one answered. I saw George's car outside, so I knew someone had to be at home." She took her compact from her patent-leather purse, gave her nose a good dusting, and then spent a few minutes fussing with her hat until she was satisfied with the results. When she was through primping, she gave the group a good looking over. Her eyes lit up when she spied Midge. "You must be Frank Hardly," she gushed, offering one tiny gloved hand. "Congratulations!" she squealed.

"Frank?" Cherry blurted out in a puzzled tone. "Why, that's Midge!"

"That's right, Cherry," Bess jumped in and cut Cherry off. "That's *Midge's* brother, Frank. She's new here," Bess explained to Mrs. Tweeds. "She's a little confused about who everyone is."

"I didn't know there were any Hardly girls," Mrs. Tweeds said in surprise.

"They're away at girls' school," Midge explained quickly in a surprisingly deep voice. "Back east."

Cherry thought something very queer indeed was going on! Then she realized it was just like at the motel, when Midge was mistaken for a man. "Well, if Midge wants everyone to think she's a fella, I'm not going to say a word," Cherry decided. "I just wish Midge would tell me in advance who she was going to be that day, that's all."

"Who are *you*, dear?" Mrs. Tweeds turned her attention to the blushing Cherry. "Are you a friend of the family?" Mrs. Tweeds suddenly got all flustered. "Oh, dear, I shouldn't say that word—family, I mean—now that Nancy hasn't one anymore. By the way, where is that girl, anyway? Nobody's seen her, and you'd think with all she has to do with her wedding coming up this week she'd be making preparations and poring over china patterns."

"Her wedding?" Cherry gasped.

"Who is this woefully uninformed girl?" Mrs. Tweeds wanted to know. She turned to Cherry and spoke to her in a patient tone that grated on Cherry's already taut nerves. "Dear, Nancy's getting married this very week. Isn't it exciting?"

George choked on her cheese sandwich. Mrs. Tweeds ignored her. Mrs. Tweeds always ignored George.

"Who is she marrying?" Cherry interrupted excitedly.

"Why, Frank here," Mrs. Tweeds said in a impatient tone. "Don't you know anything? It's the talk of the town. Everyone's coming. But I do think it's rather tacky to hold it here, don't you think?" She shuddered and looked around the sparkling clean yellow and white kitchen. She pointed to the shiny white and gold speckled Linoleum in front of the refrigerator. "That's where his body lay," she shivered.

"Do you think Nancy would like a nice knife set?" she queried the group when she had regained her composure. "I gave a set to Mrs. Gloon's daughter, Lenora, and she reports back that they're just the thing for married life." Mrs. Tweeds opened her purse and took out a piece of paper. "Here's the shower list, dear," she said to Bess. "As Nancy's best friend and maid of honor, you're responsible for giving it. Now, I've included everyone from the Women's Club, the Garden Club, and the Literary Club. Be sure to seat Mrs. McCarthy and Mrs. Hellman miles apart; they're having a little tiff over some voile draperies. You won't have time to send formal invitations; if I were you, I'd get on the telephone and call all these people today."

She sighed and shook her head. "This is a terrible time for Hannah to be in jail, what with all the work it takes to put together a bridal shower. You don't think Chief Chumley would let her out for just a few days, do you?" Mrs. Tweeds laughed. "Just to make those cute little finger sandwiches?"

Bess smiled weakly. Cherry looked sick.

"No need to thank me, dear," Mrs. Tweeds said as she snapped her purse shut and marched out the door.

"What did she mean, Nancy's getting married?" Cherry burst out the minute Mrs. Tweeds drove away.

Midge explained the mix-up that morning when Mrs. Milton Meeks had come to call. "She assumed I was one of the Hardly boys, and I didn't correct her," Midge said. "Little did I know that she would make up a story about a wedding and spread it all over town!"

"This mix-up might come in handy," George mused. "Let's keep the charade going. Of course, you'll have to stand Nancy up at the altar. Won't that be a scandal!"

Just the thought of Nancy's even *pretending* to marry anyone but her made Cherry feel funny.

"It's just a little joke, Cherry," Midge said softly, as if reading Cherry's mind. "Really. I have no interest in any girl but this one right here," she said, pulling Velma onto her lap. Velma blushed happily.

"It's just that, well..." Cherry's voice trailed off. She poured herself a cup of coffee and sat down.

"What is it?" Velma asked. "Cherry, are you and Nancy having problems?"

"That's just the thing," Cherry said. "I don't know!" A deep red flush crept up her pretty face. "What I mean is, this is my first romance, and I don't know exactly what to expect."

"Well, what do you want?" Midge quizzed her. "That's as good a place to start as any."

A dreamy look came into Cherry's eyes. "I don't know exactly what I want, but each time I think about being with Nancy, I always picture us in a little house somewhere. Oh, I'd still be a nurse and dedicate my life to helping others, but then I'd come home each night and Nancy would be there waiting for me." She blushed some more.

"I guess I want what you and Velma have, and Bess and George, too," Cherry admitted shyly. "Then everything would be perfect. But so far, all I've gotten is one night of romance, and ten days of worry," Cherry sighed unhappily.

"Can we eat the stuff the lady brought?" was all Lauren wanted to know.

Bess took the towel off the top of the casserole. "It looks yummy," she said. She got some homemade catsup from the refrigerator and a stack of plates from the china cabinet.

"You'll get what you want," Velma assured Cherry. "It's just that you don't get it right away. True and lasting love takes time to build."

"But how much time?" Cherry cried anxiously. "We've been together for over a week! You and Midge are like lovebirds, and George and Bess seem perfectly suited."

"I think you and Nancy are perfectly suited, too," Velma declared.

"I don't know about that," Cherry said sadly. "Nancy seems so different from the first night I met her. She was so bold then; now she's so, I don't know—distant and preoccupied. I don't mean to complain," she added hastily. "It's just that I don't know how Nancy feels about me anymore. Did I do something to cause Nancy to lose interest?" Cherry fretted.

"You haven't done anything," Bess said. "Nancy always gets preoccupied when she's on a case. Why, when we were solving *The Case of the Pernicious Podiatrist*, she wore mismatched shoes: a soft kid ballet flat with a navy blue canvas boating shoe!"

"Nancy hasn't lost interest in you," George reassured

Cherry. "She just has an awful lot on her mind right now. I'm sure that's it."

"I agree," Velma said. "As soon as all this is over, you two can get back to the way you were in San Francisco."

"Besides, every couple has bad times," George said soothingly. "That comes with the territory. Why, Bess and I have plenty of problems!"

"We do?" Bess cried, almost dropping the hot casserole dish. "What are they?"

George thrust her hands deep in her pockets and pouted. Her dark brown eyes flashed with anger. "Well, for one, there's your *mother*."

"What's wrong with my mother?" Bess cried indignantly. "My mother happens to be a very nice person."

"Her mother is constantly trying to fix her up," George complained to the others. "Every Sunday Bess goes off to dinner at the Marvel estate and has to fend off some jerk her mother's dredged up while I stay home alone and eat a cold sandwich. How's that for a problem?" George glowered.

"Well, what do you want me to do?" Bess retorted. "March right into my mother's house and say, 'Mother, please stop fixing me up with every eligible man you come across, as I'm already perfectly in love with George, and will love her until the day I die'?"

"You will?" George gulped, turning bright pink.

"You know that," Bess murmured. She was in George's arms in a flash.

"I know," George whispered. "I just like to hear you say it." She kissed Bess with all her might.

Lauren turned bright pink as she looked at the cooing couple. She looked to Velma, but Velma was busy kissing Midge.

"I think I'm going to cry," Cherry wailed, jumping up from the table and racing out of the room. "Oh!"

"Me, too," Lauren muttered, running right behind her.

CHAPTER 35

Nancy's Return

Cherry awoke with a start, and, for a moment, couldn't remember where she was. "I've slept in so many different beds in the last two weeks, no wonder I'm confused," she thought. She gave in to a luxury hard-working nurses could ill afford—she decided to stay in bed just a minute longer and enjoy the quiet of the dark bedroom.

In another minute, reality came flooding back, and Cherry could no longer lie still.

"Nancy must surely be home by now," was the hopeful prayer running through her head as she hastily donned her dress and raced into the little powder room adjacent to the bedroom. She hurriedly splashed water on her face, combed her mussed hair, and applied a light dusting of powder and a hint of lipstick. She was most anxious to get downstairs and see Nancy!

A good rest had cleared all of the doubts out of her heart. She was sure Nancy loved her. "After all we meant to each other in San Francisco, she's just got to," Cherry decided. She blushed when she remembered how romantic Nancy had been the night they met. "Why, she wouldn't have said all those lovely things to me if she didn't really mean them," Cherry realized. She scolded herself for giving in to her earlier fears about Nancy. She gave her outfit one last look in the mirror, and, satisfied that she presented a pleasing picture, she raced downstairs.

Lauren, Velma, and Bess were at the kitchen table, drinking soda and eating pretzels. "Lauren's teaching us to play poker," Velma winked.

"And I'm winning, too," Lauren crowed, showing Cherry her pile of pennies. From the looks of things, they had been quite busy during the time Cherry had been asleep. A fragrant stew was simmering on the stove, two pair of men's slacks had been neatly hemmed and ironed and were hanging across the back of a chair, and Bess had changed into a buttercup yellow soft chiffon frock and reset her hair so it curled softly around her fair face.

Cherry was sorely disappointed when she discovered Nancy wasn't home yet. "She's on her way," Velma assured her. "Nancy called about an hour ago and said she didn't want to drive home, so Midge went to get her."

"An hour ago? Where are they?" Cherry cried. "Did Nancy say where she had been all day? Did she ask for me when she called? Is there something wrong with her car? Why can't she drive?" Cherry fretted.

Velma took Cherry by the hand and led her to the living room. "Sit down," she said.

Cherry took a seat on the davenport. Velma sat beside her.

"How much do you know about Nancy?" Velma wanted to know.

"I know I love her," Cherry gulped. "Isn't that enough?"

Cherry could tell by the expression on Velma's face that something was wrong! "What's happened?" Cherry cried.

Velma took a deep breath. "When Nancy called, it was clear she was very drunk," Velma said. "Midge could barely understand a word she was saying."

Cherry was shocked. "Drunk?" she cried. "I can't believe it! Not Nancy!"

"Midge says Nancy's been drinking on the sly since we left Idaho," Velma added. "Lots more than what she has at meals. You didn't know that, did you?" Velma asked softly.

Cherry gasped. It just couldn't be true. Why, she was a nurse, trained to notice such things! "The night I met Nancy, we both had a few cocktails," Cherry explained. "But I wouldn't say that either one of us was *really* inebriated," she added. "Of course, for some reason, most of that night is a blur.

"I'm sure that once Midge gets Nancy home and she gets a nice, hot supper and some rest, she'll be just fine," Cherry said. "I'll bet I know what happened. Nancy didn't eat any breakfast, and she forgot the lunch I packed for her. She probably had a cocktail and it hit her too hard. That can happen when someone drinks on an empty stomach," Cherry said. "Especially if they're not accustomed to drinking very much.

"Sometimes when it seems like someone is drunk, they're

really just nutritionally deprived," she explained, adding, "I'll bet she's learned her lesson."

"I hope so," Velma said. "But I—" But she didn't get to finish, for at that moment a car screeched to a halt in front of the Clue residence. They heard a car door slam, and the muffled laughter of two girls. "Good, they're home," Velma said. "I'll go put the coffee pot on."

"Good thinking," Cherry said. "I'll wait here in case Midge needs any help." She waited, but Midge and Nancy didn't come inside.

Cherry was puzzled. Although she couldn't make out what they were saying, she could hear the girls having a rather urgent conversation on the front porch. Why weren't they coming inside?

"Maybe Nancy's fallen," Cherry worried. She flung open the door, hoping to be of some assistance, but instead found herself witness to a shocking sight! An attractive, red-haired stranger had her arms around Nancy. And she was just about to kiss her!

"Stop," Cherry yelled, before she could think of anything better to say.

"Yes, stop," Nancy murmured before collapsing in the red-head's arms.

CHAPTER 36

A Sudden Cry

"What a mess," Midge sighed. She snuggled closer to Velma. Finally, they were alone. "Poor Cherry," Midge thought. She shuddered when she remembered the ugly scene she had witnessed just a few hours before, when she had arrived home just as Nancy collapsed into the arms of a strange red-haired girl. "If only I'd found her before that girl did," Midge wished.

"When that redhead wrote down her phone number and asked Cherry to make sure Nancy got it, I thought there was going to be a fight," Midge whispered to Velma. "Cherry is never going to forgive Nancy; I just know it."

Midge ran her hand down Velma's soft curves. "Do you want to go for a ride?" she murmured as she put her hand between Velma's thighs and rubbed softly. She nuzzled Velma's neck. "Or we can take the car out and find a nice spot in the country where we can be alone under the stars. Golly, it's been days!"

Velma moaned and wriggled closer to Midge.

"I love you," Midge whispered softly. She pulled Velma's nightgown over her head.

A sudden knock at the door startled them both. Velma hastily shrugged back into her nightie.

"Midge? Velma?" they heard a girl sob plaintively. "Can I sleep with you tonight?"

It was Cherry, and from the sound of it, she was mighty upset!

CHAPTER 37

A Rocky Romance?

 "Oh," Cherry gasped as she almost dropped the breakfast tray she had prepared for Nancy. On the silver platter were two soft-boiled eggs, a plate of dry toast, a cup of tomato juice, and a pot of strong coffee. Midge jumped up just in time to catch the pot of coffee before it crashed to the floor. She poured a cup for herself and one for Velma before returning the pot to Cherry's tray.

If truth be told, Cherry was a more than a little anxious about seeing Nancy after last night. Cherry had been aghast at the sight of Nancy in the arms of another girl, but had quickly put her feelings aside when she realized Nancy was intoxicated and in need of swift medical attention.

What was it her favorite teacher, Nurse Shirley Stern, had always said? "A good nurse has no time for personal problems." Although Cherry wondered if Nurse Stern had ever felt the kind of heartbreak she had experienced the night before. "Should I tell Nancy how I feel?" Cherry wondered.

On the way up to the second floor, Cherry bumped smack into Nancy—outfitted in a pale yellow cotton dress with a wide pleated skirt and a white pique collar—creeping down the stairs, one hand over her eyes as if to shut out the morning sun, and the other clutching her stomach.

"I've fixed a nice tray of food for you!" Cherry cried.

"Oh, I couldn't possibly eat a thing!" Nancy protested as she waved Cherry aside. Nancy made her way to the living room, grabbed her purse off the coffee table, and headed for the door.

"That's odd," Nancy murmured when she opened the front door and spied her snappy convertible parked in its usual place under the old Sycamore tree. "If Midge came to get me last night, how did my car get here? Well, never mind. I haven't time to wonder about petty details." She donned her dark glasses as defense against the bright summer morning.

"You're not leaving without any breakfast, are you Nancy?" Cherry called in astonishment as she followed close behind her chum, taking care not to spill any of the delicious, piping hot food on the silver serving tray.

"I have things to attend to," Nancy insisted as she rummaged through her purse for her car keys.

"You must keep up your strength," Cherry admonished her.

Nancy paused in the doorway. She realized Cherry was right. "Maybe a cup of black coffee, then. And an aspirin," Nancy groaned.

"Anything else?" Cherry asked cheerfully.

"Some quiet!" Nancy snapped as she whirled around and headed into the kitchen for some cooling ice to put on her forehead.

Cherry raced close behind, all the while biting her lip to keep from crying. With trembling hands, she poured Nancy a big cup of steaming hot coffee and handed her two headache pills. Her keen intuition told her it was not a good time to ask Nancy about the red-haired stranger who had brought her home the night before. Cherry felt in her pocket for the slip of paper with the girl's phone number scribbled on it. She was sorely tempted to throw it away, but decided against it. "It's not your property, Aimless," she told herself. "It rightfully belongs to Nancy."

"Cherry, are you all right?" Velma asked in a concerned tone. "You seem upset."

Cherry blinked back tears. "I'm fine," she said in a shaky voice. "Don't worry about *me*." She plopped down on a kitchen chair.

"I know why you're upset," Nancy said finally, after having gulped down two cups of the strong brew and eaten the crust off a piece of toast.

Cherry's heart soared. Now that Nancy was herself again, she was going to beg Cherry's forgiveness for the ugly scene on the porch last night, Cherry was sure of it! Tears came to Cherry's eyes. There must be a reasonable explanation as to how Nancy ended up in the arms of an attractive stranger!

"You're upset because I disappeared all day and left you all here worrying frantically about my whereabouts," Nancy blurted out. "Why, I don't even remember how I got home," she admitted. "I know I called Midge from the Tin Tan Club, and then the next thing I knew, I woke up this morning with a terrible headache."

Cherry waited for more about the attractive redhead. "And?" she prompted her chum.

"And, er, it was swell of you to come and get me, Midge," Nancy added hastily. "I hope I wasn't any trouble. You all must have been terribly worried. I'm so sorry," she said.

Nancy seemed so sincere, Cherry instantly forgot all about her own broken heart. "Of course I forgive you!" Cherry cried happily. Cherry crumpled the piece of paper in her pocket. There would be no need for it now, she thought, as she flung her arms around her chum.

Midge groaned.

"What is it, Midge?" Nancy worried. "Was I a handful last night?"

"Let's just say you weren't at your best," Midge said tersely. "I didn't mean to be so harsh," Midge added quickly when she saw Nancy's eyes fill with tears. "It's just that, well, you can get into some awfully big trouble drinking like that. I almost lost Velma that way," Midge admitted.

Cherry gasped. Was Midge implying that she and Velma had once had problems?

Midge looked Nancy straight in the eye. "Don't make the same mistake," she warned.

Nancy nodded solemnly. "I'll never do it again. I promise. I don't know how it happened. One minute I was walking out of the Chief's office in a daze, and the next, I was in a bar. Many bars," she added in a low, embarrassed tone. "It's just that after my horrible encounter with the Chief, I didn't know where to go, or what to do..." her voice broke off into a sob.

"What *did* happen?" the girls chorused.

Nancy quickly explained the turn of events that had put her in such a tizzy the day before. "I went to the Chief's office to ask him why he hadn't let Hannah go, and he acted as though our phone conversation had never taken place!" Nancy cried out. "Why, he acted as though I were crazy!"

"What?" the girls chorused.

"I was so shocked, I didn't know what to say," Nancy admitted. "I began to doubt whether I had even made that call from Wyoming. But I did, didn't I Midge?"

Midge nodded.

"Oh, I don't know what to think anymore!" Nancy cried. "Why would the Chief deny having spoken with me? Why would he promise to take care of everything, and then act like I made the whole thing up?"

Cherry gasped in alarm. Suddenly, she understood what Nancy was trying to say. "Are you saying that the person you spoke with on the telephone two days ago, the one who promised to help you, wasn't the Chief at all? That it was an impostor?"

"That must be it," Nancy exclaimed in relief. "The Chief would never let me down, I'm sure of it. Why, it was the first time he had heard it! No wonder he sent me to Dr. Fraud for a thorough examination!

"But I hopped out of the patrol car at the first opportunity and ran away," Nancy quickly added when she saw her chums' alarmed expressions. "I'll bet now that the surprise of what I told him has worn off, Chief Chumley realizes I *was* telling the truth! Plus I must inform him that someone's running around impersonating him!"

"I saw something like this in a movie once," Cherry said, "but I didn't think anyone in real life could be that deceitful!"

Midge rolled her eyes in disgust. "I'll bet he'd been abducted by aliens that day and a Martian had taken his place," she commented dryly.

"Although I sincerely doubt that, no reasonable explanation should be overlooked," Cherry agreed.

Midge slammed her fist on the table so hard the coffee cups clattered in their saucers. She got up and started pacing around the sunny kitchen, her hands jammed deep into her pockets and a fierce expression on her face.

"What is it, Midge? Do you have another theory that would explain these puzzling events?" Cherry inquired.

"Don't you see?" Midge persisted. "Nancy, I don't know how to put it to you gently, so I'll just say it. *Chief Chumley is not your friend!*"

"Midge, what a terrible thing to say. Can't you see Nancy's already upset enough?" Cherry scolded. "Honestly, Midge, I know you mean well, but sometimes you can be so...so... *frank.*"

"Nancy, the Chief has no intention of helping you," Midge insisted. "Quite the opposite. He's lying! I just know it! He *did* receive that phone call from you, he *did* promise to free Hannah. Oh, Nancy, don't you see that he's the one who stole your evidence!"

"I won't listen to this!" Nancy resisted. She put her hands over her ears. "Police Chief Chumley has always been one of my best friends in River Depths! What possible reason could he have to turn on me? Me!" she cried. "I won't believe these terrible lies. Why, I'd stake my reputation on the Chief's good character!"

"Don't you think it's rather *suspicious* that he was the *only other person* who knew *exactly* where you had hidden your evidence, and now it's gone?" Midge said angrily.

"Maybe he did talk to Nancy, but now he's covering it up for a very good reason," Cherry offered. "He's probably out investigating the case right now."

"There is no case, Cherry," Midge reminded her. "They've got a dead body, a signed confession, and a murder weapon with Hannah's fingerprints all over it. Case closed."

"I'll go to the prison tonight and see Hannah," Nancy planned. "Maybe they're scheming together. Yes, that must be it. Hannah and the Chief are waiting for just the right moment to come forward with the truth."

"What's going on?" George yawned. She appeared in the kitchen, trailed by Bess. By the sleepy look on their faces, it was clear they hadn't gotten much rest the night before. "I'll bet they were awake all night worrying about Nancy," Cherry thought fondly. "As was I."

George plopped down in a chair and pulled Bess onto her lap. Bess grabbed a piece of toast, broke off a corner, and popped it in George's mouth. "Yes, what's going on?" she repeated George's words.

"Instead of speaking to the *real* Chief the other day, we believe Nancy spoke to an impostor who cleverly disguised his voice in order to trick her into telling him where her evidence was hidden," Cherry announced.

"What?" Bess and George exclaimed.

"Either that or it really was the Chief, and he's covering up for some sleuthing he's doing," Nancy hastily added.

A sharp knock on the back door interrupted their conversation.

"Who could that be?" Nancy wondered.

"Maybe it's the Chief now," Cherry said brightly. "Maybe he couldn't speak openly with you at the police station because his investigation is top-secret, so he's coming here to confer with you in private."

Midge looked utterly astonished at the thought.

Nancy opened the door and was surprised to find Mrs. Milton Meeks, Mrs. Thaddeus Tweeds, and four other River Depths matrons standing on the back porch, with furious expressions on their faces.

Mrs. Meeks marched right past Nancy, opened the refrigerator, and removed her casserole dish of tuna salad. Mrs. Tweeds was right behind her.

"My meat loaf à la king, please," Mrs. Tweeds demanded in an angry tone.

Bess handed her the empty dish. "We ate it," was all she could think to say.

"What's happening here?" Nancy asked.

"Nancy Clue, we heard all about what you did yesterday!"

Cherry gasped. Did everyone know that Nancy had come home with another girl last night?

"Who do you think you are, going to the Chief that way and insisting he release Hannah?" Mrs. Meeks snapped.

"It's all over town how you tried to bully him into letting that horrible housekeeper go," Mrs. Tweeds informed them in an icy tone. The girls gasped when they heard the sordid slander.

"We can't believe you'd take Hannah's side," the other women chorused from the porch. "Oh, Nancy, how could you?"

"So we've come to get our food," Mrs. Tweeds said coldly.

"Oh, dear," Cherry fretted. She had already mailed the thank-you notes for the delicious dishes.

"How can you take *her* side after she murdered your poor, dear father? And you didn't even bother to turn up for the funeral," Mrs. Meeks sniffed. She glared at Nancy's sunny outfit. "And you're wearing pastels, and its only been two weeks!"

"Shame on you, Nancy Clue," the matrons chorused from their position on the porch.

Mrs. Tweeds took a lace-edged hankie from her purse and wiped her eyes. "If I weren't a lady, I'd tell you exactly what I think of girls *like you!*"

"Your father was such a dear man," Mrs. Meeks added. "Why, they're building a statue in his honor right now in the town square. I'm the head of the fundraising committee. Care to contribute?"

Nancy gulped. "You don't understand," she said, tears filling her eyes.

"I think we do," Mrs. Meeks said in a frosty tone. "We understand that you are one ungrateful girl. After all your father did for you, providing you with a nice home in an exclusive neighborhood, sending you to the best private girls' school around, buying you closets full of attractive outfits, not to mention the parade of convertibles that came and went! Is this how you repay him? Is it?" she screamed. Her face was bright red when she finished with her harangue.

"Let's go, girls," she spat.

The angry matrons stalked off, leaving behind a trail of Chantilly. Nancy slammed the door behind them so hard, the entire house shook. She kicked it, too, for good measure. Then she limped into the pantry and returned a moment later with a bottle of cooking sherry. She poured a liberal amount into her coffee cup and was preparing to gulp it down when she saw the disapproving look on Midge's face.

"The answer to your problem is not in that bottle," Midge said.

Nancy tossed the drink down the drain. She leaned against the sink and gave way to a torrent of tears.

Cherry thanked her lucky stars that she had had the foresight to launder Nancy's handkerchiefs. She ran to get one.

"I must get Hannah out of jail before it kills her!" Nancy cried as she wiped her tears. "But how? Hannah's prints are all over the murder gun, and the only evidence that could possibly free her *and* exonerate me has been stolen by persons unknown!"

There was a sharp rap at the door. "If that's Mrs. Meeks come back to scold me again, why, I won't be quite so agreeable this time," Nancy declared. She flung open the door, poised for a fight. Instead, a wonderful surprise awaited her.

"Detective Jackie Jones, what are you doing here?" Nancy gasped in delight. "You're supposed to be in San Francisco!"

Jackie Jones put down her valise and swept up Nancy in a big hug.

"Oh, you couldn't have come at a better time! We're in an awful jam and need your help," Nancy said with relief.

The girls raced to greet their chum, who had started the journey with them but had been called back on official duty only minutes into the trip.

The girls had met Jackie Jones, a handsome girl with warm brown skin, sparkling black eyes, and a broad grin that always made Cherry melt just a little, in San Francisco on their last adventure. Jackie was still a beat cop when she had been drawn into *The Case of the Not-So-Nice Nurse*. Her work on the case had resulted in a happy ending for everyone. She had been promoted to detective, Midge had gotten her police record wiped clean, and a whole convent of nuns had been rescued.

"Who wouldn't like Jackie, what with her keen mind, powerful build, good looks, and warm, winning ways?" Cherry thought. In fact, Cherry's boss, Head Nurse Margaret Marstad, had begun a romance with the dapper detective the very first night they'd met!

"Your timing couldn't be any better," Midge grinned, slapping Jackie on the back.

Cherry beamed. Somehow she always felt so secure when Jackie was around. She didn't know if it was her well-developed biceps or the gun strapped in its leather case, which Jackie wore slung low over one hip. She didn't exactly know what it was, but she knew, all of a sudden, she just felt better!

They introduced Jackie to Bess and George, who were impressed to meet a police detective from a big city like San Francisco!

"Is that a *real* gun?" Bess tittered.

Jackie grinned. "How about a cup of good, strong coffee, and then I'll let you touch it."

Midge set a pot of water to boil while Bess bustled about the kitchen, preparing a scrumptious meal. Soon the room was flooded with the most delicious smells.

"I flew all night in a cargo plane to get here," Jackie said wearily as she settled into a kitchen chair. "We stopped at every big city between San Francisco and Springfield. Then I had to take three buses to get to River Depths because no cab driver would pick me up. Why, the way people stared, you'd think they'd never seen anyone like me before in Illinois!"

Bess almost dropped an egg when she heard this. "How horrid," she cried. "I hope you don't think all Illinoisans are like that!"

"I don't understand," Cherry exclaimed in a puzzled tone. "Did you tell them you were a decorated police detective? Did you show them your gold badge?" Cherry smiled when she remembered that after Jackie's swearing-in ceremony the brand-new detective had let Cherry pin her much-coveted shield on her dress for just a minute. She knew Jackie felt the same way about her badge that Cherry felt about her nurse's cap. They were symbols of the life-long commitments they had made to serve the public.

"That's probably why I feel so close to Jackie," Cherry reasoned. "We have the same desire to help others."

"I imagine that out here the color of my skin counts more than the color of my badge," Jackie said in a disgusted tone. She waved her hand as if dismissing a pesky fly. "Tell me what's happened since I jumped ship," she commanded.

"First, you eat," Cherry said, putting a plate of just-perfect fried eggs, sizzling ham, and tasty toast in front of her chum. The others helped themselves to food from the stove, and soon they were sitting around the table, emptying cups of coffee as fast as Bess could refill them, and munching happily on the delicious food.

Jackie finally pushed away her plate and rolled up her shirt sleeves. "Now tell me what I've missed," she said in a calm, authoritative tone that sent shivers down Cherry's spine.

Cherry thrilled to the sight of the strong girl taking charge. She was frankly relieved to finally be getting some professional help! "We're in a real pickle here," she proclaimed passionately.

"Tell me everything," Jackie said in a sympathetic tone. She took her detective's notebook and a pen from her inside jacket pocket.

In a trembling tone, Nancy brought Jackie up to date on the events of the last few days. "Surely you've read the scandalous things the newspapers are printing about Hannah," she said.

Jackie nodded.

"I couldn't take it any longer, so in Wyoming I called the Chief to confess to killing Father. He was so understanding and kind; he wasn't at all angry with me. Then when I told him I had evidence that would prove my father's crime, he got all excited and asked me where it was. He said he would take care of everything."

"And you told him where to find your evidence," Jackie quizzed her.

Nancy nodded. "But then someone broke in here and stole it!"

Jackie looked suspicious, but said nothing.

"I fully expected Hannah to be here when I got home, and when she wasn't, I went to the Chief's office to find out what was going on. He acted as though I had never spoken to him!" Nancy blurted out.

"My theory is that the person Nancy spoke to over the telephone was an impostor," Cherry added. "Midge speculated that the Chief was abducted by aliens."

Jackie shot Midge a swift grin. Midge just rolled her eyes.

Jackie grew grim again as she took a moment to review their statements. Then she slowly went back over the chain of events.

"On Saturday you called the Chief, confessed to murdering your father, and told him where you had hidden the evidence that would clear you."

"Or some impostor pretending to be the Chief," Cherry interjected.

"Or some impostor," Jackie smiled a little.

Nancy nodded.

"Then, that very same night, someone broke in here and stole your evidence," Jackie repeated. "Evidence that was in a secret hiding place that only you and the Chief—or the impostor—knew about."

"That's correct," Nancy said.

Jackie frowned and made a notation in her notebook. "What else has happened?"

"We just had a visit from some miffed matrons," Cherry remembered.

"They took back their casseroles," Bess added as she spread some of Hannah's heavenly homemade marmalade on a piece of toast and popped it into her mouth.

Jackie looked puzzled. "Miffed matrons? Casseroles?" she said.

Nancy explained. "Mrs. Meeks and Mrs. Tweeds; they're the ones who brought us food."

"Meat loaf à la king and tuna salad," Bess said wistfully.

"Well, they're peeved because somehow they found out I tried to get Hannah out of jail. Mrs. Meeks is one of the biggest gossips in town," Nancy said angrily. "And to think that not a year ago I risked my neck helping her rid her mansion of a ghost!"

"Who turned out to be her nefarious nephew determined to drive her mad," Bess added when she saw the alarmed expression on Cherry's face.

"Tell Jackie about the blackmailer," Cherry urged Nancy.

"Wait a minute! You're being blackmailed?" Jackie pricked up her ears. "Why didn't you tell me sooner? Have you received letters asking for money? Threatening phone calls?"

Nancy quickly told Jackie about the ominous phone call she had received at the Double-D Motor Lodge, warning her to stay away from River Depths lest a tragic fate befall her.

"And we were followed by jewel thieves, too," Cherry blurted out. Then, to Cherry's utter mortification, Midge explained in detail how the thieves had come to follow them across the plains states.

"It's not unusual for thieves to target travelers," Jackie when she saw how red Cherry had become. "Especially ones as well-groomed and fashionably dressed as you girls," she nodded at Cherry, Nancy, and Velma. "I'll do my best to track down your mother's brooch," she tried to comfort Nancy.

Cherry smiled. She knew Jackie would be relentless in her pursuit of justice!

"Hypers," George cried. "I just remembered something. Milton Meeks is the judge that will try Hannah's case!"

"Wait a minute; there's something else," Nancy concentrated hard. So much of what had happened the day before was still a fog. Suddenly, the frightful words she had heard in the bar echoed in her ears. She repeated them for her friends.

" 'It's too bad Miss Gruel's been assigned Gerald Gloon to defend her. Why, everyone knows he's just about the worst lawyer this side of the Mississippi!' "

"Doesn't Gloon work for the district attorney?" Bess wondered aloud.

"He quit a week ago to take a job at the Public Defender's office," George said, adding, "I think his timing is highly suspicious."

"Hannah doesn't stand a ghost of a chance!" Nancy cried.

Jackie nodded her head. "It seems like a perfect frame-up," she said, "except for one thing."

"What?" the girls chorused.

"There's a signed confession and iron-clad evidence, right?"

The girls nodded.

"If they've got such great evidence, why are they going to such lengths to make sure Hannah is convicted?" Jackie wanted to know. "Why give her a lousy lawyer to boot? What are they really worried about?"

Cherry looked to Midge for an answer.

"I'm not saying a word," Midge groaned.

"I think they're worried the truth about Mr. Clue will come out," Jackie finally suggested.

"But how could that be?" Cherry gasped. "That would mean there are people who would rather see an innocent woman go to jail than to acknowledge the truth!"

Jackie nodded. Her expression was grim. "Nancy, has it ever occurred to you that the Chief might be behind all this? Think of it. He's the only one with the opportunity and the knowledge to commit the theft of your evidence."

"There's got to be some other explanation for it!" Nancy cried. "I can't possibly believe the Chief is plotting to harm me."

"Okay," Jackie abruptly quit her line of questioning. She shot Midge a knowing wink.

"I'll investigate some other leads," she said. "But first, I think you should find a good lawyer and stall this trial a few days; long enough for us get your evidence back," Jackie declared.

"I tried that!" Nancy cried. "After I escaped from Deputy Drone, I went to every law office in town, and no one would even speak to me! That's why I didn't come home all day; I was so discouraged at having failed I couldn't face anyone."

"My uncle in nearby Lakeview is a lawyer," Bess cried out. "George and I will drive to his office and beg him to defend Hannah." She and George raced out the door. "We'll be back soon—and with good news," they declared.

"Surely Bess's uncle will defend Hannah," Cherry said. "Things are looking up already!" A sudden crash from upstairs made her jump. "It's the jewel thieves, back for more!" Cherry cried as she gripped Jackie's arm.

"Help, I'm stuck," a faint voice called out from somewhere above their heads.

"Lauren?" they cried in unison. Midge raced up the stairs with the others right behind her. They made a quick search of the two second-floor bedrooms, but Lauren was nowhere to be found. Gogo, who had last been seen hours earlier, basking in a sunny spot in the living room, suddenly appeared at Midge's side. "Where did you come from, girl?" Midge asked, giving the terrier a pat on the head. The dog playfully nipped at Midge's ankle, raced out of the room and down the hall. She stopped short, faced the wall, and gave a fierce little bark.

"That's the entryway to our secret attic room; Lauren must be up there!" Nancy exclaimed, running to Gogo's side. "Good girl," she murmured, before opening the panel leading to the third floor. The door was easy to overlook as it was fashioned of the same white wainscoting that lined the rest of the second-floor hallway.

"Lauren must be awfully sneaky to have found this secret passage at all," Nancy mused.

"She does have her good points," Midge admitted.

"No one is supposed to know this room exists," Nancy added. "Father caught me and George up here once, and, boy, was he angry!" She led the way up the rickety wooden stairs and into a dark, dusty room. A small bit of light streamed in through the dormer window at the one end of the room. It was just enough to make out the figure of their young friend, who was sprawled on the floor face down, pinned under a large painting!

Jackie and Midge hastily lifted the ornately framed painting off Lauren, and Cherry efficiently checked their young chum for broken bones.

"Lie still," Cherry ordered in a firm, professional tone that surprised Lauren so much that for once she didn't argue.

"I'm okay," Lauren grumbled as Cherry gently rolled her over on her back. The minute Lauren spied Jackie, she cried, "Yikes, I confess! I was snooping around where I don't belong!" She held out her hands, wrist up. "You can cuff me and take me to jail now," Lauren said dramatically.

They laughed at the sight of the young girl's serious expression. "What am I going to arrest you for, being dusty and disorderly?" Jackie chuckled.

Lauren was indeed a sight, covered from head to toe in cobwebs. Cherry helped the trembling girl to her feet.

"You could have really injured yourself, Lauren," she scolded her young friend. "You're just lucky we found you."

"What are you doing up here, anyway?" Jackie asked.

"What are *you* doing here?" Lauren asked Jackie.

Jackie looked troubled and quickly changed the subject. "You first," she ordered.

"Oh, I was just goofing around," Lauren replied, adding hastily, "I didn't hurt anything. I thought I saw a bat or something," she explained, looking up into the dark rafters. "When I jumped, I knocked over that picture and it fell on me."

Cherry was frightened. There could very well be bats in the

attic! She took a step closer to Jackie. Jackie, sensing her alarm, put a reassuring arm around her chum.

The girls turned their attention to the ornate, gilt-framed painting that had almost crushed their young friend. "It's almost impossible to make it out in this dim light, but it appears to be a portrait," Cherry remarked. "From the looks of it, it's been hidden up here for many years."

"Ah-chooo!" Lauren sneezed suddenly. Cherry was searching her pockets for a clean handkerchief when she heard Midge cry, "Look! It's a portrait of you, Nancy!" Lauren's sneeze had blown away just enough dust from the painting so they could make out a face. Midge lit a match, and they took a closer look.

The girl in the portrait had the same sparkling blue eyes, infectious grin, and lovely titian hair as Nancy. It was Nancy, but at the same time, it wasn't.

"That's not me, that's Mother!" Nancy cried.

"You look just like her," Cherry gasped.

The shrill ringing of the phone startled them. "I wonder who that could be?" Nancy mused as she raced down the stairs.

"Let's cover this portrait with those old draperies in the corner and leave this spooky place," Cherry proposed. She was still a little worried about those bats!

"Jackie?" It was Nancy, calling from downstairs. "The telephone's for you. It's Head Nurse Margaret Marstad calling from Seattle!"

"Nurse Marstad's calling you all the way from Seattle? How romantic!" Cherry cried in delight. It was so exciting the way those two had fallen in love. But she changed her mind when she saw the angry expression that flashed across Jackie's handsome face.

Could it be that their romance was on the rocks?

CHAPTER 38

A Scandalous Story

The girls sat in the kitchen, holding their breath as they waited for Jackie to emerge from the den where she had been talking furiously on the telephone for twenty minutes. Midge, Velma, Cherry, and Nancy strained to overhear Jackie's end of the conversation.

"What's she saying now?" Velma whispered.

"All I hear is, 'yes, no, yes, no,' " Midge whispered back. "But, boy, from the sound of it, Jackie sure seems angry."

"It isn't nice to eavesdrop," Cherry thought guiltily. But, after all, they were only concerned about their friend.

As soon they heard the slam of the telephone receiver, they pretended to be engrossed in other things. Midge lit a cigarette, Nancy ran to the sink and filled a glass with water, Velma jumped behind the ironing board, and Cherry ran to the refrigerator and peered intently inside. "How about a gelatin dessert tonight?" she asked brightly as Jackie strode into the kitchen and dropped into a chair.

"Cigarette?" Midge asked. Jackie nodded, lit one, and took a few short puffs before dashing it out in the nearest saucer.

"I forgot—I quit," she said ruefully. She put her face in her hands and sighed.

"Everything okay?" Midge asked.

Jackie groaned. "That nurse is driving me crazy," she said.

Cherry gasped. Was Jackie talking about Head Nurse Margaret Marstad, the most efficient and professional head nurse it had ever been Cherry's privilege to work under?

The girls stopped pretending they were otherwise engaged and sat down. "What's happened?" they gasped.

"We've broken up," Jackie admitted.

Tears came to Cherry's emerald-green eyes. Could it be true? She didn't know what to say. Why, Nurse Marstad and Jackie seemed so right for each other! "Don't you love her anymore?"

Cherry cried, her bottom lip all aquiver. "Golly, Nurse Marstad must be heartbroken!" she cried. She was tempted to dash to the telephone and call Seattle, but the look on Jackie's face stopped her. Why, Jackie was struggling mightily to hold back tears!

"It's not that," Jackie said in a shaky voice. "It's just that—" Jackie shook her head.

"I must know!" Cherry cried. Had Nurse Marstad done something to tarnish her shiny image?

"Let me say first that I believe Peg is one fine nurse," Jackie said.

Cherry nodded. Why, Nurse Marstad was practically her nurse hero!

"But as a girlfriend, she leaves a lot to be desired," Jackie added in an unmistakably bitter tone.

Cherry gasped in alarm. What could Jackie possibly mean? "What do you mean?" Cherry asked anxiously.

Lauren picked that moment to arrive in the kitchen, fresh and shiny from her bath. She had, however, neglected to brush the dust from her long auburn hair, usually worn in a single braid but now falling freely over her shoulders and in need of a good scrubbing. Cherry sent her back to the bathroom with orders "to do something about that rat's nest on your head." With Lauren safely out of earshot, Cherry demanded an answer. "Tell me what's happened," she urged her chum, adding, "People are so hesitant to let me in on anything unpleasant. After all, I am a nurse in a big-city hospital. I see lots of not-so-nice things. Honest!"

"Give us the scoop, Jack," Midge said. She put a fresh cup of coffee in front of Jackie.

"Peg already has a girlfriend," Jackie blurted out, adding, "It's a fact she neglected to mention during any of our dates."

"Are you sure?" Cherry cried. "Maybe there's just been some awful mistake. Yes, that's it. A case of mistaken identity or a terrible rumor. There *must* be some explanation."

"I know for a fact that she has a girl because she walked in on us one afternoon in the head nurse's dormitory."

"Someone at the wrong door, perhaps," Cherry said, searching for a logical explanation. Anything but that one!

"She had a key, Cherry. She's practically living there."

Cherry gasped in horror. "Who was it?"

"I don't know," Jackie said. "Just some nurse. I didn't get

a good look at her, although," Jackie laughed sourly, "she sure got a good look at me!"

Cherry blushed when she thought of that scene!

"I just threw on my clothes and raced out of the apartment. We haven't spoken until today; Peg must have called the station house and gotten this phone number. I left it in case of emergency, although I specifically requested it not be given out to any nurses!"

"I've been over it a hundred times in my head," Jackie added in a weary tone. "Maybe I should have seen it coming. It's just that Peg and I had such a good time together in San Francisco, I never dreamt she might already have a girlfriend. And I didn't think to ask, because, well, the way she pursued me—the way we pursued each other—it just didn't seem possible there could be anyone else."

But Cherry wasn't listening. She was too busy replaying the scenario in her head. "It's all my fault," she concluded.

Jackie looked incredulous.

"I'm the one who introduced you two. I practically threw you at her," Cherry gasped. She remembered the night her two favorite people had met. Nurse Marstad was wearing a snug peach top that set off her shapely figure to its best advantage, and Jackie was looking particularly handsome and well-groomed. Cherry remembered thinking how lucky Nurse Marstad was to have such a fine girl at her side. Cherry had had such hopes for them, and now those dreams had been cruelly dashed. She was almost in tears.

"Peg wanted to continue the relationship, even after her girl found out. I said no. I don't want any part of a triangle."

"I don't understand!" Cherry cried in utter confusion. "I thought Nurse Marstad loved you! How could she do that? Why, Nurse Marstad has sullied the reputation of honest nurses everywhere."

"It's not the first time I've had my heart broken," Jackie shrugged.

"You mean, this sort of thing has happened to you before?" Cherry gasped. "How horrid! Dear, brave Jackie," she wanted to cry, but she held her tongue. Especially when she realized the others were giggling. Cherry did a slow burn. Why, even Nancy was chuckling! "I don't think a broken heart is anything to laugh at," Cherry pouted.

Jackie sensed how hurt Cherry was. "It's not funny," Jackie agreed, wiping the tears of mirth from her eyes. "Although," she said, "you should have seen the expression on Peg's face when she realized we weren't alone." Jackie started to laugh again. "Peg thought I was yelling because I was enjoying myself, which, by the way, I was," she said. "But I was yelling because I saw a nurse in the doorway! Her girlfriend was supposed to be gone for the week, attending the Sputum Conference in Spokane, but she had come back early unexpectedly," Jackie explained.

Cherry gasped. Not only was she sorely disappointed that she had missed the Sputum Conference—she had meant to attend it this year!—but she was appalled at Nurse Marstad's scandalous behavior.

But before she could say anything, Bess and George waltzed through the door, each holding a paper sack.

"We had no luck getting my uncle to agree to defend Hannah, but we did get lucky at the ice cream store," Bess sighed. "We've got Butter Brickle, Peppermint Stick, Fresh Peach, and Double Chocolate." She grabbed a handful of spoons from the dish drain, opened a gallon of chocolate ice cream, and scooped out a big chunk.

"By the look on your faces, I'd say we arrived in the nick of time," George joked as she passed around containers of the creamy concoction.

"It just gets better and better around here," Midge said sourly.

Midge tossed Jackie a spoon. "Why not?" Jackie sighed.

"What are we going to do now?" Nancy wondered aloud as she dug into the Peppermint Stick ice cream.

"Maybe we'll be able to convince the Chief to turn over your evidence," Cherry said hopefully.

"I can't wait for something that might never happen," Nancy said. "I have to do something now. Right now! But what?"

" 'O ill-dispersing wind of misery!' " Cherry sighed.

Nancy cocked her head. "Where have I heard that before?" she wondered.

"It's from *Richard III*," Cherry explained. "My twin brother Charley played the Duchess of York one summer at Boys' Camp," she said, adding, "He was surprisingly good in the role. It took quite a lot of makeup to disguise his masculine good looks, but the wardrobe department did a wonderful job, and he pulled off the part to great acclaim."

"Cherry, that's it!" Nancy cried. She kissed her chum and then did a delightful little jig around the kitchen table. Cherry had no idea why Nancy was suddenly so gay, and she was too delighted even to ask. For the first time since their arrival in River Depths, Nancy seemed more like the Nancy Clue Cherry had fallen in love with—an excitable girl undaunted by any task set before her!

Nancy rushed into the den and was soon whispering excitedly on the telephone. Nancy had obviously thought of some grand scheme, but what could it be? She returned a few minutes later with a sparkle in her eyes.

"Did you find an attorney?" Jackie quizzed her.

"Better than that," Nancy said mysteriously. "Bess, George, we've been invited to visit Mr. Donald."

Bess and George gasped in delight at the thought of seeing their beloved high school drama coach. Then they looked to each other in confusion. Had Nancy gone mad? Was this really the time for a social call?

"Who's Mr. Donald?" Cherry asked.

"He's our local drama coach," George explained. "He's an expert when it comes to costume and disguise, and—" Suddenly, her handsome face lit up. She grinned at Nancy. "If you're thinking what I think you're thinking, I think it's a grand idea!" she cried. She grabbed Bess by the hand. "Let's go!"

"Take us with you," the others urged.

Nancy agreed. "But you mustn't try to talk me out of my plan," she made them promise. They each gave Nancy a smart three-finger salute. "Scout's honor," they chorused.

"Let's go, then," Nancy exclaimed. "We haven't a minute to lose!"

The seven girls squeezed into Nancy's snappy convertible. The back seat was so crowded, Cherry had to sit on top of Jackie! Nancy smoothly backed the large automobile out of the tree-lined driveway and onto Maple Street.

"We forgot Lauren!" Midge suddenly remembered. Nancy put on the brakes, and Midge raced inside the house to get the girl.

"That was awfully nice of you to go get her," Cherry remarked when Midge returned with Lauren in tow.

"Nice, nothing," Midge sneered. "It's simply a precaution. I had an image of the house burning down in our absence," she grinned.

CHAPTER 39

A Fabulous Fellow

After a smooth ride through the exclusive suburb of River Depths where the Clues had made their home, then through the bustling downtown filled with afternoon shoppers laden with packages, and over a set of bumpy railroad tracks, they reached a part of River Depths filled with dilapidated Victorian homes. Many of the once-grand homes had sat empty since Nancy was a child. People preferred the clean lines and modern living afforded them in the suburbs.

Nancy pulled her convertible in front of an old, sprawling manse that had seen better days. When she rapped on the door, it was opened tentatively by an elderly woman. "Who is it?" she called, in a high, reedy voice that quivered with age.

Nancy giggled. "It's Nancy Clue here to see Mr. Donald," she replied.

Cherry didn't see what was so funny. She hated to think of this elderly woman living in a run-down mansion. "This must be Mr. Donald's mother," Cherry realized. "At least she's not living alone in this big place."

"Follow me, dears," the woman said. They passed rooms stuffed with trunks and suitcases, piles of fabric and all sorts of bric-a-brac, to a parlor overlooking a lush garden.

The room was nicely furnished with worn but comfy furniture, two threadbare red velvet overstuffed chairs, and dark wood bookshelves packed with hundreds of leather-bound volumes. Asleep in a wicker basket were three darling little black poodles.

"That's Mitzi, Bitzi, and Fritzi," the woman said as the girls exclaimed over the darling little pets. "Would you girls care for tea?" their hostess asked. "I have fresh-baked biscuits and gooseberry jam."

"Yum," Bess replied. When the others admitted their car

ride had left them famished, the woman excused herself. "I'll be right back," she said, with a twinkle in her eye.

"Why, Mr. Donald's mother is lovely!" Cherry exclaimed. "How nice that she lives here with her son, overlooking this lovely garden."

"Yes, they get on quite famously," Bess said. Then she burst into a fit of giggles. Soon George and Nancy joined her in her merriment.

Midge frowned. Something very queer was going on here! "When are you going to let us in on the big secret?" she asked.

But Nancy only smiled and said mysteriously, "You'll see."

"Oh, look, Midge," Cherry cried. One of the poodles was walking on her hind legs—right toward Midge!

"She's smart enough to be in the circus," Midge remarked.

"They were circus dogs," a man with a thick English accent declared. A butler in full uniform carried a silver tray into the room. It was laden with plates of biscuits and fruit, a pot of jam, and a large china teapot. "They were members of Her Majesty's Royal Circus until their retirement," he explained. "Tea is served," he announced.

"Isn't Mr. Donald joining us?" Cherry wondered.

"All in due time," the butler said. Was it Midge's imagination, or did the barest flicker of a smile cross his face?

"Will there be anything else?" he asked.

"Thank you; that will be all, Jeeves," Nancy giggled.

Cherry picked up a cup of tea and a plate of goodies. She was more puzzled than ever about what they were doing there! "Who would ever have expected an elderly woman with an English butler to live in such a shabby part of town!" she cried aloud.

Just then a handsome man with short silvery hair and an impish grin, came walking through the garden. He was clad in black cashmere slacks, soft black leather slippers, and an emerald-green jacket almost the same color as his sparkling, lively eyes. The white silk scarf tossed casually around his neck gave him a dashing air, like a movie star or a pilot, Cherry thought.

"I heard you girls were here," he said casually.

"Hello Mr. Donald!" George and Bess cried in unison, thrilled to see the fellow who had, year after year, turned the annual show at the local girls' camp into the theatrical event of the summer.

Mr. Donald listened eagerly as Nancy introduced him to the rest of the gang and explained the unusual circumstances under which they had met. His eyes shone in delight when he heard the story of their adventure during *The Case of the Not-So-Nice Nurse.* "What fun!" he enthused when he heard that the girls had rescued a convent of kidnapped nuns and accidentally killed the evil priest who had masterminded the dastardly plot.

"I hope our little town doesn't prove dull to you girls after all your adventures in San Francisco," he said. "Especially you, Detective Jackie Jones. Why, as a big-city detective, you must have all sorts of adventures every day. I'm afraid this town can be a little backward."

"Backward is hardly the word," Midge groaned. Nancy quickly filled Mr. Donald in on the dramatic events of the last few days, including Mrs. Meeks's boorish behavior during her visit to the Clue household.

"I never did like that Mrs. Meeks," Mr. Donald fumed. "She's always pulling me aside at parties and asking for decorating advice. And then she never listens to a word I say, goes out and purchases the most hideous things, and tells everyone I choose them," he shuddered. "She paired nubby tweed couch covers with raw-silk floral draperies! Imagine!

"She's going to ruin my reputation one of these days," he declared.

"She's already ruined Nancy's," Bess declared hotly. The girls told him the details of her visit, including the campaign she and others like her were waging against Hannah.

"Poor dear Hannah," Mr. Donald said sadly. "I can't for a minute believe she killed your father, Nancy. I think some intruder did it, and Hannah unwittingly wiped off the gun, and left her prints by mistake. Hannah's only fault, as far as I can see, is that she's a very tidy housekeeper," he declared.

Nancy said nothing. Obviously, in her earlier phone conversation, she hadn't told Mr. Donald *all* of her story.

"She's even spread the rumor that Midge is Frank Hardly *and* Nancy's fiancée," Bess giggled, adding, "We're letting her believe what she wants."

Mr. Donald stared at Midge with a director's probing gaze and then said, "Come to think of it, Midge, you do look awfully like Frank Hardly—same strong shoulders and determined jaw." He rifled through a nearby scrapbook. "Ah, yes. Summer of 1957. Frank Hardly in *As You Like It*. Frank played Rosalind; rather well, as I remember." He held the book up so all could see. "Take away the long curls and the dress, and you have Midge!"

"Why, Frank and Midge look so similar, they could be sisters!" Cherry cried.

Mr. Donald got a sly look in his eye. "We'll take care of Mrs. Meeks," he grinned. "Later."

He snapped the book shut. "Are you ready?" he asked.

Nancy nodded. She followed him out of the room. "Wait here," she told her chums.

Cherry frowned. If she didn't know Nancy so well, she'd think she was almost sneaky sometimes! She quickly put all unpleasant thoughts out of her mind and concentrated on her delicious cup of tea. A crash from the front of the house startled her so, she almost dropped her cup.

"Where's Lauren?" Midge yelped. She left the room and was back in a flash with the young girl. "Sit down and don't touch anything," Midge scolded the youngest member of their group.

Lauren scowled but did as she was told.

"She knocked over a suit of armor," Midge explained, adding, "Thankfully, there were no dents in it."

"My brother Charley would just love Mr. Donald!" Cherry enthused. "They have an awful lot in common, what with the way they use their talents to liven up dull interiors."

She vowed to tell Mr. Donald about her brother and his artistic tendencies but forgot all about it when the door opened and Mr. Donald emerged with an attractive, older, pleasant-faced woman clad in a simple gray dress and a starched white apron.

"Oh, hi there, Hannah," Bess and George remarked casually.

"Hannah! How did you get out of jail?" Cherry cried excitedly. "Does Nancy know you're here?"

"Nancy knows I'm here," Hannah assured her.

Cherry gasped in shock, for it was Nancy's voice that came out of Hannah's mouth!

"Your own mother wouldn't know you," Cherry almost blurted out, stopping herself just before making the terrible mistake of mentioning Nancy's long-dead mother.

Bess and George examined their chum's tidy gray hair

styled in a neat bun, stern yet loving eyes, and neat-as-a-pin outfit. "Golly!" they cried. "You really do look just like Hannah!"

"Wow, Mr. Donald, you really are the King of Disguises!" George exclaimed in admiration. "You practically had me believing you had a mother!"

Everyone laughed at the expression on Cherry's face when she realized there was no Mother Donald or English butler.

Nancy quickly explained her scheme. "I'm going to visit Hannah alone in her cell, slip into this disguise, make Hannah up to look like me, and switch places with her. Hannah will walk out of prison a free woman. That way, she can recuperate in peace at home and without the strain of a trial until you girls get back the evidence and clear our names. That is, if you don't mind searching for it on your own."

"We'll do anything to help," they chorused.

"But what if they discover your ruse? Your house is the first place they'll look," Jackie said.

"Hannah will be out of sight in the secret attic room," Nancy said. "No one knows it's there but us. And even if they discover my trickery and think to search the house, they'll never find that room."

"But Lauren found it," Velma pointed out.

"Yes, she did," Midge agreed. "But then again, Lauren seems to have special skills in finding secret places. I have another question about your plan, Nancy: What if Hannah refuses? How will you convince her to go along with this scheme?"

Nancy's eyes sparkled. She obviously had thought of every detail! "Hannah won't refuse," she said. "She'll be so relaxed after Cherry gives her a cup of tea laced with Valium, she'll agree to anything."

Cherry gasped in horror. Was Nancy asking her to dupe an unsuspecting, elderly woman? Cherry gulped hard. She had taken a solemn nurse's vow, one in which she'd promised that her nursing duties would supersede all others, including those of girlfriend. "I can't administer medication against someone's will," she said firmly, hoping Nancy would realize the predicament she was placing her in.

"Then I'll do it," Nancy said. "Just give me the pills."

"I will not!" Cherry cried indignantly. "It's not something

you can learn overnight. Why, it takes years of training to become a good nurse."

Nancy shook with anger. "I can't believe you won't do this for me. Think of Hannah; it could save her life! What kind of nurse are you?" she gasped out. "Come to think of it, what kind of girlfriend are you?"

"Perhaps you should ask *that redhead* who accompanied you home last night to do it!" Cherry shot back, stung to the quick.

The girls gasped in horror. Was there going to be a fight?

"Maybe I will," Nancy retorted, although she had no idea who Cherry was talking about. What redhead? But she was too upset to ask Cherry what she meant. She focused on one thing only—freeing Hannah at any cost! "Are you going to do it or not?" she demanded.

The others held their breath. Would Cherry do as Nancy asked?

"I can't," Cherry explained plaintively. "Why, it's against my nurse's code of ethics!"

"You know what you are, Cherry Aimless?" Nancy cried. "Why, you're a good-for-nothing girlfriend!"

Cherry recoiled as if she had been slapped. She picked up her handbag and fled. Nancy collapsed into a heap on the couch and burst into tears.

"Midge, go after Cherry," Velma said worriedly as she attempted to comfort Nancy.

Midge raced through the house and outside after her chum. She spied Cherry a block away, leaning against an old sycamore tree and sobbing into a handkerchief. "Wait up, Cherry," Midge yelled.

But when Cherry spotted her, she took off around the corner, and just as Midge was about to catch up with her, she hopped onto a bus.

"You don't know where you're going, Cherry," Midge called. "Come back."

But Cherry either didn't hear her, or pretended she didn't. The bus zoomed off.

CHAPTER 40

A Sudden Awakening

 Almost an hour had passed since Cherry and Nancy had had their spat, and Cherry still hadn't appeared. The girls had driven through town searching for their distraught chum, then given up and returned to Nancy's home on Maple Street to wait for some word from Cherry. They were beginning to get mighty worried about the whereabouts of their wayward friend. Why, they could barely eat!

"Where could she be?" Midge fretted as she pushed aside her plate of franks 'n' beans "It's going to be dark soon."

"We'll give her ten more minutes, and then take the car out and look for her," Jackie said. She hadn't touched her meal either; only nibbled absentmindedly at the potato salad.

"Earlier I thought it best to leave her be for a bit, but now I'm getting worried. I don't like the idea of her wandering around with a broken heart in a strange town," Velma declared.

An anxious look flashed across Nancy's face. "What if Cherry doesn't get home in time for us to make up before I go to jail?" she worried aloud. Nancy was in a race against time for she had an appointment to see Hannah in just one hour; now that the housekeeper had recovered slightly from her heart attack, she'd been moved back to her private cell and was allowed to have visitors. Nancy still had to pack the costume and theatrical makeup that would transform her into the pleasant-faced, elderly housekeeper.

Jackie shot Midge a disgusted look. Midge could tell what she was thinking. After the blow-up today, Jackie wasn't so sure Nancy and Cherry *should* make up. She was beginning to think Nancy wasn't the best possible girlfriend for her nurse chum.

"Cherry needs someone older, more mature. Someone strong and steady. Someone who wouldn't pull the kind of stunt Nancy pulled today," Jackie thought angrily. She kept her feelings to herself, though.

Nancy would need their help to pull off her scheme, for she was determined to masquerade as Hannah and had before her the exacting task of preparing to sneak into jail carrying a complete Hannah costume, wig and all, while at the same time fretting frantically about her missing chum, Cherry.

"I was awfully hard on Cherry," Nancy moaned aloud. "I should have never said what I did. Why, Cherry's just about the best girlfriend I've ever had!"

Jackie winced.

"When you go to apologize, I'd leave out the part about the other girlfriends," Midge cautioned.

"I'll do anything I can to make it up to her," Nancy said.

"Here's your chance," Midge said, as she saw Cherry appear at the back door. "Be very nice," she added.

The girls jumped up and headed for the living room, but before they could make their getaway, Cherry walked in and announced that she had something to say to all of them.

"I'm going back to Seattle," she said in a shaky voice that belied the matter-of-fact tone she was trying to maintain. "I'm of no use to anyone here, and that way, Nancy can get on with her life without having me and my silly standards get in her way." She took a clean hankie from her purse and daintily wiped two tears trickling down her cheek.

"I'll go and pack now," she sniffed softly.

The girls gasped and glared at Nancy. "Stop her," their eyes cried out.

"I'm so sorry for what I said," Nancy blurted out. "Please stay."

Cherry bit her lip and narrowed her eyes. Nothing Nancy could say could ever change her mind!

"Please don't leave me now, Cherry," Nancy begged as she knelt next to her friend and clasped her hand to her bosom. "How could you, after all we've meant to each other? Remember our night in San Francisco? Our first kiss?" Nancy appeared to be overcome with emotion. Tears filled her eyes. She struggled to continue. "I was wrong to ask you to do something so unscrupulous," she admitted. "Why, I admire you for your strict code of conduct. It's one reason I was drawn to you in the first place."

"Nurses set an example for girls everywhere," Cherry explained proudly.

"I know that," Nancy said. "Why, I even considered becoming a nurse when I was younger," she admitted slyly.

Cherry was thrilled to hear this. She hedged a little smile.

Nancy saw that her desperate words had done the trick. "So you'll stay?" She sneaked a look at the clock on the mantle. If she was going to finish her preparations and be at the prison on time, she really needed to hurry! Time was running out!

Cherry sighed and sank into the couch. "I don't know if I could be happy here, knowing I ruined your plans to free Hannah," she whimpered.

"My plans aren't ruined," Nancy replied. "George has agreed to come with me and—er—convince Hannah to go through with the switch. George has always had a way with Hannah," Nancy chuckled. "One word of praise from George, and Hannah would bake a truckload of her famous lemon meringue pies!"

"That's right," George said with a grin. "Nancy and I will surely make Hannah see the justice of her scheme."

"So you've selected George to go instead of me?" Cherry said in dismay.

"I need you here," Nancy said. "Hannah's going to need the best nursing care possible when she gets home, and you're the only one who can do it, Cherry. You're going to nurse as you've never nursed before!"

Cherry forgot all about Nancy's earlier harsh remarks. The call to duty rang clear and true. "I'll stay!" Cherry agreed. She threw her arms around Nancy and gave her a big kiss.

"Splendid," Nancy declared when Cherry finally released her. "Then you'll prepare the attic room for Hannah's arrival and nurse her back to health?"

Cherry could only nod. Golly, she was happy! She set about putting the last-minute touches on Nancy's disguise. Nancy decided to smuggle in the costume under her own clothes after Midge warned her that prison matrons were wont to search one's purse—and thoroughly!

Nancy showed them her bag of tricks, which she had gotten from Mr. Donald: the pieces of tape to pull parts of her face into a different shape, the rubber prosthesis that would give her a new nose, and the pair of simple, steel-rimmed glasses that would make her transformation into the elderly, pleasant-faced housekeeper complete. "I'll hide them in my shoe," she decided.

Nancy then donned the gray bun meant to replicate Hannah's prim hairdo. The theatrical makeup kit was stowed in her purse and looked much like her everyday cosmetics bag.

"But how are you going to make Hannah look like *you?*" Bess wondered. "Hannah's forty years older, and, although she's a very handsome woman, you two really don't look anything alike. Plus, she's a lot taller."

"That's going to be the tricky part, since she's going to have to walk out past prison matrons," Cherry agreed.

"Easy," Nancy replied with a smile. "Remember when I was crowned Miss River Depths 1956 and Grossman's Department Store honored me by making a Nancy Clue mannequin for their Junior Deb department? Mr. Donald was the costumer hired to design it, and, lucky for me, he still has the mold in his basement! While he was serving us tea in the guise of Jeeves he was really waiting for the quick-dry rubber to harden into a mask.

"I'll merely wear it into the prison over my own face, along with my scarf and dark glasses. See?"

"Remarkable!" the girls chorused when Nancy donned the rubber face.

"And Mr. Donald loaned me this flowered frock with a false hem."

"I'll run and get my stethoscope. You can take it along in case you need it," Cherry offered helpfully.

"There's no time to waste," Nancy cried as she gave Cherry a quick kiss and raced for the door. "George, let's go! We'll take your old jalopy so we're not so conspicuous." And off they went.

"I've never seen Nancy so jumpy," Bess remarked.

"I just hope all goes as planned," Cherry said.

"If I know Nancy, it will," Bess said. "She's one girl who always gets her way, and George is always up for any adventure Nancy has in mind."

"Well, there's no time to worry now," said Cherry. "I have a job to do!"

Nurse Aimless got to work. "We've got to dust and air out that secret attic room, move a comfortable bed up there, find clean blankets and sheets, and do any number of things to get ready for our patient," she said in a brisk tone. She clapped her hands sharply, and within minutes, the girls were scurrying about the house, gathering supplies that would be needed in the sickroom while Cherry slipped into her lightweight travel uniform, perky cap, and rubber-soled nurse's shoes.

While Velma sterilized jars in a large double-boiler on the stove, Jackie and Midge got to work disassembling a bed to take upstairs. Cherry sent Bess to the store for tapioca and cottage cheese—easily digestible foods that wouldn't upset a sick person's delicate stomach.

After donning her uniform, Cherry took Lauren upstairs to dust. To her surprise, Lauren turned out to be a helpful partner, and soon the little attic room was as neat as a pin. Lauren cleverly located an old wooden box that, when turned on its side, could double as a bedside table. "Make sure there's nothing fragile in there first," Cherry cautioned.

"There's nothing in here but bunches of old love letters tied up with ribbons," Lauren said. "They're from someone named Terry."

"It's not polite to read other people's mail," Cherry was about to scold, when a commotion from the stairwell drew her attention. She forgot all about the letters as she ran to help Midge and Jackie, who were struggling to get the double-bed frame and mattress up the narrow stairwell. Cherry guided them up the stairs and, while they were setting up the bed, raced downstairs for her first-aid kit and some fresh linen. Soon the little attic room was as fine a sick room as Cherry had ever seen.

"Good work," Cherry clapped as Midge and Jackie sank to the floor in mock exhaustion.

It had been weeks since Cherry had done any real nursing, and the excitement of preparing for a patient had driven all worry about Nancy from her head.

"Get up," Cherry ordered with mock severity. "We've still got plenty of work to do. Now, who's going to be my scrub nurse in case I have to change bandages?" she asked.

"I will," Velma volunteered cheerfully. She arrived in the attic carrying a tray loaded with sterile jars covered with a clean cotton cloth, as Cherry had instructed.

Cherry saw that Velma had done a thorough job. "Good work, Nurse Velma," Cherry said brightly. "Now I'll need my own table so I can spread out my medical equipment, in case I need to get to it in a hurry."

"I know what you can use," Lauren said. She raced downstairs and returned a minute later with a small folding t.v. table.

"It's just the ticket," Cherry declared as she set up the table and began laying out the contents of her first-aid kit. She realized immediately that something was out of kilter. A good nurse knew the contents of her first-aid kit like the back of her hand. And Cherry was nothing if not a good nurse!

She took a quick visual inventory and gasped when she discovered that something indeed *was* missing! "My vial of Valium is gone," she gasped aloud. "Who could have...oh, no!" she cried, throwing up her arms in alarm when she realized who *must* have taken it. Velma tried to calm the frantic nurse while making a careful search of the first-aid kit, but she couldn't locate the vital vial of Valium anywhere.

"So that's why Nancy was in such a hurry to get out of the house!" Cherry cried. "Not only did she lie to me, she stole from me, too. And stole medication, which, in the hands of the wrong person, can be lethal!

"Why, unless you're a health professional, it's against the law to carry controlled substances. Not only that, Nancy doesn't know what she's doing."

"Nancy knows how to give medication," a small voice said. Bess was standing at the top of the stairs with a guilty look on her face and a bag of groceries in her arms. "Once when Nancy and I were volunteer nurse's aides at the county clinic, a nurse showed us how to give out pills," Bess explained. "We weren't supposed to, but there was an epidemic and people were waiting hours for that one nurse to medicate them."

"That's unethical," Cherry gasped. "Who is that nurse? Why, she ought to be reported! And Nancy must be stopped!"

"But Hannah's at no real risk," Bess pointed out. "Nancy would never do anything to harm Hannah."

"But what Nancy's doing is wrong," Cherry insisted. "Isn't it?"

She looked around the room at her chums. She could see by the expressions on their faces that they didn't share her feelings. "Midge?" Cherry said in a weak voice. "What do you think?" Surely Midge would come to her defense! "Do you find me rigid and unbending?" Cherry asked.

Midge didn't know what to say. She tried to choose her words carefully. "Sometimes, Cherry, people do the wrong thing for the right reason."

Cherry puzzled over this for a moment. "I think I understand what you mean," she finally said. "It's like when I accidentally killed that evil priest. It was wrong to beat him to death, but I did save the lives of many women. Is that what you mean, Midge?"

"Something like that," Midge nodded.

"Tell me the truth, Midge," Cherry begged. "Am I really so awfully good that I get on people's nerves?"

"Yes, Cherry, you are," Midge blurted out before she could stop herself. When Velma heard this, she crossed her arms over her bosom and glared at her girlfriend. Midge had a feeling she would be sleeping on the sofa that night.

"But we really like you anyway, don't we, girls?" Midge added hastily.

"Really and truly," Velma gushed.

"Very much," Jackie added in a sincere tone. "I like you very much," she added softly. "Very, very much."

But there was no consoling Cherry, who flung herself on the newly made bed and burst into tears. "It's true; I am a good-for-nothing girlfriend," she sobbed. "I've let Nancy down the one time she really needed me. I should be at the jail cell right now, drugging Hannah. Instead, I'm here, frantic with worry. You know, my nickname in high school was Miss Goody Two Shoes, and until today, I was always a little proud of it," she confessed between sobs. "I thought it was an honor! But now I'm ashamed of myself!"

Suddenly, a determined glint came into Cherry's eyes. She blew her nose on the handkerchief she always kept in her pocket and raced down the attic stairs. The rest of the gang followed close behind. Where could she be going in such a hurry?

Cherry grabbed a lightweight blue cardigan sweater from the hall closet, paused for a second to powder her tear-stained cheeks, and headed for the front door. "Maybe I can make it to the prison in time to offer assistance to Nancy," she explained to her chums. "Any assistance she needs." But when she opened the door, she was shocked to find an attractive brunette girl, dressed in the sharp royal blue uniform of a Navy Nurse, standing in her way.

"Terry Tickerson, what are you doing here?" Bess cried.

The attractive girl smiled, showing off a darling dimple in her left cheek. She put down a leather satchel and took off her striking nurse's cap—a snappy, white cotton number with an impressive gold navy insignia on its brim.

Cherry noted with not a little envy that the girl's uniform, with its smart black piping and gold military buttons, was much handsomer than Cherry's own plain nurse's whites. She stifled an urge to salute.

"Didn't Nancy tell you I was coming to visit?" Terry grinned. "Why, when I saw her at the Tin Tan Club last night, she invited me to stay a few days until my ship left port. So here I am," Terry said cheerfully. "Ensign Tickerson, reporting for duty," she announced, standing straight at attention.

"Nancy said you might be in the market for a nurse," she explained when she saw their puzzled expressions. "But I see you've already hired one," Terry said as she spied Cherry. Cherry looked ruefully at her own rumpled uniform, now dusty from her work in the attic. She looked downright drab in comparison with Terry!

Terry picked up her valise, pushed past Cherry, and walked into the living room. "It sure is good to be back," Terry said, looking around the attractively furnished Clue living room. "I remember this place so well. Nancy and I used to spend a lot of time on that couch," she murmured, gesturing toward the overstuffed gray wool davenport. "It's good to see this old place. And Nancy, boy, does she look good!" Terry gave a loud wolf whistle.

"By the way, where is that girl?" she asked. As she pulled off her pristine white cotton gloves, took her compact and lipstick from her modern blue handbag, and refreshed her makeup, she continued her confession to Bess. "I was thrilled when Nancy asked me to spend a few days here," she admitted. "When I ran off to join the Navy, I thought she'd never forgive me. But after the way she acted the other night, well, it seems she's not only forgiven me, but she may even be as eager as I am to pick up where we left off."

Terry snapped her compact shut and put it back in her purse. "I'll just put my bag in her bedroom and slip into a fresh uniform," she said. "And when I come back, Bess, you can introduce me to your friends."

Cherry opened her mouth, but nothing came out. "You don't need to show me the way," Terry said, patting Cherry on the shoulder. "I've been to Nancy's bedroom plenty of times." She picked up her valise and headed upstairs.

"I've got to roll some bandages," Cherry gulped as she raced for the little attic room. The girls heard the door to the secret room slam shut, then the unmistakable sound of a true heart breaking.

"Do something," Velma hissed to Midge. "I don't care how you do it, but get rid of that nurse—now!"

"Let her stay!" Jackie cried. "Let Cherry see, once and for all, what Nancy really is."

Bess gasped. "What do you mean by that?" she cried in defense of her oldest friend. "Are you saying that Nancy's a...a—" Golly, Bess could scarcely bring herself to say the word.

"Yes, I'm saying that Nancy's a flirt!" Jackie thundered.

Bess was frankly taken aback by Jackie's blunt manner. "Oh, dear, why isn't George here?" she fretted. "She'd know what to do!" Then a funny look came into her eyes. George wasn't there because she was with Nancy!

"Come to think of it, Nancy was awfully eager to have George accompany her to the prison. Why do you think that is?" she worried aloud. Could Jackie be right? Was Nancy really a shameless vixen? In that case, was George safe with her? Was anyone's girl safe with her? Suddenly, Bess's head ached from all the terrible thoughts swirling around inside it. She turned to Midge.

"Oh, Midge," she sobbed as she threw herself into Midge's arms. "Nancy's stolen George away from me!"

"Help," Midge mouthed to Velma.

"There, there," Velma patted Bess on the back. "Nancy and George aren't at all interested in one another," she said soothingly.

"Velma's right," Midge tried to comfort the weeping Bess. "Why, if George were going to fall for anyone here, would be my girl," she pointed out.

Bess started to cry even harder. She let go of Midge and threw herself on the couch. Velma raised one brow in alarm and shot Midge a withering look.

"I was just trying to help," Midge explained sheepishly.

"Sweetheart, do you really want to help?" Velma murmured as she gave Midge a long, passionate kiss while running her hands down the front of her girlfriend's shirt.

Midge moaned softly. "I'll do anything," she promised. "Just tell me what you want."

"I want you to go upstairs—" Velma murmured.

"Yes?" Midge breathed excitedly. "And?"

"And tell that Navy Nurse to put her stethoscope and tongue depressors back in her purse and march right out of here!" Velma cried.

"There will be no need for that now," Cherry snapped. The girls gasped when they saw that Cherry had swapped her simple, utilitarian uniform and sturdy, white rubber-soled nurse's shoes for a stylish evening dress of shimmering sea green chiffon, four-inch stiletto heels, and a satin evening stole of creamy white silk. With her pale, smooth skin, sparkling green eyes, and curvy figure, Cherry looked like a dream!

"Wow!" Jackie marveled. "Oh, man, and I thought you looked good in your *uniform!*" she blurted out. She whistled low, under her breath. She couldn't take her eyes off the gorgeous girl.

"I found this in Nancy's closet," Cherry explained as she whirled about, allowing them to admire the way the skirt flew up around her shapely legs. "I think the plunging neckline is just what I need for a gay night on the town, don't you agree?" she cried in a jaunty tone.

Jackie agreed, only she couldn't find her voice to say so.

"Cherry, you look positively vivacious!" Bess cried.

Cherry threw back her head and laughed merrily. She sauntered over to the gilt-edged mirror above the sofa, patted her glamorous upswept hairdo, applied another layer of lipstick to her full, luscious lips, and turned to give Bess a wicked wink.

"Two can play at this game," Cherry announced mysteriously.

"Are we going to play a game?" Bess queried. "Now?"

"Nancy will see she's not the only fish in the sea," Cherry retorted.

"Are you going to prison to see Nancy?" Bess queried her. "Dressed like that?"

"Dressed like what?" Cherry cried. "Like a vexing vixen? *Like Nancy*? No, Bess, I'm going to the Tin Tan Club to bat my eyelashes at *some nice mechanics!*" she seethed. As if on cue, a taxi pulled up in the driveway and beeped its horn. Cherry flew out the door.

"But what about Hannah?" Bess gasped. "What will we do?"

Cherry paused for just a moment in the doorway. "Have that *Navy Nurse* take care of her," Cherry spat out.

"Don't wait up," was the last thing she said to her startled chums.

CHAPTER 41

A Warning

After Cherry made her dramatic exit, Terry sat in the kitchen with the other girls and filled them in on what had happened when she had encountered her heartbroken colleague upstairs.

"Cherry came into Nancy's room while I was unpacking and showed me these letters. She asked if I was the very same Terry who had written these torrid love letters to Nancy and signed them with lipstick kisses, and before I could think straight, I admitted I was! I tried to tell her I had written them long ago, that I'd never come between Nancy and her new girl, but that nice nurse went all to pieces!" Terry cried as she flung the ribbon-wrapped onionskin letters on the kitchen table.

"Cherry told me Lauren found them in the attic. I went upstairs to see what else of mine Nancy had kept, and when I came back downstairs, Cherry was standing in front of Nancy's three-way mirror, applying mascara. She did look lovely in that sea green chiffon dress with the plunging neckline," Terry sighed. "I can see why Nancy goes for her.

"I didn't know Nancy already had a girl," she added woefully. "Why, the way she was acting last night at the Tin Tan Club, she seemed indubitably single! I should never have come here! Why did I believe Nancy might have...could have...changed? I'm such a fool," she said sadly.

Midge filled Terry in on the details of last night's drama with the strange, red-haired girl.

"So old Nancy is still up to her tricks," Terry sighed. "Poor Cherry!"

Bess's brown eyes grew big as saucers. "What do you mean?" she quizzed.

"The girl's a terrible flirt," Terry said bluntly. "But only when she's drinking. It's the funniest thing. When she's just

Nancy, she's as trustworthy and level-headed as a scout, but the minute she has a cocktail, she becomes a totally different girl. That's why I left town so suddenly. I kept finding Nancy at the bar wrapped around some glamour girl."

Bess gasped. Terry couldn't possibly be talking about the same perfectly poised, well-groomed, polite-to-strangers, respected-by-all, girl sleuth that Bess knew so well!

"She started to run wild when you and George went away to St. Agatha's," Terry explained. "I know she sorely missed you two, but there must have been other reasons for her reckless behavior. It was as if she were running from something terrible."

"Did you know Nancy was the one who shot her father?" Midge blurted out. After first swearing the Navy Nurse to secrecy, she filled her in on Hannah's attempt to take the blame for the murder, and Nancy's scheme to switch places with Hannah.

Terry gasped. "She told me the very same thing last night, but I thought it was just one of her wild stories," she confessed. "One night years ago, she got really drunk and told me some of the most unbelievable things about her father." Terry stopped talking when she saw the expression on Midge's face. "You mean Nancy wasn't making it up?" she gasped. "Golly! No wonder she shot him! How could I have not believed her?" Terry castigated herself.

"I was one of her closest chums and didn't know anything was going on," Bess cried. "Nancy had a whole, horrible secret life and it's news to me!"

"I guess, when you really think about it, it's easy to understand Nancy's behavior," Midge admitted. "Although I'm sure it's little comfort to Cherry."

"What a pickle we're in!" Bess groaned. "Whatever will we do now?"

"I know what I'm going to do," Jackie declared. She jumped up from the table and put on her coat. "I'm going to find Cherry. The poor kid must be miserable. Where did she say she was going?"

"The Tin Tan Club," Bess answered. She wrote down the address.

"We'd better go with you," Velma and Midge declared.

"I can handle her by myself," Jackie said.

"I have no doubt whatsoever about that," Midge replied. "But I still think it's best for all concerned if we go with you."

"Cherry might need a shoulder to cry on," Velma pointed out.

Jackie shrugged her own broad shoulders. "What's wrong with mine?" she wanted to know. "I'm a cop; I know what to do with a distraught citizen."

"Especially an attractive femme wearing a stylish chiffon cocktail dress?" Midge wanted to know. "A helpless nurse with a broken heart and an eagerness to please?"

Jackie flushed indignantly. "You're not saying I'd use my professional status to take advantage of a vulnerable girl, are you?" she cried.

Midge suddenly grew serious. "Let's go out on the porch and have a smoke, shall we?" she proposed.

"What gives?" Jackie urged once they were safely out of earshot of the others. "What do you know?"

"I know that you've got a big thing for that little nurse, that's what," Midge shot back in a serious tone. "You have since you first laid eyes on her in San Francisco. What's more, I think the reason you flipped for Head Nurse Margaret Marstad is because she reminds you of Cherry. I'd dismiss it as a simple nurse fetish, but I think it's more than that. I think you've got it bad for our Miss Aimless. Real bad."

Jackie opened her mouth to protest, but nothing came out. What Midge was saying was true!

"Want more?" Midge offered.

Jackie nodded.

"I'd love to see you two together," Midge admitted.

"Nothing would thrill me more. I think you're tops and Cherry's a swell kid. What's more, I think you'd be a whole lot better for her than Nancy, but she's all ga-ga over the girl dick, so what's there to do about it? I'm not so much worried about Cherry," Midge admitted. "The first heartbreak's a given, so she may as well get it over with. It might do her some good, in fact. But, Jack..." Midge shook her head. "You don't want her cutting her baby teeth on you, do you?"

Jackie looked glum. "No, I guess not," she confessed.

"Cherry's a young one. She's sweet and loyal and would probably love you to pieces if she ever got her mind off that Clue girl. Maybe tonight she will. I say, let her be. Let her get over this thing she has for Nancy—on her own. Then it's just a matter of time before she puts two and two together."

"You think so, Midge? You think Cherry and I have a chance?" Jackie cried excitedly. She quickly regained her composure. "Not that I've actually thought it through that far," she added hastily.

"Right," Midge laughed. Then she grew serious again. "Normally I would never encourage anyone to go after someone else's girl, but after the way Nancy's treated Cherry, I'd say she's ripe for the picking," Midge said, not even trying to disguise the angry tone in her voice. "Besides, I've seen how Cherry looks at you," Midge added with a sly smile. "She's already halfway there. You've just got to let her come the rest of the way on her own."

"You're right, Midge," Jackie sighed.

"I'm always right, and it's about time someone around here realized that," Midge said smugly. Then she smiled a sad, sweet little smile that let Jackie know she only half meant it. If that.

"Thanks, Midge!" Jackie cried. "You're swell."

"The doctor is always in," Midge replied. "Besides, the way these femmes boss us around, we've got to stick together!"

Jackie nodded. "Yeah, I really respect how you keep a real tight reign on Velma."

"You said it, Jack," Midge said as she playfully punched her chum on the arm. "Shall we solve the mystery at hand and let Cherry puzzle the enigma of love on her own?"

"Sounds good to me," Jackie grinned. "Let's go find this police chief and teach him some manners," she proposed.

"Although I'm willing to admit I'd love to steal Nancy's girl, I'm not about to let the sleuth stew in jail!" She took her gun from her hip harness, snapped out the cylinder, and loaded the revolver.

"We've got six chances to persuade him to hand over the evidence. Think it's enough?" she smiled slyly.

Midge grinned and showed Jackie something she had been hiding in her pocket. It was a black leather gun case and a box of bullets. "Courtesy of the San Francisco Police Department," Midge said, adding, "Although they don't know it."

She loaded the revolver and tucked it into the waistband of her trousers. "During your promotion ceremony, some rookie left his gun on his chair, so I snatched it. I used Velma's nail file to remove the serial number."

Jackie's eyes grew wide in wonder. "Midge, you're amazing," she grinned.

Midge winked. "Let's go," she said.

Inside, they discovered Bess, Velma, and Terry sitting at the kitchen table, drinking coffee and gossiping in a half-hearted way.

"Everything okay?" Velma asked softly.

"Fine," Jackie assured her.

"Grab your purse, babe," Midge ordered. "We're going sleuthing." Velma shivered in delight. She loved it when Midge talked rugged.

"Aren't we going to wait for George to return with Hannah?" Bess queried. She was more than a little anxious to see her girlfriend again, and to be reassured of her deep and abiding love.

Jackie shook her head. "We've already lost enough time with all the crying and wailing going on around here. Why don't you wait here, Bess," she suggested. "You can help Terry with Hannah. Terry, you're Head Nurse now," she added. "How's that sit with you?"

Terry smiled and gave Jackie a smart salute. "I already went upstairs and looked over Cherry's equipment, and I must say, she's one well-stocked nurse. Everything I'll need for a bedridden patient is already sterilized and arranged in alphabetical order," she said.

Jackie smiled when she heard this. That Cherry was just so darn prepared!

Velma threw some cookies in her purse, tied a chiffon scarf over her lovely locks and, with Midge on one arm and Jackie on the other, headed for the door. She gave Jackie's strong bicep a little squeeze. "I'm glad we have a girl with a gun along," she admitted.

Jackie and Midge exchanged grins. "Two girls with two guns," they boasted.

Velma became furious when she realized Midge had a gun stuck in her trousers. "What are *you* doing with a gun?" she cried.

"Jackie has a gun," Midge pointed out.

"Jackie's gun is *official!*" Velma exclaimed. "Midge Fontaine, give me that gun!" she said, her voice all atremble. She held out her hand, palm up.

Midge set her jaw in a stubborn lock and looked annoyed.

Velma stamped her foot and frowned. "I mean it—hand it over!"

Midge did as she was told.

Velma put the gun in her purse and snapped it shut. Her bottom lip quivered and her green eyes filled with tears. "You've promised me so many times that you would stop taking chances," she said. "And here you are, ready to run off half-cocked. Jackie has a gun because it's her *business* to have one!"

Velma drew herself up to her full five feet and three inches. "Life is not a detective novel, Midge," she said angrily. "It's not full of mysteries and hair-pin plot twists and crooks running around everywhere. I think it's time you grew up and realized that." With this, Velma stalked out the door, with Midge and Jackie right behind.

CHAPTER 42

A Delightful Discovery

While Terry sat in a chair polishing the brass buttons on her uniform, Bess happily hummed about the well-equipped kitchen, planning a scrumptious meal for her honey's return.

"I'll make all of George's favorite foods," she schemed as she tied a fresh apron around her plump waist and checked the pantry and icebox for supplies. Lucky for them, Hannah had stocked up right before the murder, and there were plenty of delectable things to eat.

"We'll have Cream-of-Tomato Soup, Wilted-Leaf Lettuce Salad, Stuffed Celery, Carrots Au Gratin, Swiss Steak, and fresh-baked Buttermilk Biscuits," she planned aloud. "How does that sound?"

"Yummy," Terry replied.

"And Apple Brown Betty," Bess licked her lips.

"It's been ages since I've had a home-cooked meal!" Terry cried excitedly. "How can I help? Sitting here with nothing to do is giving me the jitters," she explained. "I've already polished all my buttons and my Good Conduct medal."

Bess handed Terry the spare apron, a sharp knife, and a bunch of carrots. "Peel these, then grate them," she instructed. Terry happily set to work while Bess lit the oven and mixed a batch of biscuit batter. Soon the kitchen was filled with delightful aromas. The two girls chatted happily as they prepared the homecoming feast. Terry told Bess about her exciting adventures aboard ship, and Bess detailed the triumphs and tribulations of teaching home economics to modern girls.

"I tell them every girl needs a good recipe for white sauce to fall back on, but they just laugh and think me hopelessly old-fashioned," Bess confessed.

Terry smiled. "How do the students take to George?" she wondered.

"Oh, George is a wonderful physical education instructor," Bess told her proudly.

Terry could well imagine. "Remember our favorite gym teacher, Miss Pleats?"

"Do I!" Bess cried as she remembered her most favorite teacher ever! "Why, I adored her. I used to bake double-fudge brownies for her every Sunday night and slip them into her locker on Monday," Bess blushed. "Oh, the daydreams I used to have about her!"

"She was a dreamboat, wasn't she?" Terry cried.

Bess nodded. "You know who reminds me of her?" she realized. "Midge!"

"You're right!" Terry exclaimed. "Same thick blond hair, cut short and worn off her handsome face."

"Big, strong shoulders."

"And long, muscular legs."

"That dry wit."

"Her playful, teasing manner."

"Stop!" Bess cried. "My biscuits are burning!" She jumped up from the table and flew to the oven just in the nick of time.

Just then they heard someone in the hallway outside the kitchen.

Terry opened the door to find Lauren standing there with a packet of letters in her hand.

"Haven't those caused enough trouble already?" Terry cried as she snatched up the bundle, went over to the stove, and turned the flame up high. Lauren grabbed them just before they ignited.

"Lauren! What are you doing? Eek!" Bess added in alarm when she got a good look at their auburn-haired young friend. Lauren's hair stuck out in short, uneven tufts all over her head.

"She's a friend of Midge and Velma's," she hurriedly explained to Terry. "And she used to have a beautiful, long auburn braid. Where have you been? And what did you do to your hair?" Bess shrieked.

"I've been up in the attic," Lauren explained. "I just came downstairs to show you these letters I found."

"Give those back," Terry demanded. "I believe they're mine."

"I don't think so," Lauren said in a smug tone. "Unless your name is Rebecca or Helen."

Terry flushed slightly. "My name is Terry," she said.

"Yes, I know," Lauren replied coolly. "You're that Navy Nurse who took Cherry's place. I know all about you," she said. "I know a lot of things."

"Like what?" Bess wanted to know. She whipped off her apron, put her hands on her round, shapely hips, and said in her best schoolmarm manner, "Stop beating around the bush, Lauren. What do you know?"

Lauren turned pale with alarm. She dropped the letters on the table. "I found these letters. They're from a girl named Helen, to someone named Rebecca. That's all I know. Honest."

Bess gasped when she read the envelope on the top of the stack. "They're not from *a girl* named Helen," she gasped in realization, "They're from Helen Clue, Nancy's attractive, spinster aunt. You know, Terry, she was a buyer for a big department store in New York. No one has seen her for years! She disappeared soon after Nancy's mother died."

"She must have written these to Nancy's mother," Terry said in amazement. "They were in-laws, and, by all accounts, good friends."

"*More* than good friends," Bess murmured after she had opened the top envelope, slid out the thin, yellowed paper and examined its contents. "It's a love letter, and it's signed, 'Your One True Love, Helen,' " Bess gasped. "With a beautiful Robert Burns poem!

'To see her is to love her,
And love but her for ever;
For Nature made her what she is
And never made anither!'

"These are so wonderful," Bess whispered as she gently slipped the letters out of the aged envelopes and read through them. "They were so in love," she sighed. "Right from the beginning.

"Lauren, why didn't you show us these earlier?"

"Every time I came downstairs, someone was yelling, so I beat it back upstairs," Lauren explained, adding, "They were taped to the bottom of a bureau drawer in the attic room."

"This is a real find," Bess praised the young girl. "You're some detective."

"And thorough," Terry noted. Lauren beamed with pride.

"But we're going to have to do something with that hair!" Bess exclaimed. Bess popped the steaks in the oven and turned down the soup. She took a pair of kitchen shears from a drawer, tied a towel around Lauren's neck, and sized up the job before her.

"We're going to have to cut it pretty short," she declared. "Lauren, what possessed you?"

"I thought it would look good," Lauren said weakly.

Bess set about tidying Lauren's sloppy hairdo. But after a few minutes of snipping, Lauren still looked like a ragamuffin.

"Let me try," Terry urged. "It's all uneven in back. Oops!" she cried. "I slipped. Sorry."

"Now you're going to have to cut the other side shorter," Bess instructed her.

"There's no saving this," Terry said as she chopped off all but an inch of Lauren's thick hair.

"It's severe, but awfully cute," Bess decided after surveying their young friend.

Lauren jumped up all excited and raced for the washroom. "It's really keen!" they heard her cry. She came racing back, running her hands through her hair. She had swiped some Butch Wax from Midge and was greasing back her short locks with the strong goo. "Do you think Velma will like it?" Lauren fretted.

Bess and Terry exchanged an amused glance. "I imagine she will," Bess replied. Actually, she was beginning to take a liking to the severe hairstyle herself. Oh, it wouldn't complement every face, but it showed off Lauren's boyish good looks to their best advantage. She was just about to tell her so when she heard the rattle of George's jalopy.

The three girls ran to the window and peered out. Was the girl in George's arms Nancy, or Hannah wearing the clever disguise? They hurriedly opened the front door so George could deliver her precious parcel to the couch. Bess could see that the plan had been a grand success, for fast asleep before her very eyes was the disguised but unmistakable figure of kindly housekeeper Hannah Gruel!

"Let's get Hannah upstairs and out of sight before anyone comes barging in here," Terry suggested. She sent Lauren to Hannah's bedroom at the back of the house for a flannel nightgown, and helped George transport her patient upstairs.

"Terry's in charge of this case," Bess explained as they climbed the stairs to the attic room. She filled George in on Cherry's dramatic exit.

"Did you have a hard time convincing Hannah to make the switch?" Bess asked.

"Not after we secretly gave her a heaping dose of Valium," George grinned.

"I didn't hear that," Terry declared sternly. Then she smiled. "Now you two scoot—I've got a patient to attend to," she declared. "Lauren can be my aide for now, right Lauren? You look like you've got extremely capable hands. We're going to give Hannah a nice, soothing sponge bath." Lauren blushed happily under the attractive brunette's gaze. She helped Terry fill a basin with soapy water and stood ready with a terrycloth towel over one arm.

"Don't you have something for George?" Terry teased Bess.

Bess blushed. "Oh, honey, I'm so glad you're home!" she purred into George's ear as they left the room.

George grinned and gave Bess a little squeeze. "Me, too!" she admitted. "Jeepers, I held my breath all the way there, hoping this wild plan would work. I have something special in my pocket," George suddenly blurted out. It was a note for Cherry, and although George was unaware of its contents, she had a feeling it was very important! Why, Nancy had sealed it with a kiss and sprayed it with her favorite perfume before begging George to deliver it to Cherry.

Bess giggled and snuggled closer to George. "I missed you so much, well, I planned a big surprise for you," she whispered in George's ear as they descended the stairs to the second floor. "It's your favorite thing," she added coyly.

"Oh, Bess!" George cried. Her interest was definitely getting piqued!

"Perhaps I'd just better show you," Bess teased.

George grinned, grabbed Bess's hand, and pulled her toward Nancy's bedroom.

"No, in the kitchen, silly," Bess murmured.

"Okay," George grinned affably. "Wherever you want."

Terry heard George's cries of delight all the way up on the third floor.

"Swiss steak? My favorite!"

CHAPTER 43

Follow That Car!

"I hope *somebody's* having good luck tonight," Midge groaned as she took a sip of her tepid coffee. Midge, Velma, and Jackie had been sitting outside the police station for over an hour, hoping to catch a glimpse of the man they suspected of stealing Nancy's evidence, Chief Chumley himself! Although Jackie hadn't said anything to Nancy, she had confirmed Midge's suspicion that all trails led to Nancy's old colleague.

His deputies insisted the Chief was away on a fishing holiday, but the girls knew he was really hiding in his office. So they were parked under a birch tree down the street, waiting for him to make his exit. From where they sat, they had a clear view of the station house. Eagle-eyed Jackie had spotted the Chief's car parked nearby. "You can tell it's the Chief's car because it has the official Police Chief decal on the back window," she had pointed out. "That's a clear sign."

Jackie checked her sturdy detective's watch with its radium glow-in-the-dark dial that proved so useful in late-night stakeouts such as this. "It's just after eleven o'clock," she announced. "Hannah should be sound asleep in the attic room by now, while Nancy's getting ready to spend her first night behind bars."

"Poor Nancy," Velma mused. She touched Jackie's arm lightly. "I know you are engineering some romantic rendezvous with Cherry, but I'd advise you to wait until Nancy's out of jail. Don't judge a girl until you've walked a mile in her pumps. Same goes for you, honey," she turned to Midge.

Midge hung her head in mock shame.

"Cookies?" Velma offered, opening her purse for her two companions. The three girls sat for a minute, munching on coconut macaroons. Midge and Jackie were like two well-oiled springs set to go off at any moment.

"I know he's in there," Jackie grumbled. "I'm tempted to

march right in and drag him out," she added angrily. "I *am* a cop, you know."

"Yeah, and if you go in there with a gun, they'll shoot first and ask questions later," Midge scowled. "Cigarette?" she offered. Jackie shrugged and took one. But she didn't light it. She just rolled it around in her hand.

Velma daintily wiped the crumbs from her lips and opened the glove box to shed some light on the scene. She handed her compact to Midge. "Hold this, babe, while I do my lips," she said. When Velma was satisfied that her shapely mouth was perfectly painted, she pulled her shoulder-length mane of thick black curly hair atop her head and gave herself a good looking over in the little round mirror. "Should I get one of those new short Italian haircuts?" she wondered aloud.

"Cherry looks awfully cute with her short hairdo!" Jackie enthused. "And since you two look so much alike, I'll bet you'd look great."

"Hrmph," Midge cleared her throat and shook her head. She handed Velma her compact.

"Then again, maybe it's not such a good idea," Jackie said.

"I wasn't asking you, babe," Velma said to Midge in a flirty tone. She looked at herself again in the compact mirror. "I'm sick of having to set my hair every day. You're lucky, Midge; a trip to the barber every week, and you're all set, while every day I have to wash and set and spray and tease...Wait! Who's that coming out of the police station now?" she cried. She had spotted something in her mirror!

The girls watched as a hunched-over figure wearing an old raincoat and a head scarf shuffled out of the station. In one hand was a mop, in the other, a bucket. "That must be the cleaning lady," Midge said. "The poor thing looks exhausted. Imagine having to clean police headquarters! Why, I'll bet they're pigs in there. Oops! Sorry, Jackie."

"They are pigs," Jackie assured her. "Why, where I work, you should see the mess the boys make! You'd think they were raised in a barn."

"I hate to interrupt," Velma said politely. "But if you two would stop chatting for one minute, I have something to say."

"What is it?" Midge and Jackie chorused.

"Follow that car!" Velma cried as she snapped her compact shut, dropped it in her purse, and pointed excitedly in the direction of the Chief's automobile.

Midge and Jackie gasped, for the figure had jumped behind the wheel and was zooming off! And where the car had been parked was a pile of clothing—an old raincoat and a head scarf!

They tailed the car through downtown but lost it when it turned down a one-way alley with its siren-light flashing. The girls raced around the block, hoping to head it off, but were stuck at a light behind a slow-moving tow truck. Midge angrily hit the steering wheel with her fist.

"Where would he be going this time of night?" Velma wondered aloud.

"We know he's not going home," Midge said. "This map Bess drew of River Depths shows his residence is at the other end of town. Where does a police chief of a small town go at night?" Midge wondered aloud.

They checked the pool hall, both all-night diners, and the donut shop, but couldn't locate the Chief's car anywhere.

"Let's head for the red-light district. Maybe he's there, shaking down some girls," Jackie guessed. "The boys always find that good for a few laughs before going home to their wives and kids. My guess is head south a mile or two."

Midge followed Jackie's suggestion, and they were relieved when they spied the Chief's car parked next to a black and white paddy wagon outside a bar. She parked the car on the other side of the street and turned off the headlights.

"It's the Tin Tan Club!" Velma gasped. "That's where Cherry was headed. Oh no, I hope there's not a raid going on!"

They leapt out of the car and raced toward the club just as a chorus line of tall girls in sparkly dresses and dramatic beehive hairdos danced out the door, smack into a half dozen burly cops.

"Is that Cherry, doing the can-can?" Velma cried. "Look, right there in the middle of that line of dancing girls!"

A gorgeous blond girl outfitted in a slinky black cocktail dress and a tiara snatched a billy club away from one cop and smacked him over the head with it. Then she kicked him in the shins with her red stilettos.

Soon, the best of River Depths' finest was quickly discouraged from entering the bar.

"Let's go close that jazz joint over on Third Avenue," an officer exclaimed as they jumped into the paddy wagon and drove away.

Jackie chuckled. "It's enough to make you wish you wore high heels, huh, Midge?" She rushed over to pluck Cherry out of the chorus line, but, to her dismay, found the perky nurse attached to a handsome girl attired in a man's black suit.

"Jackie, did you see me dance?" Cherry giggled as she stood in front of the Tin Tan Club, holding hands with the strange girl. "This is my new friend Micky," Cherry added. "You'll never guess who she is. Go on, *guess*."

"Are you a mechanic?" Jackie growled suspiciously.

"Cherry, have you seen anyone who might be the Chief?" Midge interrupted.

"Who?" Cherry replied. "No, Nancy's seen the Chief. Midge, don't you remember anything?" Cherry started to giggle again.

Midge groaned. Cherry was intoxicated!

"If you're looking for the Chief, I think he's around back," Cherry's chum said helpfully. She gestured toward a narrow side alleyway.

"Get in the car, Cherry," Midge ordered. "Let's go."

Cherry hopped in the car. So did Micky.

Midge turned on the ignition but kept her lights off as she steered the car down the narrow alley. "We've got to find him tonight," she muttered.

"Midge!" Velma cried. "Look!"

Velma had spied a shadowy figure at the far end of the alley. Midge snapped on the headlights. It was the Chief, and he was counting a pile of money. He looked up, saw the car, and went for his gun.

"Everybody down!" Jackie cried as she grabbed her pistol, kicked open the door, dropped to her knees behind it, and took aim. The man shot at Jackie and succeeded in knocking the gun from her hand. He then ran down the alley, passing the car on the left.

Midge opened her door to block his exit, but he shoved it so hard, Midge fell back into the seat. She felt something snap in her left shoulder. But the pain was nothing compared to the rage she felt.

"Duck, Jack!" she yelled as she put the car in reverse and

hit the gas. Jackie jumped out of the way and, as the car careened backward down the narrow alley, Velma grabbed Midge's gun from her purse.

"Catch up to him, honey, and I'll shoot him," she ordered, one manicured finger on the trigger. She steadied herself on Midge's right shoulder and pointed the gun at the escaping man.

"Aim low!" Midge cried. "We need him alive at least long enough to tell us where he's hidden Nancy's letters."

But before Velma could get the Chief in her sights, he slipped on a patch of oil and fell right into the path of their oncoming, two-ton automobile!

"Oops!" Midge cried as she felt Chief Chumley slip under the wheels. Velma covered her ears when she heard the horrible crunch he made. Midge jammed on the brakes. She got out of the car and glanced underneath.

"Oh, no, he's dead!" she exclaimed. She gingerly stepped over the pool of blood seeping from under the car. "Ugh! What a mess!"

Cherry jumped out of the car and cradled Jackie in her arms. "I'm okay," Jackie said. "The bullet only nicked my hand."

"Oh, why don't I have my first-aid kit with me?" Cherry admonished herself. She gave Jackie a quick going-over and was relieved to find her friend was fine.

"Oh, no, we've killed the Chief," Jackie noticed.

"No big loss," Micky scowled.

"I won't argue with you there," Midge agreed. "It's just that he's got something we desperately need."

"Maybe he's got it on him," Velma suggested.

Jackie grimaced. "We'll have to search him then," she shuddered.

"First I have to move the car," Midge groaned. She gingerly rolled the car off the Chief's body.

"Oh dear," Velma said when she spied the flattened form of former Police Chief Chumley. Midge led her away. "Why don't you slip around front and search his car, honey?" she suggested gently. Velma nodded and raced off. Midge gulped. Jackie took a deep breath to steady her nerves. They searched his pockets, but to no avail.

"He doesn't have the letters on him," Midge declared. She shook her head. "Cripes! What are we going to do with him?"

"We'll have to dispose of the body somehow," Cherry murmured shakily as she stared at the corpse. "I'm a trained professional. I can handle anything. If I could only think clearly for a minute, I could come up with a plan. Goodness, there's a lot of blood, isn't there? Good thing I packed stain remover," she muttered before pitching forward in a dead faint. Jackie swooped Cherry up in her arms and laid her across the front seat.

"Let's hide the body in the trunk and then figure out what to do with it," Midge suggested. Jackie and Midge shoved the Chief into the trunk as best they could. Golly, Midge's shoulder hurt something awful!

"Darn Lauren and her rocks," Midge scowled as she watched Jackie struggle to close the trunk lid. "We barely have room for a body in here!"

"We can't leave him in there forever," Jackie commented.

"Yeah, he'll start to stink," Midge declared.

Velma returned from searching the Chief's car.

"There's nothing that looks like Nancy's personal property in his car," she reported. "But I did find a sack of unmarked bills." She showed them a pillowcase stuffed with hundred-dollar bills. Velma blanched when she saw the pool of blood left on the ground. "Shouldn't we wash that away?" she wondered. "So no one gets suspicious?"

"No one will even notice," Micky assured them. "There's always blood back here."

"Let's get out of here then," Jackie commanded. She was keen to leave the scene before they were discovered. Her status as a big-city detective would be of little help if she were caught riding in a car with the body of a small-town police chief in the trunk!

They piled into the car, hurriedly backed out of the alley, and sped off. Midge was eager to put as many miles as possible between them and that blood-spattered site.

"I don't even know where I'm going," Midge admitted. She lit a cigarette to steady her nerves. She took a big gulp of the cool evening air. She had to clear her head. She had to think. Where could they dump the body?

Jackie puzzled over the same dilemma. "Maybe there's a quarry around here," she proposed. "We could bury him and hope by the time they dig him up we're long gone."

"Or we could weigh him down and throw him in the River Depths River and pray for rain," Micky suggested.

"We do have plenty of rocks," Midge grinned ruefully.

"If we could only get rid of him permanently, I could have my mother—the biggest gossip in town—spread the rumor that he's run off with money from last week's bank heist," Micky suggested.

"Her mother is Mrs. Milton Meeks, the matron who brought us that tuna salad," Cherry explained. She was awake, but her head was still in a fog. She continued to babble—a sure sign of trauma, Jackie thought. "She's head of the fundraising committee for Mr. Clue's commemorative statue," Cherry added. "They're erecting a bronze statue in his honor in the town square," she recalled. "She asked us for donations. Then she yelled at Nancy for not attending her father's funeral."

"That's my mother, all right," Micky laughed sourly.

"Repeat that, would you, Cherry?" Jackie asked.

"She brought us tuna salad," Cherry replied.

"No, I mean about the statue in the town square."

"It's going to be made of bronze, just like the statue of Abraham Lincoln we saw in Nebraska on the way to River Depths. In the glove box you'll find a fascinating brochure telling all about it." Golly, her head felt funny.

Midge laughed. "Let's bronze him," she joked.

"That will never work," Micky said. "But if we wanted to cover him with quick-dry concrete and then paint him bronze, I do believe we could pass him off as a park statue," she said in all seriousness. "I know where the Clue memorial is being made," she added. "No one will be there this time of night, and I can bust any lock in town."

"Let's!" Jackie and Midge chorused.

"Oh, Midge," Cherry giggled. "You always think of the silliest things!" It felt good to laugh again.

But Cherry wasn't laughing twenty minutes later when she found herself inside a sculptor's studio, watching Midge, Jackie, and Micky strip down to their undershirts and prepare the body for dipping. The trio worked quickly to position the Chief in a convincing posture before rigor mortis set in.

"Too bad we don't have a horse to sit him on," Midge joked as they tried different poses before settling on a simple yet stately stance.

"Who should he be?" Velma queried. She was making a plaque for the pedestal. "A general? A politician? A war hero?"

"We've already got one of each of those in the town square," Micky mused.

"How about a Founding Father?" Midge suggested. "Every town square's got one of those."

"Perfect," Velma said.

"Dedicated to the memory of fathers everywhere," Velma inscribed on the plaque.

"Although I prefer his final expression of surprise and fear, I guess a benevolent smile will do," Midge remarked as she finished posing the body.

"Ready to dip?" Jackie cried.

"Ready!" her chums replied.

"Golly," Cherry exclaimed as she watched them carefully pick up the Chief and dip him, bit by bit, into a vat of concrete; then, using a trowel, they smoothed the quick-drying mixture over his form. In minutes they had created a nifty statue, ready for painting. When they were finished coating him in bronze-colored paint, they stepped back to admire their handiwork.

"This is just like the pair of bronzed baby shoes Mother has on her bedroom bureau, only bigger!" Cherry cried. "Mother says they make an excellent paperweight!"

They carefully loaded the stiff figure into car, covered it with a tarp they had found in the studio, and made their way to the town square. Lucky for them, the place was deserted, and the installation went off without a hitch.

"What's next?" Cherry yawned. It had been a pretty busy night, and she was desperate to get home and out of her four-inch heels.

"Now we've got to find that evidence," Jackie declared. They piled into the car and headed for the police station to search the Chief's office.

Using Velma as a diversion, the girls were able to lure the night officer away from his post long enough for Midge and Jackie to slip inside and give the place a good going-over. They came up empty-handed, except for stacks of crisp, neatly-wrapped hundred-dollar bills and a box of official-looking documents they had discovered in the Chief's top drawer.

When they rejoined Velma outside, she told them, "I've

learned from that helpful Deputy Drone that Hannah's jury has been selected. The trial starts tomorrow!"

The girls, now growing ever more anxious to find the evidence, decided to pay a call to the Chief's suburban ranch house.

"But first I need some coffee," Midge admitted. She pulled into an all-night hamburger joint, and Velma hopped out and ran inside.

A sporty convertible pulled into the spot beside them, and a man called out, "Yoo hoo, girls!"

"Hello there," Cherry called back.

"Ignore him, Cherry," Midge groaned. "Great. Now some strange man's coming over here," she grumbled when she heard a car door slam. But to her great delight, it wasn't a stranger at all.

It was Mr. Donald—attractively attired in a cream-colored silk shirt, snug white trousers, and soft kid loafers—and his little dogs, too!

"Girls, what's wrong?" he cried. "Did something happen to Nancy?" he fretted. "Oh, dear, perhaps I did the wrong thing, teaching her to disguise herself as Hannah."

"Nancy *is* in trouble, Mr. Donald," Velma admitted as she returned to the car with cups of coffee for all. She saw that Mr. Donald was genuinely concerned about their sleuthing friend and added, "But it happened long before she came to you for help."

"We haven't time to explain now," Midge said. "We've got some evidence to track down."

"Oh, take me with you," Mr. Donald squealed. "This town is nowhere tonight. In fact, I'm so bored, I was just going home to wash my hair."

"Hop in!" the girls invited.

Mr. Donald, Mitzi, Bitzi, and Fritzi squeezed into the back seat next to Jackie, Cherry, and Micky.

"We may be heading into dangerous territory," Midge warned him as she started the engine. "Are you up to it?"

"Drive on, mister!" Mr. Donald cried in delight. "Danger's my middle name!"

CHAPTER 44

An Exhaustive Search

On the way to the Chief's house, Midge filled in Mr. Donald on their mission—to find the letters that belonged to Nancy, but had fallen into the Chief's hands. "The letters will clear up any mystery about Mr. Clue's death," Midge added mysteriously. "And if we find them at the Chief's house, well, it won't bode well for him, either."

Mr. Donald seemed to accept this explanation. Then he fell into a conversation with Micky and was thrilled when he realized she was the daughter of leading socialite Mrs. Milton Meeks.

The girls gave him a blow-by-blow account of Mrs. Meeks's visit to the Clue house.

"It's a terrible thing when matrons go bad," Mr. Donald said sadly. Then Micky got them all laughing with a perfect imitation of her mother, complete with fluttering hands and heaving bosom, culminating in a convincing swoon. Soon Mr. Donald, who was an excellent mimic, picked up Mrs. Meeks's grating mannerisms.

"Why, it's like watching two Mrs. Meekses," Cherry exclaimed. "Bravo!"

But once at the Chief's house, all laughter subsided.

"So this is where the Chief of Police lives," Mr. Donald murmured as Jackie jimmied the front-door lock of the ranch house on Lindy Lane and led the way in. "Lucky for us he's gone for the night. Let's hope he doesn't come back unexpectedly.

"This place is a nightmare," Mr. Donald lamented as they shut the curtains and turned on a lamp. "Look at that tartan sofa with those awning-stripe drapes! Who picked those out?" he shuddered. "What do I tell people over and over? Never mix plaids with stripes. But do they listen to me? No. I *do* wish people would call a professional before taking such drastic steps as picking out their own furnishings," he added. "That's what we're here for. So things like this don't happen."

Cherry had to agree with him. It was *always* better to get an expert's opinion. That's why she so often turned to Velma for advice about matters of the heart. "Why, Velma knows practically all there is to know about love," Cherry thought.

Cherry gave a little gasp of alarm when she spied a moose-head mounted over the fireplace, its big, glittery, unblinking amber eyes staring back at her.

"That is a perfect example of what I'm talking about," Mr. Donald groaned. "The wall above the fireplace is the focal point of the living room, but instead of a lovely oil painting or a mirror—which would open up this space—he chooses to mount the head of some poor dead animal."

Mitzi, Bitzi, and Fritzi whimpered in alarm. Mr. Donald patted each on its little head in a reassuring manner.

"This room could certainly use a woman's touch," Cherry murmured as she surveyed the bowling trophies and stuffed, wall-mounted fish that gave the room all the charm of a pool hall.

"I would love to get my hands on this place," Mr. Donald agreed.

"Was there ever a Mrs. Chief?" Cherry wondered aloud as she looked around the stale, dark room, which smelled of hair tonic and cheap cigars.

"She died a few years ago," Micky informed her. "She was a mousy woman with a mild manner who let the old man boss her around their whole married life."

"Here's the plan," Jackie interrupted. "We'll split up and each take a different part of the house. Now, everyone knows what we're looking for, right? Letters written to Nancy from Mr. Clue. Micky and Mr. Donald, you search down here, Cherry and I will take the basement and, Midge and Velma, how's the upstairs bedroom sound to you?"

"Perfect!" Midge and Velma cried in unison. They raced off to do their duty. But a half hour later, after an exhaustive search, they had to admit defeat. They rejoined Mr. Donald and Micky downstairs in the living room, poring through a stack of papers they had found in a desk drawer.

"There's nothing here besides the usual correspondence," Mr. Donald bemoaned. "Electric bill, grocery list—the man ate a lot of beans," he noted. "A shoe-repair bill, a receipt for some bullets, what's this?" he cried suddenly as he came across something in a plain brown wrapper. He ripped it open. "*American Nudist Magazine*," Mr. Donald read aloud. "Hmmn," he said as he flipped through the publication.

Mr. Donald opened the magazine to a photo of a co-ed playing volleyball. Midge stared at the statuesque brunette wearing only sunglasses and a smile.

Cherry and Jackie returned from the basement, which they had searched thoroughly, but to no avail. Nancy's letters were not downstairs!

"Did you find the evidence?" Cherry asked when she saw Midge bending over the desk in concentrated study. "What are you looking at?" She blushed when she saw what was in Midge's hands. "My, she's a healthy girl," she stammered.

"She certainly *is*," Velma agreed after she had taken a good look for herself.

Midge hurriedly closed the magazine and slipped it back into the desk drawer.

"Girls, we'd better get out of here," Mr. Donald fretted. "The bars are closed by now and the Chief is sure to be home soon."

"No, he won't," Cherry blurted out. "He's dead."

Mr. Donald looked surprised.

"Er, did we forget to tell you the Chief had a little accident tonight that resulted in his unfortunate demise?" Midge asked.

"What a pity," Mr. Donald exclaimed. "And I was so looking forward to seeing that man put in his place!"

"I have a feeling you'll get your wish," Midge promised their new chum. She sighed as she thought of Nancy, sitting alone in a cold, dark jail cell. Where could those letters be? "We've got to look again!" Midge cried. "Every inch of this house has to be searched. We've got five hours until court opens. Let's go!"

CHAPTER 45

A Sudden Realization

Nancy washed out her underthings in the little sink at one end of her tiny cell, humming a gay tune as she soaped and then rinsed her easy-care nylon half slip, silk stockings, and white cotton panties. "If I don't hum, I'll cry," she thought with a sigh as she surveyed the eight- by ten-foot cell. Drab gray stone walls and a curtainless, barred window set high above her head made for a cheerless interior. "Even a colorful rag rug and some starched gingham curtains wouldn't make this a sunny place," Nancy thought in dismay.

Although she could see Hannah's touch everywhere she looked—the single iron bed with its scratchy wool blanket was neatly made up and boasted crisp hospital corners, and her prison-issue tin drinking cup had been shined to a warm luster—it wasn't enough to soften the gloomy room.

And try as she might to keep busy performing the little tasks that make up a girl's evening toilet, Nancy soon found herself mulling over the mystery of the missing evidence. She had been so intent on making the switch with Hannah a success, she had pushed all other thoughts out of her mind. But now Jackie's words were back to haunt her, and in the silence of her cold, lonely cell, she could no longer ignore them.

"He's the only one with the opportunity and the knowledge to commit the theft of your evidence."

"If I could just get those words out of my head," she thought. She grabbed her hairbrush, took off the gray bun, and gave her trademark titian mane one hundred swift strokes.

"Face it, Nancy. Chief Chumley is not your friend!"

"Midge is wrong!" Nancy cried aloud. She clapped a hand over her mouth. She mustn't give herself away now, now that she had come so far! She peered out of her cell and down the dark hallway. Her closest neighbor, Miss Hildy Harms, a chronic shoplifter three cells down, appeared to be fast asleep.

Luckily, murderesses were kept at the far end of Cell Block B, away from the general population.

"Thank goodness I haven't any neighbors to see me remove my nose," Nancy thought. Mr. Donald had warned her not to sleep in the rubber prosthesis, as it could easily be stretched out of shape. Nancy had decided to keep the precious organ in her purse next to her bed.

"That way I can easily slip it on during the night if the need should arise," she schemed.

Her thoughts returned to the suspicions raised by Jackie and Midge.

"If they only knew the Chief as I do, they'd realize how mistaken their crazy accusations are," Nancy told herself as she laid out her outfit for the morning—a tidy gray house dress and a crisp white apron. Sensible tan tie shoes would complete her look.

Her tasks finished, she donned a plain white cotton nightgown and slipped into bed. She pulled the thin, scratchy blanket over her head. If a guard were to shine her light into the cell during the night, she would find nothing more than a sleeping housekeeper, securely tucked in bed.

"Lights out, ladies," a woman's voice boomed through the corridor. The cell block grew dark. Suddenly Nancy wished she was home in her own bed with Cherry by her side.

"I wonder what everyone's doing tonight?" she thought wistfully. She had to grin. She knew what Midge and Velma were doing! Then she sighed. "When I get out of here, I'm going to take Cherry into my arms and do the very same thing!"

Just then a terrible thought came to her. What if her evidence was never found, and Hannah was convicted of murder?

"Will I have to stay here for life?" Nancy wondered, shivering as she peered around the darkened cell. "What happens when Hannah makes a full recovery and wants to leave the house to go to the store? What then?"

Nancy realized she hadn't thought through her plan in a very orderly fashion. "I haven't been thinking clearly for some time," Nancy mused. "Not since the day after I killed Father, when I started having martinis for breakfast. I'll just have to stop that!

"Some detective you've turned out to be!" she chastised herself. "In the old days, you would have had this case sewn up long before now." She had never faced such a quandary! "There's virtually no evidence as to who stole the letters, and the only likely suspect is someone who couldn't possibly have committed the crime!"

She remembered what her instructor at Mr. Peeper's Professional School of Detecting had cautioned. "A good detective must put aside her own emotions and prejudices. Never go into a mystery with your eyes shut and your mind made up. Examine every clue, even if it leads to the most unlikely of suspects!"

Could Midge and Jackie be right about Chief Chumley? Could he be the one behind the nefarious plot to railroad Hannah into jail?

"Let's say Chief Chumley did it," Nancy reasoned. She shuddered to even think it. But it was her duty as a card-carrying detective to eliminate all possible suspects. She went over the events of the last few days carefully. Those she could remember, at any rate.

"Since nothing valuable was missing from the house, I can rule out a cat burglar who happened upon the secret drawer in my hope chest.

"Plus, when I think of it, it is odd that I received a threatening phone call in Wyoming, when the only person who knew I was there was the Chief!"

The horrible incident in the Chief's office came flooding back. She could see the scene as clear as day—the queer expression on the Chief's face when she surprised him and his ugly and mean words when she confronted him with the truth.

"And I'll never forget the way he pounded his fist on his desk," Nancy shivered. "Golly, I'm lucky he didn't throw that big entomology book at me!"

It struck Nancy as odd that the Chief would have such an impressive tome on his desk. Why, she had never known him to read anything but true crime magazines and police rap sheets. "Before he came to me to solve *The Case of The Insistent Insect* he didn't even know the difference between a common house fly and a moth. He told me at the time that just the thought of bugs made his skin crawl," Nancy suddenly remembered. "So why is he suddenly reading a book called *Exotic Entomology Made Easy*?" Nancy wondered.

She shot straight up. "Exotic Entomology? Golly! Bees!"

Suddenly, everything made sense. "When Velma took that threatening phone call for me, she recalled hearing a buzzing sound over the telephone. At the time I dismissed it as a bad connection, but now I see it was an important clue. The Chief must have been calling me from his office, where he was housing the deadly bee while awaiting my return.

"And to think I fell right into his trap. I'm the one who sent him straight to the evidence! Oh, how could I have been so trusting?" she chastised herself.

Nancy tossed and turned on the stiff narrow cot. There was one thing she didn't understand. "Why is the Chief so anxious to get rid of both me and Hannah? What could he possible gain?

"And where are my letters?

"Tomorrow I've got to let Cherry and the others know that it *is* Chief Chumley who's behind all this!" Nancy thought in horror. "If he's underhanded enough to let a killer bee loose in my basement, there's no telling what he'll do next!"

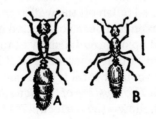

For an hour she lay awake, trying to think of where he could have hidden her letters. "Where would the Chief hide something that important? If they were in his desk drawer, the one I saw him slam shut, he's no doubt found a better hiding place by now, and probably at his home where fewer people are likely to congregate."

"Put yourself in your suspect's shoes," the Chief had once told her while they were tracking a dangerous dognapper. Nancy knew people often hid important things in, around, or under a favorite or sentimental place or belonging—often right under the nose of the sleuths.

"Why, in *The Case of the Purloined Poodle*, old Miss Pringle's prize-winning pet Pierre turned up in the pianoforte!

"What means more than anything in the world to Chief Chumley?" Nancy mused. "The tommy gun he took off Shifty Malone early on in his career? His professional bowling ball in its handsome black leather monogrammed case, a gift from the River Depths Merchants Association?"

But neither of these possessions seemed right for hiding a packet of letters. Nancy put her fingertips to her temples and thought hard. She closed her eyes and pictured Chief Chumley's living room—the musty curtains, dark paneled walls, disheveled furniture, the ash-filled fireplace adorned by a matted, ragged moosehead. The moosehead!

"It's the moosehead!" Nancy stifled a cry. The very same moosehead that had fallen off the wall at the Men's Club and killed Ted Tickerson had been confiscated by the police, and eventually ended up on proud display at the Chief's house.

"He's as proud of that moosehead as if he had stuffed it himself," Nancy thought. And if she remembered correctly from her work on *The Mystery of the Squashed Squirrel*, that head should be hollow—the perfect place to hide important documents!

"Tomorrow I have to get this information to my chums before the courtroom proceedings begin, so they can snatch back the letters. But until the letters are in my hand—until the moment I'm free to speak the truth—I have to convince everyone that I am Hannah.

"Tomorrow I have to give the performance of my life!"

CHAPTER 46

A Shocking Rumor

 "We are going to be late!" Midge bellowed up the stairs. She jangled the car keys in her pocket in frustration. "We are not going to a fashion show, ladies, we are going to court. Cherry and Velma, let's go!" She rolled her eyes at Jackie. "Whadda we gonna do with them?" she grinned.

They had spent most of the night turning the Chief's house upside down without results. Nancy's letters were nowhere to be found. Midge began to wish they hadn't run over the Chief. "Not at least until we got him to sing," she sighed.

"A little cranky this morning, are we?" Velma teased as she raced down the stairs holding a can of hair spray in one hand and comb in the other. "You know, if I had short hair, I'd be ready by now," she pointed out.

"Get in the car," Midge ordered.

Velma raced out the door, but not before giving Midge a good pinch on her right bicep. "Yes, dad," Velma laughed.

Midge chased after her. "Where's Cherry?" she grumbled when she got to the car. Bess, George, and Lauren had already roared off in George's old jalopy, and Terry was upstairs nursing Hannah, who was making a swift recovery. But Cherry was nowhere to be seen.

"I'm here," Cherry sniffled. She was standing on the front porch holding the letter Nancy had penned to her on the way to prison. In the other hand was a damp hankie, and on her face was an expression of woe.

"Come and sit in the back seat with me, Cherry," Jackie offered generously. Cherry got into the car and lay her head on Jackie's shoulder. "Tell me everything, baby," Jackie said softly as she stroked Cherry's hair. "Is it a Dear John letter?"

Cherry looked puzzled. "No, it's addressed to me," she replied. Jackie had to smile. That Cherry! But her grin turned into a grimace when she heard what came next.

"Nancy's asked me to forgive her for her scandalous behavior of the other evening and is begging me to stay here in River Depths," Cherry blurted out. "Forever!"

"After all Nancy's put you through, you're not going to go back with her, are you?" Jackie wanted to cry, but she held her tongue. She remembered Midge's wise words. She would let Cherry come to her on her own!

Midge and Velma, who had been sitting in the front seat quarreling lightly, were shocked into silence. "I guess we'd better go," Midge muttered as she started the engine and pulled Nancy's convertible, which George had graciously scrubbed clean, out of the circular drive. Midge kept her eyes on the road and her ears tuned to the drama unfolding in the back seat.

"Are you going to?" Jackie asked quietly, struggling to keep her tone nonchalant.

"I don't know," Cherry admitted. She breathed a big sigh of relief. There. She had said it. "For days I've dreamt of the moment when Nancy would declare her love for me, but now I don't know if that's even what I want!" she admitted ruefully. "Last night, when I was at the Tin Tan Club, and everyone was being so nice to me, I realized something shocking," she wailed.

"What?" the girls chorused eagerly.

"I really don't think Nancy's been a very good girlfriend lately!" Midge bit her lip. Velma gripped her thigh.

"And now she's saying all the right things, and I feel all cold inside. But I want to be in love, I really do. Oh, Jackie, what's wrong with me?"

"Right feeling, wrong girl," Jackie almost blurted out. Instead she hugged Cherry even harder.

"Will I ever love again?" Cherry cried.

"Maybe sooner than you think," Midge exclaimed. "Ouch! No pinching the driver. Besides, we're here," she announced as she pulled the car into a spot near the courthouse. They hopped out of the car and made their way to the majestic marble building surrounded by weeping willow trees. It was only nine o'clock, but the summer sun was already heating up the day. People had taken refuge in the shade and were sitting on blankets, sipping cool lemonade. A man was selling hot pretzels from a cart in front of the stairs.

"Oh, look," Cherry exclaimed. "Someone's selling little miniature replicas of the Clue memorial statue. Oh, they're pencil sharpeners; what a clever idea." She wondered if she should get one for Nancy.

"It looks like a carnival," Midge proclaimed as they passed people carrying picnic baskets and folding lawn chairs. "Look, there are George and Bess on the courthouse steps. Who's that fella with them?" Midge wondered. "Oh, that's Lauren," she quickly corrected herself. "I'm still not used her funny new haircut."

"I think Lauren looks mighty cute with her hair all cut off like that," Velma asserted.

"You do?" Midge scowled. "I think she looks like a scrub brush."

"Yoo hoo!" a woman called to them. "Over here!" It was Mrs. Milton Meeks, and she was attractively attired in her sedate gray morning suit, simple pearls, and plain pumps. She gestured wildly at them.

"This will be interesting," Midge grinned. "Let's see if Micky managed to get the news out about the Chief. That's her mother, Mrs. Meeks, the meanest matron in town," she quickly explained to Jackie.

"Oh girls!" Mrs. Meeks ran over to them. "You'll never guess what's happened!" She dropped her voice. "I have the most scandalous information about Chief Chumley," she whispered conspiratorially.

"You do?" the girls chorused, doing their best to look surprised. Mrs. Meeks looked around furtively. "Now don't go spreading this around, but I have heard from a very reliable source that Chief Chumley has run off with money confiscated in last week's River Depths Savings and Loan robbery!"

"He has?" Cherry said in alarm. She shot a nervous glance across the street to the town square, where the Chief had taken his place among other honored River Depthians. People were admiring the new addition to the park, and a few birds had already perched on his shoulders.

"What a surprise," Midge said.

"Isn't it?" the matron exclaimed. "Early this morning I went to the Chief's office to speak to him about a pressing community matter, but he wasn't there. Deputy Drone said his top drawer had been cleaned out and his papers thrown all asunder, as if the Chief had left in a hurry.

"Gracious!" the girls gasped.

"That's not all. A large sum of unmarked bills—evidence from the bank robbery—is missing!"

Mrs. Meeks grabbed a hankie from her purse and started to fan herself. "Oh, I just remembered; I found this under his desk." She showed them the linen handkerchief with the initials NC monogrammed on it. Cherry gasped. It was Nancy's hankie!

"It's Nancy's," Cherry blurted out without thinking.

"Why, so it is!" Mrs. Meeks realized. She puzzled over the scrap of cloth in her hand. "Why isn't Nancy with you, Frank?"

"I don't know," Midge confessed sadly in a deep, masculine manner. A mischievous gleam came into her eyes. "Mrs. Meeks, Nancy's disappeared!"

"Isn't it an odd coincidence that both the Chief *and* Nancy are suddenly nowhere to be found?" Mrs. Meeks remarked.

"Are you insinuating that the Chief and my fiancée have run off together?" Midge cried.

"That's *exactly* what I mean!" Mrs. Meeks exclaimed.

Cherry interjected with, "But she's—"

"Young enough to be his daughter," Midge quickly finished Cherry's sentence.

"I know! Isn't it shocking?" the matron moaned in delight. "Those two have run off together, and I have the proof linking them! But don't worry, Frank dear," Mrs. Meeks clasped Midge's hand. "This shameful secret will stay right here. Although, if it's really true that Nancy's run off with that man, I wonder if you would be interested in meeting my own lovely daughter?"

"Thank you, Mrs. Meeks," Midge said. "You are a true friend."

"I can't talk now, dear, I've got some people to see," the matron hurried away.

"Midge, why did you tell her that horrible lie?" Cherry castigated her chum.

"Don't you see, Cherry? This way, no one will ever suspect what is really going on—that Nancy has disguised herself as Hannah and is standing trial in her stead, that Hannah is hiding out in the attic, being nursed back to health by a Navy Nurse, and the Chief, well, that he's become a park fixture."

"You're right, Midge. It would be dreadful if anyone guessed the truth!"

CHAPTER 47

The State of Illinois v. Hannah P. Gruel

"Oh, did you hear that the Chief and Nancy have run off together with the money from the bank robbery?" Mrs. Thaddeus Tweeds exclaimed when she spied the girls sitting in the back row of the courtroom. "Someone saw them at the train station at the crack of dawn!" she reported. "Frank, you poor dear. You must be nearly frantic with worry about your fiancée," Mrs. Tweeds twittered.

"All rise," the bailiff barked. "The Honorable Judge Milton Meeks presiding." Mrs. Tweeds raced to her front-row seat. The spectators jumped to their feet. The courtroom was so packed the girls were lucky to have found seats at all, even in the very last row of the gallery. Cherry craned her neck to see as Nancy was brought out. She breathed in sharply when she saw the sad, stooped little figure bound in leg irons and handcuffs.

"She really does look just like Hannah," Bess whispered in George's ear. "Right down to the pressed, gray house dress and starched white apron." She squeezed George's hand. The trial was about to begin. Golly, she was nervous.

The prosecuting attorney stood and faced the jury, made up of twelve of River Depths' leading businessmen. "The state will prove, gentlemen, that on July 5, 1959, housekeeper Hannah P. Gruel did wantonly murder her longtime employer, Carson Clue, in the kitchen of his tidy, three-story brick house at 36 Maple Street."

The girls sat in shocked silence as the prosecution laid out a solid case against the hapless housekeeper. The Chief's top deputy positively identified Mr. Clue's hunting rifle as the murder weapon, and matched the prints on the barrel to those taken from Hannah the day of her arrest. Then Hannah's signed confession was passed around the jury box, and a murmur rippled through the courtroom.

"It's going to be the shortest murder trial in history," a man in front of them whispered to his companion. "I'll be surprised if it lasts the week!"

With deadly precision, the district attorney painted a picture of a frustrated housekeeper constantly at odds with her employer.

The girls gasped when Mrs. Milton Meeks was called to the stand. Bess grew red with anger. What would that horrid woman say?

Mrs. Meeks held up her gloved right hand, swore to tell the truth, the whole truth, and nothing but the truth. She sat down in the witness chair, primly smoothed her skirt over her knees, and proceeded to tell one falsehood after the other.

"I saw this coming a mile away," Mrs. Meeks declared when she was asked if she had been shocked by news of the murder. "I knew one day that woman was going to snap," she declared. "Some people do, you know. They snap. Just like that."

"Mrs. Meeks, could you characterize Hannah's relationship with her employer?" the district attorney asked.

"Yes, I'd be delighted to," she replied haughtily. "Perhaps an anecdote will serve. I remember it like it was yesterday. Hannah had been hired at a good wage to help tidy up after a Ladies' Club Luncheon. After the other maids had done their chores and caught their buses home, Hannah cornered me and begged me to let her come clean my house! She said she hated Mr. Clue and that Nancy was a demanding, spoilt child whose extensive wardrobe required hours of ironing. 'If I don't get out of that house, I promise you something terrible will happen!' were her exact words!"

"But you didn't hire her, did you?"

"Of course not," Mrs. Meeks cried indignantly. "I would never dream of stealing someone else's maid!"

"She'd make a nice statue," Midge growled to Jackie.

"A short time later, I asked Miss Gruel to bake me a huckleberry pie," Mrs. Meeks remembered. "Oh, I paid her for it—a whole fifty cents! I took one bite, and I knew there was something awfully wrong with it. Why, it was poison, I tell you. Poison! She was trying to get back at me for not employing her!" Mrs. Meeks swooned into the arms of the district attorney and had to be helped to her place beside her friend Mrs. Tweeds.

Members of the jury were on the edges of their seats. Mrs. Meeks was one of the town's most respected community leaders, and her testimony had proven to be quite damaging for Hannah!

Just then, an unexpected thing happened. Nancy struggled to her feet, clutching the long, oak table in front of her for support. She turned and faced the back of the courtroom. She looked Cherry straight in the eye.

"Miss Gruel, please take your seat," the judge demanded.

"I...fear...I...am...going...to...faint," she whispered right before she pitched forward. Everyone jumped up in alarm. Lucky for Cherry, she had had the foresight to throw bandages, germicidal ointment, smelling salts, aspirin, and her spare nurse's cap in her purse that very morning. "I'm a nurse," she cried as she pinned on her cap. "Stand back!"

Cherry leapt over the railing and caught Nancy just before she hit the floor. "Give her some air," Cherry ordered. The crowd took a step back. Nancy opened one eye and smiled slyly. "I fooled them didn't I?" she whispered. Cherry realized Nancy had been putting on a very convincing act. Why, she hadn't fainted at all!

"I just had to talk to you," Nancy whispered urgently. "I've figured out where the Chief has hidden the evidence."

Cherry grew alarmed at the mention of the Chief. "Lie back," she said in a shaky voice. "I'm going to check your heart rate."

"We haven't much time," Nancy whispered. "Listen carefully. The evidence has got to be in the moosehead hanging in the Chief's living room. I'm sure of it!"

Cherry nodded. "Your heartbeat is dangerously fast, Nancy," she whispered.

"You know why, don't you?" Nancy murmured. "It's because you're here. Did you get my letter?" she asked softly. "I've got to know, Cherry. Will you be waiting for me when I get out?"

Cherry blinked back tears. She couldn't answer. She didn't know!

"Maybe this will convince you," Nancy murmured. She swung her handcuffed hands around Cherry's head and pulled her girlfriend down, kissing her full on the lips. At first Cherry struggled to break the embrace, but soon found that her body had a mind of its own. She surrendered to Nancy's warm kiss.

A murmur went through the crowd. "What's going on?" someone yelled.

"It's the kiss of life," a woman explained knowingly.

"The court will recess for lunch," Judge Meeks pounded his gavel. Two prison guards came to take Nancy away.

Jackie fled the courtroom with Midge at her heels. "That Nancy! I'll bet she's playing on Cherry's naturally sympathetic nature to win her back," she exclaimed. She buried her head in her hands. "What am I saying here? Where's my professional distance? What's wrong with me?" she groaned.

Midge slapped her on the back. "You're in love," she said. "Ain't it grand?"

Cherry raced out of the courtroom, her cheeks all aflame. "The letters are in the moosehead!" she cried. "Let's go. I'll explain later."

They crowded in George's jalopy and raced across town to Lindy Lane. On the way Cherry told them everything she knew. It wasn't much.

"Then Nancy asked if I was going to be waiting for her when she got out of prison," Cherry practically sobbed.

"What did you say?" her friends chorused.

"I didn't have time to tell Nancy the truth—that I don't know what I want!" Cherry cried. "Everything happened so fast. Then she kissed me, and I got all confused. I just don't know. Velma, is it cruel to let Nancy think things that might not be true?" Cherry wondered.

"I wouldn't break up with someone in the middle of her murder trial, if that's what you're asking," Velma said softly.

CHAPTER 48

Drop That Moose!

Jackie, Midge, and George strained under the weight of the gigantic moosehead. "This thing weighs a ton and it stinks, besides," George complained.

"Careful, honey," Bess said worriedly as the three girls finally got the stuffed head off the wall and lowered it into Cherry and Velma's arms.

"Golly!" Cherry exclaimed when she saw the massive beast up close. "Look how its eyes sparkle yellow in the sunlight. Why, if I didn't know any better, I'd say these eyes were made of amber!"

"Drop the moose or I'll shoot," a sinister voice rang out from behind them. When Cherry turned and saw who was on the other end of the gun—a middle-aged man in a straw hat and a dark-haired woman in a simple Navy suit, the very same woman she had found crouched in their convertible in Kornville—she released her grip on the stuffed head and it crashed to the floor.

"The jewel thieves!" Cherry gasped.

"Look!" the others cried as a veritable treasure chest of jewelry laden with rubies, diamonds, pearls, emeralds, garnets, and opals—came pouring from the hollow head. The woman took a pearl-handled revolver from her purse and trained it on the girls while her accomplice removed his straw hat and scooped the gems into it. Cherry gasped.

"Thanks for finding the Chief's booty," the woman laughed. "After we heard the news that our boss left town, we were afraid he'd taken the loot with him." She came closer. Cherry was only a few feet away from the gun!

"Well, if it isn't that cute little nurse—the one who practically gave us her friend's jewelry," the woman chuckled. "Your friend's things brought a pretty penny in this town. Hey, doll, you want to come over to our side? Harold, think we could use a nurse?" But Harold was too busy playing with his new-found treasure to pay attention.

Cherry was near tears. Jackie was livid. "If only Cherry wasn't directly in the line of fire, why I'd—"

At that moment, Lauren came into the room, saying, "Hey, you guys, look at the keen rose quartz the Chief had on his bedroom bureau!"

The armed jewel thief, startled by Lauren's sudden appearance, whirled around just as the teen took quick aim and beaned the woman on the head with the sharp rock.

The woman stumbled and dropped her gun.

"You're under arrest," Jackie proclaimed as she whipped out her handcuffs and secured both crooks with them. She flashed her badge. "Detective Jackie Jones, SFPD."

"I'll tell you everything!" the woman cried out. She pointed an accusing finger at her husband. "He was behind all this," she insisted.

"It was all her idea," he shot back.

"No, it's all your fault," the woman cried. "If you hadn't racked up all those gambling debts that were sold to the Chief, we wouldn't have been forced to go out and do his bidding in the first place!"

"You mean Chief Chumley is your leader?" Cherry gasped. "That means he sent you all the way to Pocatello so you could follow us practically across the whole country and steal Nancy's jewels?"

The woman shook her head. "It was just dumb luck that we met up with you," she said bitterly. "I told Harold we shouldn't follow you girls so far. We normally don't work the Midwest. Besides, I wanted to stay in Pocatello and work the philatelist convention. Now *those* are people with money!"

While the others were mesmerized by the woman's tale, Velma was the one who remembered a girl sitting in leg irons, awaiting a special delivery. She reached inside the moosehead and felt around until she laid her hands on what they had come for—the crucial evidence.

"Look everyone!" she exclaimed. "I've found Nancy's letters!"

CHAPTER 49

The Secret Revealed

 At the courthouse, the girls quickly found seats and waited for the trial to resume. This afternoon would mark the beginning of the defense's case, and everyone was eager to see how Hannah's attorney would staunch the flood of damage from that morning's shocking revelations from Mrs. Meeks. Mr. Donald, who had been unable to get a seat for the morning's proceedings, squeezed in next to Bess, and she filled him in on Mrs. Meeks's outrageous testimony and the exciting events that had unfolded at the Chief's house.

"And we've found Nancy's evidence," Velma said triumphantly.

"It's in my purse," Bess added with a smile.

Mr. Donald glared at Mrs. Meeks when he heard about her false testimony. The matron, who was sitting in the front row behind the district attorney, had run home to slip into a fresh outfit—a lavender summer suit with black piping, a purple cloche hat with a veil that fell to just above her little pug nose, and a silver-and-diamond brooch pinned over her right bosom. She smiled and waved at the group.

Mr. Donald smiled back through clenched teeth. "One of these days I'll get the opportunity to pay her back for all the misery she's caused," he promised himself.

Mrs. Meeks busied herself greeting other townswomen, all decked out in their finest summer outfits for the afternoon's event.

"It's like she's holding court up there while Hannah's life hangs in the balance," Velma said angrily.

"The nerve of her, showing up after what she said earlier," Bess hissed.

"You'd never know she was such a monster; she's always so well dressed and looks every bit the lady!" Cherry exclaimed. She took Nancy's binoculars from her purse and trained them on Mrs. Meeks.

257

"That suit is awfully flattering for a fuller-busted figure," Cherry thought as she examined every inch of the meddlesome matron's form. "And she was wise to choose a simple brooch as an ornament instead of fussy beads that would call attention to her rather large endowment. And what a pretty brooch it is, and so unusual, too," Cherry thought to herself as she got a closer look at the simple silver horseshoe pin studded with sparkling diamonds.

"A simple silver horseshoe studded with sparkling diamonds!" she gasped. Why, Mrs. Meeks was wearing Nancy's missing brooch!

"Cherry, what is it?" her chums cried. She passed around the binoculars. "Look at Mrs. Meeks's bosom," she whispered urgently. Her chums looked perplexed. "I mean, look at the brooch pinned to her bosom. It's Nancy's; it's just got to be!"

Midge saw that Cherry was right. She handed the binoculars back to Cherry. "Check out all her chums," Midge whispered. "I may be wrong, but doesn't it look like they're all wearing some of Nancy's jewelry?"

Cherry, who knew Nancy's gems better than anyone, gasped when she trained the spyglass on the crowd of socialites hanging on Mrs. Meeks's every word. She was able to identify most of their accessories.

"I'm going up there and snatch that brooch off her suit," Cherry declared angrily.

"No, don't," Mr. Donald implored.

"Why not?" the girls chorused.

"Because Nancy may need some insurance," he said mysteriously. A mischievous grin spread over his handsome face. His green eyes sparkled with delight. "I think I've got the perfect plan," he whispered. "Midge, Jackie, George, I may need some muscle on this. You interested?"

"And how!" they cried. Just then Micky Meeks slipped into the bench beside them. "Hey," she said softly. "I hear it's all over town about the Chief and Nancy."

"Good job, Micky," Midge praised their new chum.

"Want to do another job?" Mr. Donald asked with a sly grin. Micky nodded eagerly.

"Go persuade your mother to go to the ladies' lounge," Mr. Donald directed. "Tell her her slip is showing. That will send her off in a panic," he chuckled.

Micky eagerly obeyed. Soon Mrs. Meeks was racing out of the courtroom, gingerly holding the hem of her skirt.

"The Leading Lady exits," Mr. Donald said with delight.

The girls exchanged puzzled glances. Something very exciting was going to happen; but what?

"Now, girls," he said to Cherry, Velma, and Bess. "I'll need to borrow your cosmetics." They gladly turned their compacts and lipsticks over to their friend, who stowed them in the pocket of his white canvas summer slacks. A matching white duck smock brightened by a lime-green neck scarf tied in a gay knot at his throat completed Mr. Donald perfect-for-a-summer's-day ensemble.

"Let's go," he said to Jackie, Midge, Micky, and George, with a twinkle in his eyes. The grin lighting up his handsome face told the girls they were in for a delightful surprise! They raced out of the courtroom.

"All rise."

The spectators eagerly jumped to their feet. Nancy was led to her table from a side door and sat down next to Defense Attorney Gerald Gloon.

The girls could scarcely keep their minds on the courtroom drama at hand, so curious were they about Mr. Donald's plan. They soon stopped wondering about Mr. Donald, however, when Attorney Gloon stood up and declared, "The defense rests, your honor."

Everyone gasped. He hadn't cross-examined any of the prosecution's witnesses that morning, and now it looked as if he wasn't planning to call any of his own! Why, it was practically unheard of! "That's it?" Bess cried. "The trial's over? Just like that?" An excited roar raced through the courtroom. The bailiff spent several minutes restoring order.

"Sit down!" Judge Milton Meeks ordered. Just then, Mrs. Milton Meeks raced into the courtroom with Midge, Jackie, George, and Micky right behind.

But where was Mr. Donald?

"I've got something to say," Mrs. Meeks stated as she clutched her purse to her bosom and gasped for breath.

"No, *I've* got something to say!" Nancy said suddenly. The courtroom grew still.

Nancy turned around in her seat and searched the gallery until she found her friends. "Did you get the letters?"

her glance asked. Bess nodded and pointed to her purse.

Nancy stood and ripped off her mask and wig, revealing her true identity!

"It's not Hannah at all; why, it's Nancy Clue!" everyone gasped in alarm. Matrons fainted; somewhere outside a dog began to howl.

"What a story!" Miss Gladys Gertz cried from the press gallery as Miss Mannish snapped Nancy's picture. "Stop the presses!"

"What is the meaning of this?" Judge Milton Meeks pounded his gavel. "Order in the court. Sit down, I tell you. Sit!" Once a semblance of order had been restored, Judge Meeks pointed his thick wooden gavel at Nancy and declared, "You've got quite a bit of explaining to do, young lady! The first order of business is to determine the location of the real murderess!"

A hush fell over the courtroom.

Nancy broke the silence: "She's right here in the courtroom, your honor."

The spectators looked around the room with dread. Was Hannah hiding somewhere in their midst?

"She must be in disguise!" a man cried out. People began peering at one another in suspicion. "It could be anyone," a woman replied. "Oh, horrors!"

The courtroom again dissolved into general mayhem.

"Let her speak!" someone shouted.

Nancy took a deep breath. Her next words were perhaps the most important of her life. She had waited years for this moment. She wanted to make sure she said it just right.

"I killed Father!" she blurted out.

"What?" everyone cried in alarm. "It just can't be!"

"But it's true!" Nancy cried. She told them the whole sordid story, sparing no detail.

"I have a secret; a secret I've kept for many years," Nancy began in a low tone. Everyone crowded close to hear with the young sleuth had to say. A murmur spread through the crowd. "Nancy? A secret?"

Nancy put up her hands to quiet the court. Her voice was shaky, but her words rang loud and true.

"It was only to protect me and my secret that Hannah confessed to the murder," she said dramatically.

"My father was not who you thought he was," Nancy revealed. "To you he was a civic leader and a respected attorney, but in his own home he was a bully," she paused for a moment, "and worse!"

"Worse than a bully? How can that be?" someone cried.

"He forced me to do things!" Nancy exclaimed. "At night. In my bedroom." She shook in anger. There was a fire in her eyes.

"Go, Nancy," Midge murmured. She squeezed Velma's hand.

Everyone recoiled in horror as it became clear Nancy was talking about something so monstrous, so evil, there were scarcely words to describe it. "Don't tell us any more," someone gasped.

"No, I must!" Nancy cried.

She struggled to continue. "I would awake in the mornings and tell myself I'd had another bad dream. But they weren't dreams at all. What happened to me was all too real!

"After a few years, Father stopped coming to my room, and I thought it was all over. I did my best to forget and after a while I even believed, sometimes, that I had made the whole thing up. That it *had* been a bad dream.

"But it all came flooding back one dreadful day when I found Father in the back yard behind the lilac bushes paying particular attention to the neighbor girl.

"When I saw him with that little girl, I knew I had to do something! I ran and told Hannah, and when she threatened to report him to the proper authorities, Father attacked her!"

Nancy trembled when she remembered the sight of the elderly, gray-haired housekeeper pinned in the strong grasp of her angry, evil father. "I was so afraid he really *would* kill her, I ran to the den to telephone someone, anyone, and that's when I spied father's hunting rifle on the gun rack above the mantle. I grabbed it and raced back to the kitchen.

"I had no intention of shooting him," Nancy explained earnestly, adding, "I thought I could...could...*scare* him into releasing her. But I *must* have pulled the trigger, because the next thing I knew, he was lying on the floor, right in front of our two-door Goldenrod Frigidaire. And there was blood everywhere."

Bess clucked in sympathy. "They redecorated the kitchen just last summer, and Hannah was so proud of the way it looked," she whispered sadly.

"I threw some frocks in a bag and headed for San Francisco to start a new life. But I found I couldn't! I had to come home and tell the truth.

"And I'm not sorry I shot him," Nancy cried out angrily.

"I'd do it again!"

There was not one sound in the courtroom save the surprising, soft sobs coming from Mrs. Milton Meeks. Then an angry murmur started.

"How can you possibly think we'd believe such loathsome libel about our beloved Carson Clue?" a man cried from the back of the room.

"You shouldn't have come home, Nancy Clue!" someone joined his protest. "You should have stayed away and kept your filthy lies to yourself!"

"Wait! I have the evidence to prove beyond a shadow of a doubt what my father truly was!" she cried. "Letters written in his own hand. Letters whose contents would sicken and shock any decent person's sensibilities."

"How could evidence of this nature possibly exist?" someone demanded.

"I'll tell you how, if you only let me!" Nancy retorted. "One summer, while I was away at Camp Winnebago, father wrote me letters revealing his feelings for me. Although he didn't sign them, anyone who knew him will surely recognize his bold, slanted penmanship," she added hastily.

"I was so afraid someone would see these dreadful letters," Nancy confessed. "I was tempted to throw them in the bonfire at the nightly weenie-roast, but I changed my mind and when I returned home, I hid them in the false bottom drawer of my hope chest, where they sat for years. Until now." Nancy turned an eager eye to Bess. She held out her hand. "The letters please," she said.

Bess opened her purse and handed Nancy a packet of letters. When Nancy unfolded one so she could present it to the court, a queer look crossed her face. She caught a glimpse of the words, "Darling Rebecca," written in the girlish penmanship of her Aunt Helen Clue. "Oh no, Bess, these are another mystery!" Nancy half-smiled as she handed the packet back to her chum.

"Oops," Bess giggled nervously. She gave Nancy the correct bundle.

Nancy triumphantly waved the letters around the courtroom. "Who wants to read them?" she cried. "These prove everything I just told you."

The crowd pulled back. No one wanted anything to do with the sordid missives. "What about you, Mrs. Meeks?" Nancy exclaimed bitterly. "Surely you want a peek at these. I know you don't believe me, Mrs. Meeks."

"I do believe you, Nancy Clue!" Mrs. Milton Meeks cried out suddenly. The crowd gasped as River Depths' most influential and respected matron jumped up and hugged Nancy to her ample bosom. Nancy's chums gasped. What had happened to Mrs. Milton Meeks to make her change her tune? Sudden tears came to Nancy's eyes.

Mrs. Meeks took a hankie from her black alligator bag and wiped Nancy's tears. "There, there, dear," she comforted the crying girl. "Mrs. Meeks will make it all better." Nancy looked gratefully at the transformed matron. But to her great surprise, instead of Mrs. Meeks's beady little blue eyes, Mr. Donald's sparkling green eyes—the kindest she had ever seen—looked back. Mr. Donald winked.

Mr. Donald straightened his skirt and adjusted his bosom. He cleared his throat, and when he opened his mouth, the voice of Mrs. Meeks came out.

"I've seen those letters with my own eyes, don't ask me how. I'm sworn to secrecy, but I can tell you they're every bit as disgusting as Nancy claims!" he cried. "And, what's more, anyone who doesn't believe her can just leave town as far as I'm concerned. After all the good Nancy's done—exposing horse-theft rings, finding stolen heirlooms, ridding more than one mansion in this town of a ghost—I'd think you'd all rush to her defense. Nancy deserves our utmost sympathy and deep respect, and no less!"

He hiked up his fitted, straight skirt and sat down. He was so angry, the veil on his cloche hat was all askew. He hastily straightened it.

Judge Meeks dropped his gavel in alarm. Had Mrs. Meeks gone mad?

"I have something to add to that, Myra," Mrs. Tweeds declared as she rose to her feet. The crowd buzzed with excitement. Mrs. Tweeds was the head of the Ladies' Auxiliary, the second most influential society woman in River Depths, and Myra Meeks's best girlfriend. What could she possibly have to add to the perplexing puzzle?

Mrs. Tweeds was too overcome with emotion to speak for a moment. She appeared ready to faint. Cherry accepted the call to duty and raced to her side with a jar of smelling salts.

"Thank you, my dear," Mrs. Tweeds said softly. "I certainly don't deserve such kindness after the way I treated you girls the other day," she murmured. Then she took a deep breath.

"I have something terrible to confess, too," she cried. *"I know Nancy is telling the truth about her father!"* She held up a hand to silence people's protests. "Late one evening, many years ago, I barged into the Clue house with a casserole in hand, and found Mr. Clue," she stopped for a moment to steady her voice, took a deep breath, and whispered, "somewhere he shouldn't have been.

"I was so frightened, I ran out of that house and didn't go back for years. I'm ashamed to say I never told anyone what I had seen. Who would have believed me, anyway?" she cried to the crowd.

"Would you?" she pointed to a businessman in a gray flannel suit. He hung his head in shame.

"I say we put an end to this terrible injustice right now, dismiss all charges against kindly housekeeper Hannah Gruel, and beg Nancy's forgiveness for ever doubting her story," Mrs. Tweeds proposed.

"But she killed her father," the row of townswomen chorused in unison. "And for that, she must be punished!"

Mr. Donald walked up to the women, all the while fingering the horseshoe brooch pin over his right bosom. "I love your new jewels, girls," he purred, in Mrs. Meeks's high, reedy voice. "They're so unusual. I haven't seen anything like them in the shops in town. You'll have to let everyone in on *your* little secret!"

"We've changed our minds," the matrons cried. "Set Nancy free!"

Midge had to grin when she saw the women furtively rip off their jewelry and sneak it into their purses.

"Set Nancy free! Set Nancy free!" became the cry of the crowd. The citizens of River Depths surged around the young sleuth and offered their sincerest congratulations.

"I don't believe this," Bess whispered in relief. "This is almost too good to be true."

Midge jumped out of her seat. "I'd better untie the real Mrs. Meeks," she grinned. She paused in the doorway of the courtroom to reflect on the amazing events she had just witnessed.

"Who would ever have guessed the truth that could be uncovered by one man in a dress?" Midge shook her head and smiled.

CHAPTER 50

Trouble!

 "More sherbet?" Bess asked brightly. She was fixing a tray to be brought upstairs to Hannah, whose condition had greatly improved when she'd heard she was a free woman.

"And Nancy's come home," Hannah had cried right before bursting into tears and engulfing the girl in a big hug. Now Hannah was sleeping peacefully with Gogo at her feet, and Terry was getting some much-needed rest. Bess was fussing around the kitchen, preparing a sumptuous celebration meal. The others lounged about the house, too stunned by the day's events to do more than pinch themselves in relief.

Nancy shook her head. She was frankly too worried to eat another bite of the delicious dessert. She stared out the kitchen window at the garden, where Jackie and Cherry had their heads together in deep discussion. "I've come home too late," Nancy frowned as she watched the attractive, dark-haired nurse giggling while Jackie demonstrated the correct way to pat down a prisoner.

"What did you say, Nancy?" Bess asked as she bustled about. Her cake would be done soon, and she still had to mix the yummy frosting that would go on top. "I need a jar of cherries," Bess decided aloud. "For garnish."

"What did you say about Cherry?" Velma wondered. She had wandered into the kitchen for another cool glass of minty iced tea. "Uh, oh," Velma warned when she glanced out the window and saw Jackie and Cherry together. "I'd get out there if I were you," she suggested to Nancy.

"I can't make Cherry love me if she doesn't," Nancy cried. "Can I?" she looked hopefully at Velma.

Velma shook her head. "No, but you can give her plenty of reasons to try," she said.

Bess smiled. All this love talk just made her even more glad

she had fallen for George, who was as faithful as a dog. "I'm going to bring Hannah an early supper," she announced. "I'll be right back. Someone stir the soup."

Nancy hopped up to help Bess with the tray. "I'll go with you," she sighed. "Anything's better than watching the garden show."

Midge meandered into the kitchen. "Hey, babe, whatcha doing?" she gave Velma a peck on the neck. Then she smiled when she saw Cherry and Jackie together in the garden.

"They make a nice couple, don't they?" she grinned.

"You're pretty happy with yourself, aren't you?" Velma frowned. "Tell me, Midge, how does it feel to break up a happy couple?"

Midge thought Velma was teasing until she saw the stern expression on her pretty face. "I didn't break them up," Midge defended herself.

"You didn't help matters any," Velma scowled. "I can forgive Jackie; she's in love. But what's your excuse, Midge?"

"Hey!" Midge cried angrily. "Nancy's the one who went out drinking all day and left her girl at home. And when she finally did come home, why—"

Velma's green eyes flashed with anger. *"At least Nancy came home,"* she seethed. "How can you pass judgment on her when what you did was so much worse!" Velma yelled. "What if someone had encouraged me to leave you? Would you have liked that?"

"You did leave me," Midge pointed out. "For a whole week." That week, ten years ago, had been the worst of Midge's life.

"I still remember the morning you stumbled in with lipstick all over your shirt, stinking of *somebody else's* cheap perfume!" Velma pouted.

"Oh, Velma, I'm sorry," Midge tried to hug her. Velma pushed Midge away.

"That was *years* ago!" Midge cried. "I thought you had forgiven me."

"Well, I've discovered I haven't," Velma retorted angrily.

Midge trembled. She lit a cigarette and tried to compose her thoughts. She had had no idea Velma even remembered that one ugly episode of an otherwise perfect relationship.

"The night Nancy brought that girl home, the whole thing came back to haunt me all over again. I realize I haven't forgotten. Not completely," Velma said sadly.

Midge didn't know what to say. The sordid affair had been a horrible mistake. "We had had that terrible fight about my drinking, and you threatened to leave me. I was scared. So, like a jerk, I went out and got drunk and ended up at some strange girl's house."

"You ended up in her *bed*," Velma corrected in an ice-cold tone.

"There's no excuse for what I did," Midge admitted. "You mean everything to me, Velma. Nothing like that has ever happened again. And it never will."

"How can I be sure of that?" Velma said bitterly.

"Are you telling me that after all these years you still don't trust me?" Midge cried out.

Velma burst into tears. "I don't know what I'm saying," she admitted. "I just get so jealous sometimes. Why, I'm even a little jealous of you and Cherry."

"I'm amazed that you're worried about me and Cherry," Midge cried indignantly, "especially considering the way you've flaunted your crush on Lauren!"

"My *what*?" Velma cried. "What on earth are you talking about?"

"You and Lauren spent the entire trip running off together to have private chats," Midge shouted. "What else am I to think?"

"The reason I spent so much time with Lauren is that," Velma dropped her voice and continued, "she got her *visitor* for the first time while we were driving to River Depths. She turned to me for guidance," Velma explained vehemently.

"I supposed that's *all* she wanted," Midge scowled.

Velma gasped. "Lauren is a *child*," she retorted furiously.

"She's not a child," Midge reminded her. "You said so yourself—she's just a year younger than I was when I went to prison. Well, by the time I was locked up, I had had *plenty* of girlfriends. Older girls, too."

"Thanks for reminding me," Velma snapped. "I *need* reminders of what a runaround you used to be."

"Don't try to change the subject," Midge said angrily. "You always do that. That's how you win every argument, Velma. You get me all confused and excited."

Velma folded her arms over her shapely chest and took a step back. "Don't worry, Midge, I have no intention of getting you excited today," she said smoothly.

"That suits me fine," Midge said.

"Good," Velma spat out. "Oh, Midge, sometimes you make me so mad!" She looked around frantically. "Where's my purse? I've got to get out of this house!"

"I saw it on the coffee table," Midge informed her in an icy tone. Velma stormed out of the house, but not before snatching up her purse and the keys to Nancy's car.

Lauren wandered in from the garage where she had been sorting and labeling her rocks according to classification. She had overheard the whole argument. Everyone had heard it.

"Where is Velma off to in such a rush?" Lauren asked.

"Who cares?" Midge slammed around the kitchen.

"Velma shouldn't have talked to you like that," Lauren scoffed. "She'll be sorry she said those things. Whadda ya bet, in another minute she comes back and asks for your forgiveness?"

Midge snorted and lit a cigarette. She leaned against the sink. "You obviously don't know Velma very well," Midge laughed bitterly. "If anyone's gonna have to get down on her knees, it's going to be me. But I'm not going to do it. This time, I'm right."

"Just go find her and say you're sorry, Midge!" Lauren cried. Golly, hearing those two fight had put her in a panic! "Then everything will be okay."

"That'd be like saying I was wrong, and the minute you admit you were wrong, well, then it's all over," Midge warned. "There's one thing you gotta learn about femmes, Lauren. They're jumpy and excitable and are wont to fly off the handle for no reason at all. Oh, you could be minding your own business and then all of a sudden, boom, you're in the dog house."

"Huh?" Lauren mused.

"Don't you see? That's exactly what they want. From that day on, they lead you around like a little dog on a leash. Besides, Velma's the one who's wrong here. She's going to have to come to me."

Midge decided to sit on the porch and have a smoke while she waited for Velma to come to her senses.

A few hours later, the front door burst open and a gorgeous, dark-haired girl with a short, modern Italian haircut, a black circle skirt, a snug white shell sweater, and large hoop earrings, walked in.

"You're not here to see Nancy, are you?" Cherry gasped in alarm. She had to look twice at the glamorous stranger before realizing it was Velma! "Velma, you've cut off all your hair!" Cherry cried.

"I know. How do you like it?" Velma preened.

"Oh, Velma, you *really* look like a movie star now!" Cherry enthused. "But what is Midge going to say?"

"I don't care!" Velma asserted as she slammed her purse on the coffee table and hurled herself face-down on the davenport cushions. To Cherry's great distress, Velma burst into tears.

"I meant it when I said it looked good," Cherry consoled her.

"I'm *not* crying about my hair," Velma said. "It's Midge!" She sniffed. "By the way, where is she? Has she been asking for me?"

"She's soaking in the tub," Cherry reported. "She and Jackie helped George work on her jalopy all afternoon, and Midge got awfully dirty."

"So Midge spent the day tinkering with the guys, huh?" Velma quizzed her. "She didn't leave the house or anything?"

Cherry shook her head. "Is something wrong with Midge?" Cherry wanted to know. "She's in an awfully bad mood."

"There are *several* things wrong with Midge," Velma steamed on her way up the stairs.

Cherry heard the bathroom door burst open and slam shut. Soon there were muffled shouts, and although Cherry couldn't make out any of the words, she had never heard such screaming in her life. Finally there was a loud smack and a big splash. Velma raced down the stairs and out the front door, taking time to slam it hard, twice.

"I am never speaking to you again, Midge Fontaine," she yelled from outside the house. "You can go back to Warm Springs all by yourself. From now on, consider yourself a single Midge."

"That's fine with me," Midge bellowed from the top of the stairs. She had a bath towel wrapped around her waist, and her tee-shirt on backward, and she was rubbing a red spot on her cheek. Cherry wanted to warn her that she was getting soapy water all over the rug, but now didn't seem like the time.

"That's fine with me," Midge repeated angrily. "Because you know what you are, Velma? You're...you're..." Cherry was shocked when she saw Midge sink to the carpet, put her head in her hands, and sob, "You're the best girlfriend I've ever had."

CHAPTER 51

An Agonizing Decision

"Midge has smoked every cigarette in River Depths, and Velma's locked herself in the powder room and refuses to open the door. I can't believe all this is happening!" Cherry cried.

Midge and Velma had spent the evening shouting at one another while their chums huddled in the kitchen, pretending not to hear the angry remarks and tortured sobs. Even Gogo had hidden from them. The morning had proven little better. It was quiet, all right, but that kind of dreadful quiet that came after a battle no one had won. The imperiled couple had simply grown too tired to fight.

"What more could possibly happen today?" Cherry cried to Bess as she threw up her hands in dismay.

Nancy came running from the den where she and George had been sequestered all morning, going over the box of papers taken from the Chief's desk drawer. Little by little, Nancy was piecing together a paper trail that would completely destroy the Chief's reputation as an upstanding citizen. "After I get through with him, no one will even care what happened to Chief Chumley," Nancy had made that happy announcement earlier. "No wonder he was trying to get rid of me. I would have uncovered his dastardly deeds sooner or later!"

Cherry thrilled to the sight of Nancy in her natural surroundings—her cheeks rosy from hard work, her pretty eyes flashing with excitement each time she came into the kitchen to announce a new discovery. This was the Nancy of her dreams: hard at work, level-headed, and outfitted in a charming jumper and dotted blouse. "Gosh, I wish I had Velma to talk to," Cherry thought. "Yesterday I was so sure that Nancy and I could never be more than just friends, and today I think I've changed my mind!"

"Cherry, your long-distance call to Pleasantville, Idaho, has finally gone through," Nancy informed her.

All thoughts of her own quandary flew out of Cherry's head when she realized she was finally going to get a chance to speak to her mother!

"Mother? It's Cherry," she exclaimed when she picked up the telephone. But to Cherry's surprise, it wasn't her mother on the other end. It was Visiting Nurse Katie Klempke, an attractive, pleasant-faced girl with lovely blond hair and sparkling blue eyes, who had been Cherry's classmate at Stencer Nursing School. "Is mother ill?" Cherry gasped.

"Both your parents have had complete mental breakdowns," the pleasant-voiced nurse replied.

Cherry quickly relived her last moments at her parents' house in Pleasantville. She had just finished dressing for an early supper when her mother informed her that there was a carload of rather noisy girls waiting for her. "We'll explain *everything*," her brother Charley and his close chum Johnny, partners in a successful interior design shop in New York City, had promised as Cherry raced out the door and into Nancy's arms.

What could the boys have said that could have caused her parents to go into complete and utter shock?

"Oh, no," Cherry cried. "I must come right home!"

"There's no need for that," Nurse Klempke replied in a brisk tone. "Your parents are being moved to the Pleasantville Sanitarium later today. Besides, Charley and his handsome friend Johnny are here. And they've taken care of everything!"

Cherry could see that!

"Hello, Charley? It's Cherry."

"It's good to hear your voice, Cherry," Charley cried. "Are you having fun?"

"In a way," Cherry said. "It's hard to say. Oh, Charley, what's happened to Mother and Father?"

"Nothing too terrible," Charley chuckled. "They had rather a shock the day you left, but they'll recover in time."

"Did you tell Mother about me and Nancy?" Cherry wondered.

"Mother's stopped planning your wedding, dear," Charley admitted. "I was going to tell her about me and Johnny next, but she collapsed, so I told Father instead."

"Oh dear!" Cherry cried. She shut the door to the den so she could speak her mind. "I almost wish you hadn't done that," she said.

"We mustn't blame ourselves for Mother's collapse," Charley warned. "She's been due for a good long vacation for years."

"It's not that," Cherry cried. "It's just that now something has happened, and I'm not sure if what you told Mother is true. Oh, Charley, you're going to have to go and tell her I'm in love with two girls now!"

Charley let out a whistle. "Is this the shy nurse who used to be my sister?" he teased. "Tell me everything, sis," he said. So Cherry did. But when she got off the phone with her brother, she was no closer to a decision. "You'll know what's right when it's time to choose," her brother advised.

Cherry went back to the kitchen with a heavy heart. As she was telling Nancy all about her parents' complete and utter nervous breakdowns, there was a knock at the door. It was Mrs. Milton Meeks—the *real* Mrs. Milton Meeks. "At least, I think it is," Cherry puzzled. She got a closer look at the matron. "Oh, yes, it is you, Mrs. Meeks!" she cried when she spied the beady eyes and small, determined chin.

"Oh course it's me, dear," Mrs. Meeks pushed past Cherry into the kitchen. "Will you help me with this cake?" she asked, struggling to keep her balance under the weight of a pink and white iced, three-layer wedding cake.

"How nice," Cherry cried, "Someone you know is getting married!"

Mrs. Meeks laughed. "You're such a goose. You know good and well this is the day Nancy Clue and Frank Hardly are tying the knot. Remember when I said I'd help with the wedding? Well, I felt so blue about our little misunderstanding in court, I decided to take it upon myself to provide a lavish wedding the likes of which River Depths will never forget. Now, hurry, dear. We've got little sandwiches to cut into triangles and punch to make. And it all begins in exactly one hour!

"Nancy, hadn't you better go and get dressed? Of course you're wearing your dear mother's wedding gown, aren't you?"

Jackie came into the room to see what all the fuss was about.

"Oh, good, you've hired more help. Will you be a good girl and get the fancy punch bowl out of storage?" Mrs. Meeks cried when she spied Jackie. "And, goodness, dear, put on an apron. We have guests arriving soon."

Jackie raised one eyebrow, crossed her arms over her chest, and gave Mrs. Milton Meeks a fearless look. Cherry put one arm through Jackie's and said, "I guess you don't recognize our friend; you met her in court yesterday." She continued with pride, "Mrs. Meeks, this is Detective Jackie Jones from the San Francisco Police Department."

When Nancy saw Cherry take Jackie's arm, she hurried out of the room.

"Oh, really," Mrs. Meeks thrilled. She put on her spectacles and took a good look at Jackie. "Goodness," she said. "You're with the police," she tittered. "Oh, my."

"Jewel heists are my specialty," Jackie said dryly.

"But she does many other things equally well," Cherry boasted.

"Dear, do you have a powder room free?" Mrs. Meeks cried. Cherry directed her toward the downstairs washroom.

"That was nice, Cherry," Jackie grinned.

"You mean, the way she ran off with that look in her eyes?" Cherry giggled.

"No, I mean the way you took my arm and showed me off," Jackie said softly.

Cherry blushed to the roots of her hairdo. Golly, a few minutes ago she was feeling all tingly about Nancy, and now suddenly her heart was pounding something terrible because of Jackie!

Suddenly, she felt like crawling into Jackie's strong embrace and staying there forever. "Love is supposed to be such a many splendored thing, but it's really full of heartbreak and sorrow," Cherry exclaimed. Golly, she had done a lot of growing up in the last few days!

"Midge and Velma swear they'll never speak to one another again, and Nancy and I...well, I don't know what we are to each other anymore. Only last week I was sure she was my one true love. But now I don't know. Oh, I'm so confused," Cherry cried. "Why can't things be simple, like in the movies?"

"Because life's not like that. Because girls aren't like that," Jackie grinned.

Cherry had to laugh. "You sound like Midge now," she smiled. Then she grew somber. As bad as her own problems were, as much as her own heart was aching, she knew there

were two people who were hurting much worse.

"If Midge and Velma really do break up, then there's no hope for love!" she cried.

Jackie agreed. "We've got to bring them back together."

"Girls, stop standing there gossiping and help Mr. Donald with the decorations," Mrs. Meeks ordered. "And where's that other dark-haired girl? The one who looks like you?" she asked Cherry. "Nancy would look so lovely at the altar, flanked by two brunettes."

Cherry was delighted to see Mr. Donald standing in the living room, holding a big tissue-paper bell and a box of assorted theatrical supplies. He was clad in mustard yellow sporty cashmere slacks, a matching silk shirt, and soft white suede loafers.

"When I heard Frank and Nancy were getting married, I just had to see for myself!" he cried. Under Mrs. Meeks's watchful eye, Mr. Donald got to work transforming the attractive yet staid formal living area into a dream. Using crepe paper, fresh flowers from Hannah's garden, and a bolt of the softest pink velvet, he created a milieu straight out of a fairy tale.

"We haven't any music!" Mrs. Meeks suddenly gasped.

Mr. Donald opened his box of tricks and took out a Liberace recording of a wedding march. "Will this do?" he asked.

Mrs. Meeks lit up. "I love him!" she cried. "I practically swooned when I saw him perform last year at the River Depths

Symphony Hall." She raced out of the room to call her friend Mrs. Tweeds and ask her to bring her new portable phonograph along with the clam dip.

"What's really going on here?" Mr. Donald wondered as soon as she had left the room. "Darlings, you all look so weepy-eyed."

"Oh, Mr. Donald, we're all having troubles today of the most wretched kind," Cherry sighed.

"Love problems, I'll bet," Mr. Donald guessed. "Tell me everything," he urged. "If there's one thing I am, it's lucky in love."

Jackie and Cherry quickly explained the argument that had led to the break-up of everyone's favorite couple.

"And even though they love each other madly, they're both too proud to give in," Cherry exclaimed.

"It sounds like those two need a good swat," he declared.

"I believe Velma already tried that," Cherry said.

"Then we'll go with Plan B!" Mr. Donald cried.

"Sounds great!" the girls enthused. "What is it?"

"It goes like this." Soon the trio was whispering furiously and giggling hysterically.

"The wedding will begin in fifteen minutes!" Mrs. Meeks cried as she came into the room holding a tray of canapés. Guests began arriving, all excited by the turn of events in the Clue house. Gifts piled up, and soon the dining room was overflowing with gaily wrapped packages.

Mrs. Meeks shrieked with delight when she spotted Miss Gladys Gertz and Miss Martha Mannish outfitted in crisp summer suits and wearing their press badges pinned to their lapels.

"The reporters I met in court are here!" Mrs. Meeks called. "Now this is one wedding that should be on the front page!" She raced past them, all aflutter.

Miss Gertz grinned and winked at Cherry. "Have you seen the latest edition of *The River Depths Defender*?" she asked.

"I haven't had time to read a thing," Cherry explained earnestly. "Last-minute weddings can be such a headache!"

Miss Gertz laughed merrily and handed Cherry the newspaper. "I'm so glad I didn't run you down in Dust Bin, dear," she smiled. "You're such a delight!"

Cherry gasped when she saw Miss Gertz's by-line on the front page.

GIRL DETECTIVE CRACKS CASE

River Depths, Illinois—Intrepid girl detective Nancy Clue, with selfless disregard for her own well-being, revealed herself as the true murderer of her father, respected attorney Carson Clue, thus causing the judge to free accused murderess and housekeeper Hannah Gruel, who had been like a mother to the titian-haired sleuth since the death of her own mother twenty-two years ago.

In a startling courtroom confession, Miss Clue revealed heretofore unknown diabolical aspects of her late father's nature that shocked and stunned the court. In recounting the events that led up to the justifiable homicide, Nancy described a side to Mr. Clue that startled even his most ardent fans.

"He was really going to kill Hannah! Oh, it was just awful!" Miss Clue recalled after describing how she rescued the frail, elderly housekeeper from her father's clutches.

In a decision that surprised few courtroom spectators, Judge Milton Meeks exonerated Miss Clue of all wrongdoing in the unhappy shooting.

"I knew all along she must have had good reason," Mrs. Milton Meeks declared as the courtroom cleared.

In related news, Police Chief Charles "Chick" Chumley has reportedly fled the state after admitting to this reporter that he fabricated evidence against Hannah Gruel.

"The Chief was trying to cover for his friend, Carson Clue, by framing the housekeeper," Deputy Dwight Drone admitted. "Why, everyone knows Hannah wouldn't harm a fly!"

Right next to the story was a photograph of Cherry, Nancy, Midge, Velma, and Lauren, taken at the square dance in Dust Bin. The caption read, "A disguised Nancy Clue stopping for some brief recreation at the Round-Up Club in Dust Bin, Wy., on her way to save housekeeper Hannah Gruel from wrongful conviction—*Photo by Miss Martha Mannish*."

"I don't know what you girls did with the Chief, and I don't think I want to know, but according to my sources, he deserved everything he got," Miss Gertz giggled.

Cherry raced upstairs to prepare the bride while Mr. Donald, dismayed that Midge hadn't packed a tuxedo, hopped in his sports car and raced home for one of his.

"What are we going to do?" Nancy wondered aloud when she peeked down the banister and saw there really was going to be a wedding. "I put on my mother's dress just to placate Mrs. Meeks," she explained.

"I'll spell out everything later!" Cherry cried. "Get in your bedroom and take off that dress," she ordered. Nancy blushed happily, hummed a gay tune, and raced for her room. By the time she got there, she had stripped off the ivory taffeta gown with its majestic flounced chapel sweep train, lace-trimmed veil, and chantilly lace elbow-length gloves.

"The shoes, too," Cherry cried. Nancy kicked off her satin slippers. "Shall I take off my panties and stockings?" she wondered shyly. Cherry pondered this.

"No, that would be unhygienic," Cherry replied. She scooped up the finery and raced down the hall to the washroom, where Velma had sequestered herself hours earlier.

Using a handy hairpin, Cherry picked the lock and barged in. Velma was sitting on the side of the tub, her head in her hands.

"Put this on," Cherry ordered.

"But, Cherry, this is a wedding dress," Velma protested.

"Yes, Velma, it is. You're getting married today. To Midge."

"What!" Velma cried.

"In ten minutes, Midge, pretending to be Frank Hardly, is going to be downstairs waiting at the altar. Well, the fireplace, really. Anyway, we need a bride, and you're just the right size, so get in the dress."

"If this is some sort of scheme to bring us together, forget it," Velma cried. "I'll never go back to her. Never!"

"Don't you love Midge anymore?" Cherry wailed.

"Of course I love Midge," Velma sighed. "But you heard the horrible things we said to each other."

Cherry nodded. Everyone had.

"I know Midge too well to think she'd ever get over this fight!" Velma cried. "The things I said to her—and in front of everyone! Midge is a proud girl, Cherry."

"Don't you think Midge is a big bluffer, too?" Cherry cried. "Don't you think she cares more about you than she does about her pride?"

Velma grinned, then her grin faded into a sad smile. "No," she said. "I know Midge loves me, but I'm afraid I've injured her beyond repair."

Cherry gasped. "So now you two are going to part ways and live lives of loneliness and despair just because . . . because . . . Miss Velma Pierce, if you'll forgive me for saying so, you're just about the most obstinate girl I have ever met!" Cherry cried.

"Here I am, torn between two loves, walking around with my head held high but my heart wrenched in two. You have the most wonderful girl *ever* waiting downstairs for you, and you sit up here feeling sorry for yourself! Sure, Midge can be a big jerk sometimes, and her teasing can be wearing, plus she's not the tidiest person I've ever met—I for one am sick of cigarette butts lying about," Cherry confided.

"Midge is not a big jerk!" Velma cried. "She's the most wonderful girl in the world!"

Cherry smiled and put the wedding gown on the dressing table. Velma giggled and threw her arms around her chum. "Oh, Cherry, for such a simple little nurse, you sure can be smart!"

Cherry smiled with pride when she heard those words.

"Mr. Donald will give you away," she said. "I'll send him up for you in a few minutes." Velma nodded excitedly. She stripped to her slip and pulled the dress over her head. She was fiddling with her new hairdo when Cherry left the room to check on Midge.

"Midge, you look so handsome," Cherry gasped when she saw her chum wearing a luxurious black tuxedo. "Doesn't she look spiffy?" Mr. Donald agreed. "Luckily, we're the same size, so everything fits to a tee."

"I don't want to do this," Midge complained.

"It's not legally binding," Mr. Donald assured her. He winked at Cherry. "You and Nancy are just doing it for show."

"It's not that," Midge groaned. "I don't want to face anyone after what happened between me and Velma," she sighed.

"Why, Midge?" Cherry wondered. "No one cares that you yelled the roof off. We've all forgotten about that by now. Everyone needs to let off steam now and then. It's nothing to be ashamed of."

"Velma wasn't letting off steam," Midge said miserably. "She was getting rid of me once and for all."

"Oh, Midge," Cherry wanted to cry. "You don't how wrong you are." But she held her tongue.

Someone had put on the Liberace record. The wedding march began. "Time to go," Mr. Donald chuckled. "Do you and I need to have that father-son talk?" he joked.

Tears filled Midge's eyes. She gave Mr. Donald a hug.

"Hurry, Mr. Donald," Cherry cried. "You're giving away the bride. Jackie's the best man, and I'm the flower girl. Jeepers, if I'm the flower girl, I'd better get out there." She raced to Nancy's room, selected a darling mint green dinner dress and dyed-to-match satin pumps, powdered her nose, raced downstairs, and grabbed the basket of rose petals.

As Cherry walked up the makeshift aisle, her heart filled with a kind of sad joy. "Even if I am doomed to be unlucky in love, I can at least take comfort in the knowledge that I have helped bring others together," she told herself as she made her way to the altar, Mr. Donald and Midge right behind her.

"Oh, isn't she beautiful," the guests gasped when they spied the shrouded figure of the bride descending the stairs. Cherry could see Midge glancing furtively around the room, looking for her beloved Velma. "She looks as though her heart would break," Cherry thought, blinking back a tear.

Midge looked puzzled when she spied Nancy in the crowd, clad in a frock of the palest blue and wearing her mother's diamond-studded horseshoe-shaped brooch. Then a delighted grin broke over Midge's handsome features. With shaking hands, she lifted the bride's veil.

"Why, that's not Nancy," everyone murmured in surprise.

"What's going on?" Mrs. Meeks cried. "Oh, Nancy, have you been left at the altar? Oh, dear," she cried as she fanned herself with a hankie.

Nancy silenced the guests. "The wedding will proceed as planned." She looked over to Midge and Velma. "Right?"

"Right," they chorused happily.

"I'm not marrying Frank Hardly because I'm in love with someone else," Nancy declared. Cherry's heart started pounding when she realized Nancy was looking straight at her!

"Will there be another wedding?" everyone cried as they glanced around the room, trying to spot Nancy's beau.

"Not today," Nancy said shyly. "But maybe very soon." She shot Cherry a searching look.

Cherry felt dizzy with confusion. Could she and Nancy iron out their problems and recapture the splendor of their earlier love? "I won't think about that today," Cherry told herself. "Today is Midge and Velma's special day." She gave Nancy a little smile. Just maybe, the smile said.

"Dearly beloved..." the minister began, and before Cherry could wipe the tears of joy from her eyes, Midge and Velma were married!

"My, that was a lovely ceremony," she overheard a nearby matron remark as they sat in the garden and ate slices of the delicious cake. "Although," she added, "have you ever seen a groom weep like that?"

"I timed their kiss," she heard someone else remark. "It lasted ten whole minutes. Why, I was beginning to feel faint!"

"Goodness, they do make an awfully attractive couple," a girl added. "I wish I could find someone like that Frank Hardly. He's even more handsome than I remember!"

"Where did they go on their honeymoon?" someone asked Cherry. "Niagara Falls?"

"Lake Merrimen?"

"The Poconos?"

"Did you see how quickly they left? Why, the bride didn't even bother to throw her bouquet," someone whispered loudly.

"They must have rushed off to catch a train," another girl speculated.

Cherry blushed. What would these society mavens think, she wondered, if they knew the honeymoon had already begun right above their heads, in the secret attic room upstairs? Cherry smiled as she recalled the sight of Velma hiking up her long gown and racing to the attic with Midge hot on her heels.

Jackie joined her on the wrought-iron garden bench. "I'll bet we won't see them for a few days," Jackie guessed as she peered up to the third floor. Was it her imagination or was the house shaking just a bit?

"What are you going to do now, Cherry?" Jackie quizzed her. "Go back to ward work at Seattle General? Stay here while the dust settles? If you decide to go back West, you're welcome to hitch a ride with me. I'll be leaving in a few days for San Francisco.

"You don't have to decide now, Cherry," Jackie added softly.

Cherry looked into those warm black eyes. She knew if she turned her head just another inch, their lips would meet and the decision would be made.

"I mustn't let my heart rule my head," Cherry told herself. "I don't have to decide anything today. For tomorrow is the day after today, and that will be soon enough."

The End

Coming soon—a gay adventure!

Nancy Clue and her chums meet up with the Hardly boys in *A Ghost in the Closet*, available fall 1995.

About the Author

Mabel Maney was born at All Saint's Hospital in Appleton, Wisconsin, to Marge Muldoon Maney, a former beauty queen whose titles include Miss Muskie Queen 1949 and Miss Cheese Log 1951, and Milton Maney, a traveling footwear salesman specializing in sensible shoes.

After her parents were lost at sea, Mabel's spinster aunt, Miss Maude Maney, a successful women's undergarments buyer for a local department store, enrolled Mabel at St. Agatha's School for Girls in nearby Bear Lake, where she excelled in Conversational Skills and Table Manners. After an idyllic four years spent in the highest academic pursuits, Mabel was expelled for behavior too unpleasant to mention here.

Mabel enjoyed a short stint at the Appleton Home for Wayward Girls, after which she made her way West where she found employment in the film industry, training miniature collies to jump through hoops. Following many years devoted to canine education, Mabel retired to San Francisco, where she now resides.

Her key to success? "Never mix plaids with stripes!"

Mabel Maney is the author of *The Case of the Not-So-Nice Nurse* (Cleis Press, 1993), the first in her series of Nancy Clue mysteries. Her installation art and hand-made books, self-published under the World O'Girls Books imprint, have earned her fellowships from the San Francisco Foundation and San Francisco State University, where she received her MFA in 1991. Her art has been exhibited in numerous galleries throughout the United States. *Artspace* wrote of her hand-made World O'Girls edition of *The Case of the Not-So-Nice Nurse*: "In Maney's refigured narrative, gay heroine Cherry Ames moves unhampered through a world populated by lesbian nuns and adventuresses, even engaging in a one-nighter with Nancy Drew. Entertainment aside, by appropriating and redefining the sexual orientation and cultural limits placed upon her fictional female characters, Maney provides a powerful reminder of the exclusionary nature of the ruling (in this case, straight) culture, with its power to define specific roles and acts as 'natural' while denying or marginalizing others."

Be a Good-for-Nothing Girlfriend!

Nancy and Cherry and the rest of the gang are tickled to offer you this swell tee-shirt featuring the cover of *The Case of the Good-for-Nothing Girlfriend,* the exciting new adventure story by Mabel Maney.

Full-color image on white 100% cotton tee-shirt. Specify size when ordering: M L X L X X L . $15.00 plus shipping. See page 291 for order information.

BOOKS FROM CLEIS PRESS

LESBIAN STUDIES

Boomer: Railroad Memoirs
by Linda Niemann.
ISBN: 0-939416-55-7 12.95 PAPER.

**The Case of the
Good-For-Nothing Girlfriend**
by Mabel Maney.
ISBN: 0-939416-90-5 24.95 CLOTH;
ISBN: 0-939416-91-3 10.95 PAPER.

**The Case of the
Not-So-Nice Nurse**
by Mabel Maney.
ISBN: 0-939416-75-1 24.95 CLOTH;
ISBN: 0-939416-76-X 9.95 PAPER.

Dagger: On Butch Women
*edited by Roxxie, Lily Burana and
Linnea Due.*
ISBN: 0-939416-81-6 29.95 CLOTH;
ISBN: 0-939416-82-4 14.95 PAPER.

**Daughters of Darkness:
Lesbian Vampire Stories**
edited by Pam Keesey.
ISBN: 0-939416-77-8 24.95 CLOTH;
ISBN: 0-939416-78-6 9.95 PAPER.

**Different Daughters:
A Book by Mothers of Lesbians**
edited by Louise Rafkin.
ISBN: 0-939416-12-3 21.95 CLOTH;
ISBN: 0-939416-13-1 9.95 PAPER.

**Different Mothers:
Sons & Daughters of Lesbians
Talk About Their Lives**
edited by Louise Rafkin.
ISBN: 0-939416-40-9 24.95 CLOTH;
ISBN: 0-939416-41-7 9.95 PAPER.

**Girlfriend Number One:
Lesbian Life in the '90s**
edited by Robin Stevens.
ISBN: 0-939416-79-4 29.95 CLOTH;
ISBN: 0-939416-8 12.95 PAPER.

**Hothead Paisan:
Homicidal Lesbian Terrorist**
by Diane DiMassa.
ISBN: 0-939416-73-5 14.95 PAPER.

A Lesbian Love Advisor
by Celeste West.
ISBN: 0-939416-27-1 24.95 CLOTH;
ISBN: 0-939416-26-3 9.95 PAPER.

**Long Way Home:
The Odyssey of a Lesbian
Mother and Her Children**
by Jeanne Jullion.
ISBN: 0-939416-05-0 8.95 PAPER.

**More Serious Pleasure:
Lesbian Erotic Stories
and Poetry**
edited by the Sheba Collective.
ISBN: 0-939416-48-4 24.95 CLOTH;
ISBN: 0-939416-47-6 9.95 PAPER.

**The Night Audrey's Vibrator
Spoke: A Stonewall Riots
Collection**
by Andrea Natalie.
ISBN: 0-939416-64-6 8.95 PAPER.

**Queer and Pleasant Danger:
Writing Out My Life**
by Louise Rafkin.
ISBN: 0-939416-60-3 24.95 CLOTH;
ISBN: 0-939416-61-1 9.95 PAPER.

**Rubyfruit Mountain:
A Stonewall Riots Collection**
by Andrea Natalie.
ISBN: 0-939416-74-3 9.95 PAPER.

**Serious Pleasure: Lesbian
Erotic Stories and Poetry**
edited by the Sheba Collective.
ISBN: 0-939416-46-8 24.95 CLOTH;
ISBN: 0-939416-45-X 9.95 PAPER.

SEXUAL POLITICS

**Good Sex:
Real Stories from Real People**
by Julia Hutton.
ISBN: 0-939416-56-5 24.95 CLOTH;
ISBN: 0-939416-57-3 12.95 PAPER.

**The Good Vibrations Guide
to Sex: How to Have Safe, Fun
Sex in the '90s**
*by Cathy Winks and
Anne Semans.*
ISBN: 0-939416-83-2 29.95 CLOTH;
ISBN: 0-939416-84-0 14.95 PAPER.

Madonnarama: Essays on Sex and Popular Culture
edited by Lisa Frank and Paul Smith.
ISBN: 0-939416-72-7 24.95 CLOTH;
ISBN: 0-939416-71-9 9.95 PAPER.

Public Sex: The Culture of Radical Sex
by Pat Califia.
ISBN: 0-939416-88-3 29.95 CLOTH;
ISBN: 0-939416-89-1 12.95 PAPER.

Sex Work: Writings by Women in the Sex Industry
edited by Frédérique Delacoste and Priscilla Alexander.
ISBN: 0-939416-10-7 24.95 CLOTH;
ISBN: 0-939416-11-5 16.95 PAPER.

Susie Bright's Sexual Reality: A Virtual Sex World Reader
by Susie Bright.
ISBN: 0-939416-58-1 24.95 CLOTH;
ISBN: 0-939416-59-X 9.95 PAPER.

Susie Sexpert's Lesbian Sex World
by Susie Bright.
ISBN: 0-939416-34-4 24.95 CLOTH;
ISBN: 0-939416-35-2 9.95 PAPER.

POLITICS OF HEALTH

The Absence of the Dead Is Their Way of Appearing
by Mary Winfrey Trautmann.
ISBN: 0-939416-04-2 8.95 PAPER.

AIDS: The Women
edited by Ines Rieder and Patricia Ruppelt.
ISBN: 0-939416-20-4 24.95 CLOTH;
ISBN: 0-939416-21-2 9.95 PAPER

Don't: A Woman's Word
by Elly Danica.
ISBN: 0-939416-23-9 21.95 CLOTH;
ISBN: 0-939416-22-0 8.95 PAPER

1 in 3: Women with Cancer Confront an Epidemic
edited by Judith Brady.
ISBN: 0-939416-50-6 24.95 CLOTH;
ISBN: 0-939416-49-2 10.95 PAPER.

Voices in the Night: Women Speaking About Incest
edited by Toni A.H. McNaron and Yarrow Morgan.
ISBN: 0-939416-02-6 9.95 PAPER.

With the Power of Each Breath: A Disabled Women's Anthology
edited by Susan Browne, Debra Connors and Nanci Stern.
ISBN: 0-939416-09-3 24.95 CLOTH;
ISBN: 0-939416-06-9 10.95 PAPER.

FICTION

Another Love
by Erzsébet Galgóczi.
ISBN: 0-939416-52-2 24.95 CLOTH;
ISBN: 0-939416-51-4 8.95 PAPER.

Cosmopolis: Urban Stories by Women
edited by Ines Rieder.
ISBN: 0-939416-36-0 24.95 CLOTH;
ISBN: 0-939416-37-9 9.95 PAPER.

Dirty Weekend: A Novel of Revenge
by Helen Zahavi.
ISBN: 0-939416-85-9 10.95 PAPER.

A Forbidden Passion
by Cristina Peri Rossi.
ISBN: 0-939416-64-0 24.95 CLOTH;
ISBN: 0-939416-68-9 9.95 PAPER.

In the Garden of Dead Cars
by Sybil Claiborne.
ISBN: 0-939416-65-4 24.95 CLOTH;
ISBN: 0-939416-66-2 9.95 PAPER.

Night Train To Mother
by Ronit Lentin.
ISBN: 0-939416-29-8 24.95 CLOTH;
ISBN: 0-939416-28-X 9.95 PAPER.

The One You Call Sister: New Women's Fiction
edited by Paula Martinac.
ISBN: 0-939416-30-1 24.95 CLOTH;
ISBN: 0-939416031-X 9.95 PAPER.

Only Lawyers Dancing
by Jan McKemmish.
ISBN: 0-939416-70-0 24.95 CLOTH;
ISBN: 0-939416-69-7 9.95 PAPER.

Unholy Alliances: New Women's Fiction
edited by Louise Rafkin.
ISBN: 0-939416-14-X 21.95 CLOTH;
ISBN: 0-939416-15-8 9.95 PAPER.

The Wall
by Marlen Haushofer.
ISBN: 0-939416-53-0 24.95 CLOTH;
ISBN: 0-939416-54-9 PAPER.

We Came All The Way from Cuba So You Could Dress Like This?: Stories
by Achy Obejas.
ISBN: 0-939416-92-1 24.95 CLOTH;
ISBN: 0-939416-93-X 10.95 PAPER.

Woman-Centered Pregnancy and Birth
by the Federation of Feminist Women's Health Centers.
ISBN: 0-939416-03-4 11.95 PAPER.

LATIN AMERICA

Beyond the Border: A New Age in Latin American Women's Fiction
edited by Nora Erro-Peralta and Caridad Silva-Núñez.
ISBN: 0-939416-42-5 24.95 CLOTH;
ISBN: 0-939416-43-3 12.95 PAPER.

The Little School: Tales of Disappearance and Survival in Argentina
by Alicia Partnoy.
ISBN: 0-939416-08-5 21.95 CLOTH;
ISBN: 0-939416-07-7 9.95 PAPER.

Revenge of the Apple
by Alicia Partnoy.
ISBN: 0-939416-62-X 24.95 CLOTH;
ISBN: 0-939416-63-8 8.95 PAPER.

You Can't Drown the Fire: Latin American Women Writing in Exile
edited by Alicia Partnoy.
ISBN: 0-939416-16-6 24.95 CLOTH;
ISBN: 0-939416-17-4 9.95 PAPER.

AUTOBIOGRAPHY, BIOGRAPHY, LETTERS

Peggy Deery: An Irish Family at War
by Nell McCafferty.
ISBN: 0-939416-38-7 24.95 CLOTH;
ISBN: 0-939416-39-5 9.95 PAPER.

The Shape of Red: Insider/Outsider Reflections
by Ruth Hubbard and Margaret Randall.
ISBN: 0-939416-19-0 24.95 CLOTH;
ISBN: 0-939416-18-2 9.95 PAPER.

Women & Honor: Some Notes on Lying
by Adrienne Rich.
ISBN: 0-939416-44-1 3.95 PAPER.

ANIMAL RIGHTS

And a Deer's Ear, Eagle's Song and Bear's Grace: Relationships Between Animals and Women
edited by Theresa Corrigan and Stephanie T. Hoppe.
ISBN: 0-939416-38-7 24.95 CLOTH;
ISBN: 0-939416-39-5 9.95 PAPER.

With a Fly's Eye, Whale's Wit and Woman's Heart: Relationships Between Animals and Women
edited by Theresa Corrigan and Stephanie T. Hoppe.
ISBN: 0-939416-24-7 24.95 CLOTH;
ISBN: 0-939416-25-5 9.95 PAPER.

REFERENCE

Putting Out: The Essential Publishing Resource For Gay and Lesbian Writers
by Edisol W. Dotson.
ISBN: 0-939416-86-7 29.95 CLOTH;
ISBN: 0-939416-87-5 12.95 PAPER.

SINCE 1980, Cleis Press has published progressive books by women. We welcome your order and will ship your books as quickly as possible. Individual orders must be prepaid (U.S. dollars only). Please add 15% shipping. Pennsylvania residents add 6% sales tax. **Mail orders:** Cleis Press, PO Box 8933, Pittsburgh PA 15221. **MasterCard and Visa orders:** include account number, expiration date, and signature. Fax your credit card order to (412) 937-1567. Or, phone Monday–Friday, 9am–5pm EST at (412) 937-1555.